MURDER FOR HALLOWEEN

MURDER FOR HALLOWEEN

TALES OF SUSPENSE

EDITED BY
MICHELE SLUNG AND **ROLAND HARTMAN**

THE MYSTERIOUS PRESS

Published by Warner Books

A Time Warner Company

Mysterious Press books are published by Warner Books, Inc.,
1271 Avenue of the Americas, New York, NY 10020.

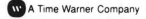 A Time Warner Company

The Mysterious Press name and logo are registered trademarks of Warner Books, Inc.
Printed in the United States of America
First printing: October 1994
10 9 8 7 6 5 4 3 2 1

Library of Congress Cataloging-in-Publication Data

Murder for Halloween / edited by Michele Slung and Roland Hartman.
p.   cm.
ISBN 0-89296-581-9
tective and mystery stories, American.   2. Halloween—
I. Slung, Michele B., 1947–   . II. Hartman, Roland.
PS648.D4M857 1994
87208—dc20   94-22500
CIP

k design by L. McRee

D
Murder
1270946

For Joan Kahn,
who introduced us

The editors would like to thank Nat Sobel and
their colleagues Linda Parisi, Kate Stine and Lorraine Lamm
for their assistance in putting this collection together.

TABLE OF CONTENTS

Preface xiii

Monsters
by **Ed McBain** 1

The Lemures
by **Steven Saylor** 9

The Adventure of the Dead Cat
by **Ellery Queen** 43

The Odstock Curse
by **Peter Lovesey** 65

The Theft of the Halloween Pumpkin
by **Edward D. Hoch** 81

Hallowe'en For Mr. Faulkner
by **August Derleth** 99

Deceptions
by **Marcia Muller** 111

CONTENTS

The Black Cat
by **Edgar Allan Poe**... 135

OMJAGOD
by **James Grady**.. 147

The Cloak
by **Robert Bloch**.. 173

What a Woman Wants
by **Michael Z. Lewin** 191

Yesterday's Witch
by **Gahan Wilson** 211

Walpurgis Night
by **Bram Stoker** 221

Trick or Treat
by **Judith Garner**... 237

One Night at a Time
by **Dorothy Cannell**.. 243

Night of the Goblin
by **Talmage Powell**... 267

Trick-or-Treat
by **Anthony Boucher**... 279

Pork Pie Hat
by **Peter Straub** 297

About the Editors 363

PREFACE

For tapping into the imagination, Halloween, unlike any other of the year's special days, provides an absolutely unbeatable combination of the ordinary and the strange. But it's not just a matter of bizarre masks or costumes transforming familiar figures into sinister apparitions, it's about mood—October thirty-first is the one night out of three hundred and sixty-five when we are not only allowed but encouraged to embrace the darkness.

Why this pagan celebration, originally a Celtic festival called Samhain, has endured for over two thousand years, winding up in contemporary America, at least, as a frenzy of candy amassment for the under-twelve set, is itself something of a sociocultural mystery: The fact that, in the if-you-can't-beat-them-join-them spirit, Christianity around the seventh century tried to coopt this ritual, virtuously recasting it as All Saints' or All Hallows' Eve, is really only one of the strands woven into that bursting bag of tricks from which, late every autumn, we see emerge witches on broomsticks, grinning ghosts and jack-o'-lanterns, skeletons, black cats, bats and wraiths of all descriptions.

Yet hardly anyone, save the sort of sectarians convinced that the forces of evil conspire to turn America's children into godless imps every time they carve a pumpkin, pauses to think about Halloween's origins much at all. For the truth is, what it's really about is a chance to put just a touch of mystery, a little "safe" danger, into the humdrum fabric of our lives—in an otherwise rational republic, it's a national moment dedicated to the weird.

Yet, though Halloween has long been seen as a time for mild pranks, along with usually unverifiable eerie activity, the dread it inspires seems to us to be more mock than real. Not only are those caramel apples and miniature Snickerses positively delicious but, for many of us, so is the contemplation of those awful things briefly going "bump!" in the night beyond our windows—that is, as long as we're safe inside.

Similarly, mystery fiction represents the temporary banishment of the normal order of things, the intrusion of chaotic forces into tidy reality, offered up in a way that, appalling body counts and all, can be equally tasty—even addictively so. Thus, what could be a more natural blend of elements than a collection of stories by favorite mystery writers who take as their inspiration Halloween's moonlit spell?

For example, you can never be sure, can you, who'll be grinning up at you when you respond to the importunate knock of trick-or-treaters. Then imagine how cleverly this possibility for mayhem might be exploited by a writer of Ed McBain's skill. (And if "Monsters" seems to strike a little too close to home for comfort, simply remember, next year, to turn off all the lights and not to open the door to anyone until morning.)

Or what about the dashing costume you impulsively rented, only to find that clinging to it was a peculiar odor and that wearing it wasn't quite the lark you'd intended? In "The Cloak," Robert Bloch understands, as only he can, the unpleasantness of certain old clothes, and probably after you read it, you'll be politely declining invitations to Halloween parties for some years to come. Meanwhile, Gahan Wilson wants to introduce us to the sweet little old lady down the block—you know, the one who has the stuffed heads of Hansel and Gretel mounted over the mantelpiece.

Hmm. Maybe we were wrong. The power of Halloween to spook us may not be so illusory after all. Anyone for Thanksgiving?

MURDER FOR HALLOWEEN

Monsters

BY ED MCBAIN

Nowadays, when we open the door to the familiar catchphrase "Trick or treat," we invariably hear it in its uninflected state. Or, perhaps we take it to be emphatic: trick or treat! Originally, however, it was posed as a real question—Trick or treat?—and one had then had the choice of handing over a sweet or, if not, taking the consequences.

Sometimes, though, as Ed McBain shows us, the options are even more varied . . . and infinitely more horrid.

MONSTERS

Last Halloween they rang the doorbell at around eleven o'clock, long after I'd thought the parade of ghoulies, ghosties, and goblins had finished.

Usually the little kiddies came first, before dinnertime, accompanied by Mommy or Daddy, bright expectant painted faces upturned, you dropped some pennies in their UNICEF container, you handed them a tie-tagged baggie of jelly beans, the little ones preferred the jelly beans. Molly used to ooh and ahh over their costumes and they'd stand there wide-eyed and innocent, not knowing what Halloween was all about, anyway, out here trick-or-treating only because all the other little six- and seven-year-olds were doing it. Those were the ones who came around before dinnertime; or sometimes while you were eating, the bell rang every five minutes and you had to get up from the table to go to the door, and there they were.

But there are monsters in the night as well.

You always gave them a choice, the jelly beans wrapped in their little tag-tied plastic bags, or the fresh fruit sitting in a basket. The little kids favored the jelly beans; the older kids usually took a piece of fruit—checked it out first to make sure there were no razor blades in it, lots of crazies tampered with fruit, you know—then

3

went off munching it in the night. Some kids wanted a bag of jelly beans *and* a piece of fruit *and* money for UNICEF, experienced trick-or-treaters, maybe ten, eleven years old who knew the power of a freckle-faced, gap-toothed grin. Most of them were cute as buttons, all dressed up and painted, pint-sized ghosts or fairies or Indians or spies or pirates. Every now and then, you'd get a couple of eleven-year-old-girls wearing satin gowns and pearls and high-heeled slippers, trying to look like movie stars but Molly said they looked more like hookers. Few years back there were more ETs than you could shake a stick at; you should've seen them.

The teenagers usually came around later.

Eight, nine o'clock, never later than ten, ten thirty.

Some of them wore genuine costumes, but most of them wore just their usual street clothes with rubber masks pulled over their heads, Wolfman or Dracula or Frankenstein and quite a few Freddies, with the hockey masks and the long razor-blade nails. They all seemed a little bored and a little embarrassed to be doing this silly kid stuff, but they came around, anyway, and accepted your jelly beans or your fruit or sometimes both. The two who rang the doorbell at around eleven o'clock last Halloween were both wearing Frankenstein masks.

I'd been living alone ever since Molly died four years ago, didn't want to leave this house with all its memories of her, would've been like leaving Molly herself. Besides, this is a nice neighborhood where I live, plenty of older folks like myself, some of them widowed, but also couples with smaller children and well-behaved teenagers. These two looked like any of the teenagers who'd stopped by earlier, tall and rangy, wearing identical green Frankenstein masks and dark jackets over blue jeans and high-topped sneakers.

"Come in, fellas," I said. "Care for some fruit? Some jelly beans?"

Beyond them, through the open doorway, I could see the lights of the houses everywhere around mine, people still up watching the eleven o'clock news. It had been a cold October. Wind whipped through the trees now, rattled the leaves on the walk outside. I hadn't yet put up my storms. When you're sixty-eight and living alone, it sometimes takes a while to get things done. The two

Frankensteins brought the cold in with them. I closed the door behind them, against the bitter wind outside. The fruit and jelly beans were in separate baskets on a long sort of mail table sitting opposite the entrance door. One of the monsters took an apple from the nearest basket, lifted the mask over his chin and mouth, and bit into the fruit. The other one took a switchblade knife from his pocket.

"Hey," I said, "what . . . ?"

The blade snapped open.

"Trick or treat," the one with the apple said, and bit into it again.

"Give me your wallet," the one holding the knife said.

I reached into the hip pocket of my trousers and handed him the wallet. He took out all the money in the bill compartment, and then checked out all the credit cards and took the ones I guessed he felt he could use—two department-store cards, and my American Express and Visa cards—and left where they were my AT&T calling card and my Shell card. He handed the wallet back to me, took a pear from the basket, lifted his mask the way his friend had done, and bit into the fruit. I wondered if I would later be able to identify either of them from glimpses of only their chins and mouths. The one with the knife used the blade to gesture toward the stairs. His friend had finished the apple. He lowered the mask over his chin again, tossed the core back into the basket with the rest of the fruit.

We went up to the second floor of the house. On one side of the hall, there were the master bedroom and bathroom I used to share with Molly. The guest room and bath were on the other side of the hall. The two Frankensteins led me directly to the master bedroom, which is where they figured I'd keep anything of value. They took all the jewelry Molly used to wear. They took both her fur coats. They even took some of her dresses. They took all her precious things.

I knew I would never forgive them for that.

Before they went out, they both stuffed their pockets with more fruit and jelly beans from the baskets on the table—as if they hadn't taken enough from me already—and then the one with the knife

5

laughed and said, "See you next year." But I didn't believe they'd be back, and neither did the police.

The police said lots of times, it wasn't enough these teenage punk junkies robbed you blind, they also liked to scare the hell out of you. It's a wonder they didn't stab you just for the hell of it, one of the cops told me, while the other one made out a list of all the stuff that'd been stolen. Molly's jewelry. Her furs. Her dresses. All her precious things. The cops said they would send the list to all the area pawnshops; sometimes they got lucky. They didn't get lucky this time, I guessed, because I never heard from them again after that night.

I kept wondering if the two Frankensteins would really come back. I kept thinking up ways to thwart them if they did. Like the kid in *Home Alone*, do you remember? All the things he did to torment those two burglars? I couldn't think of anything except buying a gun and learning how to shoot to kill. I'd never owned a gun in my life. The only time I'd ever fired a gun was when I was in navy boot camp during World War II, and that was a rifle. I hadn't enjoyed the recoil. Besides, I didn't think I would have the guts to shoot anyone. But I couldn't just let them come in again the way they had last year, could I? Steal my money and credit cards, take all of Molly's things! Her *things*! The things she *loved*! And then stuff their pockets with treats and strut out laughing? I couldn't let them strut out laughing again, could I?

They came at about the same time as last year.

Eleven o'clock, give or take a few minutes.

They were wearing the same Frankenstein masks.

I was expecting them. I had put out fresh fruit and fresh bags of jelly beans at around ten forty-five. Everything looked as inviting as it had last year, but the gun I'd bought was in the hall-table drawer, loaded and ready to shoot. I'd been taking lessons at a nearby range. I still did not know if I'd be able to point that gun at a human being and squeeze the trigger, but I knew I would not let them walk away from this house unharmed. Not again. That much I knew. That much I'd sworn to myself and to Molly's memory.

"Trick or treat," one of them said.

This time the other one had a gun. One of those huge guns I'd

6

seen in the newspapers and magazines. A nine-millimeter semi-automatic pistol. An Uzi or a Tec. It scared me to death just looking at it.

This time they used their names, talked back and forth to each other: Grab his wallet, Tommy; Want some jelly beans, Frankie? Tommy this and Frankie that, this time they were fearless. They knew they had a cowardly old man here, they knew I would do nothing to stop them. Just like last time.

They took all my money again, and all of my new credit cards, and they led me upstairs again, and stole everything that wasn't nailed down. Tommy was the one with the gun; he stayed with me in the entrance hall while Frankie carried their booty out to the van. Took him three trips. They stole a television set, a tape deck, a digital disc player, my binoculars, three overcoats, some rings they'd missed the last time, a pocket watch that had belonged to my father, a vacuum cleaner, a toaster, anything else they thought they could easily fence, anything, everything. They were carrying a lifetime out to that van.

When Frankie came back after his last trip to the car, he said, "Nice doing business with you again," and was reaching for a packet of jelly beans when I yanked the gun out of the table drawer.

"Oh-ho, what's *this*?" Tommy said.

"Why I do believe it's a Smith and Wesson," Frankie said.

"How much for it on the street, Frank?"

"Fifty? Sixty?"

"Take it from him," Tommy said, and held his arm straight out, the nine-millimeter pistol pointed at my head. "Mr. S," he said, "Mr. W, meet Mr. Nine."

Frankie took a step toward me.

I whirled toward him.

"Don't move!" I said.

The gun was shaking in my fist.

"Blow him away, Tom," he said softly.

I turned to Tommy again, the one with the gun, the one with Mister Nine, and that was when Frankie hit me on the side of the head. I staggered forward, almost into Tommy's arms. He swung the pistol away and out of reach, and brought his knee up into my chest. Frankie hit me again, at the back of the neck this time, with a clenched fist that felt like a mallet. I fell to my knees. Tommy picked up the gun I'd dropped and slid it into his belt. They both stuffed pears and apples, and little packets of jelly beans into their pockets. Tommy took another apple from the basket. Frankie took another pear.

"See you next year," Tommy said, and they walked out.

On my knees, I watched them as they went up the path.

On my knees, I watched them as they took off the monster masks, Tommy raising the apple to his mouth, Frankie raising the pear to his.

Then I heard them both scream, and I saw their tongues spurting blood as they bit into the razor blades.

Ed McBain *is one of the mystery genre's most successful—and beloved— practitioners. Creator of the 87th Precinct novels and the Matthew Hope series, he is also, as Evan Hunter, the author of such celebrated works as* The Blackboard Jungle *and the unforgettable screenplay for Alfred Hitchcock's* The Birds. *In 1985 the Mystery Writers of America named him a Grand Master, its most prestigious honor.*

THE LEMURES

BY STEVEN SAYLOR

Falling just after Halloween on the calendar is All Souls' Day, which has its origins in the legend of a long-ago pilgrim back from the Holy Land, convinced by an eerie chance encounter that souls trapped in purgatory could be released by the prayers of the faithful. In the last years of the tenth century, November second became the special day consecrated for these supplications.

Steven Saylor, however, moves our point of spooky reference even further back in time, to ancient Rome. Introducing us to "lemures"—troubled spirits resembling those who roam abroad at Halloween and All Souls'—he shows us that while these unwanted ha'nts might indeed be banished in the spring by priests, it takes a canny detective like Gordianus to do the trick in the autumn.

THE LEMURES

The slave pressed a scrap of parchment into my hand:

> From Lucius Claudius to his friend Gordianus, greetings.
> If you will accompany this messenger on his return, I will
> be grateful. I am at the house of a friend on the Palatine
> Hill; there is a problem which requires your attention.
> Come alone—do not bring the boy—the circumstances
> might frighten him.

Lucius need not have warned me against bringing Eco, for at
that moment the boy was busy with his tutor. From the garden,
where they had found a patch of morning sunlight to ward off the
October chill, I could hear the old man declaiming while Eco wrote
the day's Latin lesson on his wax tablet.

"Bethesda!" I called out, but she was already behind me, holding
open my woolen cloak: As she slipped it over my shoulders, she
glanced down at the note in my hand. She wrinkled her nose.
Unable to read, Bethesda regards the written word with suspicion
and disdain.

"From Lucius Claudius?" she asked, raising an eyebrow.

"Why, yes, but how—?" Then I realized she must have recog-

11

nized his messenger. Slaves often take more notice of one another than do their masters.

"I suppose he wants you to go gaming with him, or to taste the new vintage from one of his vineyards." She tossed back her mane of jet-black hair and pouted her luscious lips.

"I suppose not; he has work for me."

A smile flickered at the corner of her mouth.

"Not that it should be any concern of yours," I added quickly. Since I had taken Eco in from the streets and legally adopted him, Bethesda had begun to behave less and less like a concubine and more and more like a wife and mother. I wasn't sure I liked the change; I was even less sure I had any control over it.

"Frightening work," I added. "Probably dangerous." But she was already busy adding to the household accounts in her head. As I stepped out the door I heard her humming a happy Egyptian tune from her childhood.

The day was bright and crisp. Drifts of leaves lined either side of the narrow winding pathway that led from my house down the slope of the Esquiline Hill to the Subura below. The tang of smoke was on the air, rising from kitchens and braziers. The messenger drew his dark green cloak more tightly about his shoulders to ward off the chill.

"Neighbor! Citizen!" a voice hissed at me from the wall to my right. I looked up and saw two eyes peering down at me, sur-mounted by the dome of a bald, knobby head. "Neighbor—yes, you! Gordianus, they call you; am I right?"

I looked up at him warily. "Yes, Gordianus is my name."

"And Detectus, they call you—'the Finder,' yes?"

"Yes."

"You solve puzzles. Plumb mysteries. Answer riddles."

"Sometimes."

"Then you must help me!"

"Perhaps, Citizen. But not now. A friend summons me—"

"This will take only a moment."

"Even so, I grow cold standing here—"

"Then come inside! I'll open the little door in the wall and let you in."

"No—perhaps tomorrow."

"No! Now! They will come tonight, I know it—or even this afternoon, when the shadows lengthen. See, the clouds are coming up. If the sun grows dim, they may come out at midday beneath the dark, brooding sky."

"*They?* Whom do you mean, Citizen?"

His eyes grew large, yet his voice became quite tiny, like the voice of a mouse. "The lemures . . ." he squeaked.

The messenger clutched at his cloak. I felt the sudden chill myself, but it was only a cold, dry wind gusting down the pathway that made me shiver; or so I told myself.

"Lemures," the man repeated. "The unquiet dead."

Leaves scattered and danced about my feet. A thin finger of cloud obscured the sun, dimming its bright, cold light to a hazy gray.

"Vengeful," the man whispered. "Full of spite. Empty of all remorse. Human no longer, spirits sucked dry of warmth and pity, desiccated and brittle like shards of bone, with nothing left but wickedness. Dead, but not gone from this world as they should be. Revenge is their only food. The only gift they offer is madness."

I stared into the man's dark, sunken eyes for a long moment, then broke from his gaze. "A friend calls me," I said, nodding for the slave to go on.

"But neighbor, you can't abandon me. I was a soldier for Sulla! I fought in the civil war to save the Republic! I was wounded—if you'll step inside you'll see. My left leg is no good at all, I have to hobble and lean against a stick. While you, you're young and whole and healthy. A young Roman like you owes me some respect. Please—there's no one else to help me!"

"My business is with the living, not the dead," I said sternly.

"I can pay you, if that's what you mean. Sulla gave all his soldiers farms up in Etruria. I sold mine—I was never meant to be a farmer. I still have silver left. I can pay you a handsome fee, if you'll help me."

"And how can I help you? If you have a problem with lemures, consult a priest or an augur."

"I have, believe me! Every May, at the Lemuria, I take part in the procession to ward off evil spirits. I mutter the incantations, I cast the black beans over my shoulder. Perhaps it works; the lemures never come to me in spring, and they stay away all summer. But as surely as leaves wither and fall from the trees, they come to me every autumn. They come to drive me mad!"

"Citizen, I cannot—"

"They cast a spell inside my head."

"Citizen! I must go."

"Please," he whispered. "I was a soldier once, brave, afraid of nothing. I killed many men, fighting for Sulla, for Rome. I waded through rivers of blood and valleys of gore up to my hips and never quailed. I feared no one. And now . . ." He made a face of such self-loathing that I turned away. "Help me," he pleaded.

"Perhaps . . . when I return. . . ."

He smiled pitifully, like a doomed man given a reprieve. "Yes," he whispered, "when you return. . . ."

I hurried on.

The house on the Palatine, like its neighbors, presented a rather plain facade, despite its location in the city's most exclusive district. Except for two pillars in the form of dryads supporting the roof, the portico's only adornment was a funeral wreath of cypress and fir on the door.

The short hallway, flanked on either side by the wax masks of noble ancestors, led to a modest atrium. On an ivory bier, a body lay in state. I stepped forward and looked down at the corpse. I saw a young man, not yet thirty, unremarkable except for the grimace that contorted his features. Normally the anointers are able to remove signs of distress and suffering from the faces of the dead, to smooth wrinkled brows and unclench tightened jaws. But the face of this corpse had grown rigid beyond the power of the anointers to soften it. Its expression was not of pain or misery, but of fear.

"He fell," said a familiar voice behind me.

I turned to see my one-time client and since-then friend, Lucius Claudius. He was as portly as ever, and not even the gloomy light of the atrium could dim the cherry-red of his cheeks and nose.

We exchanged greetings, then turned our eyes to the corpse.

"Titus," explained Lucius, "the owner of this house. For the last two years, anyway."

"He died from a fall?"

"Yes. There's a gallery that runs along the west side of the house, with a long balcony that overlooks a steep hillside. Titus fell from the balcony three nights ago. He broke his back."

"And died at once?"

"No. He lingered through the night and lived until nightfall the next day. He told a curious tale before he died. Of course, he was feverish and in great pain, despite the draughts of nepenthes he was given. . . ." Lucius shifted his considerable bulk uneasily inside his vast black cloak and reached up nervously to scratch at his frazzled wreath of copper-colored hair. "Tell me, Gordianus, do you have any knowledge of lemures?"

A strange expression must have crossed my face, for Lucius frowned and wrinkled his brow. "Have I said something untoward, Gordianus?"

"Not at all. But this is the second time today that someone has spoken to me of lemures. On the way here, a soldier, a neighbor of mine—but I won't bore you with the tale. All Rome seems to be haunted by spirits today! It must be this oppressive weather . . . this gloomy time of year . . . or indigestion, as my father used to say—"

"It was not indigestion that killed my husband. Nor was it a cold wind, or a chilly drizzle, or a nervous imagination."

The speaker was a tall, thin woman. A stola of black wool covered her from neck to feet; about her shoulders was a wrap of dark blue. Her black hair was drawn back from her face and piled atop her head, held together by silver pins and combs. Her eyes were a glittering blue. Her face was young, but she was no longer a girl. She held herself as rigorously upright as a vestal, and spoke with the imperious tone of a patrician.

"This," said Lucius, "is Gordianus, the man I told you about." The woman acknowledged me with a slight nod. "And this," he continued, "is my dear young friend, Cornelia. From the Sullan branch of the Cornelius family."

I gave a slight start.

"Yes," she said, "blood relative to our recently departed and deeply missed dictator. Lucius Cornelius Sulla was my cousin. We were quite close, despite the difference in our ages. I was with dear Sulla just before he died, down at his villa in Neapolis. A great man. A generous man." Her imperious tone softened. She turned her gaze to the corpse on the bier. "Now Titus is dead, too. I am alone. Defenseless . . ."

"Perhaps we should withdraw to the library," suggested Lucius.

"Yes," said Cornelia, "it's cold here in the atrium."

She led us down a short hallway into a small room. My sometime-client Cicero would not have called it much of a library—there was only a single cabinet piled with scrolls against one wall—but he would have approved of its austerity. The walls were stained a somber red and the chairs were backless. A slave tended to the brazier in the corner and departed.

"How much does Gordianus know?" said Cornelia, to Lucius.

"Very little. I only explained that Titus fell from the balcony."

She looked at me with an intensity that was almost frightening. "My husband was a haunted man."

"Haunted by whom, or what? Lucius spoke to me of lemures."

"Not plural, but singular," she said. "He was tormented by one lemur only."

"Was this spirit known to him?"

"Yes. An acquaintance from his youth; they studied law together in the Forum. The man who owned this house before us. His name was Furius."

"This lemur appeared to your husband more than once?"

"It began last summer. Titus would glimpse the thing for only a moment—beside the road on the way to our country villa, or across the Forum, or in a pool of shadow outside the house. At first he wasn't sure what it was; he would turn back and try to find it, only to discover it had vanished. Then he began to see it inside the house. That was when he realized who and what it was. He no longer tried to approach it; quite the opposite, he fled the thing, quaking with fear."

"Did you see it, as well?"

She stiffened. "Not at first . . ."

"Titus saw it, the night he fell," whispered Lucius. He leaned forward and took Cornelia's hand, but she pulled it away.

"That night," she whispered, "Titus was brooding, pensive. He left me in my sitting room and stepped onto the balcony to pace and take a breath of cold air. Then he saw the thing—so he told the story later, in his delirium. It came toward him, beckoning. It spoke his name. Titus fled to the end of the balcony. The thing came closer. Titus grew mad with fear—somehow he fell."

"The thing pushed him?" I said.

She shrugged. "Whether he fell or was pushed, it was his fear of the thing that finally killed him. He survived the fall; he lingered through the night and the next day. Twilight came. Titus began to sweat and tremble. Even the least movement was agony to him, yet he thrashed and writhed on the bed, mad with panic. He said he could not bear to see the lemur again. At last he died. Do you understand? He chose to die rather than confront the lemur again. You saw his face. It was not pain that killed him. It was fear."

I pulled my cloak over my hands and curled my toes. It seemed to me that the brazier did nothing to banish the cold from the room. "This lemur," I said, "how did your husband describe it?"

"The thing was not hard to recognize. It was Furius, who owned this house before us. Its flesh was pocked and white, its teeth broken and yellow. Its hair was like bloody straw, and there was blood all around its neck. It gave off a foul odor . . . but it was most certainly Furius. Except . . ."

"Yes?"

"Except that it looked younger than Furius at the end of his life. It looked closer to the age when Furius and Titus knew one another in the Forum, in the days of their young manhood."

"When did you first see the lemur yourself?"

"Last night. I was on the balcony—thinking of Titus and his fall. I turned and saw the thing, but only for an instant. I fled into the house—and it spoke to me."

"What did it say?"

"Two words: *Now you*. Oh!" Cornelia drew in a quick, strangled breath. She clutched at her wrap and gazed at the fire.

I stepped closer to the brazier, spreading my fingers to catch the warmth. "What a strange day!" I muttered. "What can I say to you, Cornelia, except what I said to another who told me a tale of lemures earlier today: why do you consult me instead of an augur? These are mysteries about which I know very little. Tell me a tale of a purloined jewel or a stolen document; call on me with a case of parricide or show me a corpse with an unknown killer. With these I might help you; about such matters I know more than a little. But how to placate a lemur, I do not know. Of course, I will always come when my friend Lucius Claudius calls me; but I begin to wonder why I am here at all."

Cornelia studied the crackling embers and did not answer.

"Perhaps," I ventured, "you believe this lemur is not a lemur at all. If in fact it is a living man—"

"It doesn't matter what I believe or don't believe," she snapped. I saw in her eyes the same pleading and desperation I had seen in the soldier's eyes. "No priest can help me; there is no protection against a vengeful lemur. Yet, perhaps the thing is really human, after all. Such a pretense is possible, isn't it?"

"Possible? I suppose."

"Then you know of such cases, of a man masquerading as a lemur?"

"I have no personal experience—"

"That's why I asked Lucius to call you. If this creature is in fact human and alive, then you may be able to save me from it. If instead it is what it appears to be, a lemur, then—then nothing can save me. I am doomed." She gasped and bit her knuckles.

"But if it was your husband's death the thing desired—"

"Haven't you been listening? I told you what it said to me: *Now you*. Those were the words it spoke!" Cornelia sobbed. Lucius went to her side. Slowly she calmed herself.

"Very well, Cornelia. I will help you if I can. First, questions. From answers come answers. Can you speak?"

She bit her lips and nodded.

"You say the thing has the face of Furius. Did your husband think so?"

"My husband remarked on it, over and over. He saw the thing very close, more than once. On the night he fell, the creature came near enough for him to smell its fetid breath. He recognized it beyond a doubt."

"And you? You say you saw it for only an instant before you fled. Are you sure it was Furius you saw last night on the balcony?"

"Yes! An instant was all I needed. Horrible—discolored, distorted, wearing a hideous grin—but the face of Furius, I have no doubt."

"And yet younger than you remember."

"Yes. Somehow the cheeks, the mouth . . . what makes a face younger or older? I don't know, I can only say that in spite of its hideousness the thing looked as Furius looked when he was a younger man. Not the Furius who died two years ago, but Furius when he was a beardless youth, slender and strong and full of ambition."

"I see. In such a case, three possibilities occur to me. Could this indeed have been Furius—not his lemur, but the man himself? Are you certain that he's dead?"

"Oh, yes."

"There is no doubt?"

"No doubt at all . . ." She shivered and seemed to leave something unspoken. I looked at Lucius, who quickly looked away.

"Then perhaps this Furius had a brother?"

"A much older brother," she nodded.

"Not a twin?"

"No. Besides, his brother died in the civil war."

"Oh?"

"Fighting against Sulla."

"I see. Then perhaps Furius had a son, the very image of his father?"

Cornelia shook her head. "His only child was an infant daughter. His only other survivors were his wife and mother, and a sister, I think."

"And where are the survivors now?"

Cornelia averted her eyes. "I'm told they moved into his mother's house on the Caelian Hill."

"So: Furius is assuredly dead, he had no twin—no living brother at all—and he left no son. And yet the thing which haunted your husband, by his own account and yours, bore the face of Furius."

Cornelia sighed, exasperated. "Useless! I called on you only out of desperation." She pressed her hands to her eyes. "Oh, my head pounds like thunder. The night will come and how will I bear it? Go now, please. I want to be alone."

Lucius escorted me to the atrium. "What do you think?" he said.

"I think that Cornelia is a very frightened woman, and her husband was a frightened man. Why was he so fearful of this particular lemur? If the dead man had been his friend—"

"An acquaintance, Gordianus, not exactly a friend."

"Is there something more that I should know?"

He shifted uncomfortably. "You know how I detest gossip. And really, Cornelia is not nearly as venal as some people think. There is a good side of her that few people see."

"It would be best if you told me everything, Lucius. For Cornelia's sake."

He pursed his small mouth, furrowed his fleshy brow and scratched his bald pate. "Oh, very well," he muttered. "As I told you, Cornelia and her husband have lived in this house for two years. It has also been two years since Furius died."

"And this is no coincidence?"

"Furius was the original owner of this house. Titus and Cornelia acquired it when he was executed for his crimes against Sulla and the state."

"I begin to see . . ."

"Perhaps you do. Furius and his family were on the wrong side of the civil war, political enemies of Sulla's. When Sulla achieved absolute power and compelled the Senate to appoint him dictator, he purged the Republic of his foes. The proscriptions—"

"Names posted on lists in the Forum; yes, I remember only too well."

"Once a man was proscribed, anyone could hunt him down and bring his head to Sulla for a bounty. I don't have to remind you of the bloodbath, you were here; you saw the heads mounted on spikes outside the Senate."

"And Furius's head was among them?"

"Yes. He was proscribed, arrested, and beheaded. You ask if Cornelia is certain that Furius is dead? Yes, because she saw his head on a spike, with blood oozing from the neck. Meanwhile, his property was confiscated and put up for public auction—"

"But the auctions were not always public," I said. "Sulla's friends usually had first choice of the finest farms and villas."

"As did Sulla's relations," added Lucius, wincing. "Yes, I'm afraid that when Furius was caught and beheaded, Titus and Cornelia didn't hesitate to contact Sulla immediately and put their mark on this house. Cornelia had always coveted it; why pass up the opportunity to possess it, and for a song?" He lowered his voice. "The rumor is that they placed the only bid, for the unbelievable sum of a thousand sesterces!"

"The price of a mediocre Egyptian rug," I said. "Quite a bargain."

"If Cornelia has a flaw, it's her avarice. In that, she's hardly alone. Greed is the great vice of our age."

"But not the only vice."

"What do you mean?"

"Tell me, Lucius, was this Furius really such a great enemy of our late, lamented dictator? Was he such a terrible threat to the security of the state and to Sulla's personal safety that he truly belonged on the proscription lists?"

"I don't understand."

"There were those who ended up on the lists because they were too rich for their own good, because they possessed things that others coveted."

Lucius frowned. "Gordianus, what I've already told you is scandalous enough, and I'll ask you not to repeat it. I don't know what further implication you may have drawn, and I don't care to know. I think we should drop the matter."

Friend he may be, but Lucius is also of patrician blood; the cords that bind the rich together are made of gold, and are stronger than iron.

I made my way homeward, pondering the strange and fatal haunting of Titus and his wife. I had forgotten completely about the soldier until I heard him hissing at me from his garden wall.

"Yes, yes! You said you'd come back to help me, and here you are. Come inside!" He disappeared, and a moment later a little wooden door in the wall opened inward. I stooped and stepped inside to find myself in a garden open to the sky, surrounded by a colonnade. The scent of burning leaves filled my nostrils; an elderly slave was gathering leaves with a rake, arranging them in piles about a small brazier in the center of the garden.

The soldier smiled at me crookedly. I judged him to be not much older than myself, despite his bald head and the gray hairs that bristled from his eyebrows. The dark circles beneath his eyes marked him as a man who badly needed sleep and a respite from worry. He hobbled past me and pulled up a chair for me to sit on.

"Tell me, neighbor, did you grow up in the countryside?" he said. His voice cracked slightly, as if pleasant discourse was a strain to him.

"No, I was born in Rome."

"Ah. I grew up near Arpinum myself. I only mention it because I saw you staring at the leaves and the fire. I know how city folk dread fires and shun them except for heat and cooking. It's a country habit, burning leaves. Dangerous, but I'm careful. The smell reminds me of my boyhood. As does this garden."

I looked up at the tall, denuded trees that loomed in stark silhouette against the cloudy sky. Among them were some cypresses and yews that still wore their shaggy, gray-green coats. A weirdly twisted little tree, hardly more than a bush, stood in the corner, surrounded by a carpet of round, yellow leaves. The old slave walked slowly toward the bush and began to rake its leaves in among the others.

"Have you lived in this house long?" I asked.

"For three years. I cashed in the farm Sulla gave me and bought this place. I retired before the fighting was finished. My leg was crippled, and another wound made my sword arm useless. My shoulder still hurts me now and again, especially at this time of year, when the weather turns cold. This is a bad time of year, all around." He grimaced, whether at a phantom pain in his shoulder or at phantoms in the air I could not tell.

"When did you first see the lemures?" I asked. Since the man insisted on taking my time, there was no point in being subtle.

"Just after I moved into this house."

"Ah, then perhaps the lemures were here before you arrived."

"No," he said gravely. "They must have followed me here." He limped toward the brazier, stooped stiffly, gathered up a handful of leaves and scattered them on the fire. "Only a little at a time," he said softly. "Wouldn't want to be careless with a fire in the garden. Besides, it makes the pleasure last. A little today, a little more tomorrow. Burning leaves reminds me of boyhood."

"How do you know they followed you? The lemures, I mean."

"Because I recognize them."

"Who were they?"

"I never knew their names." He stared into the fire. "But I remember the Etruscan's face when my sword cut open his entrails and he looked up at me, gasping and unbelieving. I remember the bloodshot eyes of the sentries we surprised one night outside Capua. They had been drinking, the fools. When we stuck our swords into their bellies, I could smell the wine amid the stench that came pouring out. I remember the boy I killed in battle once—so young and tender my blade sliced clear through his neck. His head went flying off. One of my men caught it and cast it back at me, laughing. It landed at my feet. I swear, the boy's eyes were still open, and he knew what was happening to him. . . ."

He stooped, groaning at the effort, and gathered another handful of leaves. "The flames make all things pure again," he whispered. "The odor of burning leaves is the smell of innocence."

He watched the fire for a long moment. "They come at this time of year, the lemures. Seeking revenge. They cannot harm my body. They had their chance to do that when they were living, and they only succeeded in maiming me. It was I who killed their bodies, I who triumphed. Now they seek to drive me mad. They cast a spell on me. They cloud my mind and draw me into the pit. They shriek and dance about my head, they open their bellies over me and bury me in offal, they dismember themselves and drown me in a sea of blood and gore. Somehow I've always struggled free, but my will grows weaker every year. One day they will draw me into the pit and I will never come out again."

He covered his face. "Go now. I'm ashamed that you should see me like this. When you see me again, it will be more terrible than you can imagine. But you will come, when I send for you? You will come and see them for yourself? A man as clever as you might strike a bargain, even with the dead."

He dropped his hands. I would hardly have recognized his face—his eyes were red, his cheeks gaunt, his lips trembling. "Swear to me that you will come, Gordianus. If only to bear witness to my destruction."

"I do not make oaths—"

"Then promise me as a man, and leave the gods out of it. I beg you to come when I call."

"I will come," I finally sighed, thinking that a promise to a madman was not truly binding.

The old slave, clucking and shaking his head with worry, ushered me to the little door. "I fear that your master is already mad," I whispered. "These lemures are from his own imagination."

"Oh, no," said the old slave. "I have seen them, too."

"You?"

"Yes, just as he described."

"And the other slaves?"

"We have all seen the lemures."

I looked into the old slave's calm, unblinking eyes for a long moment. Then I stepped through the passage and he shut the door behind me.

"A veritable plague of lemures!" I said as I lay upon my couch taking dinner that night. "Rome is overrun by them."

Bethesda, who sensed the unease beneath my levity, tilted her head and arched an eyebrow, but said nothing.

"And that silly warning Lucius Claudius wrote in his note this morning! 'Do not bring the boy, the circumstances might frighten him'—ha! What could be more appealing to a twelve-year-old boy than the chance to see a genuine lemur!"

Eco chewed a mouthful of bread and watched me with round eyes, not sure whether I was joking or not.

"The whole affair seems quite absurd to me," ventured Bethesda. She crossed her arms impatiently. As was her custom, she had already eaten in the kitchen, and merely watched while Eco and I feasted. "As even the stupidest person in Egypt knows, the bodies of the dead cannot survive unless they have been carefully mummified according to ancient laws. How could the body of a dead man be wandering about Rome, frightening this Titus into jumping off a balcony? Especially a dead man who had his head cut off. It was a living fiend who *pushed* him off the balcony, that much is obvious. Ha! I'll wager it was his wife who did it!"

"Then what of the soldier's haunting? The old slave swears that the whole household has seen the lemures. Not just one, but a whole swarm of them."

"Fah! The slave lies to excuse his master's feeblemindedness. He is loyal, as a slave should be, but not necessarily honest."

"Even so, I think I shall go if the soldier calls me, to judge with my own eyes. And the matter of the lemur on the Palatine Hill is worth pursuing, if only for the handsome fee that Cornelia promises."

Bethesda shrugged. To change the subject, I turned to Eco. "And speaking of outrageous fees, what did that thief of a tutor teach you today?"

Eco jumped from his couch and ran to fetch his stylus and wax tablet.

Bethesda uncrossed her arms. "If you continue with these matters," she said, her voice now pitched to conceal her own unease, "I think that your friend Lucius Claudius gives you good advice. There is no need to take Eco along with you. He's busy with his lessons and should stay at home. He's safe here, from evil men and evil spirits alike."

I nodded, for I had been thinking the same thing myself.

The next morning I stepped quietly past the soldier's house. He did not spy me and call out, though I could tell he was awake and in his garden; I smelled the tang of burning leaves on the air.

I had promised Lucius and Cornelia that I would come again to the house on the Palatine, but there was another call I wanted to make first.

A few questions in the right ears and a few coins in the right hands were all it took to find the house of Furius's mother on the Caelian Hill, where his survivors had fled after he was proscribed, beheaded, and dispossessed. The house was small and narrow, wedged in among other small, narrow houses that might have been standing for a hundred years; the street had somehow survived the fires and the constant rebuilding that continually changes the face of the city, and seemed to take me into an older, simpler Rome, when rich and poor alike lived in modest private dwellings, before the powerful began to flaunt their wealth with great houses and the poor were pressed together into many-storied tenements.

A knock upon the door summoned a veritable giant, a hulking, thick-chested slave with squinting eyes and a scowling mouth—not the door slave of a secure and respectable home, but quite obviously a bodyguard. I stepped back a few paces so that I did not have to strain to look up at him, and asked to see his master.

"If you had legitimate business here, you'd know that there is no master in this house," he growled.

"Of course," I said, "I misspoke myself. I meant to say your mistress—the mother of the late Furius."

He scowled. "Do you misspeak yourself again, stranger, or could it be that you don't know that the old mistress had a stroke not long after her son's death? She and her daughter are in seclusion and see no one."

"What was I thinking? I meant to say, of course, Furius's widow—"

But the slave had had enough of me, and slammed the door in my face.

I heard a cackle of laughter behind me and turned to see a toothless old slavewoman sweeping the portico of the house across the street. "You'd have had an easier time getting in to see the dictator Sulla when he was alive," she laughed.

I smiled and shrugged. "Are they always so unfriendly and abrupt?"

"With strangers, always. You can't blame them—a house full of women with no man around but a bodyguard."

"No man in the house—ah, not since Furius was executed."

"You knew him?" asked the slavewoman.

"Not exactly. But I know of him."

"Terrible, what they did to him. He was no enemy of Sulla's. Furius had no stomach for politics or fighting. A gentle man, wouldn't have kicked a dog from his front step."

"But his brother took up arms against Sulla, and died fighting him."

"That was his brother, not Furius. I knew them both, from when they were boys growing up in that house with their mother. Furius was a peaceful child, and a cautious man. A philosopher, not a fighter. What was done to him was a terrible injustice—naming him an enemy of the state, taking all his property, cutting off

26

his . . ." She stopped her sweeping and cleared her throat. She hardened her jaw. "And who are you? Another schemer come to torment his womenfolk?"

"Not at all."

"Because I'll tell you right now that you'll never get in to see his mother or sister. Ever since the death, and after that the old woman's stroke, they haven't stirred out of that house. A long time to be in mourning, you might say, but Furius was all they had. His widow goes out to do the marketing, with the little girl; but she still wears black. They all took his death very hard."

At that moment the door across the street opened. A blonde woman emerged, draped in a black stola. Beside her, reaching up to hold her hand, was a little girl with haunted eyes and black curls. Closing the door and following behind was the giant, who saw me and scowled.

"On their way to market," whispered the old slavewoman. "She usually goes at this time of morning. Ah, look at the precious little one, so serious-looking yet so pretty. Not so much like her mother, not so fair; no, the very image of her aunt, I've always said."

"Her aunt? Not her father?"

"Him, too, of course . . ."

I talked with the old woman for a few moments, then hurried after the widow. I hoped for a chance to speak with her, but the bodyguard made it quite plain that I should keep my distance. I fell back and followed them in secret, observing her purchases as she did her shopping in the meat market.

At last I broke away and headed for the house on the Palatine.

Lucius and Cornelia hurried to the atrium even before the slave announced my arrival. Their faces were drawn with sleeplessness and worry.

"The lemur appeared again last night," said Lucius.

"The thing was in my bedchamber." Cornelia's face was pale. "I woke to see it standing beside the door. It must have been the smell that woke me—a horrible, fetid stench! I tried to rise and couldn't. I wanted to cry out, but my throat was frozen—the thing cast a spell on me. It said the words again: *Now you.* Then it disappeared into the hallway."

"Did you pursue it?"

She looked at me as if I were mad.

"But *I* saw the thing," offered Lucius. "I was in the bedchamber down the hall. I heard footsteps, and called out, thinking it might be Cornelia. There was no answer and the footsteps grew hurried. I leaped from my couch and stepped into the hall. . . ."

"And you saw it?"

"Only for an instant. I called out. The thing paused and turned, then disappeared into the shadows. I would have followed it—really, Gordianus, I swear I would have—but at that instant Cornelia cried out for me. I turned and hurried to her room."

"So the thing fled, and no one pursued it." I stifled a curse.

"I'm afraid so," said Lucius, wincing. "But when the thing turned and looked at me in the hallway, a bit of moonlight fell on its face."

"You had a good look at it, then?"

"Yes. Gordianus, I didn't know Furius well, but I had some dealings with him before his death, enough to recognize him across a street or in the Forum. And this creature—despite its broken teeth and the tumors on its flesh—this fiend most certainly bore the face of Furius!"

Cornelia suddenly gasped and began to stagger. Lucius held her up and called for help. Some of the household women gathered and escorted her to her bedchamber.

"Titus was just the same before his fall," sighed Lucius, shaking his head. "He began to faint and suffer fits, would suddenly lose his breath and be unable to catch another. They say such afflictions are frequently caused by spiteful lemures."

"Perhaps," I said. "Or by a guilty conscience. I wonder if the lemur left any other manifestations behind? Show me where you saw the thing."

Lucius led me down the hallway. "There," he said, pointing to a spot a few paces beyond the door to his room. "At night a bit of light falls just there; everything beyond is dark."

I walked to the place and looked about, then sniffed the air. Lucius sniffed as well. "The smell of putrefaction," he murmured. "The lemur has left its fetid odor behind."

"A bad smell, to be sure," I said, "but not the odor of a corpse. Look here! A footprint!"

Just below us, two faint brown stains in the shape of sandals had been left on the tiled floor. In the bright morning light other marks of the same color were visible extending in both directions. Those toward Cornelia's bedchamber, where many other feet had traversed, quickly became confused and unreadable. Those leading away showed only the imprint of the forefeet of a pair of sandals, with no heel marks.

"The thing came to a halt here, just as you said. Then it began to run, leaving only these abbreviated impressions. Why should a lemur run on tiptoes, I wonder? And what is this stain left by the footsteps?"

I knelt down and peered closely. Lucius, shedding his patrician dignity, got down on his hands and knees beside me. He wrinkled his nose. "The smell of putrefaction!" he said again.

"Not putrefaction," I countered. "Common excrement. Come, let's see where the footprints lead."

We followed them down the hallway and around a corner, where the footprints ended before a closed door.

"Does this lead outside?" I asked.

"Why, no," said Lucius, suddenly a patrician again and making an uncomfortable face. "That door opens into the indoor toilet."

"How interesting." I opened it and stepped inside. As I would have expected in a household run by a woman like Cornelia, the fixtures were luxurious and the place was quite spotless, except for some telltale footprints on the limestone floor. There were windows set high in the wall, covered by iron bars. A marble seat surmounted the hole. Peering within, I studied the lead piping of the drain.

"Straight down the slope of the Palatine Hill and into the Cloaca Maxima, and thence into the Tiber," commented Lucius. Patricians may be prudish about bodily functions, but of Roman plumbing they are justifiably proud.

"Not nearly large enough for a man to pass through," I said.

"What an awful idea!"

"Even so . . ." I called for a slave, who managed to find a chisel for me.

"Now what are you doing? Here, those tiles are made of fine limestone, Gordianus! You shouldn't go chipping away at the corners."

"Not even to discover *this?*" I slid the chisel under the edge of one of the stones and lifted it up.

Lucius drew back and gasped, then leaned forward and peered down into the darkness. "A tunnel!" he whispered.

"So it appears."

"Why, someone must go down it!" Lucius peered at me and raised an eyebrow.

"Not even if Cornelia doubled my fee!"

"I wasn't suggesting that *you* go, Gordianus." He looked up at the young slave who had fetched the chisel. The boy looked slender and supple enough. When he saw what Lucius intended, he started back and looked at me imploringly.

"No, Lucius Claudius," I said, "no one need be put at risk; not yet. Who knows what the boy might encounter—if not lemures and monsters, then booby traps or scorpions or a fall to his death. First we should attempt to determine the tunnel's egress. It may be a simple matter, if it merely follows the logical course of the plumbing."

Which it did. From the balcony on the western side of the house, it was easy enough to judge where the buried pipes descended the slope into the valley between the Palatine and the Capitoline, where they joined with the Cloaca Maxima underground. At the foot of the hill, directly below the house, in a wild rubbish-strewn region behind some warehouses and granaries, I spied a thicket. Even stripped of their leaves, the bushes grew so thick that I could not see far into them.

Lucius insisted on accompanying me, though his bulky frame and expensive garb were ill-suited for traversing a rough hillside. We reached the foot of the hill and pushed our way into the thicket, ducking beneath branches and snapping twigs out of the way.

At last we came to the heart of the thicket, where our perseverance was rewarded. Hidden behind the dense, shaggy branches of a cypress tree was the tunnel's other end. The hole was crudely made, lined with rough dabs of cement and broken bricks. It was just large enough for a man to enter, but the foul smell that issued

30

from within was enough to keep vagrants or even curious children out.

At night, hidden behind the storehouses and sheds, such a place would be quite lonely and secluded. A man—or a lemur, for that matter—might come and go completely unobserved.

"Cold," complained Lucius, "cold and damp and dark. It would have made more sense to stay in the house tonight, where it's warm and dry. We could lie in wait in the hallway and trap this fiend when he emerges from his secret passage. Why, instead, are we huddling here in the dark and cold, watching for who-knows-what and jumping in fright every time a bit of wind whistles through the thicket?"

"You need not have come, Lucius Claudius. I didn't ask you to."

"Cornelia would have thought me a coward if I didn't." He pouted.

"And what does Cornelia's opinion matter?" I snapped, and bit my tongue. The cold and damp had set us both on edge. A light drizzle began to fall, obscuring the moon and casting the thicket into even greater darkness. We had been hiding among the brambles since shortly after nightfall. I had warned Lucius that the watch was likely to be long and uncomfortable and possibly futile, but he had insisted on accompanying me. He had offered to hire some ruffians to escort us, but if my suspicions were correct we would not need them; nor did I want more witnesses to be present than was necessary.

A gust of icy wind whipped beneath my cloak and sent a shiver up my spine. Lucius's teeth began to chatter. My mood grew dark. What if I was wrong, after all? What if the thing we sought was not human, but something else . . .

"And as for jumping in fear every time a twig snaps," I whispered, "speak for yourself—"

I fell silent, for at that moment not one but many twigs began to snap. Something large had entered the thicket and was moving toward us.

"It must be a whole army!" whispered Lucius, clutching at my arm.

"No," I whispered back. "Only two persons, if my guess is right."

Two moving shapes, obscured by the tangle of branches and the deep gloom, came very near to us and then turned aside, toward the cypress tree that hid the tunnel's mouth.

A moment later I heard a man's voice, cursing: "Someone has blocked the hole!" I recognized the voice of the growling giant who guarded the house on the Caelian Hill.

"Perhaps the tunnel has fallen in." When Lucius heard the second voice he clutched my arm again, not in fear but surprise.

"No," I said aloud, "the tunnel was purposely blocked so that you could not use it again."

There was a moment of silence, followed by the noise of two bodies scrambling in the underbrush.

"Stay where you are!" I said. "For your own good, stay where you are and listen to me!"

The scrambling ceased and there was silence again, except for the sound of heavy breathing and confused whispers.

"I know who you are," I said. "I know why you've come here. I have no interest in harming you, but I must speak with you. Will you speak with me, Furia?"

"Furia?" whispered Lucius. The drizzle had ended, and moonlight illuminated the confusion on his face.

There was a long silence, then more whispering—the giant was trying to dissuade his mistress. Finally she spoke out. "Who are you?" she said.

"My name is Gordianus. You don't know me. But I know that you and your family have suffered greatly, Furia. You have been wronged, most unjustly. Perhaps your vengeance on Titus and Cornelia is seemly in the eyes of the gods—I cannot judge. But you have been found out, and the time has come to stop your pretense. I'll step toward you now. There are two of us. We bear no weapons. Tell your faithful slave that we mean no harm, and that to harm us will profit you nothing."

I stepped slowly toward the cypress tree, a great, shaggy patch of black amid the general gloom. Beside it stood two forms, one tall, the other short.

With a gesture, Furia bade her slave to stay where he was, then she stepped toward us. A patch of moonlight fell on her face. Lucius gasped and started back. Even though I expected it, the sight still sent a shiver through my veins.

I confronted what appeared to be a young man in a tattered cloak. His short hair was matted with blood and blood was smeared all around his throat and neck, as if his neck had been severed and then somehow fused together again. His eyes were dark and hollow. His skin was as pale as death and dotted with horrible tumors, his lips were parched and cracked. When Furia spoke, her sweet, gentle voice was a strange contrast to her horrifying visage.

"You have found out," she said.

"Yes."

"Are you the man who called at my mother's house this morning?"

"Yes."

"Who betrayed me? It couldn't have been Cleto," she whispered, glancing at the bodyguard.

"No one betrayed you. We found the tunnel this afternoon."

"Ah! My brother had it built during the worst years of the civil war, so that we might have a way to escape in a sudden crisis. Of course, when the monster became dictator, there was no way for anyone to escape."

"Was your brother truly an enemy of Sulla's?"

"Not in any active way, but there were those willing to paint him as such—those who coveted all he had."

"Furius was proscribed for no reason?"

"No reason but the bitch's greed!" Her voice was hard and bitter. I glanced at Lucius, who was curiously silent at such an assault on Cornelia's character.

"It was Titus whom you haunted first—"

"Only so that Cornelia would know what awaited her. Titus was a weakling, a nobody, easily frightened. Ask Cornelia; she frightened him into doing anything she wished, even if it meant destroying an innocent colleague from his younger days. It was Cornelia who convinced her dear cousin Sulla to insert my brother's name in the proscription lists, merely to obtain our house. Because the men of our line have perished, because Furius was the last, she thought that her calumny would go unavenged forever."

"But now it must stop, Furia. You must be content with what you have done so far."

"No!"

"A life for a life," I said. "Titus for Furius."

"No, ruin for ruin! The death of Titus will not restore our house, our fortune, our good name."

"Nor will the death of Cornelia. If you proceed now, you are sure to be caught. You must be content with half a portion of vengeance, and push the rest aside."

"You intend to tell her, then? Now that you've caught me at it?"

I hesitated. "First, tell me truly, Furia, did you push Titus from his balcony?"

She looked at me unwaveringly, the moonlight making her eyes glimmer like shards of onyx. "Titus jumped from the balcony. He jumped because he thought he saw the lemur of my brother, and he could not stand his own wretchedness and guilt."

I bowed my head. "Go," I whispered. "Take your slave and go now, back to your mother and your niece and your brother's widow. Never come back."

I looked up to see tears streaming down her face. It was a strange sight, to see a lemur weep. She called to the slave, and they departed from the thicket.

We ascended the hill in silence. Lucius stopped chattering his teeth and instead began to huff and puff. Outside Cornelia's house I drew him aside.

"Lucius, you must not tell Cornelia."

"But how else—"

"We will tell her that we found the tunnel but that no one came, that her persecutor has been frightened off for now, but may come again, in which case she can set her own guard. Yes, let her think that the unknown threat is still at large, always plotting her destruction."

"But surely she deserves—"

"She deserves what Furia had in store for her. Did you know Cornelia had placed Furius's name on the lists, merely to obtain his house?"

"I—" Lucius bit his lips. "I suspected the possibility. But Gordianus, what she did was hardly unique. Everyone was doing it."

"Not everyone. Not you, Lucius."

"True," he said, nodding sheepishly. "But Cornelia will fault you for not capturing the imposter. She'll refuse to pay the full fee."

"I don't care about the fee."

"I'll make up the difference," said Lucius.

I laid my hand on his shoulder. "What is rarer than a camel in Gaul?" Lucius wrinkled his brow. I laughed. "An honest man in Rome."

Lucius shrugged off the compliment with typical chagrin. "I still don't understand how you knew the identity of the imposter."

"I told you that I visited the house on the Caelian Hill this morning. What I didn't tell you was that the old slavewoman across the street revealed to me that Furius not only had a sister, but that this sister was the same age—his twin—and bore a striking resemblance to him."

"Ah! They must have been close, and her slightly softer features make her look younger than Furius."

"Who must have been quite handsome. Even through her horrid makeup . . ." I sighed. "Also, when I followed Furius's widow to market, I was struck by her purchase of a quantity of calf's blood. She also gathered a spray of juniper berries, which the little girl carried for her."

"Berries?"

"The cankers pasted on Furia's face—juniper berries cut in half. The blood was for matting her hair and daubing on her neck. As for the rest of her appearance, her ghastly makeup and costuming, you and I can only guess at the ingenuity of a household of women united toward a single goal. Furia has been in seclusion for months, which explains the almost uncanny paleness of her flesh—and the fact that she was able to cut off her hair without anyone taking notice."

I shook my head. "A remarkable woman. I wonder why she never married? The turmoil and confusion of the civil war, I suppose, and the death of her brothers ruined her prospects forever. Misery is like a pebble cast into a pond, sending out a wave that spreads and spreads."

I headed home that night weary and wistful. There are days when one sees too much of the world's wickedness, and only a long sleep in the safe seclusion of one's home can restore an appetite for life. I thought of Bethesda and Eco, and tried to push the face of Furia from my thoughts. The last thing on my mind was the haunted soldier and his legion of lemures, and yet I was destined to encounter them all before I reached my house.

I passed by the wall of his garden, smelled the familiar tang of burning leaves, but thought no more about the soldier until I heard the little wooden door open behind me and the voice of his old retainer crying out my name.

"Thank the gods you've finally returned!" he whispered hoarsely. He seemed to be in the grip of a strange malady or spell, for even though the door allowed him more room to stand, he remained oddly bent, his eyes gleamed dully, and his jaw was slack. "The master has sent messenger after messenger to your door—always they are told you are out, that your return is expected at any moment. But when the lemures come, time stops. Please, come! Save the master—save us all!"

From beyond the wall I heard the sound of moaning, not from one man but from many. I heard a woman shriek, and the sound of furniture overturned. What madness was taking place within the house?

"Please, help us! The lemures, the lemures!" The old slave made a face of such horror that I started back and turned to make my escape. My house was only a few steps up the pathway. But I turned back. I reached inside my tunic and felt for the handle of my dagger before I thought how little use a dagger would be to deal with those already dead.

It took no small amount of courage to step through the little door. My heart pounded like a hammer in my chest.

The air within was dank and smoky. After the brief drizzle a clammy cold had descended upon the hills of Rome, such as holds down plumes of smoke and makes the air unwholesome and stagnant. I breathed in an acrid breath and coughed.

The soldier came running from within the house. He tripped and staggered forward on his knees, wrapped his arms around my waist and looked up at me in abject terror. "There!" He pointed back toward the house. "They pursue me! Gods have mercy—the boy without a head, the soldier with his belly cut open, all the others!"

I peered into the hazy darkness, but saw nothing except a bit of whorling smoke. I suddenly felt dizzy and lightheaded. It was because I had not eaten all day, I told myself; I should have been less proud and presumed upon Cornelia's hospitality for a meal. Then, while I watched, the whorl of smoke began to expand and change shape. A face emerged from the murky darkness—a boy's face, twisted with agony.

"See!" cried the soldier. "See how the poor lad holds his own head in his fist, like Perseus holding the head of the Gorgon! See how he stares, blaming me!"

Indeed, out of the darkness and smoke I began to see exactly what the wretched man described, a headless boy in battle garb clutching his dismembered head by the hair and holding it aloft. I opened my mouth in awe and terror. Behind the boy, other shapes began to emerge—first a few, then many, then a legion of phantoms covered with blood and writhing like maggots in the air.

It was a terrifying spectacle. I would have fled, but I was rooted to the spot. The soldier clutched my knees. The old slave began to weep and babble. From within the house came the sound of others in distress, moaning and crying out.

"Don't you hear them?" cried the soldier. "The lemures, shrieking like harpies!" The great looming mass of corpses began to keen and wail—surely all of Rome could hear it!

Like a drowning man, the mind in great distress will clutch at anything to save itself. A bit of straw will float, but will not support a thrashing man; a plank of wood may give him respite, but best of all is a steady rock within the raging current. So my mind clutched at anything that might preserve it in the face of such overwhelming and inexplicable horror. Time had come to a stop, just as the old slave had said, and in that endlessly attenuated moment a flood of images, memories, schemes, and notions raged through my mind. I clutched at straws. Madness pulled me downward, like an unseen current in black water. I sank—until I suddenly found the rock for which I sought.

"The bush!" I whispered. "The burning bush, which speaks aloud!"

The soldier, thinking I spied something within the mass of writhing lemures, clutched at me and trembled. "What bush? Ah yes, I see it, too . . ."

"No, the bush here in your garden! That strange, gnarled tree among the yews, with yellow leaves all around. But now the leaves have all been swept in among the others . . . burnt with the others in the brazier . . . the smoke still hangs in the air . . ."

I pulled the soldier out of the garden, through the small door, and onto the pathway. I returned for the old slave, and then, one by one, for the others. They huddled together on the cobblestones, trembling and confused, their eyes wide with terror and red with blood.

"There are no lemures!" I whispered hoarsely, my throat sore from the smoke—even though I could see them hovering over the wall, cackling and dangling their entrails in the empty air.

The slaves pointed and clutched one another. The soldier hid behind his hands.

As the slaves grew more manageable, I led them in groups to my house, where they huddled together, frightened but safe. Bethesda was perplexed and displeased at the sudden invasion of half-mad strangers, but Eco was delighted at the opportunity to stay up until dawn under such novel circumstances. It was a long, cold night, marked by fits of panic and orgies of mutual reassurance, while we waited for sanity to return.

The first light of morning broke, bringing a cold dew that was a tonic to senses still befuddled by sleeplessness and poisoned by smoke. My head pounded like thunder, with a hangover far worse than any I had ever gotten from wine. A ray of pale sunlight was like a knife to my eyes, but I no longer saw visions of lemures or heard their mad shrieking.

The soldier, haggard and dazed, begged me for an explanation. I agreed readily enough, for a wise man once taught me that the best relief for a pounding headache is the application of disciplined thought, which brings blood to the brain and flushes evil humors from the phlegm.

"It came to me in a flash of inspiration, not logic," I explained. "Your autumnal ritual of burning leaves, and the yearly visitation of the lemures . . . the smoke that filled your garden, and the plague of spirits . . . these things were not unconnected. That odd, twisted tree in your garden is not native to Rome, or to the peninsula. How it came here, I have no idea, but I suspect it came from the East, where plants which induce visions are quite common. There is the snake plant of Aethiopia, the juice of which causes such terrible visions that it drives men to suicide; men guilty of sacrilege are forced to drink it as a punishment. The rivergleam plant that grows on the banks of the Indus is also famous for making men rave and see weird visions. But I suspect that the tree in your garden may be a specimen of a rare bush found in the rocky mountains east of Egypt. Bethesda tells a tale about it."

"What tale?" said Bethesda.

"You remember—the tale your Hebrew father passed on to you, about his ancestor called Moses, who encountered a bush that spoke aloud to him when it burned. The leaves of your bush, neighbor, not only spoke but cast powerful visions."

"Yet why did I see what I saw?"

"You saw that which you feared the most—the vengeful spirits of those you killed fighting for Sulla."

"But the slaves saw what I saw! And so did you!"

"We saw what you suggested, just as you began to see a burning bush when I said the words."

He shook his head. "It was never so powerful before. Last night was more terrible than ever!"

"Probably because, in the past, you happened to burn only a few of the yellow leaves at a time, and the cold wind carried away much of the smoke; the visions came upon some but not all of the household, and in varying degrees. But last night the smoke hovered in the garden and the haze spread through the house; and perhaps you happened to burn a great many of the yellow leaves at once. Everyone who breathed the smoke was intoxicated and stricken with a kind of madness. Once we escaped the smoke, with time the madness passed, like a fever burning itself out."

"Then the lemures never existed?"

"I think not."

"And if I uproot that accursed bush and cast it in the Tiber, I will never see the lemures again?"

"Perhaps not," I said. *Though you may always see them in your nightmares*, I thought.

"So, it was just as I told you," said Bethesda, bringing a cool cloth to lay upon my forehead that afternoon. Flashes of pain still coursed through my temples from time to time, and whenever I closed my eyes alarming visions loomed in the blackness.

"Just as you told me? Nonsense!" I said. "You thought that Titus was pushed from his balcony—and that his wife Cornelia did it!"

"A woman pretending to be a lemur drove him to jump—which is just the same," she insisted.

"And you said the soldier's old slave was lying about having seen the lemures himself, when in fact he was telling the truth."

"What I said was that the dead cannot go walking about unless they have been properly mummified, and I was absolutely right. And it was I who once told you about the burning bush that speaks, remember? Without that, you never would have figured the cause."

"Fair enough," I admitted, deciding it was impossible to win the argument.

"This quaint Roman idea about lemures haunting the living is completely absurd," she went on.

"About that I am not sure."

"But with your own eyes you have seen the truth! By your own wits you have proved in two instances that what everyone thought to be lemures were not lemures at all, only makeup and fear, intoxicating smoke and guilty consciences!"

"You miss the point, Bethesda."

"What do you mean?"

"Lemures *do* exist—perhaps not as visitors perceptible to the senses, but in another way. The dead do have power to spread misery among the living. The spirit of a man can carry on and cause untold havoc from beyond the grave. The more powerful the man, the more terrible his legacy." I shivered—not at lurid visions remembered from the soldier's garden, but at the naked truth, which

40

was infinitely more concrete and terrible. "Rome is a haunted city. The lemur of the dictator Sulla haunts us all. Dead he may be, but not departed. His wickedness lingers on, bringing despair and suffering upon his friends and foes alike."

To this Bethesda had no answer. I closed my eyes and saw no more monsters, but slept a dreamless sleep until dawn of the following day.

Steven Saylor won the Mystery Writers of America "Best Short Story" Edgar in 1993 for one of his Gordianus tales, set in the Rome of the first century B.C. Thus, his chronicling of the cases of this "Detectus," as he styles him, have been given classic status to match their already "classic" appeal. His novels in the Roma Sub Rosa series, featuring Gordianus, include Roman Blood, Arms of Nemesis *and* Catalina's Riddle.

The Adventure
of the Dead Cat

BY ELLERY QUEEN

Receiving an ominous-looking dead-black envelope in the day's mail is an extraordinary event—but
if it arrives around the end of October and is addressed in flashy orange ink, there's a good chance
it's simply an invitation to a Halloween party. This
is exactly the case with the peculiar missive addressed to "Miss Nikki Porter" and sent to her business address, the apartment of her employer, Ellery
Queen.

What's "peculiar" about it is that while there's
definitely a festive event in the works—"a secret
meeting of The Inner Circle of Black Cats," to be
held promptly at 9:05 on Halloween night—who's
doing the inviting has chosen for the moment to stay
anonymous. Naturally, such a coy come-on leaves
Ellery both annoyed and curious, and just as predict-
ably his curiosity wins out in this highly sophisticated
tale of masks and murder—and murder un-
masked—in old Manhattan.

THE ADVENTURE OF THE DEAD CAT

The square-cut envelope was a creation of orange ink on black notepaper; by which Ellery instantly divined its horrid authorship. Behind it leered a bouncy hostess, all teeth and enthusiastic ideas, who spent large sums of some embarrassed man's money to build a better mousetrap.

Having too often been one of the mice, he was grateful that the envelope was addressed to "Miss Nikki Porter."

"But why to me at your apartment?" wondered Nikki, turning the black envelope over and finding nothing.

"Studied insult," Ellery assured her. "One of those acid-sweet women who destroy an honest girl's reputation at a stroke. Don't even open it. Hurl it into the fire, and let's get on with the work."

So Nikki opened it and drew out an enclosure cut in the shape of a cat.

"I am a master of metaphor," muttered Ellery.

"What?" said Nikki, unfolding the feline.

"It doesn't matter. But if you insist on playing the mouse, go ahead and read it." The truth was, he was a little curious himself.

"*Fellow Spook*," began Nikki, frowning.

"Read no more. The hideous details are already clear—"

"Oh, shut up," said Nikki. *"There is a secret meeting of The Inner Circle of Black Cats in Suite 1313, Hotel Chancellor, City, Oct. 31."*

"Of course," said Ellery glumly. "That follows logically."

"You must come in full costume as a Black Cat, including domino mask. Time your arrival for 9:05 P.M. promptly. Till the Witching Hour. Signed—*G. Host.* How darling!"

"No clue to the criminal?"

"No. I don't recognize the handwriting. . . ."

"Of course you're not going."

"Of course I *am!*"

"Having performed my moral duty as friend, protector, and employer, I now suggest you put the foul thing away and get back to our typewriter."

"What's more," said Nikki, "you're going, too."

Ellery smiled his number-three smile—the toothy one. "Am I?"

"There's a postscript on the cat's—on the reverse side. *Be sure to drag your boss-cat along, also costumed.*"

Ellery could see himself as a sort of overgrown Puss-in-Boots plying the sjambok over a houseful of bounding tabbies all swilling Scotch. The vision was tiring.

"I decline with the usual thanks."

"You're a stuffed shirt."

"I'm an intelligent man."

"You don't know how to have fun."

"These brawls inevitably wind up with someone's husband taking a poke at a tall, dark, handsome stranger."

"Coward."

"Heavens, I wasn't referring to myself—!"

Whence it is obvious he had already lost the engagement.

Ellery stood before a door on the thirteenth floor of the Hotel Chancellor, cursing the Druids.

For it was Samain at whose mossy feet must be laid the origins of our recurrent October silliness. True, the lighting of ceremonial bonfires in a Gaelic glade must have seemed natural and proper at the time, and a Gallic grove fitting rendezvous for an annual convention of ghosts and witches; but the responsibility of even pagan deities must surely be held to extend beyond temporal bounds, and the Druid lord of death should have foreseen that a bonfire would be out of place in a Manhattan hotel suite, not to mention disembodied souls, however wicked.

Then Ellery recalled that Pomona, goddess of fruits, had contributed nuts and apples to the burgeoning Halloween legend, and he cursed the Romans, too.

There had been Inspector Queen at home, who had intolerably chosen to ignore the whole thing; the taxi driver, who had asked amiably, "Fraternity initiation?"; the dread chorus of meows during the long, long trek across the Chancellor lobby; and, finally, the reeking wag in the elevator who had tried to swing Ellery around by his tail, puss-pussying obscenely as he did so.

Cried Ellery out of the agony of his mortification: "Never, never, *never* again will I—"

"Stop grousing and look at this," said Nikki, peering through her domino mask.

"What is it? I can't see through this damned thing."

"A sign on the door. IF YOU ARE A BLACK CAT, WALK IN!!!!! With five exclamation points."

"All right, all right. Let's go in and get it over with."

And, of course, when they opened the unlocked door of 1313, darkness.

And silence.

"Now what do we do?" giggled Nikki, and jumped at the snick of the door behind them.

"I'll tell you what," said Ellery enthusiastically. "Let's get the hell out of here."

But Nikki was already a yard away, black in blackness.

"Wait! Give me your hand, Nikki."

"*Mister* Queen. That's not my hand."

"Beg your pardon," muttered Ellery. "We seem to be trapped in a hallway. . . ."

"There's a red light down there! Must be at the end of the hall— *eee!*"

"Think of the soup this would make for the starving." Ellery disentangled her from the embrace of some articulated bones.

"Ellery! I don't think that's funny at all."

"I don't think *any* of this is funny."

They groped toward the red light. It was not so much a light as a rosy shade of darkness, which faintly blushed above a small plinth of the raven variety. The woman's cornered the black-paper market, Ellery thought disagreeably as he read the runes of yellow fire on the plinth:

TURN LEFT!!!!!!!!!

"And into, I take it," he growled, "the great unknown." And, indeed, having explored to the left, his hand encountered outer space; whereupon, intrepidly, and with a large yearning to master the mystery and come to grips with its diabolical authoress, Ellery plunged through the invisible archway, Nikki bravely clinging to his tail.

"Ouch!"

"What's the matter?" gasped Nikki.

"Bumped into a chair. Skinned my shin. What would a chair be doing—?"

"Poooor Ellery," said Nikki, laughing. "Did the dreat bid mad hurt his—*Ow!*"

"Blast this—Ooo!"

"Ellery, where are you? Ooch!"

"Ow, my foot," bellowed Ellery from somewhere. "What is this—a tank-trap? Floor cluttered with pillows, hassocks—"

"Something cold and wet over here. Feels like an ice bucket . . . Owwwww!" There was a wild clatter of metal, a soggy crash, and silence again.

"Nikki! What happened?"

"I fell over a rack of fire tongs, I think." Nikki's voice came clearly from floor level. "Yes. Fire tongs."

"Of all the stupid, childish, unfunny—"

"Oop."

"Lost in a madhouse. Why is the furniture scattered every which way?"

"How should I know? Ellery, where *are* you?"

"In Bedlam. Keep your head now, Nikki, and stay where you are. Sooner or later a St. Bernard will find you and bring—"

Nikki screamed.

"Thank God," said Ellery, shutting his eyes.

The room was full of blessed Consolidated Edison light, and various adult figures in black-cat costumes and masks were leaping and laughing and shouting, "Surpriiiiise!" like idiot phantoms at the crisis of a delirium.

O Halloween.

"Ann! Ann Trent!" Nikki was squealing. "Oh, Ann, you fool, how ever did you find me?"

"Nikki, you're looking *wonderful*. Oh, but you're famous, darling. The great E. Q.'s secretary . . ."

Nuts to you, sister. Even bouncier than predicted. With that lazy, hippy strut. And chic, glossy chic. Lugs her sex around like a sample case. Kind of female who would be baffled by an egg. Looks five years older than she is, Antoine notwithstanding.

"But it's not Trent anymore, Nikki—Mrs. John Crombie. Johnnnnny!"

"Ann, you're *married?* And didn't invite me to the wedding!"

"Spliced in dear old Lunnon. John's British—or was. Johnny, top flirting with Edith Baxter and come here!"

"Ann darlin'—this exquisite girl! Scotch or bourbon, Nikki? Scotch, if you're the careful type—but bourbon works faster."

John Crombie, Gent. Eyes of artificial blue, slimy smile, sunlamp complexion, Olivier chin. British Club and Fox and Hounds—he posts even in a living room. He will say in a moment that he loathes Americah. Exactly. Ann Trent Crombie must have large amounts of the filthy. He despises her and patronizes her friends. He will fix me with the superior British smile and flap a limp brown hand . . . *Quod erat demonstrandum.*

"I warn you, Nikki," Ann Crombie was saying, "I'm hitched to a man who tries to jockey every new female he meets." Blush hard, prim Nikki. Friends grow in unforeseen directions. "Oh, Lucy! Nikki, do you remember my kid sister Lu—?"

Squeal, squeal. "Lucy Trent! This isn't *you?*"

"Am I grown up, Nikki?"

"Heavens!"

"Lucy's done *all* the party decorating, darling—spent the whole sordid day up here alone fixing things up. Hasn't she done an *inspired* job? But then, I'm so useless."

"Ann means she wouldn't help, Nikki. Just a lout."

Uncertain laugh. Poor Lucy. Embarrassed by her flowering youth, trying hard to be New York . . . There she goes refilling a glass—emptying an ashtray—running out to the kitchen—for a tray of fresh hot pigs-in-blankets?—*bong!* . . . the unwanted and gauche hiding confusion by making herself useful. Keep away from your brother-in-law, dear; that's an upstanding little bosom under the Black Cat's hide.

"Oh, Ellery, do come here and meet the Baxters. Mrs. Baxter—Edith—Ellery Queen . . . "

What's this? A worm who's turned, surely! The faded-fair type, hard used by wedlock. Very small, a bit on the spready side—she let herself go—but now she's back in harness again, all curried and combed, with a triumphant lift to her pale head, like an old thoroughbred proudly prancing in a paddock she had never hoped to enter again. And that glitter of secret pleasure in her blinky brown eyes, almost malice, whenever she looked at Ann Crombie. . . .

"Jerry Baxter, Edith's husband. Ellery Queen."

"Hiya, son!"

"Hi yourself, Jerry."

Salesman, or advertising-agency man, or Broadway agent. The life of the party. Three drinks and he's off to the races. He will be the first to fall in the apple tub, the first to pin the tail on Lucy or Nikki instead of on the donkey, the first to be sick, and the first to pass out. Skitter, stagger, sweat, and whoop. Why do you whoop, Jerry Baxter?

Ellery shook hot palms, smiled with what he hoped was charm, said affably: "Yes, isn't it?" "Haven't we met somewhere?" "Here, here, that's fine for now," and things like that, wondering what he was doing in a hotel living room festooned with apples, marsh-mallows, nuts, and crissscrossing crepe-paper twists, hung with grinning pumpkins and fancy black-and-orange cardboard cats, skeletons, and witches, and choked with bourbon fumes, tobacco smoke, and Chanel No. 5. Some Chinese lanterns were reeking, the noise was maddening, and merely to cross the room required the preparations of an expedition, for the overturned furniture and other impedimenta on the floor—cunningly plotted to trap groping Black Cats on their arrival—had been left where they were.

So Ellery, highball in hand, wedged himself in a safe corner and mentally added Nikki to the Druids and the Romans.

Ellery accepted the murder game without a murmur. He knew the futility of protest. Wherever he went, people at once suggested a murder game, apparently on the theory that a busman enjoys nothing so much as a bus. And, of course, he was to be the detective.

"Well, well, let's get started," he said gaily, for all the traditional Halloween games had been played: Nikki had slapped Jerry Baxter laughingly once and British Johnny—not laughingly—twice, the house detective had made a courtesy call, and it was obvious the delightful evening had all but run its course. He hoped Nikki would have sense enough to cut the *pièce de résistance* short, so that a man might go home and give his thanks to God; but no, there she was in a whispery, giggly huddle with Ann Crombie and Lucy Trent, while John Crombie rested his limp hand on her shoulder and Edith Baxter splashed some angry bourbon into her glass.

Jerry was on all fours, being a cat.

"In just a minute," called Nikki, and she tripped through the archway—kitchen-bound, to judge from certain subsequent cutlery sounds—leaving Crombie's hand momentarily suspended.

Edith Baxter said, "Jerry, get up off that floor and stop making a darned fool of yourself!" furiously.

"Now we're all set," announced Nikki, reappearing. "Everybody around in a circle. First I'll deal out these cards, and whoever gets the ace of spades, *don't let on!*—because you're the Murderer."

"Ooh!"

"Ann, you stop peeking."

"Who's peeking?"

"A tenner says I draw the fatal pasteboard," laughed Crombie. "I'm the killer type."

"*I'm* the killer type!" shouted Jerry Baxter. "Gack-gack-gack-gack!"

Ellery closed his eyes.

"Ellery! Wake up."

"Huh?"

Nikki was shaking him. The rest of the company were lined up on the far side of the room from the archway, facing the wall. For a panicky moment he thought of the St. Valentine's Day Massacre.

"You go on over there with the others, smarty-pants. You mustn't see who the murderer is, either, so you close your eyes, too."

"Fits in perfectly with my plans," said Ellery, and he dutifully joined the five people at the wall.

"Spread out a little there—I don't want anyone touching anyone else. That's it. Eyes all shut? Good. Now I want the person who drew the ace of spades—Murderer—to step quietly away from the wall—"

"Not cricket," came John Crombie's annoying alto. "*You'll* see who it is, dear heart."

"Yes," said Edith Baxter nastily. "The light's on."

"But I'm running this assassination! Now, stop talking, eyes closed. Step out, Murderer—that's it . . . quietly! No talking there at the wall! Mr. Queen is *very* bright and he'd get the answer in a shot just by eliminating voices—"

"Oh, come, Nikki," said Mr. Queen modestly.

"Now, Murderer, here's what you do. On the kitchen table you'll find a full-face mask, a flashlight, and a bread knife. Wait! Don't start for the kitchen yet—go when I switch off the light in here; that will be your signal to start. When you get to the kitchen, put on the mask, take the flashlight and knife, steal back into this room, and—pick a victim!"

"Oooh."

"Ahhhh!"

"Ee!"

Mr. Queen banged his forehead lightly against the wall. How long, O Lord?

"Now remember, Murderer," cried Nikki, "you pick anyone you want—except, of course, Ellery. He has to live long enough to solve the crime. . . ."

If you don't hurry, my love, I'll be dead of natural causes.

"It'll be dark, Murderer, except for your flash, so even I won't know what victim you pick—"

"May the detective inquire the exact purpose of the knife?" asked the detective wearily of the wall. "Its utility in this amusement escapes me."

"Oh, the knife's just a prop, goopy—atmosphere. Murderer, you just tap your victim on the shoulder. Victim—whoever feels the tap—turn around and let Murderer lead you out of the living room to the kitchen."

"The kitchen, I take it, is the scene of the crime," said Mr. Queen gloomily.

"Uh-huh. And, Victim, as soon as Murderer gets you into the kitchen, scream like all fury as if you're being stabbed. Make it realistic! Everybody set? Ready? . . . All right, Murderer, soon's I turn this light off, go to the kitchen, get the mask and stuff, come back, and pick your victim. Here goes!"

Click went the light switch. Being a man who checked his facts, Ellery automatically cheated and opened one eye. Dark, as advertised. He shut the eye, and then jumped.

"Stop!" Nikki had shrieked.

"What, what?" asked Ellery excitedly.

"Oh, I'm not talking to you, Ellery. Murderer, I forgot something! Where are you? Oh, never mind. Remember, after you've supposedly stabbed your victim in the kitchen, come back to this room and quickly take your former place against the wall. Don't make a sound; don't touch anyone. I want the room to be as quiet as it is this minute. Use the flash to help you see your way back, but as soon as you reach the wall, turn the flash off and throw flash and mask into the middle of the living room—thus, darling, getting rid of the evidence. Do you see? But, of course, you *can't*." You're in rare form, old girl. "Now, even though it's dark, people, *keep your eyes shut*. All right, Murderer—get set—*go!*"

Ellery dozed. . . .

It seemed a mere instant later that he heard Nikki's voice saying with incredible energy: "Murderer's tapping a victim—careful with that flashlight, Murderer!—we musn't tempt our Detective *too* much. All right, Victim? Now let Murderer lead you to your doom . . . the rest of you keep your eyes closed . . . don't turn ar- . . ."

Ellery dozed again.

* * *

He awoke with a start at a man's scream.

"Here! What—"

"Ellery Queen, you asleep again? That was Victim being carved up in the kitchen. Now . . . yes! . . . here's Murderer's flashback . . . that's it, to the wall quietly . . . now flash *off!*—fine!—toss it and your mask away . . . Boom. Tossed. Are you turned around, face to the wall, Murderer, like everybody else? Everybody ready? Lllllllights!"

"Now—" began Ellery briskly.

"Why, it's John who's missing," laughed Lucy.

"Pooooor John is daid," sang Jerry.

"My poor husband," wailed Ann. "Jo-hon, come back to me!"

"Ho, John!" shouted Nikki.

"Just a moment," said Ellery. "Isn't Edith Baxter missing, too?"

"My wiff?" shouted Jerry. "Hey, wiff! Come outa the wood-work!"

"Oh, darn," said Lucy. "There mustn't be two victims, Nikki. That spoils the game."

"Let us repair to the scene of the crime," proclaimed Miss Porter, "and see what gives."

So, laughing and chattering and having a hell of a time, they all trooped through the archway, turned left, crossed the foyer, and went into the Crombie kitchen and found John Crombie on the floor with his throat cut.

When Ellery returned to the kitchen from his very interesting telephone chat with Inspector Queen, he found Ann Crombie being sick over the kitchen sink, her forehead supported by the greenish hand of a greenish Lucy Trent, and Nikki crouched quietly in a corner, as far away from the covered thing on the floor as the architect's plans allowed, while Jerry Baxter raced up and down weeping: "Where's my wife? Where's Edith? We've got to get out of here."

Ellery grabbed Baxter's collar and said, "It's going to be a long night, Jerry—relax. Nikki—"

"Yes, Ellery." She was trembling and trying to stop it and not succeeding.

"You know who was supposed to be the murderer in that foul

54

game—the one who drew the ace of spades—you saw him or her step away from the living room wall while the lights were still on in there. Who was it?"

"Edith Baxter, Edith got the ace. Edith was supposed to be the murderer."

Jerry Baxter jerked out of Ellery's grasp. "You're lying!" he yelled. "You're not mixing my wife up in this stink! You're a lying—"

Ann crept away from the sink, avoiding the mound. She crept past them and went into the foyer and collapsed against the door of a closet just outside the kitchen. Lucy crept after Ann and cuddled against her, whimpering. Ann began to whimper, too.

"Edith Baxter was Murderer," said Nikki drearily. "In the game, anyway."

"You lie! You lying—"

Ellery slapped his mouth without rancor and Baxter started to cry again. "Don't let me come back and find any other throats cut," said Ellery, and he went out of the kitchen.

It was tempting to assume the obvious, which was that Edith Baxter, having drawn the ace of spades, decided to play the role of murderer in earnest, and did so, and fled. Her malice-dipped triumph as she looked at John Crombie's wife, her anger as she watched Crombie pursue Nikki through the evening, told a simple story; and it was really unkind of fate—if fate was the culprit—to place Edith Baxter's hand on John Crombie's shoulder in the victim-choosing phase of the game. In the kitchen, with a bread knife at hand, who could blame a well-bourboned woman if she obeyed that impulse and separated Mr. Crombie's neck from his British collar?

But investigation muddled the obvious. The front door of the suite was locked—nay, even bolted—on the inside. Nikki proclaimed herself the authoress thereof, having performed the sealed-apartment act before the game began (she said) in a moment of "inspiration."

Secondly, escape by one of the windows was out of the question, unless, like Pegasus, Edith Baxter possessed wings.

Thirdly, Edith Baxter had not attempted to escape at all: Ellery found her in the foyer closet against which the widow and her sister whimpered. Mrs. Baxter had been jammed into the closet by a nasty hand, and she was unconscious.

Inspector Queen, Sergeant Velie, & Co. arrived just as Edith Baxter, with the aid of ammonium carbonate, was shuddering back to life.

"Guy named Crombie's throat slit?" bellowed Sergeant Velie without guile.

Edith Baxter's eyes rolled over and Nikki wielded the smelling salts once more, wearily.

"Murder games," said Inspector Queen gently. "Halloween," said Inspector Queen. Ellery blushed. "Well, son?"

Ellery told his story humbly, in penitential detail.

"Well, we'll soon find out," grumbled his father, and he shook Mrs. Baxter until her chin waggled and her eyes flew open. "Come, come, madam, we can't afford these luxuries. What the hell were you doing in that closet?"

Edith screamed, "How should I know, you old man?" and had a convulsion of tears. "Jerry Baxter, how can you sit there and—?"

But her husband was doubled over, holding his head.

"You received Nikki's instructions, Edith," said Ellery, "and when she turned off the light you left the living room and went to the kitchen. Or started for it. What did happen?"

"Don't third-degree me, you detective!" screeched Mrs. Baxter. "I'd just passed under the archway, feeling my way, when somebody grabbed my nose and mouth from behind and I must have fainted because that's all I knew till just now and Jerry Baxter, if you don't get up on your two feet like a man and defend your own wife, I'll—I'll—"

"Slit his throat?" asked Sergeant Velie crossly, for the sergeant had been attending his own Halloween party with the boys of his old precinct and was holding three queens full when the call to duty came.

"The murderer," said Ellery glumly. "The real murderer, Dad. At the time Nikki first put out the lights, while Edith Baxter was still in the room getting Nikki's final instructions, one of us lined up at that wall stole across the room, passed Nikki, passed Edith Baxter in the dark, and ambushed her—"

"Probably intended to slug her," nodded the inspector, "but Mrs. Baxter obliged by fainting first."

"Then into the closet and away to do the foul deed?" asked the sergeant poetically. He shook his head.

"It would mean," mused Inspector Queen, "that after stowing Mrs. Baxter in the foyer closet, the real killer went into the kitchen, got the mask, flash, and knife, came back to the living room, tapped John Crombie, led him out to the kitchen, and carved him up. That part of it's okay—Crombie must have thought he was playing the game—but how about the assault on Mrs. Baxter beforehand? Having to drag her unconscious body to the closet? Wasn't there any noise, any sound?"

Ellery said apologetically, "I kept dozing off."

But Nikki said, "There was no sound, Inspector. Then or at any other time. The first *sound* after I turned the light off was John screaming in the kitchen. The only other *sound* was the murderer throwing the flash into the middle of the room after he . . . she . . . whoever it was . . . got back to the wall."

Jerry Baxter raised his sweating face and looked at his wife.

"Could be," said the inspector.

"Oh my," said Sergeant Velie. He was studying the old gentleman as if he couldn't believe his eyes—or ears.

"It could be," remarked Ellery, "or it couldn't. Edith's a very small woman. Unconscious, she *could* be carried noiselessly the few feet in the foyer to the closet . . . by a reasonably strong person."

Immediately Ann Crombie and Lucy Trent and Jerry Baxter tried to look tiny and helpless, while Edith Baxter tried to look huge and heavy. But the sisters could not look less tall or soundly made than nature had fashioned them, and Jerry's proportions, even allowing for reflexive shrinkage, were elephantine.

"Nikki," said Ellery in a very thoughtful way, "you're sure Edith was the only one to step away from the wall while the light was still on?"

"Dead sure, Ellery."

"And when the one you thought was Edith came back from the kitchen to pick a victim, that person had a full mask on?"

"You mean after I put the light out? Yes. I could see the mask in the glow the flash made."

"Man or woman, Miss P?" interjected the sergeant eagerly. "This could be a pipe. If it was a man—"

But Nikki shook her head. "The flash was pretty weak, Sergeant. And we were all in those Black Cat outfits."

"Me, I'm no Fancy Dan," murmured Inspector Queen unexpectedly. "A man's been knocked off. What I want to know is not who was where when, but—who had it in for this character?"

It was a different sort of shrinkage this time, a shrinkage of four throats. Ellery thought, They *all* know.

"Whoever," he began casually, "whoever knew that John Crombie and Edith Baxter were—"

"*It's a lie!*" Edith was on her feet, swaying, clawing the air. "There was nothing between John and me. Nothing. Nothing! Jerry, don't believe them!"

Jerry Baxter looked down at the floor again. "Between?" he mumbled. "I guess I got a head. I guess this has got me." And, strangely, he looked not at his wife but at Ann Crombie. "Ann . . . ?"

But Ann was jelly-lipped with fear.

"Nothing!" screamed Jerry's wife.

"That's not true." And now it was Lucy's turn, and they saw she had been shocked into a sort of suicidal courage. "John was a . . . a . . . John made love to every woman he met. John made love to *me*—"

"To you." Ann blinked and blinked at her sister.

"Yes. He was . . . disgusting. I . . ." Lucy's eyes flamed at Edith Baxter with scorn, with loathing, with contempt. "But *you* didn't find him disgusting, Edith."

Edith glared back, giving hate for hate.

"You spent four weekends with him. And the other night, at that dinner party, when you two stole off—you thought I didn't hear—but you were both tight . . . you begged him to marry you."

"You nasty little blabbermouth," said Edith in a low voice.

"I heard you. You said you'd divorce Jerry if he'd divorce Ann. And John kind of laughed at you, didn't he?—as if you were dirt. And I saw your eyes, Edith, I saw your eyes. . . ."

And now they, too, saw Edith Baxter's eyes—as they really were.

"I never told you, Ann. I couldn't. I couldn't. . . ." Lucy began to sob into her hands.

Jerry Baxter got up.

"Here, where d'ye think you're going?" asked the sergeant not unkindly.

Jerry Baxter sat down again.

"Mrs. Crombie, did you know what was going on?" asked Inspector Queen sympathetically.

It was queer how she would not look at Edith Baxter, who was sitting lumpily now, no threat to anyone—a soggy old woman.

And Ann said, stiff and tight, "Yes, I knew." Then her mouth loosened again and she said wildly, "I knew, but I'm a coward. I couldn't face him with it. I thought if I shut my eyes—"

"So do I," said Ellery tiredly.

"What?" asked Inspector Queen, turning around. "You what, son? I didn't get you."

"I know who cut Crombie's throat."

They were lined up facing the far wall of the living room—Ann Crombie, Lucy Trent, Edith Baxter, and Jerry Baxter—with a space the breadth of a man, and a little more, between the Baxters. Nikki stood at the light switch, the inspector and Sergeant Velie blocked the archway, and Ellery sat on a hassock in the center of the room, his hands dangling listlessly between his knees.

"This is how we were arranged a couple of hours ago, Dad, except that I was at the wall, too, and so was John Crombie . . . in that vacant space."

Inspector Queen said nothing.

"The light was still on, as it is now. Nikki had just asked Murderer to step away from the wall and cross the room—that is, toward where you are now. Do it, Edith."

"You mean—"

"Please."

Edith Baxter backed from the wall and turned and slowly picked her way around the overturned furniture. Near the archway, she paused, an arm's length from the inspector and the sergeant.

"With Edith about where she is now, Nikki, in the full light, instructed her about going to the kitchen, getting the mask, flash, and knife there, coming back in the dark with the flash, selecting a victim, and so on. Isn't that right?"

"Yes."

"Then you turned off the light, Nikki—didn't you?"

"Yes . . ."

"Do it."

"D-do it, Ellery?"

"Do it, Nikki."

When the darkness closed down, someone at the wall gasped. And then the silence closed down, too.

And after a moment Ellery's voice came tiredly: "It was at this point, Nikki, that you said 'Stop!' to Edith Baxter and gave her a few additional instructions. About what to do after the 'crime.' As I pointed out a few minutes ago, Dad—it's during this interval, with Edith standing in the archway getting Nikki's afterthoughts, and the room in darkness, that the real murderer must have stolen across the living room from the wall, got past Nikki and Edith and into the foyer, and waited there to ambush Edith."

"Sure, son," said the inspector. "So what?"

"How did the murderer manage to cross this room in pitch darkness without making any noise?"

At the wall, Jerry Baxter said hoarsely, "Y'know, I don't have to stand here. I don't have to!"

"Because, you know," said Ellery reflectively, "there wasn't any noise. None at all. In fact, Nikki, you actually remarked in that interval: 'I want the room to be as quiet as it is this minute.' And only a few moments ago you corroborated yourself when you told Dad that the first sound after you turned off the light was John screaming in the kitchen. You said the only other sound was the sound of the flashlight landing in the middle of the room after the murderer got back to the wall. So I repeat: How did the murderer cross this room in darkness without making a sound?"

Sergeant Velie's disembodied bass complained from the archway that he didn't get it at all, at all.

"Well, Sergeant, you've seen this room—it's cluttered crazily with overturned furniture, pillows, hassocks, miscellaneous objects. Do you think *you* could cross it in darkness without sounding

60

like the bull in the china shop? Nikki, when you and I first got here
and blundered into the living room—"

"In the dark," cried Nikki. "We bumped. We scraped. I actually
fell—"

"Why didn't the murderer?"

"I'll tell you why," said Inspector Queen suddenly. "*Because no
one did cross this room in the dark.* It can't be done without making
a racket, or without a light—and there was no light at that time or
Nikki'd have seen it."

"Then how's it add up, Inspector?" asked the sergeant patheti-
cally.

"There's only one person we know crossed this room—the one
Nikki saw cross while the light was on, the one they found in the
closet in a 'faint,' Velie. *Edith Baxter!*"

She sounded nauseated. "Oh no," she said. "No."

"Oh yes, Mrs. Baxter. It's been you all the time. You did get to
the kitchen. You got the mask, the flash, the knife. You came back
and tapped John Crombie. You led him out to the kitchen and
there you sliced him up—"

"No!"

"Then you quietly got into that closet and pulled a phony faint,
and waited for them to find you so you could tell that cock-and-
bull story of being ambushed in the foyer, and—"

"Dad," sighed Ellery.

"Huh?" And because the old gentleman's memory of similar
moments—many similar moments—was very green, his tone became truculent. "Now tell me I'm wrong, Ellery!"

"Edith Baxter is the one person present tonight who couldn't
have killed John Crombie."

"You see?" moaned Edith. They could hear her panting.

"Nikki actually saw somebody with a flash *return* to the living
room after Crombie's death-scream, go to the wall, turn off the
flash, and she heard that person hurl it into the middle of the room.
Who was it Nikki saw and heard? We've deduced that already—
the actual murderer. Immediately after that, Nikki turned up the
lights.

"If Edith Baxter were the murderer, wouldn't we have found
her *at the wall with the rest of us* when the lights went on? But she

61

wasn't. She wasn't in the living room at all. We found her in the foyer closet. So she *had* been attacked. She *did* faint. She *didn't* kill Crombie."

They could hear her sobbing in a great release.

"Then who did?" barked the inspector. His tone said he was tired of this fancy stuff and give him a killer so he could book the rat and go home and get to sleep.

"The one," replied Ellery in those weary tones, "who was able to cross the room in the dark without making any noise. For if Edith is innocent, only one of those at the wall could have been guilty. And that one had to cross the room."

There is a maddening unarguability about Ellery's sermons.

"But how, Son, how?" bellowed his father. "It couldn't be done without knocking *something* over—making *some* noise!"

"Only one possible explanation," said Ellery tiredly; and then he said, not tiredly at all, but swiftly and with the slashing finality of a knife, "I thought you'd try that. That's why I sat on the hassock, so very tired. That's why I staged this whole . . . silly . . . scene. . . ."

Velie was roaring: "Where the hell are the lights? Miss Porter, turn that switch on, will you?"

"I can't find the—the damned thing!" wept Nikki.

"The rest of you stay where you are!" shouted the inspector.

"Now drop the knife," said Ellery, in the slightly gritty tones of one who is exerting pressure. "Drop it. . . ." There was a little clatter, and then a whimper. "The only one who could have passed through this jumbled maze in the dark without stumbling over anything," Ellery went on, breathing a bit harder than usual, "would be someone who'd *plotted a route through this maze in advance of the party* . . . someone, in fact, who'd plotted the maze. In other words, the clutter in this room is not chance confusion, but deliberate plant. It would require photographing the details of the obstacle course on the memory, and practice, plenty of practice— but we were told you spent the entire day in this suite *alone*, my dear, fixing it up for the party."

"Here!" sobbed Nikki, and she jabbed the light switch.

"I imagine," said Ellery gently to the girl in his grip, "you felt *someone* had to avenge the honor of the Trents, Lucy."

THE ADVENTURE OF THE DEAD CAT

Ellery Queen *is the name chosen by two Brooklyn-born first cousins, Frederic Dannay and Manfred B. Lee, for their now-immortal sleuth, hero of thirty novels and dozens of short stories. It is also the pseudonym by which they identified themselves, beginning with their debut work,* The Roman Hat Mystery, *in 1929. Their diverse and always important contributions to the genre—creating popular magazines and story collections, engaging in historical scholarship out of which came seminal reference books, the discovery and encouragement of new writers—made them perhaps the most significant figures in the world of twentieth-century crime and suspense fiction. Recipients of Edgar awards in several categories, they were named Grand Masters in 1960.*

THE ODSTOCK CURSE

BY PETER LOVESEY

The rites and customs of Halloween have always provided folklorists and anthropologists with rich source material, a fact cleverly exploited by Peter Lovesey in this story within a story within a story. Lecturer Tom Staniforth, who on this last night of October has just held an audience spellbound in the village hall, describing his investigations into the Odstock curse, a notorious local legend, knows enough to be fascinated by the academic side of Halloween. Unfortunately, ever the unemotional scholar, he's unable to take its hauntings seriously—which proves to be a problem when the footnotes to the evening's topic turn out to be the sort that leave footprints!

THE ODSTOCK CURSE

"Finally, ladies and gentlemen, finally I want to come close to home, to your home, that is to say, to Odstock and the bizarre events that happened in your village almost two hundred years ago, events that I venture to suggest still have the capacity to chill your spines."

Dr. Tom Staniforth peered over half-glasses at his awestruck audience. Truth to tell, he felt uneasy himself, not at his spine-chilling material so much as the fact that he had consented to give this talk to an open meeting in a village hall on—of all evenings—October thirty-first. The timing had not been his suggestion and neither had the title, "Horrors for Halloween." He dreaded the possibility that some university colleague had seen the posters or otherwise got wind that a senior member of the Social Anthropology Department was sensation-mongering in the wilds of Wiltshire. He had come simply because Mother had insisted upon it. Pearl Staniforth had arranged the whole thing as a personal tribute to a former colleague of her late husband. And now, wearing one of her appalling red velvet hats, Mother was seated beside this old gentleman in the second row giving a sub-commentary and beaming maternally at regular intervals.

He was almost through, thank God.

"Forgive me if what I have to say about the Odstock curse is familiar to most of you, but I suggest it can still bear telling. I thought it would be instructive in the first place to relate the legend and afterwards to pick out the truth as far as one can verify it from reliable sources—by which I mean parish records, legal documents and, perhaps less reliable, the memoir of a contemporary witness, the village blacksmith. In the anthropological scale of things, it is all very recent." He paused, widening his eyes. Having abandoned his academic scruples, he might as well milk the subject for melodrama. Spacing his words, he went on, "In the churchyard is an old gravestone partially covered by a briar rose. The stone has an intriguing inscription: *'In memory of Joshua Scamp who died April 1st, 1801. May his brave deed be remembered here and hereafter.'* "

With strange timing came a distant rumble of thunder that cued an uneasy murmur in the audience. The storm had been threatening for hours.

"Thank you, Josh, we heard the commercial," Tom Staniforth adroitly remarked, giving the opportunity for everyone to laugh aloud and ease the tension. "The brave deed is a matter of record. The unfortunate Mr. Scamp allowed himself to be hanged for a crime he did not commit. He was a Gypsy accused of stealing a horse, which was a capital offence in those Draconian times. The real thief and villain of the piece was his feckless son-in-law, Noah Lee, who not only stole the horse but planted a coat belonging to Joshua at the scene of the crime. Joshua was arrested. He refused to plead and maintained a stoic silence throughout his interrogation and trial. He went to the gallows—a public execution in Salisbury—without naming the true culprit. You see, his daughter Mary was expecting a child and he could not bear to see her bereft of a husband, facing a life of misery and destitution.

"Joshua's heroic act might have gone unremarked were it not for the Gypsy community, who protested his innocence. They recovered the corpse of the hanged man from the prison authorities, brought him home to Odstock and gave him a Christian burial. Hundreds attended. And later the same year the real horse-thief, Noah Lee, was arrested at Winchester for stealing a hunter. He was duly hanged, which you may think made a mockery of Scamp's

68

noble sacrifice. But the truth emerged because Joshua's daughter, Mary, no longer felt constrained to remain silent. Great sympathy was extended to her and she was well cared for. And Joshua Scamp became a Gypsy martyr. The briar rose was planted at the head of his grave and a yew sapling at the foot. Each year on the anniversary of his execution they would make a pilgrimage here, large numbers from all the surrounding counties.

"Now it seems that after some years the annual visit of the Gypsies became a nuisance." Another clap of thunder tested Staniforth's powers of improvisation.

"Have it your way, Josh," he quipped, and earned more laughter, "but there must have been some justification for the rector of Odstock to have sworn in twenty-five special constables to keep the peace. Well, the blacksmith's memoir claims that the yew tree by the grave had become unsightly and the rector insisted that it was pulled up by the roots—a job that the sexton duly carried out. Unfortunately this measure deeply upset the Gypsies and a mob of them descended on the church. There were scuffles as attempts were made to keep them off the sacred ground. The crowning insult was when Mother Lee, the Gypsy Queen, was evicted from the church, where she had come to pray, and the door locked behind her. The lady in question was venerated by the Gypsies. She was the elderly mother of Noah Lee, the horse-thief, and she had earned enormous respect for disowning her son and praising the bravery of Joshua Scamp.

"Whatever the rights and wrongs of it—and I imagine there was cause for grievance on both sides—the Gypsies were deeply angered. They took their revenge by breaking into the church and attacking everything inside. The pews, the windows, the communion plate, the vestments, the bell-ropes: nothing was spared. The constables were vastly outnumbered and powerless to prevent the desecration. This is all on record.

"Late in the evening, Mother Lee, having allegedly spent some hours in the Yew Tree Inn, returned to the churchyard where her people were still at work uprooting trees. Perched on the church gate, she called them to order and addressed a crowd that included most of the villagers as well as her own flock. Gypsies, as you know, have always claimed powers of divination. Speaking in a voice of doom Mother Lee pointed to the rector and told him that he would not be preaching in Odstock at that time next year. She told the church warden who had engaged the special constables, a farmer by the name of Hodding, 'For two years bad luck shall tread upon thy heels. No son of thine shall ever farm thy land.' The sexton was informed that by next April he would be in his own grave. Two half-Gypsy brothers unwise enough to have been employed as special constables were told, 'Bob and Jack Bachelor, you will die together, sudden and quick.' And finally she dealt with the door that had been slammed in her face: 'I put a curse on this church door. From this time whoever shall lock 'un shall die within a year.' And legend has it that all the curses came true."

Tom Staniforth let the drama of the story hold sway for a moment. He looked out at his audience and made brief eye contact with several. How gullible people are, he thought. They patently believe this codswallop.

"However, I promised to deal in facts, not legend," he resumed in a businesslike tone. "Let us see what survives of the Odstock curse when we test it against reliable sources. The parish records are helpful. They tell us that the rector retired within a year, so that part is true, though we have no contemporaneous evidence for the throat cancer which was said to have robbed him of his power of speech. Nothing is known of bad luck afflicting Farmer Hodding except that his wife had a series of stillborn infants, which was not unusual in those days. I was unable to verify the story that his crops failed and his herd had to be slaughtered after contracting anthrax. The sexton, it is true, appears in the records of burials a few months after he was cursed. As for the Bachelor brothers, they are not mentioned in the register again, but superstition has it that a pair of skeletons found in 1929 in a shallow grave on Odstock Down belonged to them." Staniforth raised his hands to the audience. "So what? Even if they *were* the brothers, a supernatural explanation is unlikely. The possibility is high that the Gypsies took revenge and disposed of the bodies. The so-called power of the Gypsy's curse is undermined if they had to resort to murder to make it come true. To sum up, ladies and gentlemen, I have to say that I find the Odstock curse a beguiling story that, sadly for believers in the occult, falls well within the bounds of coincidence and manipulation."

He stepped from behind the table. "That concludes my talk. I hope you are reassured and will sleep peacefully tonight. I certainly intend to, and I have spent more time on these legends than most."

The reception he was given was gratifying. Pearl Staniforth, smiling this way and that as she clapped, prolonged it by at least ten seconds.

And there was a curious effect when the clapping died, because the storm outside had just broken over Odstock, and the beating of rain on the roof appeared to sustain the applause. While the downpour continued no one was eager to leave, so the speaker invited questions.

A man at the back of the hall got up. He was one of the committee; earlier he had taken the money at the door. "What a wonderful talk, sir—a fitting subject for the occasion, and so eloquently delivered. I can't remember applause like that. Just one question, sir. I don't know if it was deliberate, only when you were discussing the evidence for the curse, you omitted to mention the Gypsy's warning about the church door. What are your views on that?"

"I apologize," said Staniforth at once. "An oversight. I didn't mean to ignore it. The story goes that in the years since the curse was made, two people locked the door and suffered the promised fate within a year. But one is bound to ask how many hundreds, or thousands, must have turned the key and survived. You are up against statistical probability, you see." He smiled, a shade too complacently.

"No, sir," said the questioner in his broad South Wiltshire tones. "With respect, you're misinformed. The door has been locked twice since the curse, and only twice in almost two hundred years. The first time was in nineteen hundred, in defiance of the curse, when a carpenter was employed to make new gates. He was given the story, but he mocked it, turned the key and paid the price within the twelvemonth. They buried him under the path, between the gates he made and the door he locked. The second time was in the nineteen thirties, when a locum was appointed while the rector was away. This locum dismissed the story as blasphemous and locked the door to uphold the power of the Lord, as he saw it.

He was gathered shortly after. When the rector returned, he threw the key into the River Ebble just across the road, and the church has never been locked since."

Deflated, Staniforth said, "I'm obliged to you. I stand corrected then, but I'd still like to see paper evidence of the two alleged deaths."

"If it didn't happen, why would the rector throw the key away?"

"Oh, the church rejects superstition as much as modern science does. No doubt he thought it the best way to put an end to such foolishness."

Happily for Staniforth the questioner was too polite to pursue the matter. The questions turned to the safer topic of witchcraft and after ten minutes a vote of thanks was proposed, coupled with the suggestion that as the rain had eased slightly it might be timely to call the evening to a halt.

For Tom Staniforth it had scarcely begun.

Old Walter Fremantle had invited the Staniforths back to his cottage for supper, not a prospect Tom relished, although he felt some obligation for the sake of his late father. Piers Staniforth and Walter Fremantle had gone through Cambridge together as history students and remained close friends even after their careers had diverged. Walter had become a museum curator and Piers a nationally known television archaeologist until his death abroad in the 1960s. From things Pearl had let slip occasionally it seemed that Walter had helped them financially after Piers died.

"Your father would have been so proud tonight," Pearl enthused while Tom cringed with embarrassment. "You had that audience in the palm of your hand—didn't he, Walter?"

"Oh, emphatically," said Walter, as he tried to pour brandy with a tremulous hand.

Tom offered to help. It was a case of all hands to the pump. Already his mother had supervised the microwave cooking and he had served the soup and the quiche. And it tasted good. Convenience food—but less of a risk than home cooking by a seventy-five-year-old bachelor.

They had not been settled long in deep armchairs in front of the fire when Walter launched into a confession. Frail as he appeared, he was still articulate, and there could be no doubt that what he told Tom and his mother was profoundly important to him. "Your talk tonight has stirred me to raise a matter that has troubled me for many years. I didn't know you were an expert on the curse—didn't even realize you would mention it. Up to now I have hesitated to bring up the subject, mainly, I think, because I am a coward by nature."

"Far from it, Walter!" Pearl strove to reassure him.

Mother, will you shut up? thought Tom.

"It concerns Piers, your father. It was, I think, in nineteen sixty-two, towards the end of his life, that he came to see me for lunch one day. He was between expeditions, as I recall, just back from Nigeria and about to leave for South America in two or three weeks."

"Our life was like that." Pearl now chose to reminisce. "I scarcely saw him unless I went on the digs. I could have gone. The television people would have paid for me, but it was the travel, the packing and the unpacking. I was weary of it."

"Mother, Walter is trying to tell us something."

"Does that mean the rest of us have to be silent? It was never like that in the old days, was it, Walter?"

Walter gave a nod and a faint smile. "We were back from lunch and unpacking some of the objects Piers had generously brought back from Africa to present to the museum when I was phoned from downstairs and told that a woman had come into the museum and wished to donate an item to the local history collection. I'm afraid one gets all sorts of rubbish brought in and I was skeptical. This lady was apparently unwilling to return at some more convenient moment. However, Piers, ever the gentleman, insisted that I spoke to her, so I invited her up to my office. The woman who presently came in was a Gypsy, dressed like Carmen herself in a black skirt, white blouse and red shawl, which was most unsuitable because she was sixty at least, and large. I've nothing personal against such people, but she struck me immediately as someone I didn't care to deal with. My guess was that she wished to sell me something."

"They always do," said Pearl, "and if you don't buy they spit on your doorstep and give you the evil eye."

"Is that so? In fact, this person, who wouldn't give her name,

73

incidentally, made herself a nuisance in another way, by relating the legend of the Odstock curse, at interminable length."

"How tedious," said Pearl, without much tact.

"I was familiar with the story," said Walter, "and I tried to tell her as much, but she would insist on giving us her version, which she claimed was Gypsy lore. At another time I might have been more inclined to listen, because there is a lot of interest in preserving oral folklore, but my time with Piers was precious and she was invading it. Piers was extremely patient and good-mannered about the whole thing. I think it interested him."

"What was behind it?" Pearl asked.

"Mother, Walter is coming to that."

"Well, I've no need to keep you in suspense," said Walter. "She produced an iron key, heavily coated with rust, from under her shawl and placed it on my desk. Her son, she said, had found it on the river bank during the summer when the water level went down several feet. As a true Romany she knew it to be the cursed key of Odstock Church."

"Good Lord! And she expected you to buy it?"

"She was making a gift of it to the museum. She said she wouldn't offer it to the church in case someone tried to defy the curse. She said it would be safer in a display cabinet in a museum. I asked her if she seriously believed that the so-called curse was still potent. She gave me a look fit to shatter my skull and said that Joshua Scamp himself would deal with anyone so foolish as to lock the church door."

"The hanged man?"

"Yes. The curse is everlasting."

"Are you saying she actually believed that Scamp had some influence in the world of the living?"

"My dear boy, it's the Gypsy version of the tale. I thought it poppycock myself."

"Exactly the point I was about to make," said Tom. "You were being asked to believe in a malevolent spirit, as well as the curse. There are limits."

Walter nodded. "That was my view when she presented me with the key. After she had finally been persuaded to leave, Piers asked me how much of the story I believed and I told him it was no doubt founded on a real incident that had been much embroidered over the years. Piers asked whether I proposed to display the key in the museum and I said certainly not. It seemed to me unlikely in the extreme that a key recovered from the river would be the very one that the rector had thrown in thirty years ago. Piers was more cautious in delivering a verdict."

"That's Piers all over," Pearl commented with a smile.

"My point was that we had nothing with which to authenticate the key except the Gypsy woman's assertion. I said the only way to test it was to take the damned thing to the church and see if it fitted the lock. Piers advised me most adamantly not to take such a risk. He said the woman had impressed him and the power of the Gypsies should never be underestimated. We had an amiable dispute. I remember accusing him of superstition and he said he'd rather be superstitious and safe than skeptical and dead." Walter hesitated and stared into the fire. Some of the rain was penetrating the chimney and hissing as the droplets touched the embers.

Tom asked, "Did you ever try the key in the door?"

Walter turned, and Tom noticed that his eyes were suddenly moist and red at the edges. "Yes, I did. It was from vanity, really. I wanted the satisfaction of telling my old friend that I had been right. I rose early the very next day, determined to prove my point. I was ninety percent sure the key wouldn't fit, but if it did, I'd display it in my local collection with a note about the execution of Joshua Scamp and its aftermath. I remember it was a glorious morning and the rooks in the tall trees outside seemed to be chorusing me as I walked up the path to the door of St. Mary's."

Pearl said impatiently, "Did it fit?"

"Oh, yes. It turned the mechanism inside. The bolt engaged. Only briefly, because I turned it back in the same movement. I was shaking at the discovery."

"Remarkable."

"And you lived to tell the tale," Tom said robustly to the old man. "Well done, Walter! You struck a blow for rational thought. What happened to the key? Did you put it on display?"

"It's in front of you, hanging on that nail over the fireplace."

Tom looked up at the notorious key, a rusty, corroded thing with a shank no longer than his smallest finger. It appeared innocuous enough. "May I handle it?"

"Please don't."

"It doesn't frighten me in the least."

"No. For God's sake hear me out."

"I thought you'd finished."

Walter shook his head. "Bear with me. This is painful. A month or so after trying the key in the door, I was afflicted with physical symptoms I couldn't account for. I became weary after no exertion at all and I lost weight steadily. My doctor put me through no end of tests. I had a full body scan. Everything. There was nothing they could diagnose, yet anyone could see I was wasting away. It was obvious to me that I wouldn't see the year out unless some miracle reversed the process. I kept remembering how I had defied the curse and locked the church door."

"It wouldn't have been that," said Tom. "Whatever was amiss with you, it wouldn't have been that."

"May I continue?" asked Walter quietly. "One morning I was shopping in Salisbury and a woman approached me and asked if I would buy a sprig of heather for good luck. She was the Gypsy who had presented me with the key. I said I needed all the good luck that was going and told her what I had done. She hadn't recognized me, I had lost so much weight. She was visibly shocked by what I told her. I'm afraid I was feeling so wretched that I begged for her help. I offered her any money if she would help me to lift the curse. She could name the sum. She would accept nothing, not even a silver coin for the heather. She said my only chance was to wait for Hallows' Eve and then to invoke the spirit of Joshua Scamp by chanting his name three times. I was so desperate about my health that I was perfectly willing to try, but the rest of her advice was more difficult. I had to find a believer in the curse and speak that person's name aloud." His voice was faltering. "The curse would then be lifted from me and transferred."

Pearl's hand went to her throat. "Oh, my God!"

Tom felt his muscles tighten.

The old man said, "Yes, I thought of Piers. I rememberd how he had almost pleaded with me not to try the key in the church door. He was a believer. In the few days left before Halloween, I wrestled with my conscience, telling myself it was all hocus-pocus anyway and Piers was an ocean away in South America. How could the shade of a dead Gypsy who had never traveled out of England trouble a modern man in Peru? Yet I still hesitated. If I had not felt so wretchedly ill I would not have taken the risk. When you are reduced to shaking skin and bones, you will try anything. So on the night of Halloween, thirty years ago this night, I did as the Gypsy advised. When I had three times invoked the spirit of Joshua Scamp, I spoke the name of my oldest friend." Walter bent forward and covered his eyes.

"What happened?"

His answer came in sobs. "Nothing. Nothing that night. For a week . . . no change. Then . . . the second week, my appetite returned . . . I felt stronger, actually recovering." He looked up, weeping uncontrollably, "In three months I was back to my old weight. The only thing I wanted was a postcard from my old friend in Peru." He paused in an effort to control his emotions and added, barely audibly, "It never came. I heard one evening on the television news about the mud-slip, the fatal accident to Piers. Devastating. What can I say to you both? Through my selfishness you lost a husband and a father."

Before Pearl could respond, Tom said gently but firmly, "Walter, it's typical of your generosity to tell us this, and I'm sure it seemed to make sense to you at the time, but really it's a misconstruction of events. It doesn't bear analysis. I'm sure I speak for Mother when I say you can sleep easy in the knowledge that you had nothing whatsoever to do with Dad's death. It was an accident."

"No."

"Your health improved because you threw off the effects of the virus, or whatever it was. We've all had mysterious illnesses that come and go. Yours was more severe than most."

"I know what happened, my son. Believe me, I was dying. I know why it went away. I don't deserve to be here. Your father should have been at that lecture tonight, not me."

Tom leaned closer to him and said earnestly, "The whole tenor of my talk was that superstitions are founded on coincidence and false reasoning, and this is a classic example. You were too close to events to judge them analytically. You accepted the supernatural explanation. Come on, Walter, you're an intelligent man of good education.''

Pearl chimed in with, "I forgive you, Walter."

Tom swung around in his chair. He was incensed. "For God's sake, Mother—there's nothing to forgive! He had nothing to do with Father's death. This whole thing about the curse is mumbo jumbo—and I'm about to prove it." He got up and snatched the key from its place over the hearth.

"Don't!" cried Walter.

Tom's mother shrieked his name, but he had already crossed the room, grabbed his coat off the hook and stepped outside.

Pearl screamed.

Tom strode along the road towards the church, regardless of the driving rain.

Odstock Church stands alone, a few hundred yards from the rest of the village. Distant lightning gave Tom Staniforth intermittent glimpses of the agitated trees along each side of the road. The castellated tower and steep tiled roof of St. Mary's came into view, silvering dramatically each time a flash came. He refused to be intimidated.

Too far behind Tom to influence events, his mother and Walter Fremantle had started in pursuit. Neither was in any condition to move fast, yet they were trying to run.

Tom reached the church gates. Without pause, he stepped under the archway formed by two pollarded trees and up to the timber-framed porch. A lantern mounted on the highest beam lighted the path. The church doors were of faded oak fitted into a stone arch, with iron strap-hinges and a turning latch with a ring handle. A brighter flash of lightning turned the whole thing white. Tom found the rusted key-escutcheon, thrust in the key and turned it. The mechanism was a devil to shift. He was afraid that the key would snap under the strain. Finally it turned through a full arc and he heard the movement of the bolt sliding home.

Done.

He didn't withdraw the key. He wanted others to know that someone with a mind free of superstition had defied the Gypsy's curse.

Hearing the footsteps of his mother and old Walter Fremantle,

Tom stepped aside, away from the door. They would see the key in the lock. He was triumphant.

The glory was brief. Lightning struck the church roof. The thunder—an immense clap—was instantaneous. The ground itself vibrated. Scores of tiles loosened, slid down the pitched roof and fell. Two, at least, razor-sharp, cracked against Tom's skull and felled him like a pin in an alley.

Neither Walter nor Pearl saw the body when they first came through the gate. The porch light had blown when the lightning struck. They groped at the door, feeling for the key in the lock.

Walter located it and gasped, "He did it. I tried to stop him. I tried!"

Pearl found her son lying insensible against a gravestone, with blood oozing from a head wound. Whimpering, she got to her knees and cradled his damaged head. He made no sound.

Pearl rocked her son.

"Is he . . . ?" Walter could not bring himself to speak the word.

Pearl ignored him anyway. The pride she had felt in the village hall when Tom was speaking with such authority had ended in blood and tears. She sobbed for the limp burden in her arms and the bigotry of rational thinking. She mourned her wise, never-to-be-forgotten husband and her rash, misguided son.

Gently, Pearl let Tom's bloodied head rest in her lap. She brought her hands together in front of her, fingers tightly intertwined. Then in a clear voice she called the name of Joshua Scamp. She called it three times. She cried out passionately, "Take Walter Fremantle. He knows the power of the curse better than any man, having used it to kill my husband. He is a believer. Take him. For pity's sake, take him instead."

She remembered nothing else. She didn't see old Walter unlock the church door, remove the key, and take it across the road to the river and throw it in. She didn't see him collapse as he tried to climb up the bank.

The next morning, in the intensive care ward at Odstock Hospital, Tom Staniforth's eyelids quivered and opened. His mother, in a hospital dressing gown, watching through a glass screen, turned to the young policeman beside her, gripped his hand and squeezed it. "He's going to live!"

"I'm happy for you, ma'am," said the constable. "Happy for

myself, too. Maybe your son can tell me what happened last night. What with you having passed out as well, and old Mr. Fremantle dead of a heart attack, I was afraid we'd have no witnesses. I'm supposed to write a report of the incident, you see. I know it was the lightning that struck the church, but it's difficult working out what happened, with all three of you going down like that."

"However did you find us?" Pearl asked.

"Wasn't me, ma'am. Now I'd really like to trace the man who alerted us, but I'm not optimistic. No one seems to know him. Right strange chap, he was. Came bursting into a farm cottage soon after midnight, in fancy dress from one of them Halloween parties. Top hat and smock and a piece of rope around his neck. He nearly scared the family out of their wits, ranting on about a dead'un at the church door. Didn't leave his name. Just raced off into the storm. Drunk, I expect. But I reckon you owe him, you and your son."

Author's footnote: I should like to pay credit to three sources for the story of Joshua Scamp and the Curse of Odstock. *Wiltshire Folklore*, by Kathleen Wiltshire (Salisbury, England: Compton Russell, 1975) gives the version told by Canon Bouverie about 1904; *Wiltshire Folklore and Legends*, by Ralph Whitlock (London: Robert Hale, 1992) has Hiram Witt the blacksmith's memoir of 1870; and the fictional story of the lecture and its consequences was suggested by my son, Philip, who visited Odstock with me at Easter, 1993.

Peter Lovesey has won both Gold and Silver Dagger awards from the Crimes Writers Association of Great Britain, as well as the coveted Grand Prix de Littérature Policière given in France. Though celebrated for his ability to bring the past to life in two series set in the Victorian era—one featuring the period police officers Sergeant Cribb and Constable Thackeray, the other King Edward VII, cleverly reimagined as a monarch-turned-sleuth—Lovesey is equally at home in the twentieth century. Among his novels with contemporary settings are The Last Detective *and* Diamond Solitaire, *both featuring that veteran of the London police, Peter Diamond.*

THE THEFT OF THE HALLOWEEN PUMPKIN

BY EDWARD D. HOCH

What's in a name? Well, for starters, try to imagine
how the title of this story would sound if it had been
called "The Theft of the Halloween Turnip." Yet,
according to some Halloween lore, long ago in Scot-
land, at harvest time, the custom of lighting a candle
inside the hollowed-out roundness of a plant's edible
part began—and that plant was not the pumpkin but
the turnip.

Similarly, would we accept the irrepressible Nick
Velvet as the smooth and delicately artful thief he is
if he were named something else? Nick Tweed, for
example? No, you're right, we wouldn't, and in this
delightful caper, Velvet and pumpkin make an unlikely pairing to solve a vicious crime and satisfy a
gorgeous dame.

THE THEFT OF THE HALLOWEEN PUMPKIN

Nick Velvet first saw the big multicolored hot-air balloons at an autumn rally on a farm in upstate New York one pleasant weekend when he and Gloria were driving aimlessly through the countryside.

"Oh, *look*, Nicky! Let's stop!" she cried—and since he was at least as interested as she was he pulled off the road into a field where other cars were parked.

There were about a dozen of the big balloons in all, crowded onto a farmer's field and looking a bit like some weird October crop come suddenly to maturity. Nick and Gloria walked among them, watching preparations for what was to be a cross-country balloon race. "Could *you* go up in one of those things?" Gloria asked.

"If I had to," Nick decided, viewing the gradually inflating balloons a bit uncertainly.

"They're perfectly safe," a freckle-faced young man assured them, overhearing their conversation. "Man has been flying in hot-air balloons for two hundred years."

"Is this one yours?" Nick asked.

"I don't own it but I fly it." He held out his hand. "My name's Roger Enfield." His red hair and a thin red mustache went well with the freckles. Nick guessed he was still in his early twenties.

He introduced himself and Gloria and Nick shook the young man's hand. "Where are you racing to today?"

"Where the wind takes us," Enfield answered with a laugh. "But we hope to head southeast across the Hudson and come down in Dutchess County."

"Can't you steer these things?"

"Oh, a little. You can go up and down by turning the burner on and off, regulating the amount of heated air in the balloon. Sometimes you can catch a stream of faster air aloft that's going in your direction. And we can always drop ballast if we have to. But a lot depends on the wind."

"Ready to go, Roger?" a tall man asked, striding through the crowd like an officer inspecting his troops. He wore riding boots and a tan leather jacket reminiscent of the sort pilots wore during the barnstorming Twenties.

"Yes, Mr. Melrose," Enfield replied, and both of them climbed into the little gondola beneath the candy-striped balloon.

"That's Horace Melrose, the publisher," Gloria whispered. "I read somewhere that he's a nut about ballooning."

Melrose was snapping out commands as the ground crew released the ropes holding the balloon in place. Gradually it began to rise, clearing the trees and hovering for a moment as if seeking its way. Then a draft of air took it and it began drifting southeast toward the river.

"It looks like he's right on course," Gloria remarked as they strolled back to the car.

That was the first weekend in October, and Nick thought no more about Melrose, Enfield, and the balloon rally until three weeks later when he was far away, sunning himself on the beach of an expensive Acapulco resort. It was a nice place to visit in late October when the weather around New York began to turn damp and rainy, but Nick wouldn't have chosen it on his own without the urging of his latest client, who gave her name on the telephone as Rita Spangles.

"I can't come up there," she'd informed him. "And I can't do business over the telephone. Fly down here for a couple of days and I'll pay your expenses, in addition to your regular fee."

"All right," he'd agreed. "I'll phone you when I get in."

"No. Be on the beach the day after tomorrow. Have you got a bathing suit?"

"Yes."

"What color?"

"You get your choice of black or red trunks. Like a roulette wheel."

She laughed. "Wear the red. I always win on red."

"What will you be wearing?"

"A white maillot. I'll look for you around one o'clock."

So there he was, a half hour early, basking in the sun with a copy of yesterday's *New York Times*, looking, he hoped, like a typical businessman on vacation. Then he saw her, a few minutes before the appointed hour, strolling across the sand in her white one-piece bathing suit, carrying a striped beach jacket over one shoulder.

He tried not to look up too obviously as she passed, and she paused at his feet to ask, "Velvet?"

"Hello there," he said, glancing up with a smile. "Join me on my blanket?"

She sank down beside him. "From what people told me about you, I expected a younger man."

"Don't let the gray hairs fool you. I'm in disguise."

"I see." She picked up a handful of sand. "You steal things, right?"

"Right. Nothing of value. No money, art works, or securities. Worthless stuff only. My fee's twenty-five thousand."

"I know all that. Would you steal a pumpkin?"

"What kind of pumpkin?"

"A Halloween pumpkin. A jack-o'-lantern. Next Sunday's Halloween."

"So it is. Where will the pumpkin be? In a store? In a farmer's field?"

"On the front porch of a friend of mine."

Nick rolled over on his stomach. "Miss Spangles, pardon me for mentioning it, but you could hire a couple of neighborhood kids to steal a pumpkin off somebody's front porch. They'd probably do it for a couple of candy bars."

"Not from this porch, they wouldn't. It's on an estate that's surrounded by a wall and has guards and dogs patrolling the grounds."

"Then why do they bother with a pumpkin if they don't encourage visitors?"

"A family custom. I think it's his wife's idea."

"Where is this place?"

She'd uncapped a plastic bottle and was spreading suntan lotion carefully along her firm thighs. Her hair was blonde and her complexion fair. She probably burned easily. "Dutchess County, north of New York. Do you know the area?"

"Sure."

"He's a publisher, name of Horace Melrose. He owns a chain of newspapers in cities around the country."

"I've met him briefly," Nick said.

"Can you do it? Steal the pumpkin from his porch on Halloween night?"

"It sounds easy enough. What's your connection with Melrose?"

"We were friends—" she began, and then corrected herself. "Hell, I was his mistress for eight years. Now I'm in exile down here. He pays the bills as long as I stay away."

"And the pumpkin?"

"That's a personal matter. You don't need to know any more."

"You want me to steal it as a sign? To remind him you're still around?"

"Something like that." She looked away, out to sea. "Just bring me the pumpkin."

"Is it a real one, or—"

"I know they use the same decorations every year, and then store them away. It's probably plastic or something." She reached into the drawstring bag she carried with her. "Here's a check for your travel expenses. You'll get your fee when you deliver."

Nick Velvet nodded. She was the sort of woman he liked to deal with, and not just because of the way she looked in a bathing suit. "You'll have it the day after Halloween," he assured her.

Roger Enfield was having a beer in a Poughkeepsie bar when Nick found him. It took a moment for recognition to dawn. "Sure,

I remember you. At the balloon race. You had a nice-looking woman."

"Gloria will be happy to hear that," Nick murmured, signaling the bartender. "Who won the race?"

"Fella from New Mexico. Hot-air balloons are a big thing down there. They have races all the time."

"You work for Horace Melrose?"

"Hell, no! He acts like I do sometimes, though. For the races he hires the balloon *and* me from the promotion company I work for."

"Then your balloon's for hire?" Nick said with interest, ordering a beer for himself.

"Sure. What'd you have in mind?"

"A sort of promotion. On Halloween night."

"I don't take it up after dark. It's too easy to get tangled in power lines."

"Late afternoon, then. Just before dark." Nick hoped the pumpkin would be out on the porch then. It was a chance he'd have to take. "I'd want to go up, touch down at a certain spot, and then go up again. Could you do that?"

"Sure, if the weather cooperates. I don't go up if it's rainy or windy."

"The pay would be good," Nick assured him. "I'd want you to land on the Melrose property."

"What—on Halloween?" Enfield's voice rose in alarm. "Not a chance, mister! Not after what happened there last year!"

"Oh? I wasn't aware anything happened there last year. Why don't we move over to a booth and you can tell me about it."

Enfield wiped the foam from his red mustache and picked up his half-finished beer. "Sure, I'll tell you. It's no secret. It was in all the papers." They settled down in one of the wooden booths where there was more privacy and Nick ordered another round of beers.

The story Enfield told him was simple enough. On Halloween of the previous year, a man had been shot on Melrose property near the front porch of the house. A security guard had mistaken him for a prowler, and when the man started running the guard had fired. The man's name was Tom Reynolds and he was a sportswriter for a Philadelphia newspaper. He'd died at the hospital a few hours later. No one ever established what he was doing on the Melrose property.

"So you see what I mean about Halloween," Roger Enfield said. "If I landed that balloon there Sunday night, the guards would probably pump it full of holes."

"What's Melrose got to hide?" Nick wondered.

"Nothing. He just likes his privacy. He told me once he's around so many people every day he likes to get away from them on weekends."

Nick was struck by a thought. "He's a newspaper publisher. Did this man Reynolds work for him?"

"No. Melrose doesn't own any big-city papers. They didn't even know each other. That's why no one could figure out what Reynolds was doing there."

"Did the police bring charges against anyone?"

Enfield shook his head. "The Melroses are pretty important people up here. And Reynolds was trespassing, after all."

Rita Spangles had mentioned a wife. "What about Mrs. Melrose?"

"Jenny? She's a fine woman—very involved with social issues. She serves on a lot of committees."

Nick finished his beer. "Are you sure you won't change your mind about the balloon?"

"On Halloween? Not a chance! Take my advice. If you don't want to get shot, stay away from the Melrose place. If anything, those guards are more trigger-happy now than they were a year ago."

Until then, it had seemed like a simple and uncomplicated assignment. In fact, it had seemed so simple that Nick had dreamed up the balloon landing to spice it up a bit. The idea of using a hot-air balloon to steal a pumpkin and then escaping the same way appealed to his sense of the dramatic. If it couldn't be done, there were plenty of other ways to accomplish the theft. But the news about the man named Tom Reynolds being shot and killed there the previous Halloween bothered him. What if Rita Spangles had hired Reynolds to steal the pumpkin, too? What if the whole thing was some sort of bizarre ritual to lure someone to his death each Halloween?

Later when he told Gloria of this idea, she scoffed. "Honestly, Nicky, you get the craziest ideas sometimes! You should be writing these horror movies the kids like so much. You could call this one *Halloween 4½* or something."

"I suppose I did let my imagination go too far," he admitted. "But Tom Reynolds is dead, there's no denying that. And he was trespassing on their property, the same as I'll be doing."

"Can't you find out if there was any connection between Reynolds and this woman who hired you?"

It was a good suggestion and he wondered why he hadn't thought of it. "I've only got a few days but maybe I can find out something," he decided.

The following morning Nick was in Philadelphia, calling on Tom Reynolds's former editor at the newspaper office on Market Street. The editor's name was Paul Karoski, and his thin hair and pale skin indicated that his was a sporting life spent mainly indoors.

"Reynolds was one of the best young sportswriters I had," he told Nick. "It was a shame what happened to him."

"Exactly what did happen?"

"He was onto a story of some sort. He never did tell me what it was. It brought him to the Melrose estate for some reason and he got himself shot. That's about all I know."

"The story must have been involved with sports somehow," Nick reasoned.

"Sure. Football, I think, because for a couple of days before he died he kept replaying a videotape from the Eagles-Rams game of a few weeks earlier. I even looked at it myself after the shooting, but I couldn't see anything unusual on it."

"Do you still have that tape?" Nick asked.

Karoski thought about it. Then he got up and shuffled through a stack of videotapes on top of a filing cabinet. "Maybe I erased—no, here it is. Eagles-Rams, from last October."

"Could I borrow it?"

The sports editor frowned at Nick. "What's your connection with all this? Are you a detective or something?"

"An investigator. I'm working on another matter and someone suggested I look into Tom Reynolds's death."

"All right," Karoski decided. "Take the tape, bur bring it back. Give me a receipt for it."

"Gladly." Nick slipped the video cassette into the briefcase he'd brought along and reached for a pen. "One other thing. Did you or Reynolds know a woman named Rita Spangles?"

Karoski thought about it. "I don't, but I had no way of knowing all Tom's friends. He was a good-looking fellow, unmarried— Hold on. Wait a minute. Rita Spangles—I think that was the name of the woman at the hospital."

"What woman?"

"After he was shot, Reynolds lived about five hours. The hospital phoned me because they found his press card on him. I drove right up there, but he was dead by the time I reached the hospital. It was about a three-hour drive. They told me the only person he'd seen was this woman, and I think her name was Rita Spangles. I saw her only briefly, as she was leaving the hospital. I figured it was one of his girlfriends."

"Did she seem upset by his death?"

"Yes. But she didn't talk to me."

"I'll get this tape back to you," Nick promised, giving Karoski his asked-for receipt as he left.

That evening he played it on their machine at home. Gloria looked in from the kitchen and sighed. "Don't we get enough football on Sundays and Monday nights?"

"This is work. It's a tape Reynolds was studying before he was killed."

"It looks like any other football game to me," Gloria said after watching it a while.

"That's the trouble," Nick agreed. He sat through the entire game—nearly three hours of it—without seeing anything unusual. It was just like any other football game.

* * *

THE THEFT OF THE HALLOWEEN PUMPKIN

On Friday night he looked for and found Roger Enfield in the same bar. "Are you back with your balloon plan?" the young man asked.

"A new one this time. You don't have to take me up, and you don't have to land the balloon. But could you fly over the Melrose place Sunday evening, just before dark?"

Enfield thought about it. "Daylight Savings Time ends Saturday. It'll be dark a little after five o'clock on Sunday."

"All right—around that time, then."

"Where'll you be?"

Nick took some money from his wallet and slid it across the table. "I'll be around. You just come in low and attract lots of attention."

The following morning Nick drove up to the Melrose place, stopping along the way to phone Jenny Melrose for an appointment. He represented himself as a free-lance writer wanting to interview her for an article he was preparing on gracious living in the Hudson Valley. He suspected that would perk her interest, and it did.

She was a pleasant woman in her late thirties, a bit younger than her husband but with the same commanding personality. The sunny living room in which she greeted him had been decorated in expensive good taste—a bit old-fashioned by Nick's standards but still attractive. "Where will your article appear, Mr. Nicholas?" she asked, arranging herself on the sofa opposite him.

"I'm hoping for the *New York Times Magazine*, or perhaps *Country Gentleman*."

"I see."

"Could you tell me a bit about your style of living here?" Nick asked. "How you celebrate holidays, Halloween, for instance, since it's coming up tomorrow. Do you get any trick-or-treaters here?"

"Heavens, no. The gate is closed and there are guards. My husband is very security-conscious."

"How about decorations? Do you do anything special?"

"For Halloween?" She smiled at his question, perhaps at the absurdity of it. "No, no special decorations."

Nick pursued doggedly, "Not even a pumpkin?"

"Oh, we put a couple out on the porch with candles in them. They can be seen from the road. But that's as far as we go."

"I'd like to get a picture of those if I could."

She spread her hands helplessly. "I don't even know where they're stored. I must remember to have one of the servants get them out tomorrow."

"Perhaps I could come back then. The front of your house is so lovely it would make a very effective picture in my story."

"I'm afraid tomorrow wouldn't be convenient."

"I wouldn't have to disturb you. You could just leave word at the gate that I'm expected. One of your security men can stay with me while I snap a photograph of the house on Halloween evening."

"Very well," she agreed. "I suppose there's no harm in that."

Nick forced himself to remain for another forty-five minutes, pursuing his line of questioning about holiday celebrations. Then he departed, confident that he had prepared the way. She had surprised him when she mentioned two pumpkins but that wouldn't stop him. He'd steal them both.

Halloween proved to be a crisp autumn day in Dutchess County, with the last of the leaves drifting down through sunlit skies. Wearing a black turtleneck sweater and slacks, Nick arrived back at the Melrose estate a little after four o'clock, let himself in the chained entranceway, and drove up the curving driveway. He was just taking a camera from his car when Horace Melrose, coming around from the side of the house, accosted him.

"What are you doing here?" the publisher asked.

"Nicholas is the name," Nick said, extending his hand. "I had a most informative interview with Mrs. Melrose yesterday and she gave me permission to return today for some pictures of the outside of the house."

Melrose ignored Nick's hand. "There's supposed to be a security guard with you. We've had trouble before with reporters."

"I'm not a reporter, Mr. Melrose. I'm a free-lance writer doing a magazine article."

"Nevertheless, no one's allowed on these grounds unaccompanied." He walked quickly down the drive to speak some brief harsh words to the security guard on duty. The man came hurrying up to Nick.

"Get your pictures and be on your way, mister," he growled.

"The lighting has got to be right," Nick answered, looking at the sky. Enfield's balloon was due any minute.

As Nick fussed with the camera, Jenny Melrose appeared in the doorway with two large glowing plastic pumpkins. "Here they are," she announced. "I'm sorry to have kept you waiting." She placed one on either side of the wide steps and inspected the scene with a critical eye. "Can you get them both in the photo?"

"I think so," Nick said, looking through the viewfinder and taking a step backward, thinking ironically that the pumpkins were reasonable copies of the real thing and would actually photograph very well. "Let me just move them slightly," he said, noticing that Horace Melrose was no longer on the scene and the guard was taking only a casual interest in the proceedings. He lifted the nearer pumpkin, careful not to disturb the flickering candle inside. There seemed nothing unusual about it to make it valuable to Rita Spangles or anyone else. A grease-penciled number on the bottom—274—seemed to indicate what its price had been.

"What's that?" the guard said, pointing at the sky.

"It looks like Roger Enfield's balloon," Jenny Melrose said. She and the gaurd moved out beyond Nick's car for a better view. "I wonder what he's doing up so late in the afternoon."

Nick had a look at the second pumpkin by then, but there was no price marked on it. While Mrs. Melrose and the guard watched the descending balloon, he blew out both candles and tossed the pumpkins through the open window of his car.

"I think he's trying to land," the guard said, unsnapping the holster at his side.

The big striped balloon, settling toward the front lawn of the Melrose estate, did indeed look as if it might land. Nick climbed quickly into his car. "Thanks a lot," he called out to Jenny Melrose. "I've got my pictures!"

"What?" She turned, startled. "Already?"

Nick was already wheeling the car around the circular driveway. He heard her say something about the pumpkins, and then the guard shouted at him, but he kept going.

His car hit the slender chain across the gate and snapped it like a string. He saw a little puff of white in the rearview mirror and thought he heard the bark of the guard's gun fired after him. Overhead, Roger Enfield's balloon lifted high into the twilight sky, out of harm's way.

"What did *you* do for Halloween?" Nick asked Rita Spangles the following day, gazing out of her hotel-room window at the golden sand of the Acapulco beach.

"Trick or treat, like everyone else," she answered. "The treat was a bottle of French champagne in a nice man's room." She lit a cigarette and studied the two plastic pumpkins on the table in front of her. "Don't think I'm paying you *fifty* thousand just because you stole *two* of them."

"The second one's on me," Nick said generously. "I didn't know which one you needed."

She continued staring at them. "To tell you the truth, I don't either. How come the heat from the candle doesn't melt the plastic?"

"They make it with a high melting point for uses like this."

"You think there's something inside the candles?"

Nick shook his head. "I checked on that. They're solid. Look, maybe I can help with your problem if you tell me about it."

"Is that included in your fee?"

"Sometimes."

"All right," she agreed with a sigh, sitting on the edge of the bed. "As you know, I was Horace's mistress. I still am, I suppose, though I haven't seen him in a long time. Just over a year ago, this reporter named Tom Reynolds, a sportswriter and photo editor for a Philadelphia paper, started nosing around. That's when Horace sent me out of town. Reynolds tracked me to Florida and started asking questions."

"What sort of questions?"

"Horace's firm wanted to buy a paper in the Midwest and someone out there tried to block the sale by claiming he had links to organized crime. They said he was a business associate of Norman Elba, who's involved in illegal sports gambling."

"The sports connection—that's what interested Reynolds!"

Nick remembered the videotape of the football game. Luckily he'd brought it in his suitcase on the off-chance Rita knew something about it.

"I suppose so," she agreed. "Anyway, Reynolds asked me about Horace, about what we did on certain dates he named. At first I clammed up, but later, when I knew Horace was about to ditch me, I started talking. I didn't have any solid information about Norman Elba, though."

"What was Reynolds doing at the Melrose home last Halloween?"

"He'd learned something and he went to confront Horace with it. Horace thought it was a routine interview and agreed to see him. I told Reynolds he should have settled for a statement over the phone, but he wanted to see Horace's face. He saw it, all right, and got a bullet for his trouble."

"You were at the hospital when he died," Nick said.

She looked surprised. "How did you know that?"

"His editor told me."

"Yeah, well, I went up there with him. You know. He was a handsome guy, young."

"Then you saw the shooting?"

"Not really. I was waiting in the car out on the main road, so Horace wouldn't see me. I followed the ambulance to the hospital and told them I was his fiancée."

"Did he talk to you?"

"Just a few words before he died. He said to get the pumpkin. 'It's on the pumpkin.' Those were his exact words."

"*On* the pumpkin, not *in* it?"

"*On.* I'm sure of that. But the next day when I returned to Horace's place, the pumpkins were gone—stored away for another year. Horace didn't want me snooping around with his wife there— he sent me away and warned me not to come back. He promised to send me money, and he has, but I keep remembering Tom Reynolds, a nice guy who didn't deserve what he got. And I keep remembering the dirty deal Horace handed me. When another Halloween rolled around I decided I should try to even the score, for Reynolds and me both."

Nick turned over the orange plastic globes, searching again for markings. "There's only the price on this one. Unless—"

"What is it?"

"This 274 scrawled on here with a black grease pencil. You said Reynolds was a photo editor besides being a sportswriter. He might have carried a grease pencil to mark photos, and when he saw the Melrose security guards drawing their guns he managed to mark this number on the pumpkin."

"I thought it was the price," Rita said.

"So did I. But $2.74 isn't a likely price for it. And there's no decimal point. It's not a price at all, but a number."

"A date?"

"February 1974? I doubt it. He'd have had time to put a line or dash separating the numbers if he meant them to be separated."

"Then what could it be?"

"Something important to him. The key to whatever he'd uncovered about Melrose and Norman Elba. I wonder—"

Nick was interrupted by a knock at the door. "Room service!"

Rita Spangles looked blank. "I didn't order anything."

"Open the door slowly," Nick whispered, slipping behind it.

But as soon as her hand turned the knob the door sprang open, propelled by a brawny man who barreled forward to grab Rita and cover her mouth before she could scream. Nick shoved back on the door, knocking a second man off balance, then dove for the one holding Rita. As they toppled, wrestling, to the floor, the second man recovered enough to shout, "Get the pumpkins!"

Rita snatched up a lamp and brought it down on the head of Nick's adversary, stunning him. Then she turned toward the man who had spoken. "I know you," she said, "you're Norman Elba!"

The gambler smiled and reached inside his jacket. Nick moved fast, almost by reflex, hurling the broken lamp at Elba's head just as a snubnosed revolver appeared in his hand.

It was a brief battle. When it was over, Nick and Rita had Norman Elba and his henchman tied hand and foot with a haphazard collection of pantyhose, neckties, and a torn-up pillowcase.

"Melrose knew where to find you," Nick explained to Rita. "He guessed you hired me to steal the pumpkins and sent Elba after you." He turned to the gambler. "Isn't that right?"

"Go to hell!"

Nick held up the pumpkin. "What does 274 mean?"

"You tell me. You wanted it bad enough to steal it."

"It was Tom Reynolds's dying message, hidden for a year after his murder, and somehow it ties you and Melrose together."

Elba merely smiled. Rita appealed to Nick. "We can't hold him here forever."

"No," he agreed. There was a sound from the room next door. It sounded like a football game on television, and he remembered that the games from the States were shown here on cable. It would be Monday evening back East. Then he thought again of the videotape Paul Karoski had loaned him. "Of course—that's it!"

"What is?"

"Does the hotel have a video recorder somewhere?"

"There's one in the lounge downstairs. They play tapes of horse races in the afternoon and the guests make small wagers."

"Come on," Nick said. "I've got a tape in my room I want to play."

The lounge was unoccupied when they reached it and he slipped the tape into the machine. Then he turned on the set and pushed the Fast Forward button on the video recorder.

"What are you doing?" Rita asked.

"These machines all have digital counters to indicate the relative position of programs or scenes on a tape. See it there? It's almost to one hundred already. When it nears 274 we'll stop it and play the tape at its regular speed. I think we'll see something interesting— something Reynolds's editor missed because he didn't know where to look."

He waited another moment and stopped the tape at 270. Then he pushed the Play button. "But they're not even showing the game," Rita complained. "The camera's panning over the crowd in the stands."

"And there it is!" Nick quickly pressed the Pause button and the image froze on the screen. It was a picture of Horace Melrose and Norman Elba with their heads together in deep conversation. "There's the proof Tom Reynolds spotted! When he confronted

Melrose with what he had, Melrose ordered his security guards to shoot him. But Reynolds managed to scrawl that number on the pumpkin, and to tell you about it before he died."

"But why didn't Horace try to recover this tape?"

"Reynolds may not have been that specific about the nature of his evidence. Or Melrose might have figured it was better not to call attention to the tape at all. If he led Karoski to believe it was valuable, he could have gotten another copy easily enough and looked at it a bit more carefully."

"What should we do now?" she asked.

Nick thought about it as he rewound the videotape. "Phone Paul Karoski in Philadelphia and tell him what we've got. Then we'll turn Elba and his friend over to the local police and I'll be heading home—as soon as you pay me my fee."

Edward D. Hoch has been called the last surviving member of an endangered species—the professional writer of short mysteries. It's a vocation he began practicing in 1956 when his first effort was bought; today the list of his published stories numbers well into the hundreds. He is also a distinguished archivist of the mystery short story and has produced numerous anthologies, including the two popular series The Year's Best Mystery and Suspense Stories *and* Best Detective Stories of the Year. *His best-known recurring characters are Nick Velvet and the police officer Captain Leopold; in 1968, he won a Best Short Story Edgar for a tale featuring Leopold.*

Hallowe'en For Mr. Faulkner

By August Derleth

For moments of dread and superstition, the calendar is indeed crowded around the end of October and the beginning of November. But Guy Fawkes Day, celebrated on November 5 in the British Isles, has its origins not in ancient Celtic practice but in a harrowing episode of actual history—the famous Gunpowder Plot of 1605, which threatened not only the life of the king, James I, but also the members of both houses of Parliament.

Miraculously, the conspiracy was thwarted on the fourth, the very day before it was to take place, though the means by which Guy Fawkes and his fellow traitors were themselves betrayed has ever since been a matter of conjecture. Today the holiday, with its annual burnings of "guys" in straw effigy, provides for English schoolchildren the equivalent of the frenzied excitement of Halloween in the United States.

For August Derleth's very proper Mr. Faulkner,

an American visiting London one autumn in the aftermath of World War II, however, Halloween starts out as a night like any other—except for the impenetrable fog and the masked and costumed figures who emerge from it.

Hallowe'en For Mr. Faulkner

There was simply no use going farther; so Guy Faulkner stood where he was, as helpless as if he were in the midst of a chartless sea. He was somewhere in London, in a sea of fog. Was it in Lambeth? And had he not heard the bells of St. Clement's? He deplored his insistence on going out that afternoon in trace of some faint lead to supplement the work now being done by Inigo Gunter, who was an expert in matters historical and genealogical, and whose report had been promised him this very day. A pox on his own impatience! Now there was no telling just when he would escape the fog.

He stood resolutely still. Sooner or later someone was bound to come along. If it were a bobby, he would be given good conduct to his hotel. If it were anyone at all familiar with the district, he might at least learn where he had wandered to. The fog swirled around him, growing ever more dense—not yellow, as he had been led to believe, but a kind of gray shot through with a glow rising as from distant lights which had no separate identity. He quelled his impatience; he had no alternative but to wait. He would have been almost as helpless in Chicago or New York, for all his familiarity with those cities, so thick was the fog.

Quite suddenly a dark shape loomed beside him.

"Pardon me," he said.

"Match, Guvnor?"

Faulkner took out his lighter. Fortunately, it lit at once. He held it up.

The fog played tricks on him. The face he looked into might have been his own. It bent to light a pipe, seemed to flatten, to dissolve—the fog again.

"I'm afraid I'm lost," said Faulkner.

"Come along," said the other, beginning to move away.

Faulkner followed. His companion walked with sureness and ease; he at least could find his way.

"I want to go to the Chelsea," he said.

But the other did not reply, and Faulkner had all he could do to keep up with him, trying to keep from falling over curbs and colliding with lampposts. Should there not have been more light as they approached the hotel? he wondered. But abruptly his silent companion turned off the walk, and mounted a few steps. Faulkner was conscious of a typical iron railing at either side. Coming up behind his guide, Faulkner lit his lighter again; the figure 16 gleamed on the heavy door. Then the door swung open upon a darkened hall, and immediately his guide was engulfed. Faulkner hesitated only a moment—anything was better than the oppressive fog. The door closed behind him, and another opened before upon a dimly lit room into which he had hardly stepped before he was aware of the strangeness of it—a room, as it were, of invaluable antique furnishings; it might have been lifted completely from a museum. He turned to his companion to ask—and found himself alone.

The door behind was closed. Down along one wall of the room was another door, beneath which showed a brighter light; and behind it rose the murmur of voices. Had his companion gone that way? But no, how could he? There had not been time. A sudden panic assailed Faulkner and he turned to go back the way he had come.

But even as his hand fell upon the knob, the door at the end of the room opened, a yellow glow spread into the room, and a hearty voice said to someone behind, "Here's Guy now. We were waiting for you."

Faulkner turned, surprised. The man was masked with a domino. And in costume. Behind him, grouped about a table, were others, likewise costumed and masked. But, of course, the night was near to All Hallows and some people celebrated the time of masks throughout the week; these were doubtless traditional maskers, and known to him, perhaps, behind their masks. He hesitated but a moment more; the man before him held the door invitingly open, and his smile bade Faulkner welcome as no words need have done.

"You're late, Guy . . ."

"We thought you'd failed of coming . . ."

"What kept you? . . ."

A chair was pushed forward for him.

Bewildered, he sat down. He was aware of a strange kind of apprehension within him, as if something ominous lay behind this mask of comradeship. He could not remember a voice, a face, a gesture. And yet, so familiar were these men, that he could not but wonder how he could have forgotten them. In a moment, certainly, their names would come to them; someone would mention them.

"I say, Wright, now Guy's here, we can get on with it."

Wright—John Wright, Faulkner said to himself. And that man talking was Tom Winter. And that, Robert Catesby. And the fourth, Tom Percy. And finally, Ambrose Rokewood. Faulkner could not recall where he had met them, yet their names were now certainly coming back to him. But the feeling of apprehension did not leave him.

He waited.

The bottles and glasses were pushed aside, and Catesby leaned over.

"The day's been chosen, you'll recollect, Guy."

"The fifth," said Winter.

One of them chuckled. "Was it not a clever thing to have chosen a night of this week for our last meeting? When one and all are in costume, and the most improbable of all excites no question?"

"But for your own, Guy," said Wright. "A strange costume, indeed. And unmasked! How bold!"

"Ah, I am but a humble servant of Mr. Percy," Faulkner said, and grinned.

But simultaneously he thought: Percy. But of course, he was employed by Percy. Had he not come over the sea from Flanders not long since? And spoken there with Stanley of Deventer? What nagged in his mind was a perplexity indeed. A broader ocean, a strange land, great cities . . .

"The powder's laid," continued Catesby.

"Aye, and the fuse is placed," said Percy. "He had good time in which to do these things from my house next door to parliament house. A good and willing servant, indeed. Once this business is done with, I commend him to you. He will go to heights."

"One way or t'other," said Wright sourly. "High by his skill or by the scaffold if we're caught."

"Come, come, let us not speak of being caught," protested Catesby. "We've come a long way; we are on the threshold of success. Victory will be ours within the week, mark me."

"Who will light the fuse?" asked Rokewood. "I offer myself."

"Noble and generous Rokewood," said Catesby. "But this would scarce be fair to the others who are as eager to consummate this task. Shall we not draw for it?"

"Aye," said Wright.

And "Aye," said Percy.

Winter nodded, without saying anything, and Rokewood made no protest.

"It will be arranged before this night is done. Come now, let us look to plans to which we must adhere once the thing has been accomplished. Draw closer."

Catesby produced a map and spread it before them. Six heads circled it. Catesby's elegant fingers, dark against the white ruff at his wrist, descended to the map.

"The moment it is done, I will ride to my mother's house at Ashby St. Legers. We shall, several of us, ride through Warwickshire to rally the country behind us. I myself will ride straight to Digby and enlist his aid, by which time he will be ready, if I tell them both James and Salisbury are dead."

"And what if they are not?" asked Rokewood.

"We dare not fail."

"There are thirty-six barrels of gunpowder under coal and faggots in the cellar. More than a ton of the stuff," said Percy.

"But, since it's been there so long—May, was it not?—what assurance have we that it has not got wet?"

"It was put in a dry place on purpose," said Percy, and turned to Faulkner. "Was it not, Guy?"

Faulkner nodded.

"And the Jesuits?"

"We have Garnet's blessing, at least. But Greenway and Gerard know our plan and have not spoken against it."

A doubt beset Faulkner. He closed his eyes. Instantly all this elaborate play was alien. He was Guy Faulkner of New York, in London pursuing his genealogical studies. The year was 1953. But when he opened his eyes a moment later, he could have taken solemn oath that it was some other year. The candles flickered, and appurtenances of the house loomed grotesque in their age in the candlelight, the five masked men who stood about him, leaning over the map on the table, were impeccably dressed in the costumse of the turn of the seventeenth century.

An elaborate hoax. Who could have been responsible for it? Or, for that matter, for his own words, spoken so glibly? Or was it a plot, indeed? Was it by some accident that he had stumbled upon an attempt to repeat history, to blow up Parliament? Apprehension took hold of him again.

"Guy says little," said Wright suddenly.

"I am no man for words," Faulkner responded without hesitation.

"True," agreed Gatsby. "Would that all others had to their credit Guy's deeds. We should not now be in doubt of the success of our plot. Where is Tresham?"

"No one knows. Safe in his bed, most likely," said Percy.

"I said it was a mistake to invite Tresham to take part in this," said Rokewood heavily. "Monteagle is his brother-in-law; can he contrive to keep him from Parliament and be destroyed with James and Salisbury?"

"He dare not."

"Who will say him nay? Was he not all eagerness and will at the beginning; but now that the thing is all but done, where is Tresham?" demanded Rokewood. "A peer's brother-in-law has no place among us."

"A man's a man not by any accident of blood," said Catesby.

"Nor of religion, then," said Percy.

"Agreed," said Catesby. "Or color, age, or temper."

All this time Winter had said nothing. Now he put on the table six sticks he had been fashioning. All save one were of equal length; the one was shorter.

"How say we?" he asked.

"He who draws the short stick shall light the fuse," said Catesby.

There was an immediate chorus of agreement.

Catesby slipped on his gloves, so that he might not himself feel which was the short one among them, picked up the sticks, rolled them about a little, and held them out, stuck in his fist.

Percy drew first.

Then Rokewood. Since both had sticks of equal length, neither had drawn the short one.

Winter drew—a long stick.

Wright—another of similar length.

Catesby grinned sardonically, and held the two remaining sticks before Faulkner. "It lies between us, Guy. Fate would have it so."

Faulkner drew. He had the short stick.

Catesby opened his hand, let the remaining stick fall. "I congratulate you, Guy. None could better perform this task to free our great country from the oppressions of James and Salisbury."

Faulkner smiled. Uncertainty, apprehension, astonishment vied for revelation, but none showed on his features.

"You'll remember what was agreed upon," Catesby went on. "You'll get into the cellar in the night, and, as soon as the King has arrived, light the fuse and make your escape at once. Fly to join me at Ashby St. Legers."

Rokewood came to his feet, a heavy man, dark of feature. He reached behind him for his cloak. "The thing's as good as done. I bid you good-night, gentlemen. May God attend our plans."

One by one they withdrew, until only Catesby was left.

"You have not moved, Guy. Is anything wrong?"

"I must have time to think on this," said Faulkner.

"Ten days, no more. The calendar marks the twenty-fifth of the month. In six more, November's upon us. Aye, and within the week beyond that James and Salisbury will be no more!" He stuck out his hand to shake Faulkner's. "Good luck, Guy. We'll to victory or hang with you." At the threshold he turned for a final word. "I trust when again we meet at this place, 'twill be Old Paradise no longer, but New!"

Then he was gone.

Faulkner sat alone and for the moment, unmoving. How quixotic were his thoughts! Were it possible for a man to step back into time, he might have done so. The time would be 1605, the event the Gunpowder Plot against James I and Lord Salisbury. But in his mind was a core of turgid confusion. How was it possible for him to remember so well these people with whom he had sat this night and yet never met?

Was there, indeed, a hoax that intended him for victim? Or was there, on the other hand, a danger that there was indeed some plan afoot to blow up Parliament. He grew cold with fear. Something must be done to prevent such a plan's fulfillment. But what?

Who was it had mentioned Tresham and Lord Monteagle?

He looked wildly about him; there was not much time. At any moment he might be interrupted. The householder might come back. Wright, it seemed, was owner here. Or was it but another of Catesby's houses?

He came upon paper, a quill pen, ink.

"My lord, out of the love I bear to some of your friends, I have a care for preservation. Therefore I would advise you, as you tender your life, to devise some excuse to shift of your attendance of this Parliament, for God and man hath concurred to punish the wickedness of this time. And think not slightly of this advertisement, but retire yourself into your country, where you may expect the event in safety, for though there be no appearance of any stir, yet I say they shall receive a terrible blow, the Parliament, and yet they shall not see who hurts them. This counsel is not to be condemned, because it may do you good and can do you no harm, for the danger is past as soon as you have burnt the letter; and I hope God will give you the grace to make good use of it, to whose holy protection I commend you."

Without hesitation, he signed it, "Tresham." His own name would have no meaning to Lord Monteagle. He folded the letter, folded another paper around it so devised to hold it as might an envelope, of which he saw none, wrote Lord Monteagle's name in a bold hand on the outside, and, without another glance for his surroundings, fled the room, fled the next, and in a few moments was outside and running through the fog as fast as possible, until he found a postman's box, and there dropped his letter, trusting that it would reach Monteagle in time. Ten days. He felt for his lighter, but he had left it, as he had his hat. He would not retrace his steps.

The air stirred him, the close-pressing fog brought him once again to awareness that he was lost. But, no, not quite. Was not that Westminster Bridge ahead? He walked on, and soon found himself above the Thames, with the fog beginning to thin.

Though it was past midnight, Gunter was still waiting for him. Not because he had intended to do so, but because he had fallen asleep in Faulkner's room. He started away under Faulkner's touch.

"I've been asleep," he said, ruefully, looking at his watch. "And missed a nightcap with Barry."

"Have one with me," said Faulkner, moving toward the decanter. "I've had an evening."

"In this fog?"

"It's beginning to lift." Faulkner came back with glasses and the decanter. "What have you found?"

"Ah, something of interest, indeed," said Gunter, becoming alert at once. "Though I've no way of knowing how you'll take it." He tossed off a drink and complimented Faulkner. "It's all in these papers." He took them out of his pocket, tapped them intimately where he held them in his hand, and gave them to Faulkner.

"I've got you back as far as York. The name was changed, you see, in 1605. Used to be Fawkes. Family of Edward Fawkes of York. It was Edward's son, Guy . . ."

"The Gunpowder Plot!"

"Of course. The disgrace of it upon the family brought about the change in name. One understands that, of course. But no doubt you Americans look upon these things in a more romantic light."

Faulkner's mouth went dry; his whisky was tasteless on his tongue.

He opened the papers and read of the succession of the line of Edward Fawkes, father of Guy Fawkes, who lent his name forever

108

to the Gunpowder Plot to blow up Parliament with King James I and his ministers . . .

In the clear light of morning, he knew what he must do. He had a perfect excuse—to look for his hat and lighter. True, he did not know the address, but had not one of them spoken of "Old Paradise," and was there not a street by that name not far from the Thames, off Westminster Bridge?

On that chance he called a cab. "Take me to Old Paradise Street."

There was no question. He got in, settled back and was soon rolling toward his destination. The number, he remembered, was 16.

Someone had made game of him for Hallowe'en. Who they were, Faulkner would soon know. There was no fog this morning to confuse him.

The cab rolled over Westminster Bridge and soon after came to a halt.

"Old Paradise, sir," said his driver.

Faulkner got out, paid him and let him go. He walked slowly up the street. He could hardly hope to find any familiar facet, for the thick fog of the preceding evening had shrouded everything unrecognizably. Even the walk beneath his feet felt different. It had had the feel of cobbles in the night.

A short street. But there was no number 16.

He stood for a moment puzzled. But a postman coming along gave him hope and he stopped him.

"Number 16?" said the postman. "I'm old enough to remember that. Before the war, it's rubble now. Come along, I'll show you where it was."

Faulkner followed him, and they came presently to a cellar filled with rubble. There had once been a house there, and steps leading up to it, and iron railings about it. The railings were still there. Beyond all was rubble. But not far from where they stood, in the rubble, lay the same numerals Faulkner had seen less than a day ago—not bright and gleaming now, but old, worn, bent. And beyond that . . . ?

"They've not got around to cleaning up here yet," said the postman apologetically. "The place was hit not long after Coventry.

Historic house, too. Said to have been used as a meeting place for the Gunpowder plotters. Oh, I say now, you'd better not go climbing about in that rubble—it's posted and dangerous."

But Faulkner had gone ahead.

He felt he had the best right in the world to do so. Hoax, hallucination, dream—whatever had happened to him, he meant to retrieve his hat and the lighter which lay gleaming not far from it in the middle of the ruin and a little toward the rear . . . just where the room with the table would have been . . . if there had been such a room . . . and such a house . . . New Paradise indeed!

He went back to his hotel and telephoned Inigo Gunter.

"Tell me, did they ever find out who wrote that letter to Lord Monteagle in the Gunpowder affair?"

"No, Mr. Faulkner, to the best of my knowledge, they did not. They thought it was Tresham, but he denied it and died in the Tower. He might have won his freedom."

"Never mind, Mr. Gunter. I did it myself."

That was a break he had not meant to make, he told himself after he had cut off. He had meant to voice his belief that Guy Fawkes had written Monteagle and disclosed the plot. But to call Gunter again and explain would only complicate matters more.

Inigo Gunter entertained his colleagues for weeks with his anecdote about the mad American and his delusion.

August Derleth was a man of varied literary output: biography, regional writing, poetry, crime fiction, horror and fantasy tales, children's books, and more. A cofounder of Arkham House, a landmark publishing enterprise devoted primarily to science fiction and the macabre, he is perhaps best known to the mystery genre as the creator of Solar Pons stories, a series of Sherlockian pastiches collected in such volumes as The Casebook of Solar Pons *and* The Chronicles of Solar Pons.

DECEPTIONS

BY MARCIA MULLER

Halloween plays only a small role in this tale of a beautiful young woman attempting to win for herself the freedom to live her life as she chooses—but it's a crucial one. After hearing the anecdote of Vanessa DiCesare's behavior at a carefree Halloween bash, Sharon McCone begins to intuit the layers of deceit she will have to peel back in order to solve the case at hand.

"Deceptions" is the fourth short story featuring the popular legal investigator who made her debut nearly twenty years ago in *Edwin of the Iron Shoes.* It was inspired by a casual visit the author once paid to Fort Point, a historic site at the mouth of San Francisco Bay, which here provides the setting for Sharon's dramatic final encounter with a killer fully ready to repeat his crime.

DECEPTIONS

San Francisco's Golden Gate Bridge is deceptively fragile-looking, especially when fog swirls across its high span. But from where I was standing, almost underneath it at the south end, even the mist couldn't disguise the massiveness of its concrete piers and the taut strength of its cables. I tipped my head back and looked up the tower to where it disappeared into the drifting grayness, thinking about the other ways the bridge is deceptive.

For one thing, its color isn't gold, but rust red, reminiscent of dried blood. And though the bridge is a marvel of engineering, it is also plagued by maintenance problems that keep the Bridge District in constant danger of financial collapse. For a reputedly romantic structure, it has seen more than its fair share of tragedy: Some eight hundred-odd lost souls have jumped to their deaths from its deck.

Today I was there to try to find out if that figure should be raised by one. So far I'd met with little success.

I was standing next to my car in the parking lot of Fort Point, a historic fortification at the mouth of San Francisco Bay. Where the pavement stopped, the land fell away to jagged black rocks; waves smashed against them, sending up geysers of salty spay. Beyond the rocks the water was choppy, and Angel Island and Alcatraz were mere humpbacked shapes in the mist. I shivered, wishing I'd worn something heavier than my poplin jacket, and started toward the fort.

This was the last stop on a journey that had taken me from the toll booths and Bridge District offices to Vista Point at the Marin County end of the span, and back to the National Parks Service headquarters down the road from the fort. None of the Parks Service or bridge personnel—including a group of maintenance workers near the north tower—had seen the slender dark-haired woman in the picture I'd shown them, walking south on the pedestrian sidewalk at about four yesterday afternoon. None of them had seen her jump.

It was for that reason—plus the facts that her parents had revealed about twenty-two-year-old Vanessa DiCesare—that made me tend to doubt she actually had committed suicide, in spite of the note she'd left taped to the dashboard of the Honda she'd abandoned at Vista Point. Surely at four o'clock on a Monday afternoon *someone* would have noticed her. Still, I had to follow up every possibility, and the people at the Parks Service station had suggested I check with the rangers at Fort Point.

I entered the dark-brick structure through a long, low tunnel—called a sally port, the sign said—which was flanked at either end by massive wooden doors with iron studding. Years before I'd visited the fort, and now I recalled that it was more or less typical of harbor fortifications built in the Civil War era: a ground floor topped by two tiers of working and living quarters, encircling a central courtyard.

I emerged into the court and looked up at the west side; the tiers were a series of brick archways, their openings as black as empty eyesockets, each roped off by a narrow strip of yellow plastic strung across it at waist level. There was construction gear in the courtyard; the entire west side was under renovation and probably off limits to the public.

As I stood there trying to remember the layout of the place and wondering which way to go, I became aware of a hollow metallic clanking that echoed in the circular enclosure. The noise drew my eyes upward to the wooden watchtower atop the west tiers, and

114

then to the red arch of the bridge's girders directly above it. The clanking seemed to have something to do with cars passing over the roadbed, and it was underlaid by a constant grumbling rush of tires on pavement. The sounds, coupled with the soaring height of the fog-laced girders, made me feel very small and insignificant. I shivered again and turned to my left, looking for one of the rangers.

The man who came out of a nearby doorway startled me, more because of his costume than the suddenness of his appearance. Instead of the Parks Service uniform I remembered the rangers wearing on my previous visit, he was clad in what looked like an old Union Army uniform: a dark blue frock coat, lighter blue trousers, and a wide-brimmed hat with a red plume. The long saber in a scabbard that was strapped to his waist made him look thoroughly authentic.

He smiled at my obvious surprise and came over to me, bushy eyebrows lifted inquiringly. "Can I help you, ma'am?"

I reached into my bag and took out my private investigator's license and showed it to him. "I'm Sharon McCone, from All Souls Legal Cooperative. Do you have a minute to answer some questions?"

He frowned, the way people often do when confronted by a private detective, probably trying to remember whether he'd done anything lately that would warrant investigation. Then he said, "Sure," and motioned for me to step into the shelter of the sally port.

"I'm investigating a disappearance, a possible suicide from the bridge," I said. "It would have happened about four yesterday afternoon. Were you on duty then?"

He shook his head. "Monday's my day off."

"Is there anyone else here who might have been working then?"

"You could check with Lee—Lee Gottschalk, the other ranger on this shift."

"Where can I find him?"

He moved back into the courtyard and looked around. "I saw him start taking a couple of tourists around just a few minutes ago. People are crazy; they'll come out in any kind of weather."

"Can you tell me which way he went?"

The ranger gestured to our right. "Along this side. When he's done down here, he'll take them up that iron stairway to the first tier, but I can't say how far he's gotten yet."

I thanked him and started off in the direction he'd indicated.

There were open doors in the cement wall between the sally port and the iron staircase. I glanced through the first and saw no one. The second led into a narrow dark hallway; when I was halfway down it, I saw that this was the fort's jail. One cell was set up as a display, complete with a mannequin prisoner; the other, beyond an archway that was not much taller than my own five-foot-six, was unrestored. Its waterstained walls were covered with graffiti, and a metal railing protected a two-foot-square iron grid on the floor in one corner. A sign said that it was a cistern with a forty-thousand-gallon capacity.

Well, I thought, that's interesting, but playing tourist isn't helping me catch up with Lee Gottschalk. Quickly I left the jail and hurried up the iron staircase the first ranger had indicated. At its top, I turned to my left and bumped into a chain link fence that blocked access to the area under renovation. Warning myself to watch where I was going, I went the other way, toward the east tier. The archways there were fenced off with similar chain link so no one could fall, and doors opened off the gallery into what I supposed had been the soldiers' living quartesr. I pushed through the first one and stepped into a small museum.

The room was high-ceilinged, with tall, narrow windows in the outside wall. No ranger or tourists were in sight. I looked toward an interior door that led to the next room and saw a series of mirror images: one door within another leading off into the distance, each diminishing in size until the last seemed very tiny. I had the unpleasant sensation that if I walked along there, I would become progressively smaller and eventually disappear.

From somewhere down there came the sound of voices. I followed it, passing through more museum displays until I came to a room containing an old-fashioned bedstead and footlocker. A ranger, dressed the same as the man downstairs except that he was bearded and wore granny glasses, stood beyond the bedstead lecturing to a man and a woman who were bundled to their chins in bulky sweaters.

"You'll notice that the fireplaces are very small," he was saying, motioning to the one on the wall next to the bed, "and you can imagine how cold it could get for the soldier garrisoned here. They didn't have a heated employees' lounge like we do." Smiling at his own little joke, he glanced at me. "Do you want to join the tour?"

I shook my head and stepped over by the footlocker. "Are you Lee Gottschalk?"

"Yes." He spoke the word a shade warily.

"I have a few questions I'd like to ask you. How long will the rest of the tour take?"

"At least half an hour. These folks want to see the unrestored rooms on the third floor."

I didn't want to wait around that long, so I said, "Could you take a couple of minutes and talk with me now?"

He moved his head so the light from the windows caught his granny glasses and I couldn't see the expression in his eyes, but his mouth tightened in a way that might have been annoyance. After a moment he said, "Well, the rest of the tour on this floor is pretty much self-guided." To the tourists, he added, "Why don't you go on ahead and I'll catch up after I talk with this lady."

They nodded agreeably and moved on into the next room. Lee Gottschalk folded his arms arcoss his chest and leaned against the small fireplace. "Now what can I do for you?"

I introduced myself and showed him my license. His mouth twitched briefly in surprise, but he didn't comment. I said, "At about four yesterday afternoon, a young woman left her car at Vista Point with a suicide note in it. I'm trying to locate a witness who saw her jump." I took out the photograph I'd been showing to people and handed it to him. By now I had Vanessa DiCesare's features memorized: high forehead, straight nose, full lips, glossy wings of dark-brown hair curling inward at the jawbone. It was a strong face, not beautiful but striking—and a face I'd recognize anywhere.

Gottschalk studied the photo, then handed it back to me. "I read about her in the morning paper. Why are you trying to find a witness?"

"Her parents have hired me to look into it."

"The paper said her father is some big politician here in the city."

I didn't see any harm in discussing what had already appeared in print. "Yes, Ernest DiCesare—he's on the Board of Supes and likely to be our next mayor."

"And she was a law student, engaged to some hotshot lawyer who ran her father's last political campaign."

"Right again."

He shook his head, lips pushing out in bewilderment. "Sounds like she had a lot going for her. Why would she kill herself? Did that note taped inside her car explain it?"

I'd seen the note, but its contents were confidential. "No. Did you happen to see anything unusual yesterday afternoon?"

"No. But if I'd seen anyone jump, I'd have reported it to the Coast Guard station so they could try to recover the body before the current carried it out to sea."

"What about someone standing by the bridge railing, acting strangely, perhaps?"

"If I'd noticed anyone like that, I'd have reported it to the bridge offices so they could send out a suicide prevention team." He stared almost combatively at me, as if I'd accused him of some kind of wrongdoing, then seemed to relent a little. "Come outside," he said, "and I"ll show you something."

We went through the door to the gallery, and he guided me to the chain link barrier in the archway and pointed up. "Look at the angle of the bridge, and the distance we are from it. You couldn't spot anyone standing at the rail from here, at least not well enough to tell if they were acting upset. And a jumper would have to hurl herself way out before she'd be noticeable."

"And there's nowhere else in the fort from where a jumper would be clearly visible?"

"Maybe from one of the watchtowers or the extreme west side. But they're off limits to the public, and we only give them one routine check at closing."

Satisfied now, I said, "Well, that about does it. I appreciate your taking the time."

He nodded and we started along the gallery. When we reached the other end, where an enclosed staircase spiraled up and down, I thanked him again and we parted company.

The way the facts looked to me now, Vanessa DiCesare had

faked this suicide and just walked away—away from her wealthy old-line Italian family, from her up-and-coming liberal lawyer, from a life that either had become too much or just hadn't been enough. Vanessa was over twenty-one; she had a legal right to disappear if she wanted to. But her parents and her fiancé loved her, and they also had a right to know she was alive and well. If I could locate her and reassure them without ruining whatever new life she planned to create for herself, I would feel I'd performed the job I'd been hired to do. But right now I was weary, chilled to the bone, and out of leads. I decided to go back to All Souls and consider my next moves in warmth and comfort.

All Souls Legal Cooperative is housed in a ramshackle Victorian on one of the steeply sloping sidestreets of Bernal Heights, a working-class district in the southern part of the city. The co-op caters mainly to clients who live in the area: people with low to middle incomes who don't have much extra money for expensive lawyers. The sliding fee scale allows them to obtain quality legal assistance at reasonable prices—a concept that is probably outdated in the self-centered 1980s, but is kept alive by the people who staff All Souls. It's a place where the lawyers care about their clients, and a good place to work.

I left my MG at the curb and hurried up the front steps through the blowing fog. The warm inside was almost a shock after the chilliness at Fort Point; I unbuttoned my jacket and went down the long deserted hallway to the big country kitchen at the rear. There I found my boss, Hank Zahn, stirring up a mug of the Navy grog he often concocts on cold November nights like this one.

He looked at me, pointed to the rum bottle, and said, "Shall I make you one?" When I nodded, he reached for another mug.

I went to the round oak table under the windows, moved a pile of newspapers from one of the chairs, and sat down. Hank added lemon juice, hot water, and sugar syrup to the rum; dusted it artistically with nutmeg; and set it in front of me with a flourish. I sampled it as he sat down across from me, then nodded my approval.

He said, "How's it going with the DiCesare investigation?"

Hank had a personal interest in the case; Vanessa's fiancé, Gary

119

Stornetta, was a longtime friend of his, which was why I, rather than one of the large investigative firms her father normally favored, had been asked to look into it. I said, "Everything I've come up with points to it being a disappearance, not a suicide."

"Just as Gary and her parents suspected."

"Yes. I've covered the entire area around the bridge. There are absolutely no witnesses, except for the tour bus driver who saw her park her car at four and got suspicious when it was still there at seven and reported it. But even he didn't see her walk off toward the bridge." I drank some more grog, felt its warmth, and began to relax.

Behind his thick horn-rimmed glasses, Hank's eyes became concerned. "Did the DiCesares or Gary give you any idea why she would have done such a thing?"

"When I talked with Ernest and Sylvia this morning, they said Vanessa had changed her mind about marrying Gary. He's not admitting to that, but he doesn't speak of Vanessa the way a happy husband-to-be would. And it seems an unlikely match to me—he's close to twenty years older than she."

"More like fifteen," Hank said. "Gary's father was Ernest's best friend, and after Ron Stornetta died, Ernest more or less took him on as a protégé. Ernest was delighted that their families were finally going to be joined."

"Oh, he was delighted all right. He admitted to me that he'd practically arranged the marriage. 'Girl didn't know what was good for her,' he said. 'Needed a strong older man to guide her.' " I snorted.

Hank smiled faintly. He's a feminist, but over the years his sense of outrage has mellowed; mine still has a hair trigger.

"Anyway," I said, "when Vanessa first announced she was backing out of the engagement, Ernest told her he would cut off her funds for law school if she didn't go through with the wedding."

"Jesus, I had no idea he was capable of such . . . Neanderthal tactics."

"Well, he is. After that Vanessa went ahead and set the wedding date. But Sylvia said she suspected she wouldn't go through with it. Vanessa talked of quitting law school and moving out of their home. And she'd been seeing other men; she and her father had a

120

bad quarrel about it just last week. Anyway, all of that, plus the fact that one of her suitcases and some clothing are missing, made them highly suspicious of the suicide."

Hank reached for my mug and went to get us more grog. I began thumbing through the copy of the morning paper that I'd moved off the chair, looking for the story on Vanessa. I found it on page three.

> The daughter of Supervisor Ernest DiCesare apparently committed suicide by jumping from the Golden Gate Bridge late yesterday afternoon.
>
> Vanessa DiCesare, 22, abandoned her 1985 Honda Civic at Vista Point at approximately four P.M., police said. There were no witnesses to her jump, and the body has not been recovered. The contents of a suicide note found in her car have not been disclosed.
>
> Ms. DiCesare, a first-year student at Hastings College of Law, is the only child of the supervisor and his wife, Sylvia. She planned to be married next month to San Francisco attorney Gary R. Stornetta, a political associate of her father. . . .

Strange how routine it all sounded when reduced to journalistic language. And yet how mysterious—the "undisclosed contents" of the suicide note, for instance.

"You know," I said as Hank came back to the table and set down the fresh mugs of grog, "that note is another factor that makes me believe she staged this whole thing. It was so formal and controlled. If they had samples of suicide notes in etiquette books, I'd say she looked one up and copied it."

He ran his fingers through his wiry brown hair. "What I don't understand is why she didn't just break off the engagement and move out of the house. So what if her father cut off her money? There are lots worse things than working your way through law school."

"Oh, but this way she gets back at everyone, and has the advantage of actually being alive to gloat over it. Imagine her parents' and Gary's grief and guilt—it's the ultimate way of getting even."

"She must be a very angry young woman."

"Yes. After I talked with Ernest and Sylvia and Gary, I spoke briefly with Vanessa's best friend, a law student named Kathy Graves. Kathy told me that Vanessa was furious with her father for making her go through with the marriage. And she'd come to hate Gary because she'd decided he was only marrying her for her family's money and political power."

"Oh, come on. Gary's ambitious, sure. But you can't tell me he doesn't genuinely care for Vanessa."

"I'm only giving you her side of the story."

"So now what do you plan to do?"

"Talk with Gary and the DiCesares again. See if I can't come up with some bit of information that will help me find her."

"And then?"

"Then it's up to them to work it out."

The DiCesare home was mock-Tudor, brick and half-timber, set on a corner knoll in the exclusive area of St. Francis Wood. When I'd first come there that morning, I'd been slightly awed; now the house had lost its power to impress me. After delving into the lives of the people who lived there, I knew that it was merely a pile of brick and mortar and wood that contained more than the usual amount of misery.

The DiCesares and Gary Stornetta were waiting for me in the living room, a strangely formal place with several groupings of furniture and expensive-looking knickknacks laid out in precise patterns on the tables. Vanessa's parents and fiancé—like the house—seemed diminished since my previous visit: Sylvia huddled in an armchair by the fireplace, her gray-blonde hair straggling from its elegant coiffure; Ernest stood behind her, haggard-faced, one hand protectively on her shoulder. Gary paced, smoking and clawing at his hair with his other hand. Occasionally he dropped ashes on the thick wall-to-wall carpeting, but no one called it to his attention.

They listened to what I had to report without interruption. When I finished, there was a long silence. Then Sylvia put a hand over her eyes and said, "How she must hate us to do a thing like this!"

Ernest tightened his grip on his wife's shoulder. His face was a conflict of anger, bewilderment, and sorrow.

There was no question of which emotion had hold of Gary; he smashed out his cigarette in an ashtray, lit another, and resumed pacing. But while his movements before had merely been nervous, now his tall, lean body was rigid with thinly controlled fury. "Damn her!" he said. "Damn her anyway!"

"Gary." There was a warning note in Ernest's voice.

Gary glanced at him, then at Sylvia. "Sorry."

I said, "The question now is, do you want me to continue looking for her?"

In shocked tones, Sylvia said, "Of course we do!" Then she tipped her head back and looked at her husband.

Ernest was silent, his fingers pressing hard against the black wool of her dress.

"Ernest?" Now Sylvia's voice held a note of panic.

"Of course we do," he said. But the words somehow lacked conviction.

I took out my notebook and pencil, glancing at Gary. He had stopped pacing and was watching the DiCesares. His craggy face was still mottled with anger, and I sensed he shared Ernest's uncertainty.

Opening the notebook, I said, "I need more details about Vanessa, what her life was like the past month or so. Perhaps something will occur to one of you that didn't this morning."

"Ms. McCone," Ernest said, "I don't think Sylvia's up to this right now. Why don't you and Gary talk, and then if there's anything else, I'll be glad to help you."

"Fine." Gary was the one I was primarily interested in questioning, anyway. I waited until Ernest and Sylvia had left the room, then turned to him.

When the door shut behind them, he hurled his cigarette into the empty fireplace. "Goddamn little bitch!" he said.

I said, "Why don't you sit down."

He looked at me for a few seconds, obviously wanting to keep on pacing, but then he flopped into the chair Sylvia had vacated. When I'd first met with Gary this morning, he'd been controlled

123

and immaculately groomed, and he had seemed more solicitous of the DiCesares than concerned with his own feelings. Now his clothing was disheveled, his graying hair tousled, and he looked to be on the brink of a rage that would flatten anyone in its path.

Unfortunately, what I had to ask him would probably fan that rage. I braced myself and said, "Now tell me about Vanessa. And not all the stuff about her being a lovely young woman and a brilliant student. I heard all that this morning—but now we both know it isn't the whole truth, don't we?"

Surprisingly he reached for a cigarette and lit it slowly, using the time to calm himself. When he spoke, his voice was as level as my own. "All right, it's not the whole truth. Vanessa *is* lovely and brilliant. She'll make a top-notch lawyer. There's a hardness in her; she gets it from Ernest. It took guts to fake this suicide. . . ."

"What do you think she hopes to gain from it?"

"Freedom. From me. From Ernest's domination. She's probably taken off somewhere for a good time. When she's ready she'll come back and make her demands."

"And what will they be?"

"Enough money to move into a place of her own and finish law school. And she'll get it, too. She's all her parents have."

"You don't think she's set out to make a new life for herself?"

"Hell, no. That would mean giving up all this." The sweep of his arm encompassed the house and all of the DiCesares' privileged world.

But there was one factor that made me doubt his assessment. I said, "What about the other men in her life?"

He tried to look surprised, but an angry muscle twitched in his jaw.

"Come on, Gary," I said, "you know there were other men. Even Ernest and Sylvia were aware of that."

"Ah, Christ!" He popped out of the chair and began pacing again. "All right, there were other men. It started a few months ago. I didn't understand it; things had been good with us; they still *were* good with us physically. But I thought, okay, she's young; this is only natural. So I decided to give her some rope, let her get it out of her system. She didn't throw it in my face, didn't embarrass me in front of my friends. Why shouldn't she have a last fling?"

"And then?"

"She began making noises about breaking off the engagement. And Ernest started that shit about not footing the bill for law school. Like a fool I went along with it, and she seemed to cave in from the pressure. But a few weeks later, it all started up again—only this time it was purposeful, cruel."

"In what way?"

"She'd know I was meeting political associates for lunch or dinner, and she'd show up at the restaurant with a date. Later she'd claim he was just a friend, but you couldn't prove it from the way they acted. We'd go to a party and she'd flirt with every man there. She got sly and secretive about where she'd been, what she'd been doing."

I had pictured Vanessa as a very angry young woman; now I realized she was not a particularly nice one, either.

Gary was saying, ". . . the last straw was on Halloween. We went to a costume party given by one of her friends from Hastings. I didn't want to go—costumes, a young crowd, not my kind of thing—and so she was angry with me to begin with. Anyway, she walked out with another man, some jerk in a soldier outfit. They were dancing. . . ."

I sat up straighter. "Describe the costume."

"An old-fashioned soldier outfit. Wide-brimmed hat with a plume, frock coat, sword."

"What did the man look like?"

"Youngish. He had a full beard and wore granny glasses."

Lee Gottschalk.

The address I got from the phone directory for Lee Gottschalk was on California Street not far from Twenty-fifth Avenue and only a couple of miles from where I'd first met the ranger at Fort Point. When I arrived there and parked at the opposite curb, I didn't need to check the mailboxes to see which apartment was his; the corner windows on the second floor were ablaze with light, and inside I could see Gottschalk, sitting in an armchair in what appeared to be his living room. He seemed to be alone but expecting company, because frequently he looked up from the book he was reading and checked his watch.

In case the company was Vanessa DiCesare, I didn't want to go barging in there. Gottschalk might find a way to warn her off, or simply not answer the door when she arrived. Besides, I didn't yet have a definite connection between the two of them; the "jerk in a soldier outfit" *could* have been someone else, someone in a rented costume that just happened to resemble the working uniform at the fort. But my suspicions were strong enough to keep me watching Gottschalk for well over an hour. The ranger *had* lied to me that afternoon.

The lies had been casual and convincing, except for two mistakes—such small mistakes that I hadn't caught them even when I'd read the newspaper account of Vanessa's purported suicide later. But now I recognized them for what they were: The paper had called Gary Stornetta a "political associate" of Vanessa's father, rather than his former campaign manager, as Lee had termed him. And while the paper mentioned the suicide note, it had not said it was *taped* inside the car. While Gottschalk conceivably could know about Gary managing Ernest's campaign for the Board of Supes from other newspaper accounts, there was no way he could have known how the note was secured—except from Vanessa herself.

Because of those mistakes, I continued watching Gottschalk, straining my eyes as the mist grew heavier, hoping Vanessa would show up or that he'd eventually lead me to her. The ranger appeared to be nervous: He got up a couple of times and turned on a TV, flipped through the channels, and turned it off again. For about ten minutes, he paced back and forth. Finally, around twelve thirty, he checked his watch again, then got up and drew the draperies shut. The lights went out behind them.

I tensed, staring through the blowing mist at the door of the apartment building. Somehow Gottschalk hadn't looked like a man who was going to bed. And my impression was correct: In a few minutes he came through the door onto the sidewalk carrying a suitcase—pale leather like the one of Vanessa's Sylvia had described to me—and got into a dark-colored Mustang parked on his side of the street. The car started up and he made a U-turn, then went right on Twenty-fifth Avenue. I followed. After a few minutes, it became apparent that he was heading for Fort Point.

When Gottschalk turned into the road to the fort, I kept going until I could pull over on the shoulder. The brake lights of the Mustang flared, and then Gottschalk got out and unlocked the low iron bar that blocked the road from sunset to sunrise; after he'd driven through he closed it again, and the car's lights disappeared down the road.

Had Vanessa been hiding at drafty, cold Fort Point? It seemed a strange choice of place, since she could have used a motel or Gottschalk's apartment. But perhaps she'd been afraid someone would recognize her in a public place, or connect her with Gottschalk and come looking, as I had. ANd while the fort would be a miserable place to hide during the hours it was open to the public—she'd have had to keep to one of the off-limits areas, such as the west side—at night she could probably avail herself of the heated employees' lounge.

Now I could reconstruct most of the scenario of what had gone on: Vanessa meets Lee; they talk about his work; she decides he is the person to help her fake her suicide. Maybe there's a romantic entanglement, maybe not; but for whatever reason, he agrees to go along with the plan. She leaves her car at Vista Point, walks across the bridge, and later he drives over there and picks up the suit-case. . . .

But then why hadn't he delivered it to her at the fort? And to go after the suitcase after she'd abandoned the car was too much of a risk; he might have been seen, or the people at the fort might have noticed him leaving for too long a break. Also, if she'd walked across the bridge, surely at least one of the people I'd talked with would have seen her—the maintenance crew near the north tower, for instance.

There was no point in speculating on it now, I decided. The thing to do was to follow Gottschalk down there and confront Vanessa before she disappeared again. For a moment I debated taking my gun out of the glove box, but then decided against it. I don't like to carry it unless I'm going into a dangerous situation, and neither Gottschalk nor Vanessa posed any particular threat to me. I was merely here to deliver a message from Vanessa's parents asking her to come home. If she didn't care to respond to it, that was not my business—or my problem.

I got out of my car and locked it, then hurried across the road and down the narrow lane to the gate, ducking under it and continuing along toward the ranger station. On either side of me were tall, thick groves of eucalyptus; I could smell their acrid fragrance and hear the fog-laden wind rustle their brittle leaves. Their shadows turned the lane into a black winding alley, and the only sound besides distant traffic noises was my tennis shoes slapping on the broken pavement. The ranger station was dark, but ahead I could see Gottschalk's car parked next to the fort. The area was illuminated only by small security lights set at intervals on the walls of the structure. Above it the bridge arched, washed in fog-muted yellowish light; as I drew closer I became aware of the grumble and clank of traffic up there.

I ran across the parking area and checked Gottschalk's car. It was empty, but the suitcase rested on the passenger seat. I turned and started toward the sally port, noticing that its heavily studded door stood open a few inches. The low tunnel was completely dark. I felt my way along it toward the courtyard, one hand on its icy stone wall.

The doors to the courtyard also stood open. I peered through them into the gloom beyond. What light there was came from the bridge and more security beacons high up on the wooden watchtowers; I could barely make out the shapes of the construction equipment that stood near the west side. The clanking from the bridge was oppressive and eerie in the still night.

As I was about to step into the courtyard, there was a movement to my right. I drew back into the sally port as Lee Gottschalk came out of one of the ground-floor doorways. My first impulse was to confront him, but then I decided against it. He might shout, warn Vanessa, and she might escape before I could deliver her parents' message.

After a few seconds I looked out again, meaning to follow Gottschalk, but he was nowhere in sight. A faint shaft of light fell through the door from which he had emerged and rippled over the cobblestone floor. I went that way, through the door and along a narrow corridor to where an archway was illuminated. Then, realizing the archway led to the unrestored cell of the jail I'd seen earlier, I paused. Surely Vanessa wasn't hiding in there. . . .

DECEPTIONS

I crept forward and looked through the arch. The light came from a heavy-duty flashlight that sat on the floor. It threw macabre shadows on the water-stained walls, showing their streaked paint and graffiti. My gaze followed its beams upward and then down, to where the grating of the cistern lay out of place on the floor beside the hole. Then I moved over to the railing, leaned across it, and trained the flashlight down into the well.

I saw, with a rush of shock and horror, the dark hair and once-handsome features of Vanessa DiCesare.

She had been hacked to death. Stabbed and slashed, as if in a frenzy. Her clothing was ripped; there were gashes on her face and hands; she was covered with dark smears of blood. Her eyes were open, staring with that horrible flatness of death.

I came back on my heels, clutching the railing for support. A wave of dizziness swept over me, followed by an icy coldness. I thought: He killed her. And then I pictured Gottschalk in his Union Army uniform, the saber hanging from his belt, and I knew what the weapon had been.

"God!" I said aloud.

Why had he murdered her? I had no way of knowing yet. But the answer to why he'd thrown her into the cistern, instead of just putting her into the bay, was clear: She was supposed to have committed suicide; and while bodies that fall from the Golden Gate Bridge sustain a great many injuries, slash and stab wounds aren't among them. Gottschalk could not count on the body being swept out to sea on the current; if she washed up somewhere along the coast, it would be obvious she had been murdered—and eventually an investigation might have led back to him. To him and his soldier's saber.

It also seemed clear that he'd come to the fort tonight to move the body. But why not last night, why leave her in the cistern all day? Probably he'd needed to plan, to secure keys to the gate and fort, to check the schedule of the night patrols for the best time to remove her. Whatever his reason, I realized now that I'd walked into a very dangerous situation. Walked right in without bringing my gun. I turned quickly to get out of there. . . .

And came face-to-face with Lee Gottschalk.

His eyes were wide, his mouth drawn back in a snarl of surprise. In one hand he held a bundle of heavy canvas. "You!" he said. "What the hell are you doing here?"

I jerked back from him, bumped into the railing, and dropped the flashlight. It clattered on the floor and began rolling toward the mouth of the cistern. Gottschalk lunged toward me, and as I dodged, the light fell into the hole and the cell went dark. I managed to push past him and ran down the hallway to the courtyard.

Stumbling on the cobblestones, I ran blindly for the sally port. Its doors were shut now—he'd probably taken that precaution when he'd returned from getting the tarp to wrap her body in. I grabbed the iron hasp and tugged, but couldn't get it open. Gottschalk's footsteps were coming through the courtyard after me now. I let go of the hasp and ran again.

When I came to the enclosed staircase at the other end of the court, I started up. The steps were wide at the outside wall, narrow at the inside. My toes banged into the risers of the steps; a couple of times I teetered and almost fell backwards. At the first tier I paused, then kept going. Gottschalk had said something about unrestored rooms on the second tier; they'd be a better place to hide than in the museum.

Down below I could hear him climbing after me. The sound of his feet—clattering and stumbling—echoed in the close space. I could hear him grunt and mumble: low, ugly sounds that I knew were curses.

I had absolutely no doubt that if he caught me, he would kill me. Maybe do to me what he had done to Vanessa . . .

I rounded the spiral once again and came out on the top floor gallery, my heart beating wildly, my breath coming in pants. To my left were archways, black outlines filled with dark-gray sky. To my right was blackness. I went that way, hands out, feeling my way.

My hands touched the rough wood of a door. I pushed, and it opened. As I passed through it, my shoulder bag caught on something; I yanked it loose and kept going. Beyond the door I heard Gottschalk curse loudly, the sound filled with surprise and pain; he must have fallen on the stairway. And that gave me a little more time.

The tug at my shoulder bag had reminded me of the small flashlight I keep there. Flattening myself against the wall next to the door, I rummaged through the bag and brought out the flash. Its beam showed high walls and arching ceilings, plaster and lath pulled away to expose dark brick. I saw cubicles and cubbyholes opening into dead ends, but to my right was an arch. I made a small involuntary sound of relief, then thought *Quiet!* Gottschalk's footsteps started up the stairway again as I moved through the archway.

The crumbling plaster walls beyond the archway were set at odd angles—an interlocking funhouse maze connected by small doors. I slipped through one and found an irregularly shaped room heaped with debris. There didn't seem to be an exit, so I ducked back into the first room and moved toward the outside wall, where gray outlines indicated small high-placed windows. I couldn't hear Gottschalk anymore—couldn't hear anything but the roar and clank from the bridge directly overhead.

The front wall was brick and stone, and the windows had wide waist-high sills. I leaned across one, looked through the salt-caked glass, and saw the open sea. I was at the front of the fort, the part that faced beyond the Golden Gate; to my immediate right would be the unrestored portion. If I could slip over into that area, I might be able to hide until the other rangers came to work in the morning.

But Gottschalk could be anywhere. I couldn't hear his footsteps above the infernal noise from the bridge. He could be right here in the room with me, pinpointing me by the beam of my flashlight. . . .

Fighting down panic, I switched the light off and continued along the wall, my hands recoiling from its clammy stone surface. It was icy cold in the vast, echoing space, but my own flesh felt colder still. The air had a salt tang, underlaid by odors of rot and mildew. For a couple of minutes the darkness was unalleviated, but then I saw a lighter rectangular shape ahead of me.

When I reached it I found it was some sort of embrasure, about four feet tall, but only a little over a foot wide. Beyond it I could see the edge of the gallery where it curved and stopped at the chain link fence that barred entrance to the other side of the fort. The fence wasn't very high—only five feet or so. If I could get through this narrow opening, I could climb it and find refuge. . . .

The sudden noise behind me was like a firecracker popping. I whirled, and saw a tall figure silhouetted against one of the seaward windows. He lurched forward, tripping over whatever he'd stepped on. Forcing back a cry, I hoisted myself up and began squeezing through the embrasure.

Its sides were rough brick. They scraped my flesh clear through my clothing. Behind me I heard the slap of Gottschalk's shoes on the wooden floor.

My hips wouldn't fit through the opening. I gasped, grunted, pulling with my arms on the outside wall. Then I turned on my side, sucking in my stomach. My bag caught again, and I let go of the wall long enough to rip its strap off my elbow. As my hips squeezed through the embrasure, I felt Gottschalk grab at my feet. I kicked out frantically, breaking his hold, and fell off the sill to the floor of the gallery.

Fighting for breath, I pushed off the floor, threw myself at the fence, and began climbing. The metal bit into my fingers, rattled and clashed with my weight. At the top, the leg of my jeans got hung up on the spiky wires. I tore it loose and jumped down the other side.

The door to the gallery burst open and Gottschalk came through it. I got up from a crouch and ran into the darkness ahead of me. The fence began to rattle as he started up it. I raced, half-stumbling, along the gallery, the open archways to my right. To my left was probably a warren of rooms similar to those on the east side. I could lose him in there . . .

Only I couldn't. The door I tried was locked. I ran to the next one and hurled my body against its wooden panels. It didn't give. I heard myself sob in fear and frustration.

Gottschalk was over the fence now, coming toward me, limping. His breath came in erratic gasps, loud enough to hear over the noise from the bridge. I twisted around, looking for shelter, and saw a pile of lumber lying across one of the open archways.

I dashed toward it and slipped behind, wedged between it and the pillar of the arch. The courtyard lay two dizzying stories below me. I grasped the end of the top two-by-four. It moved easily, as if on a fulcrum.

Gottschalk had seen me. He came on steadily, his right leg dragging behind him. When he reached the pile of lumber and started over it toward me, I yanked on the two-by-four. The other end moved and struck him on the knee.

He screamed and stumbled back. Then he came forward again, hands outstretched toward me. I pulled back further against the pillar. His clutching hands missed me, and when they did he lost his balance and toppled onto the pile of lumber. And then the boards began to slide toward the open archway.

He grabbed at the boards, yelling and flailing his arms. I tried to reach for him, but the lumber was moving like an avalanche now, pitching over the side and crashing down into the courtyard two stories below. It carried Gottschalk's thrashing body with it, and his screams echoed in its wake. For an awful few seconds the boards continued to crash down on him, and then everything was terribly still. Even the thrumming of the bridge traffic seemed muted.

I straightened slowly and looked down into the courtyard. Gottschalk lay unmoving among the scattered pieces of lumber. For a moment I breathed deeply to control my vertigo; then I ran back to the chain link fence, climbed it, and rushed down the spiral staircase to the courtyard.

When I got to the ranger's body, I could hear him moaning. I said, "Lie still. I'll call an ambulance."

He moaned louder as I ran across the courtyard and found a phone in the gift shop, but by the time I returned, he was silent. His breathing was so shallow that I thought he'd passed out, but then I heard mumbled words coming from his lips. I bent closer to listen.

"Vanessa," he said. "Wouldn't take me with her. . . ."

I said, "Take you where?"

"Going away together. Left my car . . . over there so she could drive across the bridge. But when she . . . brought it here she said she was going alone. . . ."

So you argued, I thought. And you lost your head and slashed her to death.

"Vanessa," he said again. "Never planned to take me . . . tricked me. . . ."

I started to put a hand on his arm, but found I couldn't touch him. "Don't talk anymore. The ambulance'll be here soon."

"Vanessa," he said. "Oh God, what did you do to me?"

I looked up at the bridge, rust red through the darkness and the mist. In the distance, I could hear the wail of a siren.

Deceptions, I thought.

Deceptions. . . .

Marcia Muller *has been given credit for helping to revitalize the role of the female detective in modern mystery fiction. Her novels spotlighting her different heroines, Sharon McCone, Elena Oliverez and Joanna Stark,* include The Shape of Dread, Beyond the Grave, There Hangs the Knife *and, most recently,* Wolf in the Shadows. *With her husband, Bill Pronzini, she has edited numerous successful anthologies, among them* The Web She Weaves *and* Chapter and Hearse. *Another of their collaborations is* 1001 Midnights: The Aficionado's Guide to Mystery and Detective Fiction.

THE BLACK CAT

BY EDGAR ALLAN POE

If there was ever a story that could be said to have introduced more readers to the purest concept of Suspense than Poe's "The Black Cat," we don't know what it is. Yet despite its seeming familiarity, many of you will have never actually read it. Our advice is, even if you think you know it well, think again . . . and read it, slowly. Central to our most common cultural clichés in the realm of fright, it is, in fact, stranger and more awful than any of the peculiar films that bear its name (and often, at the same time, bear little if any resemblance to the original).

The elements that Poe so long ago and so definitively made his own—the pervasive sense of encroaching, inexorable dread; feverish dreams that seep into waking reality; the gothic excesses of self-torturing madness—are all here, along with the inexplicable and ghastly act of cruelty that sets the plot into motion. Cat-lovers, beware, but for everyone else, it's the perfect tale to read aloud each and every Halloween.

THE BLACK CAT

For the most wild, yet most homely narrative which I am about to
pen, I neither expect nor solicit belief. Mad indeed would I be to
expect it, in a case where my very senses reject their own evidence.
Yet, mad am I not—and very surely do I not dream. But to-morrow
I die, and to-day I would unburthen my soul. My immediate purpose is to place before the world, plainly, succinctly, and without
comment, a series of mere household events. In their consequences, these events have terrified—have tortured—have destroyed me. Yet I will attempt to expound them. To me, they have
presented little but Horror—to many they will seem less terrible
than *baroques*. Hereafter, perhaps, some intellect may be found
which will reduce my phantasm to the common-place—some intellect more calm, more logical, and far less excitable than my own,
which will perceive, in the circumstances I detail with awe, nothing
more than an ordinary succession of very natural causes and effects.

From my infancy I was noted for the docility and humanity of
my disposition. My tenderness of heart was even so conspicuous as
to make me the jest of my companions. I was especially fond of
animals, and was indulged by my parents with a great variety of
pets. With these I spent most of my time, and never was so happy
as when feeding and caressing them. This peculiarity of character

grew with my growth, and, in my manhood, I derived from it one of my principal sources of pleasure. To those who have cherished an affection for a faithful and sagacious dog, I need hardly be at the trouble of explaining the nature or the intensity of the gratification thus derivable. There is something in the unselfish and self-sacrificing love of a brute, which goes directly to the heart of him who has had frequent occasion to test the paltry friendship and gossamer fidelity of mere *Man*.

I married early, and was happy to find in my wife a disposition not uncongenial with my own. Observing my partiality for domestic pets, she lost no opportunity of procuring those of the most agreeable kind. We had birds, gold fish, a fine dog, rabbits, a small monkey, and *a cat*.

This latter was a remarkably large and beautiful animal, entirely black, and sagacious to an astonishing degree. In speaking of his intelligence, my wife, who at heart was not a little tinctured with superstition, made frequent allusion to the ancient popular notion, which regarded all black cats as witches in disguise. Not that she was ever *serious* upon this point—and I mention the matter at all for no better reason than that it happens, just now, to be remembered.

Pluto—this was the cat's name—was my favorite pet and playmate. I alone fed him, and he attended me wherever I went about the house. It was even with difficulty that I could prevent him from following me through the streets.

Our friendship lasted, in this manner, for several years, during which my general temperament and character—through the instrumentality of the Fiend Intemperance—had (I blush to confess it) experienced a radical alteration for the worse. I grew, day by day, more moody, more irritable, more regardless of the feelings of others. I suffered myself to use intemperate language to my wife. At length, I even offered her physical violence. My pets, of course, were made to feel the change in my disposition. I not only neglected, but ill-used them. For Pluto, however, I still retained sufficient regard to restrain me from maltreating him, as I made no scruple of maltreating the rabbits, the monkey, or even the dog, when by accident, or through affection, they came in my way. But my disease grew upon me—for what disease is like Alcohol!—and at length even Pluto, who was now becoming old, and consequently somewhat peevish—even Pluto began to experience the effects of my ill temper.

One night, returning home, much intoxicated, from one of my haunts about town, I fancied that the cat avoided my presence. I seized him; when, in his fright at my violence, he inflicted a slight wound upon my hand with his teeth. The fury of a demon instantly possessed me. I knew myself no longer. My original soul seemed, at once, to take its flight from my body; and a more than fiendish malevolence, gin-nurtured, thrilled every fibre of my frame. I took from my waistcoat-pocket a pen-knife, opened it, grasped the poor beast by the throat, and deliberately cut one of its eyes from the socket! I blush, I burn, I shudder, while I pen the damnable atrocity.

When reason returned with the morning—when I had slept off the fumes of the night's debauch—I experienced a sentiment half of horror, half of remorse, for the crime of which I had been guilty; but it was, at best, a feeble and equivocal feeling, and the soul remained untouched. I again plunged into excess, and soon drowned in wine all memory of the deed.

In the meantime the cat slowly recovered. The socket of the lost eye presented, it is true, a frightful appearance, but he no longer appeared to suffer any pain. He went about the house as usual, but, as might be expected, fled in extreme terror at my approach. I had so much of my old heart left, as to be at first grieved by this evident dislike on the part of a creature which had once so loved me. But this feeling soon gave place to irritation. And then came, as if to my final and irrevocable overthrow, the spirit of PER-VERSENESS. Of this spirit philosophy takes no account. Yet I am not more sure that my soul lives, than I am that perverseness is one of the primitive impulses of the human heart—one of the indivisible primary faculties, or sentiments, which give direction to the character of Man. Who has not, a hundred times, found himself committing a vile or a silly action, for no other reason than because he knows he should *not*? Have we not a perpetual inclination, in the teeth of our best judgment, to violate that which is *Law*, merely because we understand it to be such? This spirit of perverseness, I say, came to my final overthrow. It was this unfathomable longing of the soul *to vex itself*—to offer violence to its own nature—to do wrong for the wrong's sake only—that urged me to continue and finally to consummate the injury I had inflicted upon the unoffending brute. One morning, in cool blood, I slipped a noose about its neck and hung it to the limb of a tree;—hung it with the tears streaming from my eyes, and with the bitterest remorse at my heart;—hung it *because* I knew that it had loved me, and *because* I felt it had given me no reason of offence;—hung it *because* I knew that in so doing I was committing a sin—a deadly sin that would so jeopardize my immortal soul as to place it—if such a thing were possible—even beyond the reach of the infinite mercy of the Most Merciful and Most Terrible God.

On the night of the day on which this cruel deed was done, I was aroused from sleep by the cry of fire. The curtains of my bed were in flames. The whole house was blazing. It was with great difficulty that my wife, a servant, and myself, made our escape from the conflagration. The destruction was complete. My entire worldly wealth was swallowed up, and I resigned myself thenceforward to despair.

I am above the weakness of seeking to establish a sequence of cause and effect, between the disaster and the atrocity. But I am detailing a chain of facts—and wish not to leave even a possible link imperfect. On the day succeeding the fire, I visited the ruins. The walls, with one exception, had fallen in. This exception was found in a compartment wall, not very thick, which stood about the middle of the house, and against which had rested the head of my bed. The plastering had here, in great measure, resisted the action of the fire—a fact which I attributed to its having been recently spread. About this wall a dense crowd were collected, and many persons seemed to be examining a particular portion of it with very minute and eager attention. The words "strange!" "singular!" and other similar expressions, excited my curiosity. I approached and saw, as if graven in *bas relief* upon the white surface, the figure of a gigantic *cat*. The impression was given with an accuracy truly marvellous. There was a rope about the animal's neck.

When I first beheld this apparition—for I could scarcely regard it as less—my wonder and my terror were extreme. But at length reflection came to my aid. The cat, I remembered, had been hung in a garden adjacent to the house. Upon the alarm of fire, this garden had been immediately filled by the crowd—by some one of whom the animal must have been cut from the tree and thrown, through an open window, into my chamber. This had probably been done with the view of arousing me from sleep. The falling of other walls had compressed the victim of my cruelty into the substance of the freshly-spread plaster; the lime of which, with the flames, and the *ammonia* from the carcass, had then accomplished the portraiture as I saw it.

Although I thus readily accounted to my reason, if not altogether to my conscience, for the startling fact just detailed, it did not the less fail to make a deep impression upon my fancy. For months I could not rid myself of the phantasm of the cat; and, during this period, there came back into my spirit a half-sentiment that seemed, but was not, remorse. I went so far as to regret the loss of the animal, and to look about me, among the vile haunts which I now habitually frequented, for another pet of the same species, and of somewhat similar appearance, with which to supply its place.

One night as I sat, half stupefied, in a den of more than infamy, my attention was suddenly drawn to some black object, reposing upon the head of one of the immense hogsheads of Gin, or of Rum, which constituted the chief furniture of the apartment. I had been looking steadily at the top of this hogshead for some minutes, and what now caused me surprise was the fact that I had not sooner perceived the object thereupon. I approached it, and touched it with my hand. It was a black cat—a very large one—fully as large as Pluto, and closely resembling him in every respect but one. Pluto had not a white hair upon any portion of his body; but this cat had a large, although indefinite splotch of white, covering nearly the whole region of the breast.

Upon my touching him, he immediately arose, purred loudly, rubbed against my hand, and appeared delighted with my notice. This, then, was the very creature of which I was in search. I at once offered to purchase it of the landlord; but this person made no claim to it—knew nothing of it—had never seen it before.

I continued my caresses, and, when I prepared to go home, the animal evinced a disposition to accompany me. I permitted it to do so; occasionally stooping and patting it as I proceeded. When it reached the house it domesticated itself at once, and became immediately a great favorite with my wife.

For my own part, I soon found a dislike to it arising within me. This was just the reverse of what I had anticipated; but I know not how or why it was—its evident fondness for myself rather disgusted and annoyed. By slow degrees, these feelings of disgust and annoyance rose into the bitterness of hatred. I avoided the creature; a certain sense of shame, and the remembrance of my former deed of cruelty, prevented me from physically abusing it. I did not, for some weeks, strike, or otherwise violently ill use it; but gradually—very gradually—I came to look upon it with unutterable loathing, and to flee silently from its odious presence, as from the breath of a pestilence.

What added, no doubt, to my hatred of the beast, was the discovery, on the morning after I brought it home, that, like Pluto, it also had been deprived of one of its eyes. This circumstance, however, only endeared it to my wife, who, as I have already said, possessed, in a high degree, that humanity of feeling which had once been my distinguishing trait, and the source of many of my simplest and purest pleasures.

With my aversion to this cat, however, its partiality for myself seemed to increase. It followed my footsteps with a pertinacity which it would be difficult to make the reader comprehend. Whenever I sat, it would crouch beneath my chair, or spring upon my knees, covering me with its loathsome caresses. If I arose to walk it would get between my feet and thus nearly throw me down, or, fastening its long and sharp claws in my dress, clamber, in this manner, to my breast. At such times, although I longed to destroy it with a blow, I was yet withheld from so doing, partly by a memory of my former crime, but chiefly—let me confess it at once—by absolute *dread* of the beast.

This dread was not exactly a dread of physical evil—and yet I should be at a loss how otherwise to define it. I am almost ashamed to own—yes, even in this felon's cell, I am almost ashamed to own—that the terror and horror with which the animal inspired me, had been heightened by one of the merest chimæras it would be possible to conceive. My wife had called my attention, more than once, to the character of the mark of white hair, of which I have spoken, and which constituted the sole visible difference between th strange beast and the one I had destroyed. The reader will remember that this mark, although large, had been originally very indefinite; but, by slow degrees—degrees nearly imperceptible, and which for a long time my Reason struggled to reject as fanciful—it had, at length, assumed a rigorous distinctness of outline. It was now the representation of an object that I shudder to name— and for this, above all, I loathed, and dreaded, and would have rid myself of the monster *had I dared*—it was now, I say, the image of a hideous—of a ghastly thing—of the GALLOWS!—oh, mournful and terrible engine of Horror and of Crime—of Agony and of Death!

And now was I indeed wretched beyond the wretchedness of mere Humanity. And *a brute beast*—whose fellow I had contemptuously destroyed—*a brute beast* to work out for *me*—for me a man, fashioned in the image of the High God—so much of insufferable woe! Alas! neither by day nor by night knew I the blessing of Rest any more! During the former the creature left me no moment alone; and, in the latter, I started, hourly, from dreams of unutterable fear, to find the hot breath of *the thing* upon my face, and its vast weight—an incarnate Night-Mare that I had no power to shake off—incumbent eternally upon my *heart*!

Beneath the pressure of torments such as these, the feeble remnant of the good within me succumbed. Evil thoughts became my sole intimates—the darkest and most evil of thoughts. The moodiness of my usual temper increased to hatred of all things and of all mankind; while, from the sudden, frequent, and ungovernable outbursts of a fury to which I now blindly abandoned myself, my uncomplaining wife, alas! was the most usual and the most patient of sufferers.

One day she accompanied me, upon some household errand, into the cellar of the old building which our poverty compelled us to inhabit. The cat followed me down the steep stairs, and, nearly throwing me headlong, exasperated me to madness. Uplifting an axe, and forgetting, in my wrath, the childish dread which had hitherto stayed my hand, I aimed a blow at the animal which, of course, would have proved instantly fatal had it descended as I wished. But this blow was arrested by the hand of my wife. Goaded, by the interference, into a rage more than demoniacal, I withdrew my arm from her grasp and buried the axe in her brain. She fell dead upon the spot, without a groan.

This hideous murder accomplished, I set myself forthwith, and with entire deliberation, to the task of concealing the body. I knew that I could not remove it from the house, either by day or by night, without the risk of being observed by the neighbors. Many projects entered my mind. At one period I thought of cutting the corpse into minute fragments, and destroying them by fire. At another, I resolved to dig a grave for it in the floor of the cellar. Again, I deliberated about casting it in the well in the yard—about packing it in a box, as if merchandize, with the usual arrangements, and so getting a porter to take it from the house. Finally I hit upon what I considered a far better expedient than either of these. I determined to wall it up in the cellar—as the monks of the middle ages are recorded to have walled up their victims.

For a purpose such as this the cellar was well adapted. Its walls were loosely constructed, and had lately been plastered throughout with a rough plaster, which the dampness of the atmosphere had prevented from hardening. Moreover, in one of the walls was a projection, caused by a false chimney, or fireplace, that had been filled up, and made to resemble the rest of the cellar. I made no doubt that I could readily displace the bricks at this point, insert the corpse, and wall the whole up as before, so that no eye could detect anything suspicious.

And in this calculation I was not deceived. By means of a crowbar I easily dislodged the bricks, and, having carefully deposited the body against the inner wall, I propped it in that position, while, with little trouble, I relaid the whole structure as it originally stood. Having procured mortar, sand, and hair, with every possible precaution, I prepared a plaster which could not be distinguished from the old, and with this I very carefully went over the new brickwork. When I had finished, I felt satisfied that all was right. The wall did not present the slightest appearance of having been disturbed. The rubbish on the floor was picked up with the minutest care. I looked around triumphantly, and said to myself—"Here at least, then, my labor has not been in vain."

My next step was to look for the beast which had been the cause of so much wretchedness; for I had, at length, firmly resolved to put it to death. Had I been able to meet with it, at the moment, there could have been no doubt of its fate; but it appeared that the crafty animal had been alarmed at the violence of my previous anger, and forebore to present itself in my present mood. It is impossible to describe, or to imagine, the deep, the blissful sense of relief which the absence of the detested creature occasioned in my bosom. It did not make its appearance during the night—and thus for one night at least, since its introduction into the house, I soundly and tranquilly slept; aye, *slept* even with the burden of murder upon my soul!

The second and the third day passed, and still my tormentor came not. Once again I breathed as a freeman. The monster, in terror, had fled the premises forever! I should behold it no more! My happiness was supreme! The guilt of my dark deed disturbed me but little. Some few inquiries had been made, but these had been readily answered. Even a search had been instituted—but of course nothing was to be discovered. I looked upon my future felicity as secured.

Upon the fourth day of the assassination, a party of the police came, very unexpectedly, into the house, and proceeded again to make rigorous investigation of the premises. Secure, however, in the inscrutability of my place of concealment, I felt no embarrassment whatever. The officers bade me accompany them in their search. They left no nook or corner unexplored. At length, for the third or fourth time, they descended into the cellar. I quivered not in a muscle. My heart beat calmly as that of one who slumbers in innocence. I walked the cellar from end to end. I folded my arms upon my bosom, and roamed easily to and fro. The police were thoroughly satisfied and prepared to depart. The glee at my heart was too strong to be restrained. I burned to say if but one word, by way of triumph, and to render doubly sure their assurance of my guiltlessness.

"Gentlemen," I said at last, as the party ascended the steps, "I delight to have allayed your suspicions. I wish you all health, and a little more courtesy. By the bye, gentlemen, this—this is a very well constructed house." [In the rabid desire to say something easily, I scarcely knew what I uttered at all.]—"I may say an

145

excellently well constructed house. These walls—are you going, gentlemen?—these walls are solidly put together;" and here, through the mere frenzy of bravado, I rapped heavily, with a cane which I held in my hand, upon that very portion of the brick-work behind which stood the corpse of the wife of my bosom.

But may God shield and deliver me from the fangs of the Arch-Fiend! No sooner had the reverberation of my blows sunk into silence, than I was answered by a voice from within the tomb!—by a cry, at first muffled and broken, like the sobbing of a child, and then quickly swelling into one long, loud, and continuous scream, utterly anomalous and inhuman—a howl—a wailing shriek, half of horror and half of triumph, such as might have arisen only out of hell, conjointly from the throats of the damned in their agony and of the demons that exult in the damnation.

Of my own thoughts it is folly to speak. Swooning, I staggered to the opposite wall. For one instant the party upon the stairs remained motionless, through extremity of terror and of awe. In the next, a dozen stout arms were toiling at the wall. It fell bodily. The corpse, already greatly decayed and clotted with gore, stood erect before the eyes of the spectators. Upon its head, with red extended mouth and solitary eye of fire, sat the hideous beast whose craft had seduced me into murder, and whose informing voice had consigned me to the hangman. I had walled the monster up within the tomb!

Edgar Allan Poe is acknowledged as the "father" of the modern detective story, and such illustrations of the deductive process as "The Purloined Letter," "The Gold Bug" and "The Murders in the Rue Morgue" remain influential to this day. However, his writing fed the stream of literature devoted to horror, the grotesque and the fantastic as much as it did the one in the process of evolving into the mystery puzzle, and he will be equally remembered for such hallucinatory works as "The Fall of the House of Usher," "The Pit and the Pendulum" and "The Tell-Tale Heart."

OMJAGOD

BY JAMES GRADY

In a tale reminiscent of both Stephen King and
Margaret O'Brien (she of the never-to-be-forgotten
Halloween walk in the film *Meet Me in St. Louis*),
James Grady puts himself into the mind of a re-
sourceful young boy with a Halloween agenda that
involves confronting several different sorts of
demons. The result is a story at once complex and
stirring, taking place amidst a sort of food chain of
villains, each battening off the lesser ones on down
the line until the level is reached where one brave
kid with a couple of devoted pals can make a difference—even in the world of indifferent grown-ups.

OMJAGOD

. . . made you look, dirty crook, stole your mother's—

"Paul!" said Mom, snapping him back to their yellow kitchen. Her purse lay on the counter. "Where's your costume?"

Don't look at me! he prayed. Don't see me!

"Mom, I'm too old to dress up." Don't stammer. Don't cry.

"Then maybe you're too old for Halloween."

"I just gotta go, Mom! I just gotta!"

She smiled: "Well, if you *just gotta* . . . I've got an idea."

Don't look in your purse!

Paul hurried behind her as she went into the living room.

The closet door was open, she was inside it, stepping out . . .

Putting an old fashioned man's hat on his head, snap brimmed and a color dark beyond any name.

"Mom!"

"It's a great costume!"

"What am I supposed to be?"

"A gangster. That was your grandfather's hat. Makes it semi-authentic." She smiled. "Hey, I got a great idea!"

From the back of the closet where Paul had hidden it, she pulled out the olive-green trench coat his aunt bought from a children's catalog to help Paul remember what he'd never forget.

"I wondered what happened to this," said his mom as she pulled the coat on Paul. "There! The complete look."

Big old hat, trench coat flapping below his knees.

"Don't lose Dad's hat. It's all he left us."

"Maybe I should—"

"No," she said, "I like it on you. Now run upstairs and show your grandmother. I want to read the newspaper before monsters start ringing our doorbell."

Paul flew up the stairs. This was the house where his dad grew up, the home he'd held onto after his parents died. Walk down the hall to the bedroom that Halloweens before had been Aunt Patti's.

Knock: "Gramma? It's me. How you doing?" he asked the old lady in the bed. Outside her window, the sky turned to blood.

Paul switched on lamps. Framed photos stood on the bureau: Paul's mother and uncles when they were children; the man whose hat Paul wore—eyes blazing, mustache waxed. The photo in the center was the old woman's son-in-law in his captain's uniform.

"Mom made me wear the hat for a costume," Paul told his mother's mother. Her good hand lay across the sheets. Gray hair clung to her pillows like a spiderweb.

The old woman's good eye flicked to the olive-drab coat.

"Yeah," said Paul, "that, too."

Paul looked at his father's picture. "I know: he was the only Gaje you ever trusted."

Gramma's eye caressed her husband's hat.

"Mom says I look like a gangster."

The old lady's eye burned.

"You know, don't you. I know! I'm sorry, but . . . Believe me, Gramma, I got no choice. Please promise you won't tell Mom!"

Paul's heart slugged his ribs. A tear rolled down her cheek.

"Don't cry, Gramma, it's OK. Honest! I promise you—and I'll be OK, too. Trust me."

Her good hand crawled across the sheet to his coat. She liked to touch his cheek, so he bent his face to meet her fingers.

Her thumb pressed his forehead. Like thunder. Like lightning.

Exhausted, the hand fell. Paul lowered it gently to the sheet.

The old woman's eye blazed.

"Thank you, Gramma," he whispered. Kissed her forehead in front of blood vessels that had burst.

A dozen virgin candles on the TV table reflected in her eye.

"Gramma, if I do that, Mom might know, might figure—"

The eye narrowed.

With a sigh, Paul touched candle after candle. When his fingers were on the thickest, tallest white candle, Gramma's eye closed. Paul set the candle in the metal pan on the bureau, struck a kitchen match. The room filled with sulphur and smoke.

Downstairs, the doorbell rang. Children squealed.

Gramma's eye turned to the window. Night clouded the glass. She looked back to Paul. To the flickering candle.

"Gotta be back before it's burned out." Paul swallowed. "I'll try, Gramma, I'll do my best. I'll make it."

She blinked.

"Yeah, who am I trying to con?"

In the hall, Paul heard a tear hit her pillow.

The hat wobbled on his head and his feet were bowling balls as he clumped downstairs.

"Going to be a busy night," said his mother. She sat at the scarred dining room table, night school books on her left. On her right, work spilled out of her husband's khaki briefcase. A bowl of dwarf Hershey bars sat on the table. She brushed graying hair out of her eyes, stared at the weekly newspaper.

"Do you know a boy named Branch Pace?"

Slow, easy: "Why?"

"There's another story about him here in the paper. He won the cross-country medal. Next spring, they figure he'll be the first freshman ever to win the mile at the state meet."

"He's fast," said Paul.

"You know him? You're in sixth grade; he's a freshman."

"He went to my school. He's a big deal."

She smiled at the newspaper truth. "He must be the guy I see in sweats, running in the streets real early in the morning. Got a feeling you should keep an eye on him."

"No kidding."

"Good example, role model."

"Yeah, right."

Her eyes left the paper. "Come here, honey."

She straightened his coat lapels, tied the belt in a knot. Flipped the collar up.

"I don't give a damn if you ever get a medal," she told him.

Don't say it! Don't make me—

"You remember what your—"

"I know, Mom!" *Don't say it!*

"Do good, be happy, walk true." She smiled.

Paul's heart stopped and his face melted.

"He used to say, 'Walk like a man,' " she said, "but I reminded him not everybody understood that 'man' doesn't always mean 'male,' and what if that baby in my tummy was a—"

"Mom?"

"Yes, my *only only* son?"

"Wish Dad were here."

"Me, too." She brushed his cheek. Went to hug him, felt him stiffen, stopped. "You're a real good guy, Paul Rivers."

"No I'm not. I'm just a kid."

"I wish you were, honey! I wish you could be again!"

"I gotta go. The guys are waiting."

"Your little gang?"

She smiled when he looked away.

"Go on, lamscray. But be careful—and walk true."

The door, all he had to do was go out that door.

Can't tell her. Can't hit her with any more weight.

"Is something wrong?" she said.

"I love you, Mom." Then he hugged her, saw her surprised look that said maybe he hadn't grown up yet. Paul ran to the door.

"Honey!"

Stopped him cold, hand on the doorknob: "What?"

"Check to make sure I locked my car. The whole town's getting them stolen, and we're behind in our insurance again."

The front door closed behind him.

Mom didn't notice that he wasn't taking a treat bag.

The black sky held a full moon.

Look through the windows of her old car—locks down. If the insurance was paid, best thing would be for it to be stolen.

But then the cops would come 'round the house, then. . . .

The money burned in his jeans' pocket. Leaves skittered across the sidewalk. Mrs. Schenck had a plastic skeleton hanging from her clothesline; bones flapped in the night.

Two ballerinas, a karate kid and a troll hurried up Paul's front walk. A dad holding a flashlight watched from the sidewalk. The troll asked Paul: "What are you supposed to be?"

He pressed Grampa's hat on his head, ran.

Past houses with glowing porch lights, fierce jack-o'-lanterns and bowls of candy to the Johnson house.

Colored lights circled the Johnsons' windows, the porch; hung in the naked ash tree: twinkling red, blue and green bulbs.

Asa and Laurel met him outside their picket fence.

"Don't say anything!" Asa gestured to the rubber sword stuck in the red sash tied around his bony ribs, the colored vest with pieces of cloth safety pinned over Mr. Johnson's bowling team patches, the engineer's neckerchief tied as a headband. "I'm a pirate, OK? My mom made me wear all this, OK? She even took a thousand pictures! I have to wear three like total long underwears to keep from freezing and she's taking pictures!"

"A pirate?"

"Yeah, like right on, huh?"

"Did you get it?" his sister asked Paul. Laurel was a hair taller than Paul, a brown hair to his black. This year he could beat her arm wrestling, though she still outcharged him on the soccer field. A quirk of maternal fertility and school eligibility dates had stranded her and her brother in the same grade. She wore blue jeans, black sneakers, a jean jacket. Already her mother had given up daring to suggest what Laurel should wear.

"How much?" she said.

"Twenty-three dollars," said Paul.

"That's not enough!" said Asa. "He said we gotta have twenty-five!"

"It'll be enough," said Paul. "If it works."

"Will your mother find out you took it?" asked Laurel.

"She doesn't open her purse until she leaves for work." Paul said: "Why are there colored lights all over your house?"

Brother glanced at sister, said: "Our mom's Jewish."

"So?" said Paul.

"So . . ." Asa shrugged. "So my Dad's like anything but Jewish—a goy. We don't know what the hell we are, but—"

"We're what we want to be," snapped Laurel.

"—but we don't get to have Christmas lights because Jews don't believe in Christmas, so . . . Halloween lights."

"Our family's big on compromises and solutions," said Laurel. "Come on; if we're late . . ."

They walked as fast as they could. Around them in the night, doorbells rang, children yelled, parents oohed and ahed.

"What's your family?" asked Laurel.

"My mother's a Gypsy," said Paul. "My dad was a Marine."

" 'Marine' isn't a religion," said Laurel, "or a race."

"Says who?" answered Paul. "You guys got everything?"

"Duct tape, one Rock Star tape recorder, a cassette of that geeky baby-song singer, camera, six boxes of dental floss—"

"Dental floss?" yelled Paul. "I said fishing line!"

"Our dad, like, doesn't even *eat* fish!"

"What about getting some from your dad?" asked Laurel.

"He's dead."

"A Jeep fell on him," said Asa.

"Why didn't you ever tell me?" said Laurel. "I thought your folks were divorced like everybody else's."

"Talk later!" said Asa. "Run!"

And they did.

Elm trees scraped the night. White skeletons stenciled on black plastic trash bags flapped from telephone wires.

They ran through the schoolyard. Ran to Sligo Park, acres of trees and cobblestone paths donated by a smokestack czar whose family had cannibalized his legacy, leaving the town bricked-up factories by the railroad tracks where ghosts listened for the whistles of trains that came no more.

"Stop," gasped Asa. "Slow down."

Paul was panting, Laurel not even winded, but they were all together, so they slowed to walk with Asa.

"Hear that?" said Asa.

"What?" said both Laurel and Paul.

"Was just a truck out on the interstate," said Laurel.

"You didn't even hear it!" snapped her brother.

"Did so!"

"Did not," said Paul, "and neither did I."

"Well I did," said Asa.

"Then maybe it was an owl," said Paul.

"All the owls are dead," said the thin boy. "Like we're going to be."

"Nobody's dying," said Paul. But in that instant, he saw a candle flame, heard a heartwhisper: *Liar, liar, pants on fire.*

"That's easy for you to say," grumbled Asa. "This way."

He led them out of the watchlights' mist, off the cobblestone path. Sticks crunched underfoot, the earth rose and fell as they wove through trees they saw as dark lines in the night.

"Forgot to bring a flashlight," said Laurel. "My fault."

"We know the way," said Paul. "If we don't know that much, all the flashlights in the world won't save us."

He pushed Grampa's hat lower on his head: "Dental floss!"

"We're a very oral health–conscious family," said Asa.

"Quiet!" whispered Laurel. "OMJAGOD."

OMJAGOD—Our Magic Jungle And Garden Of Death, the name they'd sought for two days way back in third grade. Uttering that word to a stranger made your tongue turn into a firesnake. OMJAGOD stood on the crest of a knoll, a ring of trees no wind could penetrate. Inside the ring was a circle of wild grass soft enough for a fairy's bed and big enough to stable three winged horses.

There was one way into OMJAGOD: between two sheer boulders. There was one way out: a six-foot gap between two scarred oaks.

Inside OMJAGOD, they caught their breath.

"Take off your coat," said Laurel. "Smart of you to wear it."

"My mom's idea," said Paul, handing the garment to Asa. Paul unbuttoned his shirt. "She doesn't know."

As Laurel tore strips of duct tape, Asa said: "Run the cord under his arm and put the mike up close to his collar."

"Probably only hear my heart beating," said Paul.

"No," insisted Asa as they taped the book-sized machine onto their friend's shivering back. "It works. We tried it."

155

"My shirt is tight," said Paul, dressing.

"With the coat, you can't tell," said Laurel.

"He'll think, like, maybe you've turned into a hunchback."

"Oh sure!"

"It's OK," said Laurel. "It'll work."

"Got to," whispered her brother.

"I'll push the button before we split up," she said. "The tape is forty-five minutes long. Plenty of time."

Moonlight made their faces pale.

"It's the only way," said Paul.

"Who'd ever believe us?" said Laurel.

"Like, nothin' they could do anyway." Asa swallowed. "I should be the one to—"

"You should do what you can do," said Paul. "You have to. I had to be the one to make the pact, I have to be the one to go."

"He figures this way he's got you, too," Laurel told Paul. "He thinks this means you'll be afraid, too."

"I'm not afraid of him!" said Asa.

"Yes you are," said Paul. "So am I."

Asa said, "But then, like, I should be the guy who—"

"Laurel is faster than us," said Paul. "Has to be her."

"I don't like that," said Asa.

Me either, thought Paul. Me either.

"She's not faster than him," said Asa. "Nobody is."

"Says who, dork breath!" said his sister.

"Says me, dingleberry!"

"Hey!" said Paul.

"Better run," said Asa. "You better run and run and run!"

Laurel pushed her fist against her pencil-thin brother's ribs: "You just do what you have to do, you . . . You just . . . You."

"Yeah," whispered Asa. "Yeah. Don't you let her get caught," he warned Paul.

"Never happen," said Paul. *Not as long as I'm alive.*

That sound: maybe it was an owl. Or the wind outside OMJA-GOD.

Asa held his fist in front of him.

Paul's clenched hand kissed his best friend's.

Laurel's fist pressed against theirs made a triangle, the strongest shape in the universe. Mrs. Firestone said so in science.

Together, they whispered the magic oath Paul had revealed.

Shoulder to shoulder, Laurel and Paul hurried between the oaks. They were strong, didn't look back as the shadows ate them.

"Don't lose your hat," yelled Asa. "Your mom will kill you!"

Through the woods to the dimly lit cobblestone path.

"Wish it didn't have to be your mom's money." Laurel sighed. "Our family believes in plastic."

They cut through the schoolyard. Empty swings swayed.

"If it works," said Paul, "won't matter."

"If it doesn't work," said Laurel, "won't matter either."

They hurried through alleys, hid in a doorway when a car roared past. Somewhere in the night, a trick-or-treater laughed.

"Sorry about your dad," said Laurel. "Was it in a war?"

"Life," said Paul, "just life. An accident."

"Oh," she said. That was enough. That was everything.

"Thanks for saving my brother," she whispered.

"Naw," mumbled Paul, watching his shoes, pressing the hat tighter on his head. "Naw."

Took five more steps before he could say: "That's what we do."

"All the 'we' is just you," she said.

Paul felt like a lion. Felt like a mouse.

Turned the corner onto Main, saw *him* across the street, ducked back in the alley and felt like a fool.

He pulled Laurel behind a dumpster: "He's already there!"

"He's twenty minutes early!"

"Maybe he hasn't ripped off a watch yet," said Paul.

"I've gotta be between the drugstore and the office building!" said Laurel. "Where we put the refrigerator box this morning!"

"If you cross the street, he'll see you!"

"Not if I run back to Zolinsky's. The road curves and—"

"If he hears you sneaking up the passageway from the alley—"

"Too late now," she said. "Too late to be there ready."

"We can—"

"No we can't." Laurel's smile was soft over her braces.

They stared at each other for eternity.

Laurel stepped so close their noses almost touched. Her hand slid inside Paul's coat, along his ribs, under his shirt. . . .

"There," she said, "you're turned on. Count to a hundred."

"Two hundred," said Paul. "Don't make a sound!"

Then she was gone.

. . . one ninety-eight, one ninety-nine . . .

Walk out of the alley. To the curb. Face him.

Across the street a figure pranced between the nights of a boy and the days of a man. His eyes were focused in the glaze of the drugstore window. His hair was perfect; his skin was clear and clean. The yellow windbreaker he wore looked tailored for his whipcord body. Wrinkle-free slacks hugged his steel legs. Starlight glistened off his black shoes.

You see my reflection in the window, thought Paul.

From the middle of the road, Paul called, "Branch Pace."

Still that figure wouldn't turn from the glass. If his gaze widened beyond the window's mirror, he would see the refrigerator box that surely didn't belong in a passageway on Main Street.

Paul stepped on to the sidewalk, said again: "Branch Pace."

"Well, well, well," purred the handsome freshman as he faced the sixth-grader in the old hat and floppy coat. Branch's eyes were slick. "Why are you wearing junk like that, Mamma's boy?"

"It's Halloween," said Paul.

"Where's your skinny friend?"

"You told me to come alone," said Paul. *Am I close enough? Is the mike working?*

"What do I care who you bring? You're all punks. You. That skinny wimp Jew boy. His sister. 'Course," said Branch, smiling, "she's almost getting so she ain't skinny anymore."

Then he laughed. "What's the matter? You lookin' at that, too? Is the little man growing up?"

Don't blow it: "You said we had a deal."

Branch pinched Paul's collarbone: "I say what I want to say!"

Paul twisted free—*Stay close!*

"Why are you always hurting little kids like us?"

Branch drilled his forefinger into Paul's breastbone—just missed the mike. "Because I can, punk. Because I can."

Cardboard scraped in the passageway. . . .

"What's that?" Branch started to turn toward . . .

"It's a werewolf, you big dummy!" shouted Paul. "It's a vampire! It's a—Oww!"

Branch flicked Paul's nose: "What did you call me?"

"Nothing," said Paul. "I didn't say anything."

"Better not talk back to me. Better not say anything to anybody, or I'll get you and that skinny Jew boy—and his sister, yeah, I'll get her. You better believe that."

"I do," said Paul. "I do."

"Werewolf, huh? You're such a punk, you probably believe in that shit. Good thing your father's dead. You'd embarrass him. Aww," said Branch, "is the little boy going to cry?"

"You can't make me cry."

"Wanna bet?" Branch laughed. A police car rolled by. The sports star waved at the cop, who knew everybody in this ordinary American hometown, and got a hey-cool-dude nod in answer.

"So get to it, punk. You ain't the big business I got tonight. Where's my money?"

Paul handed him the folded bills—Come on, Laurel!

"It better be all there." Branch waved the bills in front of Paul's eyes. "Tell the truth."

"Twenty-three dollars. We'll have to get the rest to—"

"Tomorrow, or your ass is mowed grass." Branch smiled. "Sell your Halloween candy."

"We paid you, so you'll leave us alone, right?"

"Smart deal that you came up with. You pay me, you're cool. For now. Later, we'll see what's what. And if—"

Laurel yelled: "Hey, asshole!"

Turn with Branch and look toward the passage—

White light explodes!

Flash blind, Paul tackled the older boy around the waist.

"Hey!" yelled Branch.

The two boys fell to the sidewalk. Laurel ran down the passageway, to the alley, toward the park.

Hold on just hold on just thirty seconds, maybe less, he'll chase her, give her head start, he'll forget about me, got—

Yell: "Camera! She took a picture! We got a picture!"

Red lights blur—Branch slugged Paul's head.

159

Can't hold on, can't—

"You're gonna die, punk! Let me go!"

Branch twisted to his feet, dragging Paul with him. He grabbed Paul's back to throw the smaller boy away—

Grabbed a box under the floppy coat.

"What's . . ." Branch pulled the coat over Paul's head, pulled his shirt up. "A tape recorder! You were—"

Paul screamed as Branch grabbed the box duct-taped to Paul's ribs. The older boy pulled and twisted. Skin ripped off bones and *can't breathe, like boa constrictor squeezing ribs—*

Crashed down on his hands and knees, Paul gasped for breath as Branch ripped the tape recorder free. Crimson pain seared Paul's eyes. He felt an ankle. Pulled.

Branch tumbled. The tape recorder flew out of his hands.

Yellow headlights swung over them, winked out like a candle.

Branch pinned Paul to the ground, his knees digging into the smaller boy's arms, his hips pressing down on Paul's chest.

Car door opened, slammed.

"You're gonna—"

Hands plucked Branch off Paul, pushed the track star against the drugstore wall.

"Whacha think you doin' messin' wit' a kid?" yelled a voice Paul had never heard before.

From flat on his back on the sidewalk, he saw Branch trembling in front of a man who wore a mirror-black leather jacket. A van with its lights out was nosed to the curb.

"Hey, Harry—Mr. Scarfo!" said Branch. "I just . . . It's not my fault, it's—you're early, you're real early!"

"You ain't early, you ain't around no more!" said Harry Scarfo. "Now what's wit' da kid? You's supposed to be alone!"

"I figured he wouldn't get here until—"

"You're too much of a punk to do figurin'!"

"He was wearing a tape recorder!"

Paul sat up. . . .

"Don't move, kid," said Harry Scarfo.

Metal clicked and the van's passenger door swung open.

Two tiny black shoes dropped from the van to the curb, two tiny shoes connected to two small legs clad in gray pants. The legs walked out from behind the van's door.

The midget wore a gray suit and a natty silver tie. He had red hair. He buttoned his double-breasted jacket, then let his hands swing down below his knees. Precise steps took him to where Paul's hat had fallen.

"I didn't have you bring me out here to play with children," said the midget.

"Hey, Stubby—"

"Mr. Stubbs," snapped the midget. "Careless once is using any name. Careless twice is insulting me."

"Look, I'm sorry, I—"

"Your hat?" the midget asked Paul.

Paul nodded.

"And is this," said Stubbs, sweeping his hand toward Branch, "this is your spotter?"

"Sweetest eyes in town!" argued Scarfo. "Perfect alibi for running the streets, scouting—"

"I don't know about the tape recorder!" said Branch. "This kid was trying to trap me!"

"How?" Stubbs smiled. "Why?"

"Don't worry," said Scarfo. "He's too short to be a c—"

Stubbs swung the back of his right hand like a canoe paddle, whacked Scarfo in the face.

"Short means short!" yelled Stubbs. "That's that, that's all!"

"Hey, yeah, sure, I didn' mean no—"

"Don't say what you don't mean, you don't bleed for what you don't want." Stubbs shook his head. "You're going country simple."

"No, come on, I—"

"You come on," said Stubbs. "Don't do business on Main Street. Put the kids in the van."

"I'm not supposed to get in a car with strangers," said Paul.

"Tonight's a hell of a night, kid," said Stubbs. "If you're smart, you know that here and now, I'm the king of supposed-to's."

He pointed: "Hat like that, you don't want to lose it."

Scarfo jammed the hat on Paul's head, booted him inside the

back of the van. Threw in the tape recorder twisted with snakes of duct tape. The windowless box smelled of grease and steel, rubber. Paul sat on a wheel rim. Branch perched on a muffler. Scarfo locked the back door. Branch punched Paul.

"Do that again without permission," said the midget in the front seat, "and I'll stick your fingers in the radiator fan."

Scarfo drove the van into the night.

The van roared through streets of goblins and ghosts no taller than the King Of Supposed-To's. Well-lit houses fell away. They took Old River Road to Industrial Drive. Rusted fortresses of commerce sought shelter in the dark along their path. Scarfo pointed a plastic wand at a chain link fence. The gate slid open. When the van was past its barbed-wire-topped poles, the gate shut.

The van parked in front of a building five times taller than Paul's school and longer than the soccer field. A lone bulb illuminated two sliding doors in the brick wall. Scarfo unlocked the van's back door: "Roll out."

Wind howled off the river. Paul held onto his hat. Smelled welding, paint.

Stubbs in the lead, then Paul, then Branch and Scarfo, they—
Snickity-click-clang!

"Move and you're hamburger!" yelled a man from the shadows.

The van travelers froze.

"Hey," yelled Scarfo, "Twist Reels: 's me! 's us!"

A man in a tuxedo stepped out of the dark. The lone bulb glistened off the grease in his hair and the sawed-off barrel of his pump shotgun.

"You sure it's you?" Reels kept his shotgun locked on them.

No, thought Paul: locked on me!

"What's your prob'?" Scarfo shook his shoulders and made his leather jacket snap. "Some kind o' TV talk show identity crisis?"

"I just gotta be sure!" The shotgun didn't waver.

"You gotta be what you gotta be," said Scarfo. "Me, I'm me. Talking to a guy in a monkey suit who's sticking a sawed-off boomer in my face, racked to rock 'n' roll."

The shotgun dipped a full inch: "So . . . Who are they?"

"You blind? You can't tell this is Mr. Stubbs, cruised in low and slow and outta sight from the city, just like the boss said?"

"Point the shotgun somewhere else," snapped Mr. Stubbs.

"Who are those guys?" said Twist Reels.

"What's that to you?" said Stubbs. "They're with me."

"Even the one with the hat? Is he a . . . like you, I mean . . . a—"

"He's a kid," said Stubbs.

"A punk!" said Branch.

Stubbs squeezed Branch's knee. "You keep your mouth shut, you keep your legs on."

"He's the man," Scarfo told Branch's anguished face. "Least, for you and me. Big time here, he's the Little Man—no offense."

"Just so everybody understands," said Stubbs.

The shotgun pointed at the ground.

Scarfo spread his arms wide, said: "Twist, it's Halloween, but what's wit' the monkey suit?"

"We're supposed to be out of town at a wedding, right?" Twist Reels pushed his tuxedo lapel toward them; pinned there was a white carnation. "So . . ."

"What's with the sawed-off?" said Stubbs.

Twist Reels swung his eyes through the darkness: "Mojo Jones!"

"What the hell you talkin' bout?" hissed Scarfo.

"I seen him!"

"Get outta here! Nobody *sees* Mojo Jones."

"Well I seen his shadow anyway," said Twist Reels. "Long and lean and wearing that damn hat of his—just like him!"

Twist Reels thrust the shotgun toward Paul.

Don't shoot I love you Mom I love you Mom I'm sorry Gramma Laurel Asa Dad—

"Your guts are running out your eyes and you're seeing things!" said Scarfo. "This is just a kid who fell off his turf!"

"It ain't him I seen. It was Mojo Jones!"

"You mean his shadow." Stubbs sighed. "So where did you see whatever you think it was you saw?"

"Back in the city. On the wall outside Dante's."

"After you were inside fuelin' your guts." Scarfo shook his head. "Even if you saw what you saw, you ain't seein' it here. Forget about Mister Mojo Jones. He ain't hound-doggin' us. Eli's got this play covered. We be totally cool."

"Mojo Jones!" whispered Twist Reels.

"If you're expectin' Mojo an' you ain't already got your shotgun racked," said Scarfo, "you're dumber than you think."

Twist Reels stared at the sawed-off terror in his shaking hands. Scarfo opened the door and shooed Branch and Paul inside.

He sighed. "Hell is not finding competent help you can trust."

"Guess so," said Stubbs.

They entered a hollow mountain. Shadows flowed around them. From deeper inside came the scream of a compressed air wrench.

Scarfo drew a revolver, swung the cylinder open, checked the six shells, snapped the cylinder shut with a click.

"Twist's brain might be dim," said Scarfo as he tucked the gun inside his black leather jacket, "but he's got bright eyes."

Scarfo strode into the cave. Branch pushed Paul to follow. Stubbs padded behind them.

The smell of paint grew stronger. Rubber, grease. Rotting things. The air hammer whined. Somebody beat steel. A ball of light glowed up ahead, closer, closer. Heaven clinked—Paul looked up: pulleys and hooks and chains dangled from steel beams.

They walked into a white light sphere.

"Wow," said Branch. "Cool."

Cars. Cars with their bumpers off, tire-stripped cars squatting on blocks, cars with their hoods up and trunks popped, cars with their windows taped, cars sticky with fresh paint.

"Yo!" yelled Scarfo.

A workman wearing coveralls lowered his air wrench, stared at their entrance. So did two other coveralls men working on cars, one with a ball peen hammer, the other with a paint gun. Wrenchman, Hammerguy and the Painter joined their parade.

Beyond the cars, two men sat at a desk. The man in front of the desk was a Buddha with ebony skin and a rumpled brown suit. Like Twist Reels, the man sitting in the desk's executive chair wore a tuxedo. He had no neck, and a bullet-shaped bald head.

"Well hell, Eli," said the Black Buddha, "look what your crew dragged in."

Scarfo pushed Branch and Paul closer to the desk.

The fat black man laughed. "Weisberg's warriors! Damn, it's a pygmy convention!"

"Shut up, Moses!" Eli Weisberg leered across the desk. Paul shrank back, but Scarfo's hand kept him still. Eli glared at Stubbs. "What the hell did you bring these two here for?"

"Frankly," said Stubbs, "I'm still trying to think of a good answer for that."

Moses Wallace laughed out loud.

"Local boys," he said. "Local blues."

"No such thing as 'local,' " snapped Eli. "Might be fringe city out here, but I'm the main man in the big downtown up the road."

"Less'n Mr. Jack O'Bannion tumbles to your play," said Moses.

"Slick Jack ain't no Mister here!" roared Eli.

Moses ignored that interruption. "You being his trusted right hand and all. Less'n gray hairs on the Commission decide they don't want any franchise changes. Less'n the Feds get you on a wire, or the Chinatown boys—"

"I got all the lessons you need." Eli pushed an Uzi machine pistol across his desk. "Who are these punks?"

Scarfo said, "Branch's the spotter been workin' for us."

"I know you," said Moses. "You're in the sports pages."

Eli frowned. "You goin' to play college basketball?"

"I'm the fastest miler my age in the state!" said Branch.

"Big money don't cover no little-boy races!" bellowed Eli. "What the hell good are you?"

Branch trembled.

"What's with Hat Boy?" Eli growled at Paul.

"He's a citizen," said Stubbs. " 'Pears to me, your spotter was working a shakedown or joy kickin' on your time, and the guy in the hat was more stand-up than fall-down."

"Don't mix your crimes!" Eli roared at Branch.

"Leave that for big boys." Moses shook his head. "This is un-cool, Brother Eli. You tiptoe to me for muscle, you got the smarts to bankroll your play by stripping the wheels out of this nowhere town 'fore you deal it to me, then your lame-ass crew cruises in with a sawed-off citizen who'll put all our sorry ass profiles on milk cartons. This does not bode well for the future."

A voice whispered from nowhere: "What future?"

One hearbeat, nothing. Next heartbeat, there he stood, in the shimmer where darkness met light, just suddenly . . . there.

Hands in the pockets of a long black coat, collar up. White face with sharp features and diamond eyes. A dark hat, snug on top of a hatchet frame, a hat almost twin to the one on Paul's head.

"Holy—" Scarfo swallowed his words. Everyone froze, transfixed by the man at the edge of the light.

"Who the hell are you?" rumbled Moses.

"Mo-Mo-Mojo," whispered Eli.

"Call me Mr. Jones." He smiled. Saw everyone.

Scarfo's eyes flicked back toward the tunnel of darkness.

Mr. Jones said: "Your other friend's hanging around."

Eli swallowed. Made a show of leaning back in his swivel chair. "Nice to see you again—Mr. Jones."

"We met only once."

"I delivered your money."

"Yes. Money. For those who care."

"We're all businessmen," said Moses Wallace, "Mister Who-The-Hell Jones."

Jones strolled around the ring of light. "Life has so much more to offer than money. Ambition, power. Art. Religion."

Mojo Jones stopped in front of Paul. "Nice hat."

"You got business with us?" snapped Moses Wallace.

"Guess I do."

"You *guess*, right?" said Eli. Whatever your business when you came here, I can double it, triple it—get you more later."

"I have a contract," said Jones.

Paul felt the men in the room stiffen. Hammerman tapped the ball peen in the palm of his hand.

"Unlike you," said Jones, "I never betray an employer."

"Jack O'Bannion is a skirt-chasing, drunken . . . These aren't the old days. You know that better than anybody—Mojo."

"Time never changes."

"Yeah, well the tick-tock on Slick Jack says it's time for him to go. Time for new blood."

"Yes."

"You ain't that good, Mojo." Eli smiled. The Uzi lay on his desk. He looked at the Black Buddha, who carried a silver pistol in his vest, at the three men in coveralls, at Scarfo and

Stubbs. "Seven to one, even you ain't that good. So you're here to talk."

"Negotiation is not my calling," said Jones. "And you are terrible at math."

Eli blinked.

Stubbs said: "O'Bannion wouldn't want two kids mixed in the business."

"They are already here," said Mojo.

And Eli roared, "Stubbs you rat fink rat traitor rat—"

"You're the rat," said Stubbs. "The captain of the ship just sent me along for the ride."

"You're one dead midget!"

"Aren't we all. The boys, Mojo—they ain't in it if they ain't here, and them bein' here means you didn't do the job."

"I always do the job." Mojo smiled. "Have them wait outside."

"With me." Stubbs swept his paw toward the way out. Paul and Branch moved fast, knew that if they ran, Stubbs's long arm would pull them back into the light.

Dim mist covered the path.

Drip. Drip. Drip.

Ahead, in the shadows, a flower on the concrete floor beside a black pool that rippled with each falling drop.

"Don't look up!" Paul ordered Branch.

Something deep within the bully made him obey.

Outside, Stubbs made them lean against the van.

"What was that sound?" said Branch.

"What do you want me to do?" asked Paul.

"Wait," said Stubbs.

Paul pulled his hat lower. But it wouldn't cover his ears. Wouldn't cover his eyes. His coat didn't stop the cold.

A breeze, a chill. From the other side of the van, black coat and hat, he appeared. "What will I do with you two?"

Branch whispered, "How did—"

"They're boys, Mojo," said Stubbs.

"Would you challenge me, Monkey Man?"

"Fools die," said Stubbs, "not me. This is business what's gotta be done right."

"They are not right for our business."

"You got it, Mr. Jones."

"You trust them?"

"He won't talk!" yelled Branch. "I can make him not talk. I won't say anything! He ain't with me, do what you want with—"

Stubbs slapped Branch.

"I don't trust them," said Stubbs. "I know them. Mr. Mouth is a weasel liar, but he can be trained to disremember," said Stubbs. "And our friend with the hat . . . Well, he's a hero but he's smart. Knows this ain't about his people or his turf. Knows there's nothing he can do but—"

"But suffer me," said Mojo. "Call me jaded, but I sense these two have business between them that might spin out to touch us."

"What's between them is theirs," said Stubbs, "once they know you."

Mojo glided to Paul. Let him fall into diamond eyes. "That hat: you understand in your bones, don't you?"

"Yes," whispered Paul.

"But your friend needs to learn. And believe."

Mojo whirled. Black coat swirling like a cape. Arcs of silver flashed in the night. Too terrified to scream, Branch trembled as slash after slash, his pants, his yellow jacket, his shirt, all were cut from his flesh. The blade went in his mouth. Mr. Jones hissed: "Mojo!"

A flick of Jones's wrist. Branch chokes down a scream and blood from a scar no one could see. Blade out red and wiped on Branch's bare chest, silver flash in the night—gone.

Stubbs tucked a $50 bill in Paul's jeans. "Cab fare. The gate'll be open when you get there. Go back to town. Back to being a kid who knows what he don't say."

Stubbs nodded toward Branch. "Give you a head start."

"Thanks," whispered Paul. Had to know: "Why are you doing this for me?"

"Smart for business," answered Stubbs.

"More," said Paul.

"Once upon a time," said Stubbs, "I was the smaller kid, too. Now run," he said.

Out the chain link fence. Down Old River Road. Cars roar by.

Don't flag them down, faceless fiends cruising Halloween: fools die. One cab in town. Only comes when it's called. Pay phones don't take $50 bills. Run past the Catholic Church, lit crucifix, blood on His palms, feet, side. Side stitch aching, hard to breathe. Don't stop. Run.

Klaxons screaming, fire trucks roared back the way Paul had come. Orange light flickered on the horizon.

The clock on Town Hall: nine after nine. Mom would be starting to *not worry*. Laurel, Asa.

How much of the candle left to burn?

Edge of Main Street—way down, revelers spill out of a bar. A gorilla dances with a vampire.

Stagger, shuffle, walk.

Home, almost home, or—

An aluminum whiz cut the night above his head.

Duck! The hat crunched.

White-sheeted ghost with a crimson mouth, naked legs and shiny black shoes, baseball bat arcing round again—

Jump back, backhand swung bat cutting . . . *whoosh!*

Dart to the right, jump on the sidewalk—

Whoosh!

Snap the trench coat belt at the ghost's head. The ghost blinks and jumps, swings the bat—

Boing! Aluminum bat bounces off a steel light pole. The bat twists out of the ghost's hands, careens to the drugstore window.

Glass shatters.

Paul reaches between the ghost's naked legs, grabbed the sheet and pulled.

The ghost staggered. Fought clear of the sheet—almost fell through the gaping hole in the window. Naked except for his black shoes, Branch grabbed the stolen sheet, reached through the shattered window for the bat he'd snatched from a trick-or-treater.

A thousand slivered mirrors in the shattered web of glass showed the boy in the floppy hat and coat, running away.

Cyclops eye of a security camera caught Branch as he reached through the hole in the drugstore window. Branch saw its stare. . . .

Paul ran. Behind him, a rabid scream tore the night.

Up the alley. Cut through the schoolyard, stumble into the chain link swings—get free, twist around! Run! Down that street, all the lights in the houses out, people hiding from Halloween. Don't stop. Run.

Behind Paul, running shoes on concrete. Coming closer, closer.

The *whoosh* of a swinging bat fifty, forty nine steps back . . .

Sligo Park. Half the watchlights dark from civic budget woes. Uneven cobblestones, trip stumble don't-fall, run. Footsteps behind, closer, a seasoned racer closing on Paul's gasps. Into the trees, uphill and *so close* behind, crashing-snapping brush . . .

Up ahead, the sheen of moonlight on twin boulders . . . OMJA-GOD.

Scramble, he's ten feet behind, nine . . . Through the mountain pass—

Empty, an empty glen of wild grass and dead leaves.

The two oaks, the only way out—run!

The *whoosh* of a bat missing his neck. The oaks, scars in their bark Paul knew by heart.

"OMJAGOD!" he screamed, and dove flat as an arrow shot precisely between knotholes on the two oaks, sprawled on the heap of twisted sticks and jagged rocks, a sea of dead leaves as—

Behind him, the bloody-mouthed ghost roared vengeful glee, cocked the aluminum bat and charged between the two oaks—

Slammed into a transparent web of dental floss.

A hundred razor lines caught Branch's fury, snapping, twisting, tangling him—springing him back like invisible bowstrings. The aluminum bat flew away in the night.

A bed of dried leaves in OMJAGOD's circle exploded.

Rising into the night, blue-skinned from the vigil he'd promised and kept, came a righteous giant in a red sash and a patched bowling vest, a blood-eyed pirate with a hard rubber sword.

As he charged, Asa screamed the secret battle cry oath of OMJA-GOD: *"Semper fi!"*

Asa slammed the rubber sword up between Branch's shiny shoes. The older boy gasped. Asa slid under the doubled-over bully, wrapped his arm around Branch's neck, and flipped Branch over his shoulder. Branch crashed to the ground. The sheet flew off. Asa stood on Branch's hand. "This is from all the little guys!"

With one punch, he broke Branch's nose.

Sprawled on his back, naked except for his shoes, Branch raised his battered head. Saw white light explode.

"We got your pictures!" yelled Laurel. "We can prove it to the cops! You belong to us!"

Branch rolled to his hands and knees. A star soccer player kicked him in the butt like he was a whipped mongrel.

"Get out of here!" yelled Paul.

Scrambling, sobbing, obeying the jabs of a rubber sword, Branch stumbled between the two boulders, limped off naked (except for his black shoes) into the night.

"Wow," said Laurel as the sounds of Branch crashing through the thorn bushes faded. "I wonder if the pictures will turn out."

Then she made a face. "Yuck!"

Asa stared at Paul. "What happened to you?"

"Everything," was the answer.

Three friends moved close together inside the ring of trees.

"It's so light out," whispered Laurel.

"It's the full moon," said Asa.

"No it's not," said Paul.

He saw his mother, on the couch, eyes closed, ambushed by exhaustion while she waited for her *only only* son. After Paul told her he'd kept no Halloween candy, he surprised her by putting Grampa's hat in his own closet. Mother looked at son with new eyes. The next morning, as the radio talked about the awesome fire at the old factory and the sad arrest for vandalism of a juvenile the station couldn't name, Paul watched her open her purse and find that her few bucks had fused into one $50 bill. When she asked how such a thing could be, he said Gramma lit a candle.

"You know what the real worst part is?" said Asa. "That we had to fight him here. That he had to . . . Of all the people in the universe, that that creep had to be the one to find this place."

. "Maybe we were lucky he did," said Paul.

"We can never come here again, can we?" said Laurel.

OMJAGOD. The ground pressed up through the bed of scruffy weeds. Night pushed apart the trees scattered around this knoll. The sentinel boulders shrank to large rocks.

"Maybe we don't have to," said Paul.

They rode their winged horses home.

James Grady's first novel, the thriller Six Days of the Condor, *was made into a film starring Robert Redford. A screenwriter and award-winning writer of short stories, his other works include* Hard Bargains, Steeltown, *and* Thunder.

THE CLOAK

BY ROBERT BLOCH

"Extra! Extra! Read all about it! Big Halloween Horror! Extra!" If you know anything at all about the work of Robert Bloch, one of the great masters of suspense and terror, you'll realize that by the time Henderson, our hero, has encountered this shouting headline-monger, it's far too late for the situation to be remedied.

This is, in fact, a mesmerizing but pretty bleak little story and we're not sure at all if there's any lesson to be taken from it, other than the one that advises you to resist acting on impulse whenever the thirty-first of October rolls around.

THE CLOAK

The sun was dying, and its blood spattered the sky as it crept into a sepulcher behind the hills. The keening wind sent the dry, fallen leaves scurrying toward the west, as though hastening them to the funeral of the sun.

"Nuts!" said Henderson to himself, and stopped thinking.

The sun was setting in a dingy red sky, and a dirty raw wind was kicking up the half-rotten leaves in a filthy gutter. Why should he waste time with cheap imagery?

"Nuts!" said Henderson, again.

It was probably a mood evoked by the day, he mused. After all, this was the sunset of Halloween. Tonight was the dreaded Allhallows Eve, when spirits walked and skulls cried out from their graves beneath the earth.

Either that, or tonight was just another rotten cold fall day. Henderson sighed. There was a time, he reflected, when the coming of this night meant something. A dark Europe, groaning in superstitious fear, dedicated this Eve to the grinning Unknown. A million doors had once been barred against the evil visitants, a million prayers mumbled, a million candles lit. There was something majestic about the idea, Henderson reflected. Life had been an adventure in those times, and men walked in terror of what the next turn of a midnight road might bring. They had lived in a world of demons and ghouls and elementals who sought their souls—and by Heaven, in those days a man's soul meant something. This new skepticism had taken a profound meaning away from life. Men no longer revered their souls.

"Nuts!" said Henderson again, quite automatically. There was something crude and twentieth-century about the coarse expression which always checked his introspective flights of fancy.

The voice in his brain that said "nuts" took the place of humanity to Henderson—common humanity which would echo the same sentiment upon hearing his secret thoughts. So now Henderson uttered the word and endeavored to forget problems and purple patches alike.

He was walking down this street at sunset to buy a costume for the masquerade party tonight, and he had much better concentrate on finding the costumer's before it closed than waste his time daydreaming about Halloween.

His eyes searched the darkening shadows of the dingy buildings lining the narrow thoroughfare. Once again he peered at the address he had scribbled down after finding it in the phone book.

Why the devil didn't they light up the shops when it got dark? He couldn't make out numbers. This was a poor, run-down neighborhood, but after all—

Abruptly, Henderson spied the place across the street and started over. He passed the window and glanced in. The last rays of the sun slanted over the top of the building across the way and fell directly on the window and its display. Henderson drew a sharp intake of breath.

He was staring at a costumer's window—not looking through a fissure into hell. Then why was it all red fire, lighting the grinning visages of fiends?

"Sunset," Henderson muttered aloud. Of course it was, and the faces were merely clever masks such as would be displayed in this sort of place. Still, it gave the imaginative man a start. He opened the door and entered.

The place was dark and still. There was a smell of loneliness in the air—the smell that haunts all places long undisturbed; tombs, and graves in deep woods, and caverns in the earth, and—

THE CLOAK

"Nuts."

What the devil was wrong with him, anyway? Henderson smiled apologetically at the empty darkness. This was the smell of the costumer's shop, and it carried him back to college days of amateur theatricals. Henderson had known this smell of moth balls, decayed furs, grease paint and oils. He had played amateur Hamlet and in his hands he had held a smirking skull that hid all knowledge in its empty eyes—a skull, from the costumer's.

Well, here he was again, and the skull gave him the idea. After all, Halloween night it was. Certainly in this mood of his he didn't want to go as a rajah, or a Turk, or a pirate—they all did that. Why not go as a fiend, or a warlock, or a werewolf? He could see Lindstrom's face when he walked into the elegant penthouse wearing rags of some sort. The fellow would have a fit, with his society crowd wearing their expensive Elsa Maxwell take-offs. Henderson didn't greatly care for Lindstrom's sophisticated friends anyway; a gang of amateur Noel Cowards and horsy women wearing harnesses of jewels. Why not carry out the spirit of Halloween and go as a monster?

Henderson stood there in the dusk, waiting for someone to turn on the lights, come out from the back room and serve him. After a minute or so he grew impatient and rapped sharply on the counter.

"Say in there! Service!"

Silence. And a shuffling noise from the rear, then—an unpleasant noise to hear in the gloom. There was a banging from downstairs and then the heavy clump of footsteps. Suddenly Henderson gasped. A black bulk was rising from the floor!

It was, of course, only the opening of the trapdoor from the basement. A man shuffled behind the counter, carrying a lamp. In that light his eyes blinked drowsily.

The man's yellowish face crinkled into a smile.

"I was sleeping, I'm afraid," said the man, softly. "Can I serve you, sir?"

"I was looking for a Halloween costume."

"Oh, yes. And what was it you had in mind?"

The voice was weary, infinitely weary. The eyes continued to blink in the flabby yellow face.

"Nothing usual, I'm afraid. You see, I rather fancied some sort

177

of monster getup for a party—don't suppose you carry anything in that line?"

"I could show you masks."

"No. I meant werewolf outfits, something of the sort. More of the authentic."

"So. The *authentic*."

"Yes." Why did this old dunce stress the word?

"I might—yes. I might have just the thing for you, sir." The eyes blinked, but the thin mouth pursed in a smile. "Just the thing for Halloween."

"What's that?"

"Have you ever considered the possibility of being a vampire?"

"Like Dracula?"

"Ah—yes, I suppose—Dracula."

"Not a bad idea. Do you think I'm the type for that, though?"

The man appraised him with that tight smile. "Vampires are of all types, I understand. You would do nicely."

"Hardly a compliment," Henderson chuckled. "But why not? What's the outfit?"

"Outfit? Mostly evening clothes, or what you wear. I will furnish you with the authentic cloak."

"Just a cloak—is that all?"

"Just a cloak. But it is worn like a shroud. It *is* shroud-cloth, you know. Wait, I'll get it for you."

The shuffling feet carried the man into the rear of the shop again. Down the trapdoor entrance he went, and Henderson waited. There was more banging, and presently the old man reappeared carrying the cloak. He was shaking dust from it in the darkness.

"Here it is—the genuine cloak."

"Genuine?"

"Allow me to adjust it for you—it will work wonders, I'm sure."

The cold, heavy cloth hung draped about Henderson's shoulders. The faint odor rose mustily in his nostrils as he stepped back and surveyed himself in the mirror. The lamp was poor, but Henderson saw that the cloak effected a striking transformation in his appearance. His long face seemed thinner, his eyes were accentuated in the facial pallor heightened by the somber cloak he wore. It was a big, black shroud.

"Genuine," murmured the old man. He must have come up suddenly, for Henderson hadn't noticed him in the glass.

"I'll take it," Henderson said. "How much?"

"You'll find it quite entertaining, I'm sure."

"How much?"

"Oh. Shall we say five dollars?"

"Here."

The old man took the money, blinking, and drew the cloak from Henderson's shoulders. When it slid away he felt suddenly warm again. It must be cold in the basement—the cloth was icy.

The old man wrapped the garment, smiling, and handed it over.

"I'll have it back tomorrow," Henderson promised.

"No need. You purchased it. It is yours."

"But—"

"I am leaving business shortly. Keep it. You will find more use for it than I, surely."

"But—"

"A pleasant evening to you."

Henderson made his way to the door in confusion, then turned to salute the blinking old man in the dimness.

Two eyes were burning at him from across the counter—two eyes that did not blink.

"Good night," said Henderson, and closed the door quickly. He wondered if he were going just a trifle mad.

At eight, Henderson nearly called up Lindstrom to tell him he couldn't make it. The cold chills came the minute he put on the damned cloak, and when he looked at himself in the mirror his blurred eyes could scarcely make out the reflection.

But after a few drinks he felt better about it. He hadn't eaten, and the liquor warmed his blood. He paced the floor, attitudinizing with the cloak—sweeping it about him and scowling in what he thought was a ferocious manner. Damn it, he was going to be a vampire all right! He called a cab, went down to the lobby. The driver came in, and Henderson was waiting, black cloak furled.

"I wish you to drive me," he said in a low voice.

The cabman took one look at him in the cloak and turned pale.

"Whazzat?"

"I ordered you to come," said Henderson gutturally, while he

179

quaked with inner mirth. He leered ferociously and swept the cloak back.

"Yeah, yeah, OK."

The driver almost ran outside. Henderson stalked after him.

"Where to, boss—I mean, sir?"

The frightened face didn't turn as Henderson intoned the address and sat back.

The cab started with a lurch that set Henderson to chuckling deeply, in character. At the sound of the laughter the driver got panicky and raced his engine up to the limit set by the governor. Henderson laughed loudly, and the impressionable driver fairly quivered in his seat. It was quite a ride, but Henderson was entirely unprepared to open the door and find it slammed after him as the cabman drove hastily away without collecting a fare.

"I must look the part," he thought complacently, as he took the elevator up to the penthouse apartment.

There were three or four others in the elevator; Henderson had seen them before at other affairs Lindstrom had invited him to attend, but nobody seemed to recognize him. It rather pleased him to think how his wearing of an unfamiliar cloak and an unfamiliar scowl seemed to change his entire personality and appearance. Here the other guests had donned elaborate disguises—one woman wore the costume of a Watteau shepherdess, another was attired as a Spanish ballerina, a tall man dressed as Pagliacci, and his companion had donned a toreador outfit. Yet Henderson recognized them all; knew that their expensive habiliments were not truly disguises at all, but merely elaborations calculated to enhance their appearance. Most people at costume parties gave vent to suppressed desires. The women showed off their figures, the men either accentuated their masculinity as the toreador did, or clowned it. Such things were pitiful; these conventional fools eagerly doffing their dismal business suits and rushing off to a lodge, or amateur theatrical, or mask ball in order to satisfy their starving imaginations. Why didn't they dress in garish colors on the street? Henderson often pondered the question.

Surely, these society folk in the elevator were fine-looking men and women in their outfits—so healthy, so red-faced, and full of vitality. They had such robust throats and necks. Henderson looked at the plump arms of the woman next to him. He stared, without realizing it, for a long moment. And then, he saw that the occupants of the car had drawn away from him. They were standing in the corner, as though they feared his cloak and scowl, and his eyes fixed on the woman. Their chatter had ceased abruptly. The woman looked at him, as though she were about to speak, when the elevator doors opened and afforded Henderson a welcome respite.

What the devil was wrong? First the cab driver, then the woman. Had he drunk too much?

Well, no chance to consider that. Here was Marcus Lindstrom, and he was thrusting a glass into Henderson's hand.

"What have we here? Ah, a bogy-man!" It needed no second glance to perceive that Lindstrom, as usual at such affairs, was already quite bottle-dizzy. The fat host was positively swimming in alcohol.

"Have a drink, Henderson, my lad! I'll take mine from the bottle. That outfit of yours gave me a shock. Where'd you get the make-up?"

"Make-up? I'm not wearing any make-up."

"Oh. So you're not. How . . . silly of me."

Henderson wondered if he were crazy. Had Lindstrom really drawn back? Were his eyes actually filled with a certain dismay? Oh, the man was obviously intoxicated.

"I'll . . . I'll see you later," babbled Lindstrom, edging away and quickly turning to the other arrivals. Henderson watched the back of Linstrom's neck. It was fat and white. It bulged over the collar of his costume and there was a vein in it. A vein in Lindstrom's fat neck. Frightened Lindstrom.

Henderson stood alone in the ante-room. From the parlor beyond came the sound of music and laughter; party noises. Henderson hesitated before entering. He drank from the glass in his hand— Bacardi rum, and powerful. On top of his other drinks it almost made the man reel. But he drank, wondering. What was wrong with him and his costume? Why did he frighten people? Was he unconsciously acting his vampire role? That crack of Lindstrom's about make-up now—

Acting on impulse, Henderson stepped over to the long panel mirror in the hall. He lurched a little, then stood in the harsh light before it. He faced the glass, stared into the mirror, and saw nothing.

He looked at himself in the mirror, and there was no one there!

Henderson began to laugh softly, evilly, deep in his throat. And as he gazed into the empty, unreflecting glass, his laughter rose in black glee.

"I'm drunk," he whispered. "I must be drunk. Mirror in my apartment made me blurred. Now I'm so far gone I can't see straight. Sure I'm drunk. Been acting ridiculously, scaring people. Now I'm seeing hallucinations—or not seeing them, rather. Visions. Angels."

His voice lowered. "Sure, angels. Standing right in back of me, now. Hello, angel."

"Hello."

Henderson whirled. There she stood, in the dark cloak, her hair a shimmering halo above her white, proud face; her eyes celestial blue, and her lips infernal red.

"Are you real?" asked Henderson, gently. "Or am I a fool to believe in miracles?"

"This miracle's name is Sheila Darrly, and it would like to powder its nose if you please."

"Kindly use this mirror through the courtesy of Stephen Henderson," replied the cloaked man, with a grin. He stepped back a ways, eyes intent.

The girl turned her head and favored him with a slow, impish smile. "Haven't you ever seen powder used before?" she asked.

"Didn't know angels indulged in cosmetics," Henderson replied. "But then there's a lot I don't know about angels. From now on I shall make them a special study of mine. There's so much I want to find out. So you'll probably find me following you around with a notebook all evening."

"Notebooks for a vampire?"

"Oh, but I'm a very intelligent vampire—not one of those backwoods Transylvanian types. You'll find me charming, I'm sure."

"Yes, you look like the sure type," the girl mocked. "But an angel and a vampire—that's a queer combination."

"We can reform one another," Henderson pointed out. "Besides, I have a suspicion that there's a bit of the devil in you. That dark cloak over your angel costume; dark angel, you know. Instead of heaven you might hail from my hometown."

Henderson was flippant, but underneath his banter cyclonic thoughts whirled. He recalled discussions in the past; cynical observations he had made and believed.

Once, Henderson had declared that there was no such thing as love at first sight, save in books or plays where such a dramatic device served to speed up action. He asserted that people adopted a belief in love at first sight when all one could possibly feel was desire.

And now this Sheila—this blond angel—had to come along and drive out all thoughts of morbidity, all thoughts of drunkenness and foolish gazings into mirrors, from his mind; had to send him madly plunging into dreams of red lips, ethereal blue eyes and slim white arms.

Something of his feelings had swept into his eyes, and as the girl gazed up at him she felt the truth.

"Well," she breathed, "I hope the inspection pleases."

"A miracle of understatement, that. But there was something I wanted to find out particularly about divinity. Do angels dance?"

"Tactful vampire! The next room?"

Arm in arm they entered the parlor. The merrymakers were in full swing. Liquor had already pitched gaiety at its height, but there was no dancing any longer. Boisterous little grouped couples laughed arm in arm about the room. The usual party gagsters were performing their antics in corners. The superficial atmosphere, which Henderson detested, was fully in evidence.

It was reaction which made Henderson draw himself up to full height and sweep the cloak about his shoulders. Reaction brought the scowl to his pale face, caused him to stalk along in brooding silence. Sheila seemed to regard this as a great joke.

"*Pull* a vampire act on them," she giggled, clutching his arm. Henderson accordingly scowled at the couples, sneered horrendously at the women. And his progress was marked by the turning of heads, the abrupt cessation of chatter. He walked through the long room like Red Death incarnate. Whispers trailed in his wake.

"Who is that man?"

"We came up with him in the elevator, and he—"

"His eyes—"

"Vampire!"

"Hello, Dracula!" It was Marcus Lindstrom and a sullen-looking brunette in Cleopatra costume who lurched toward Henderson. Host Lindstrom could hardly stand, and his companion in cups was equally at a loss. Henderson liked the man when sober at the club, but his behavior at parties had always irritated him. Lindstrom was particularly objectionable in his present condition—it made him boorish.

"M'dear, I want you t' meet a very dear friend of mind. Yessir, it being Halloween and all, I invited Count Dracula here, t'gether with his daughter. Asked his grandmother, but she's busy tonight at a Black Sabbath—along with Aunt Jemima. Ha! Count, meet my little playmate."

The woman leered up at Henderson.

"Oooh Dracula, what big eyes you have! Oooh, what big teeth you have! Ooooh—"

"Really, Marcus," Henderson protested. But the host had turned and shouted to the room.

"Folks, meet the real goods—only genuine living vampire in captivity! Dracula Henderson, only existing vampire with false teeth."

In any other circumstance Henderson would have given Lindstrom a quick, efficient punch on the jaw. But Sheila was at his side, it was a public gathering; better to humor the man's clumsy jest. Why not be a vampire?

Smiling quickly at the girl, Henderson drew himself erect, faced the crowd, and frowned. His hands brushed the cloak. Funny, it still felt cold. Looking down he noticed for the first time that it was a little dirty at the edges; muddy or dusty. But the cold silk slid through his fingers as he drew it across his breast with one long hand. The feeling seemed to inspire him. He opened his eyes wide and let them blaze. His mouth opened. A sense of dramatic power filled him. And he looked at Marcus Lindstrom's soft, fat neck with the vein standing in the whiteness. He looked at the neck, saw the crowd watching him, and then the impulse seized him. He turned, eyes on that creasy neck—that wabbling, creasy neck of the fat man.

Hands darted out. Lindstrom squeaked like a frightened rat. He was a plump, sleek white rat, bursting with blood. Vampires liked blood. Blood from the rat, from the neck of the rat, from the vein in the neck of the squeaking rat.

"Warm blood."

The deep voice was Henderson's own.

The hands were Henderson's own.

The hands that went around Lindstrom's neck as he spoke, the hands that felt the warmth, that searched out the vein. Henderson's face was bending for the neck, and, as Lindstrom struggled, his grip tightened. Lindstrom's face was turning, turning purple. Blood was rushing to his head. That was good. Blood!

Henderson's mouth opened. He felt the air on his teeth. He bent down toward that fat neck, and then—

"Stop! That's plenty!"

The voice, the cooling voice of Sheila. Her fingers on his arm. Henderson looked up, startled. He released Lindstrom, who sagged with open mouth.

The crowd was staring, their mouths were all shaped in the instinctive O of amazement.

Sheila whispered, "Bravo! Served him right—but you frightened him!"

Henderson struggled a moment to collect himself. Then he smiled and turned.

"Ladies and gentlemen," he said, "I have just given a slight demonstration to prove to you what our host said of me was entirely correct. I *am* a vampire. Now that you have been given fair warning, I am sure you will be in no further danger. If there is a doctor in the house I can, perhaps, arrange for a blood transfusion."

The O's relaxed and laughter came from startled throats. Hysterical laughter, in part, then genuine. Henderson had carried it off. Marcus Lindstrom alone still stared with eyes that held utter fear. *He* knew.

And then the moment broke, for one of the gangsters ran into the room from the elevator. He had gone downstairs and borrowed the apron and cap of a newsboy. Now he raced through the crowd with a bundle of papers under his arm.

"Extra! Extra! Read all about it! Big Halloween Horror! Extra!"

Laughing guests purchased papers. A woman approached Sheila, and Henderson watched the girl walk away in a daze.

"See you later," she called, and her glance sent fire through his veins. Still, he could not forget the terrible feeling that came over him when he had seized Lindstrom. Why?

Automatically, he accepted a paper from the shouting pseudo-newsboy. "Big Halloween Horror," he had shouted. What was that?

Blurred eyes searched the paper.

Then Henderson reeled back. That headline! It was an *Extra* after all. Henderson scanned the columns with mounting dread.

"Fire in costumer's . . . shortly after 8 P.M. firemen were summoned to the shop of . . . flames beyond control . . . completely demolished . . . damage estimated at . . . peculiarly enough, name of proprietor unknown . . . skeleton found in—"

"No!" gasped Henderson aloud.

He read, reread *that* closely. The skeleton had been found in a box of earth in the cellar beneath the shop. The box was a coffin. There had been two other boxes, empty. The skeleton had been wrapped in a cloak, undamaged by the flames—

And in the hastily penned box at the bottom of the column were eyewitness comments, written up under scareheads of heavy black type. Neighbors had feared the place. Hungarian neighborhood, hints of vampirism, of strangers who entered the shop. One man spoke of a cult believed to have held meetings in the place. Superstition about things sold there—love philters, outlandish charms and weird disguises.

Weird disguises—vampires—cloaks—*his eyes!*

"This is an authentic cloak."

"I will not be using this much longer. Keep it."

Memories of these words screamed through Henderson's brain. He plunged out of the room and rushed to the panel mirror.

A moment, then he flung one arm before his face to shield his eyes from the image that was not there—the missing reflection. *Vampires have no reflections.*

No wonder he looked strange. No wonder arms and necks invited him. He had wanted Lindstrom. Good God!

The cloak had done that, the dark cloak with the stains. The stains of earth, grave-earth. The wearing of the cloak, the cold cloak, had given him the feelings of a true vampire. It was a garment accursed, a thing that had lain on the body of one undead. The rusty stain along one sleeve was blood.

Blood. It would be nice to see blood. To taste its warmth, its red life, flowing.

No. That was insane. He was drunk, crazy.

"Ah. My pale friend, the vampire."

It was Sheila again. And above all horror rose the beating of Henderson's heart. As he looked at her shining eyes, her warm mouth shaped in red invitation, Henderson felt a wave of warmth. He looked at her white throat rising above her dark, shimmering cloak, and another kind of warmth rose. Love, desire, and a— hunger.

She must have seen it in his eyes, but she did not flinch. Instead, her own gaze burned in return.

Sheila loved him, too!

With an impulsive gesture, Henderson ripped the cloak from about his throat. The icy weight lifted. He was free. Somehow, he hadn't wanted to take the cloak off, but he had to. It was a cursed thing, and in another minute he might have taken the girl in his arms, taken her for a kiss and remained to—

But he dared not think of that.

"Tired of masquerading?" she asked. With a similar gesture she, too, removed her cloak and stood revealed in the glory of her angel robe. Her blond, statuesque perfection forced a gasp of Henderson's throat.

"Angel," he whispered.

"Devil," she mocked.

And suddenly they were embracing. Henderson had taken her cloak in his arm with his own. They stood with lips seeking rapture until Lindstrom and a group moved noisily into the anteroom.

At the sight of Henderson the fat host recoiled.

"You—" he whispered. "You are—"

"Just leaving," Henderson smiled. Grasping the girl's arm, he drew her toward the empty elevator. The door shut on Lindstrom's pale, fear-filled face.

"Were we leaving?" Sheila whispered, snuggling against his shoulder.

"We were. But not for earth. We do not go down into my realm, but up—into yours."

"The roof garden?"

"Exactly, my angelic one. I want to talk to you against the background of your own heavens, kiss you amidst the clouds, and—"

Her lips found his as the car rose.

"Angel and devil. What a match!"

"I thought so, too," the girl confessed. "Will our children have halos or horns?"

"Both, I'm sure."

They stepped out onto the deserted rooftop. And once again it was Halloween.

Henderson felt it. Downstairs it was Lindstrom and his society friends, in a drunken costume party. Here it was night, silence, gloom. No light, no music, no drinking, no chatter which made one party identical with another; one night like all the rest. This night was individual here.

The sky was not blue, but black. Clouds hung like the gray beards of hovering giants peering at the round orange globe of the moon. A cold wind blew from the sea, and filled the air with tiny murmurings from afar.

This was the sky that witches flew through to their Sabbath. This was the moon of wizardry, the sable silence of black prayers and whispered invocations. The clouds hid monstrous Presences shambling in summons from afar. It was Halloween.

It was also quite cold.

"Give me my cloak," Sheila whispered. Automatically, Henderson extended the garment, and the girl's body swirled under the dark splendor of the cloth. Her eyes burned up at Henderson with a call he could not resist. He kissed her, trembling.

"You're cold," the girl said. "Put on your cloak."

Yes, Henderson, he thought to himself. Put on your cloak while you stare at her throat. Then, the next time you kiss her you will want her throat and she will give it in love and you will take it in—hunger.

"Put it on, darling—I insist," the girl whispered. Her eyes were impatient, burning with an eagerness to match his own.

THE CLOAK

Henderson trembled.

Put on the cloak of darkness? The cloak of the grave, the cloak of death, the cloak of the vampire? The evil cloak, filled with a cold life of its own that transformed his face, transformed his mind, made his soul instinct with awful hunger?

"Here."

The girl's slim arms were about him, pushing the cloak onto his shoulders. Her fingers brushed his neck, caressingly, as she linked the cloak about his throat.

Henderson shivered.

Then he felt it—through him—that icy coldness turning to a more dreadful heat. He felt himself expand, felt the sneer cross his face. This was Power!

And the girl before him, her eyes taunting, inviting. He saw her ivory neck, her warm slim neck, waiting. It was waiting for him, for his lips.

For his teeth.

No—it couldn't be. He loved her. His love must conquer this madness. Yes, wear the cloak, defy its power, and take her in his arms as a man, not as a fiend. He must. It was the test.

"Sheila." Funny, how his voice deepened.

"Yes, dear."

"Sheila, I must tell you this."

Her eyes—so alluring. It would be easy!

"Sheila, please. You read the paper tonight."

"Yes."

"I . . . I got my cloak there. I can't explain it. You saw how I took Lindstrom. I wanted to go through with it. Do you understand me? I meant to . . . to bite him. Wearing this damnable thing makes me feel like one of those creatures."

Why didn't her stare change? Why didn't she recoil in horror? Such trusting innocence! Didn't she understand? Why didn't she run? Any moment now he might lose control, seize her.

"I love you, Sheila. Believe that. I love you."

"I know." Her eyes gleamed in the moonlight.

"I want to test it. I want to kiss you, wearing this cloak. I want to feel that my love is stronger than this—thing. If I weaken,

189

promise me you'll break away and run, quickly. But don't misunderstand. I must face this feeling and fight it; I want my love for you to be that pure, that secure. Are you afraid?"

"No." Still she stared at him, just as he stared at her throat. If she knew what was in his mind!

"You don't think I'm crazy? I went to this costumer's—he was a horrible little old man—and he gave me the cloak. Actually told me it was a real vampire's. I thought he was joking, but tonight I didn't see myself in the mirror, and I wanted Lindstrom's neck, and I want you. But I must test it."

"You're not crazy. I know. I'm not afraid."

"Then—"

The girl's face mocked. Henderson summoned his strength. He bent forward, his impulses battling. For a moment he stood there under the ghastly orange moon, and his face was twisted in struggle.

And the girl lured.

Her odd, incredibly red lips parted in a silvery, chuckly laugh as her white arms rose from the black cloak she wore to circle his neck gently. "I know—I knew when I looked in the mirror. I knew you had a cloak like mine—got yours where I got mine—"

Queerly, her lips seemed to elude his as he stood frozen for an instant of shock. Then he felt the icy hardness of her sharp little teeth on his throat, a strangely soothing sting, and an engulfing blackness rising over him.

Robert Bloch has been a professional writer since he was seventeen. Although he invariably treats the topics of murder and mayhem, he is better known as a fiendishly inventive chronicler of psychopathy than as a writer of strict mystery fiction. However, in 1960 he was awarded an Edgar by the Mystery Writers of America for what will probably always remain his most famous work, Psycho, *and he served a term as president of the Mystery Writers in 1970–71. Recently he published* Once Around the Bloch, *a memoir of his life and times as a writer.*

WHAT A WOMAN WANTS

BY MICHAEL Z. LEWIN

Here's how the police feel about October thirty-first—at least in the words of one veteran Indianapolis cop as imagined by Mike Lewin: "I want to remind those of you who are blind as well as deaf and stupid that tonight is Halloween . . . which is a pain in the butt because of all the kids on the streets."

At the station house roll call that opens the story, the lieutenant not only has to motivate her troops—several of whom are rather distracted by other matters—but she has to introduce a visiting magazine writer, a not-quite tourist in the country of urban crime who wants to recheck his impressions of the police experience. When she grants permission for him to be odd man out on the evening's patrol while Halloween shrieks and sputters to its usual anticlimactic close, little does she know how tricky the ensuing treats will be.

WHAT A WOMAN WANTS

"John?"

John's head was hanging over the stack of roll-call documents on the table in front of him. But his mind was bright with an outboard on Sagamore Lake, with what he would do in it with Lizzie if he could just get her there, with how he might accomplish that particular goal. And with whether she liked him at all. There *were* signs of improvement in that direction; she didn't dump on him all the time now. Maybe she was playing it cool, keeping her options open, not committing herself in public. Maybe . . . maybe he could say he'd won a competition. He'd heard her tell Vince how bad she needed a vacation. Maybe that was the way . . .

"*John?*"

John's head jerked up. "Lieutenant?"

"We've got to get started. Do you know where Maxwell is?"

"Maxwell?" John looked around the room. "Isn't he here yet?"

The lieutenant tapped her roll-call clipboard impatiently.

From behind him John heard one of the patrolmen say, "Maxwell is got to be late tonight, Lieutenant."

"Why's that, Vince?" the lieutenant asked good-naturedly.

"Because girlfriend's daddy say how she got to do her homework first."

Laughter grew in the room as another officer said, "No home-work tonight, Vince. She's out trick-or-treating."

John turned to the twenty faces behind him and grinned. "Especially tricking, huh?" he said.

John heard someone say, "You wish." He couldn't tell who it was, but he smiled to show he was a good sport. And he used the moment to allow his gaze to linger on Lizzie. She was laughing with the rest, but without looking at him. He waited as long as he dared, in case she glanced his way. Eventually he turned back to the lieutenant.

At that moment Maxwell walked in, making his entrance with his customary swagger. "The man sublime as you ring your chime, Lieutenant," he said.

The lieutenant looked at her watch but did not play angry. Maxwell saw the others laughing. "What's up? Why they got the giggles, Lieutenant? Don't they know this is a *police* station?"

"They laughing 'bout your love life," Vince offered from the back.

"Ain't no laughing matter, *my* love life," Maxwell said. He made his way down the side of the room and he slid into a chair next to Vince's.

"Just how big *is* her daddy?" someone else asked. "Bigger than you?"

Maxwell looked around, searching for the speaker. He made a face suggesting he didn't like some of the ways one could take that question, but then the lieutenant began roll-call formalities. Vince winked. Maxwell smiled. Each man made a fist. The fists touched lightly.

"I want to remind those of you who are blind as well as deaf and stupid that tonight is Halloween," the lieutenant said. "Which is a pain in the butt because of all the kids on the streets. Even so, I've got a good feeling about tonight. I think you all know what I'm talking about."

From two or three places in the room the phrase "smash-and-grab" was spoken aloud, and it was not said with any humorous content. Another officer said, "Cutlass."

The lieutenant said, "Damn right. He is due, that sucker. He is *overdue.* Time the ghost of a police uniform rose up and haunted him into custody."

The room ceased to be individuals and became a team. Their enthusiasm and determination was genuine. The serial smash-and-grabber was top of the team's most-wanted list, first pick in the draft, *numero uno.*

The lieutenant said, "They put some stats together downtown. They don't make good reading, but I'm going to read them to you anyway. They add up to thirty-seven drugstores and mini-markets in six weeks." The lieutenant put her clipboard down. "I want this guy. I want him bad."

There was a chorus of agreement from around the room. As it died down, John said, "Yeah!"

The lieutenant said, "But before we get started, the captain has some things to report. You don't mind if I tell them that the results of the 'color the police car' contest are in, do you, Cap?"

There were a few catcalls, and the captain smiled from his seat at the front of the room.

The lieutenant said, "He's got worse than that for you."

General moans.

"But even before that," the lieutenant said, "I want to introduce Mr. Keith Locke to everybody."

A slight, gray-haired man of about fifty turned in his seat at the side of the room. His mouth formed a smile without his eyes harmonizing above it. He gave the officers a little wave.

The lieutenant said, "Mr. Locke is a writer. He does articles about law enforcement for all kinds of magazines, and the chief's office has asked us to give Mr. Locke a ride tonight. I was told he wants to 'refresh his experience of what real policing in a city like Indianapolis is like.' Did I get that right, Mr. Locke? But I am also assured by his friends downtown that Mr. Locke is one of the good guys. That he's on our side, and that you can speak freely in front of him."

"Why sure, honey," Sondra said to Locke for everyone to hear. "Y'all can come ride with me and tell me *all* about your friends downtown."

Many officers chuckled, but the sound was mixed. Sondra was

lively and surprising, but she was also newly transferred to North from West. Most of the North personnel did not yet know how to take her ready suggestions of eagerness to shortcut normal promotion channels.

Locke himself did not speak, but his mouth formed the smile again before he turned back to the lieutenant.

"So if you see Mr. Locke taking notes or anything, don't worry about it. If he asks you questions, do your best to help him. Mr. Locke will be riding with John."

John jerked in his chair. "He will?"

"I told you half an hour ago, John," the lieutenant said. "Weren't you listening?"

Once they were settled in John's patrol car, Locke said, "This smash-and-grab guy sounds very interesting."

"He'll be even more interesting when we catch him," John said. John's mood was heavy. He was depressed at the prospect that his rider might keep him from manufacturing meetings with Lizzie. That he might miss a chance to talk to her alone. He'd decided to say he'd entered a competition for a lake weekend. That he was in the finals. It would test her reaction.

As John pulled on to the main road, Locke continued about the smash-and-grabs. "It seems such a peculiar M.O. I can understand why the guy steals cars for his raids, but why does he always steal an Oldsmobile Cutlass? Are there any theories?"

John occupied himself with traffic and lights before turning into a residential area.

"Is a Cutlass easier to get into than other cars?"

"Nope," John said. "The dickhead probably learned on a Cutlass but doesn't have the brain to realize it works on other models too."

"A case of arrested development?" Locke asked.

"I'll arrest his development," John said, not realizing his rider had made the joke first. "Just give me the chance."

The car's radio came to life, stopping conversation for a few moments. When the radio was quiet again John said, "Did you get that?"

"Not exactly."

"A stolen car reported on Ditch Road."

"Oh."

"But not a Cutlass."

Just then John braked sharply so the patrol car came to a halt well short of a stop sign. He waved to a woman who stood waiting on the corner with several small ghosts, witches, cowboys and bats. The woman's hair was covered by a scarf and she wore a loose jacket, but she smiled brightly as she mouthed her thanks. Then she ushered her tiny trick-or-treaters across the street. John wondered if the woman had gotten a clear look at him, whether she would recognize him another time, the nice policeman who had put himself out for her. If he'd been alone he could make sure to come back this way a few times while the woman was still out with the children. Well maybe he could manage it anyway. No need to let the rider cramp his style completely.

The woman had a friendly smile, John thought as he drove on. Nice. Not as nice as Lizzie's, of course. But not a smile to say no to.

Then John felt slight guilt at his unfaithfulness to Lizzie. Well, what Lizzie didn't know couldn't hurt her. Time enough for all that when they got it together. And again John recalled warmly the surprise softness of Lizzie's touch when they shook hands two weeks ago. Sixteen days now. Funny how small things like that can start you off. Lizzie acts so tough but feels so soft. And if that's what her hands were like . . .

"A pirate," Locke said.

"What?"

"I said, maybe this guy who steals Cutlasses will dress up like a pirate tonight."

John nodded slowly and said, "Yeah," though he wondered if maybe he was riding with a lunatic.

After a few quiet moments Locke said, "So do I have this right? The pirate steals a Cutlass and *then* he steals a plastic trash can?"

"Yeah," John said. And enlivened at the memory he added, "One time he even stole a trash can from right out back of the governor's mansion!"

"Really?" Locke said.

"Sure thing," John said happily. "The governor's own goddamn trash can. All his orange peels and cereal boxes, dumped right there in the alley behind the house."

"Do you think there might be a political element to the pirate's crimes?" Locke said. "Could that be why he chose to go to the governor's mansion?"

In the face of uncongenial complexity John's spirits dropped again. "Guy wanted a trash can, that's all."

"Mmmm," Locke said. He made some notes.

As they drove on John said, "Now there's a Cutlass, see? Parked behind that rusty pickup. Maybe we should stick around."

Locke was silent for a moment before he said, "Surely the chances of your perpetrator going for this particular vehicle aren't large."

"It wasn't a serious suggestion," John said.

"Ah." Locke turned back to his notes. When he looked up he said, "And the bricks he uses to break the drugstore windows, is there one particular place that he steals them from?"

"There are a whole lot of bricks around northside Indianapolis," John said.

"Still, if they always came from the same place . . ."

"They don't."

The radio crackled.

When it was done John said, "Did you get that?"

"Not quite."

"A 'man shot,' " John said. "Hold tight." He turned on his flashing lights. He turned on his siren.

As they drew near to the address given John saw that four other police cars were already there. "Some nights," John said, "whenever there's a decent run I'm about sitting on top of it. And other nights I'm miles away every time."

"A quarter of the city," Locke said, "*is* a very large area to be responsible for out of one station, even if it does make it possible to sustain specialized teams and enjoy economies of scale."

John unharnessed himself and opened the door.

"Shall I come?" Locke asked.

"Up to you." But John didn't wait on Locke's decision. One of the cars already on the scene was Lizzie's. Well, it would be. She was that kind of gal.

The lieutenant was that kind of gal, too, and she stood between John and where Lizzie was talking to a middle-aged female civilian. "What's up?" John asked the lieutenant.

"Would you believe . . . a BB gun?"

"A . . . ?"

"A goddamn BB gun. This guy and his brother are playing cards in the kitchen. Mom goes to the door for some trick-or-treaters and while she's away the brothers start arguing. Then Mom hears a bang and one of the brothers squeals, 'He shot me, he shot me.' " The lieutenant shook her head.

From behind her Lizzie's voice carried to them both. "Well I'm telling you, ma'am," Lizzie said, "you did exactly the right thing to call us. You didn't know it was only a BB gun."

"I'm so sorry to get y'all out here like this," the woman said.

"No problem, ma'am," Lizzie said. "You did exactly the right thing, believe me."

"Time to get back on the road," the lieutenant said to John. "Let the young'uns clean up here. You and me should get out there and find us some *real* bodies."

John hesitated, but he had no choice. He walked with the lieutenant to where the cars were parked. They met Locke coming the other direction. "How's it going, Mr. Locke?" the lieutenant said.

"Fine thanks," Locke said. "Is it over?"

"It never began. But hang in there. Chances are we'll get you something juicy before we all get to go home."

When they were on the road again, Locke said, "I was thinking about roll call."

"What about it," John said.

"How often does the captain talk to the shift?"

"Whenever he wants to."

"But today he had so much to say," Locke persisted. "And a lot sounded important. It can't be like that every day."

"The end of the month," John said. "All the brass—captains and up—they meet with the mayor's people. They go through everything from health care to some idiot's idea to change the color of all our police cars."

Locke took a moment to make some notes. Then he said, "Did I understand correctly what the captain said about the officer named Wilson?"

"What about Wilson?"

"That the department wants him fired but the mayor says no?"

"That's about the size of it," John said.

"Isn't that kind of situation usually the other way around?"

"I wouldn't know," John said.

"If you don't want to talk about it . . ." Locke said.

John considered. Then he remembered the lieutenant's comment about Locke's friends downtown. "I don't mind talking," he said.

"So what's the story with Wilson?"

"It's just that he was involved in three of what they call 'incidents of bad judgment.' And we're worried he might do it again. And if he does, who gets the blame? Morale is low enough around here and it isn't helped by the media jumping on every little thing to make us look as bad as they can."

"What sort of incidents?" Locke said.

John breathed heavily. "Like one time was he chased his girl-friend all over Broad Ripple and he dragged her into the backseat of his car and he beat the shit out of her. All right? You get the picture?"

"Not a pleasant picture," Locke said.

"But the guy's still wearing the uniform, despite what we do to try to clean up our own act. So if this guy off and shoots somebody, is the newspaper going to say the force tried to get rid of him but the politicians wouldn't let them? Is that what they're going to say? You tell me. That's your line of work, isn't it?"

"But what makes the mayor want to keep the guy?" Locke asked.

"You tell me," John said again, uncomfortable now that he had talked about Wilson at all.

There was a moment of silence in the car, but it was broken as the radio came alive. After the message was complete John picked up his own receiver and asked the dispatcher to repeat a number.

As the number was repeated, John wrote it on the back of his hand. Then he said to Locke, "Did you get that?"

"Not quite."

"Trick or treat!" John said. "Stolen Cutlass."

For a while they cruised the main arteries of northside Indianapolis talking only about Cutlasses. Then Locke said, "Tell me about yourself, John. If you don't mind."

"Not much to tell."

"How long have you been on the force?"

"Thirteen years."

"Married?"

"Not now."

"Was your being a policeman a factor in the breakup?"

"It didn't help."

"And what do you do for relaxation?"

John thought of Sagamore Lake. The motel by the shore. Of Lizzie.

"John?"

"I fish," John said. "When I get the chance."

"I've met a lot of policemen who fish," Locke said.

"Yeah?"

"I think there's something about the quiet that particularly appeals to policemen."

"Policewomen too?" John said.

"Sure," Locke said. "They need to relax too."

John looked at his watch. "Do you feel like coffee?" But before Locke could answer the radio burst into life again. When it was done, John said, "Forget the coffee. Let's go arrest the suspect in a shooting instead."

But again there were several cars already on the scene when they arrived. Not, however, including Lizzie's. "Come on," John said as he got out, and Locke kept pace as they went to the open door of the apartment building. The suspect lived on the second floor.

Even before they emerged from the stairwell they heard Maxwell's voice from inside the apartment. "So when does your mother get home, Thomas?"

A younger, fearful voice said, "When the store close."

"What time is that?"

" 'Bout eleven, I guess."

Maxwell was looking at his watch as John and Locke entered. Maxwell said, "And you were going to stay here alone till she came home?"

Three officers were ringed around a twenty-year-old man who was kneeling in the middle of the room. The young man was shirtless and handcuffed behind his back.

"Yes sir," the young man said. "To keep the trick-or-treaters from soaping the door and stuff."

Two more officers, Sondra and Vince, emerged from another room in the apartment. They stood with John and Locke. "Rest of the place looks clean," Vince said to Maxwell.

"That's right," the kneeling prisoner said. "Ain't nothing bad in here."

Maxwell said, "And you deny shooting Dexter Hill?"

"I didn't even know he was shot," the prisoner said.

"But you know him?"

"Sure I know him. But I didn't know nobody shot him."

"When was the last time you saw Dexter?"

"I saw him this morning."

"Where?"

"Over outside his place. He owe me some money and I went to get it, but 'bout the time I got there, I saw him leave out the back."

"You didn't talk to him?"

"No sir."

"You didn't threaten him?"

"No sir. Well, I did shout after him to stop, 'cause I wanted my money, but it didn't look like he heard me none."

"And you didn't see Dexter again after that?"

"No sir."

"Not outside the 500 Liquors on Thirty-eighth Street?"

"No sir."

"And you didn't shoot him?"

"No sir."

"So why do you think he says you're the one that shot him, Thomas?"

"I don't know. Except maybe he think that's how to keep from paying me back the money he owe."

Behind John and Locke the lieutenant appeared. Vince saw her and nodded to the hall outside the apartment. Sondra, John and Locke followed them.

"What's it look like?" the lieutenant asked Vince.

"Maybe he's good at playing the innocent," Vince said, "but this kid was watching TV alone in the apartment when we got here and he answered the door with a bag of candy in his hand. Didn't seem like he had anything on his conscience."

"Let them sort it out downtown," the lieutenant said.

"Pity," Sondra said, "because Dexter Hill needed shooting. I knew him from out West. Whoever did shoot him, if he'd done a better job he'd have done the city a favor."

"How bad is Hill?" the lieutenant asked. "Could he still kick it?"

"No idea," Vince said.

"Hi, Mr. Locke," Sondra said. "John treating you OK? You getting what you need?"

"Just fine," Locke said.

Vince said, "Lieutenant, I was thinking."

"See, Mr. Locke?" Sondra said. "You're bringing out the best in all of us."

"About the smash-and-grabs," Vince said.

Suddenly everyone was attentive. "What about them?" the lieutenant said.

"I was driving past a Hooks a while ago and I got to wondering why the smash-and-grab guy hadn't hit it yet."

"Where?" the lieutenant said.

"Forty-ninth and Pennsylvania," Vince said.

"It hasn't been hit?"

"I checked that list downtown gave us. He's done seventeen Hooks, but he hasn't done this one."

"He sure likes a good Hooks, this sucker," the lieutenant said.

Vince said, "There's a gas station, Pete's Service, across the street. It's dark, and there are other cars. I could watch from there."

The lieutenant said, "I'll arrange cover for you. Go on. Get out of here."

203

Vince turned and went down the stairs. The lieutenant returned to the apartment. Sondra, John and Locke followed. As they entered, Maxwell was saying, "You do understand, don't you, Thomas. I got a call from downtown and they said, 'Arrest Thomas Banks.' They may have made a mistake, but that's not up to me. They tell me to arrest you, that's what I got to do."

"I understand," the young man kneeling on the floor said.

"OK," Maxwell said. "I'll call your mother at the store and let her know what's happening. Then I'll take you downtown so we can get this sorted out."

"Yes sir," the young man said.

John whispered to Locke, "We might as well go."

Locke nodded. He led the way out of the apartment, but as John followed to the stairs he heard Locke gasp and say, "Jesus!" There was also a fierce snarl.

John turned the corner on the stairwell and saw a German Shepherd baring its teeth. Behind the dog John saw Andy, one of the K-9 officers.

"This guy with you?" Andy said.

"Yeah, a rider," John said. "Y'all didn't scare him none, did you?"

"I didn't," Andy said, "but I think Baby Fritz mighta done."

When they got back on the road John said, "Now, how about that coffee?"

"Sounds good to me," Locke said.

It sounded good to John, too, because it gave him an excuse to cruise through the residential area where he'd stopped for the woman with the scarf and the nice smile.

But although the evening was warm and there were a lot of trick-or-treaters out John didn't see the woman. Ah, well. He pulled into the parking lot of a Pantry Pride.

He bought a coffee for Locke and a diet cola for himself and then passed a few comments with the owner. John drained his cola quickly and encouraged Locke to drink up.

When they were back in the car Locke said, "What's the hurry?"

"You heard when Vince said he was going to stake out a Hooks on Forty-ninth and Penn?" John said.

"Yes," Locke said.

"Well, he's lucky, Vince. Some guys are like that. It wouldn't do us no harm to wander up that way, just in case."

At that very moment the car radio burst into life with Vince saying, "I'm at Forty-ninth and Pennsylvania, outside a Hooks Drugstore. There's been a smash-and-grab raid here. Can't have been more than a few minutes ago."

"Vince, are you psychic or what?" Lizzie said.

"It's just a pity you didn't get your idea a little earlier," John said. "We'd have nailed the bastard."

Vince said, "He doesn't usually go to work till later on. Has he ever hit one this early?"

"I don't think so," Lizzie said.

"So damn close," John said. "I suppose you're sure it was him?"

"I didn't get an autograph," Vince said, "but there's a couple of bricks inside the front door and the cigarette cabinet is bust open. Is that good enough for you?"

"If we get him tonight," Lizzie said, "you're definitely down for a psychic assist, Vince."

The lieutenant came up behind them. "What are you all doing here?" she said. "There's a Cutlass with a trash can full of cigarettes out there someplace."

When they were on the road again John said, "I was hoping to get a chance to introduce you to Lizzie, the policewoman we were talking to."

"Oh?" Locke said.

"She's only been with us a couple of years, but she's good. Always quick on the scene, not afraid to bust a head if it needs busting, but she's also got that softer side they have. Yeah, she's doing good. She'll go far. A credit to her . . . to her, well, sex."

"You approve of the increasing female police presence on the force, do you, John?"

"Yeah, I guess." Having spoken out loud about Lizzie, John was thinking of something else. He said, "I was meaning to ask you, Mr. Locke, speaking as a guy who gets around a bit. I just wondered what you thought."

"What about?" Locke said. "Females in the police?"

"Not exactly. I just wondered, what do you think women respond to? What, in your experience, is the key to what a woman wants in a man?"

Locke, surprised at the question, hesitated.

"Is that too personal?" John said. "If you don't want to talk about it . . ."

"A woman?" Locke said. "Any particular woman?"

"No. In general. But we were just talking about Lizzie. That officer I'm going to introduce you to? Take her as an example. What would you say a woman like Lizzie would respond to in a man?"

"Success," Locke said.

"Success?"

"In my experience women who opt for careers in law enforcement respect success, accomplishment. Someone who has made a lot of arrests, seen a lot of action."

"So you wouldn't say they were looking for someone who was thoughtful about them?"

"I'm just guessing, John. I haven't studied the subject from this angle. Do you like Lizzie? Is that it?"

"Lizzie? You mean as herself? I hadn't really thought about it," John said.

At first John thought it was just another car running a red light. His instinct was not to bother. But then he realized he had not actually *done* anything the whole shift except arrive at other people's action. While a traffic violation didn't exactly amount to success, it was better than a blank sheet. John made a U-turn and sped after the car. Only then did he realize he was pursuing an Oldsmobile Cutlass.

In another minute—by checking twice against the number on the back of his hand—John established it was *the* Cutlass. "Jesus God!" he said aloud, and he reached for his radio.

He broadcast his location. He broadcast the plate number of the car he was in pursuit of. He requested backup. He requested the K-9 officer. He requested anybody else who was out there.

Then the Cutlass turned off the main road onto a residential street. John followed.

The Cutlass screamed through a four-way stop. So did John.

And then the driver of the Cutlass suddenly braked and slid and turned into an alley.

John tried to follow. But as he swung into the alley his car spun and he lost control. John's car came to a stop sideways across the alley mouth. Miraculously, it hit nothing in the process.

From his seat John could see the Cutlass, fishtailing away on the alley cinders.

But then, as John watched, the Cutlass braked hard. It skidded to a skewed halt and it hit a telephone pole. Then it began to back up.

John knew stories of drivers who intentionally ran into police cars so that the officers inside would be immobilized by their airbags, but John's car was already immobile.

Then, a few yards away from them, the Cutlass stopped.

The driver's door opened. A man got out with his hands in the air. As John got out of his own car all he could hear was the man saying, "Don't shoot. Don't shoot. Don't shoot." Over and over.

Behind the man, blocking the other end of the alley, John could see a party of little figures, some dressed as cowboys, others as ghosts.

"Come and look at this, John," the lieutenant said.

John was in a daze from the sea of flashing police lights that now swarmed around the scene of his arrest, but he followed the lieutenant back into the alley, past his own car to the Cutlass. The lieutenant pointed to a dark object beside the captured vehicle. The object was a trash can. "Take a look inside," she said.

John looked while the lieutenant illuminated the can's interior with her flashlight. John saw cigarette cartons. He saw liquor bottles. He saw a bag of candy corn. He took the candy corn out and held it up.

The lieutenant said, "The sucker was taking it home to give to trick-or-treaters. That's probably why he went out early."

Maxwell walked by and patted John on the back. "Well done!" he said.

The lieutenant said to Locke, "I wanted this Cutlass sucker *so* bad, you wouldn't believe it."

"Thirty-eight more clear-ups for the month, too," Locke said.

Several officers approached, all smiling. The three closest patted John's shoulder, ruffled his hair, congratulated him.

The lieutenant said, "I thought we might come up with something juicy for you, Mr. Locke."

"It was very exciting," Locke said. "But when he turned into the alley, I knew John had him."

"You did?"

"We drove by those kids partying in the alley earlier on, so John knew all he had to do was block off this end. Very cool. That's what you were thinking, wasn't it?" Locke smiled at John, and this time his eyes smiled too.

John said, "Yeah."

"I look forward to telling the chief all about my ride tonight and what a great job my new friend John here is doing," Locke said.

"Well done, man," Vince said.

"Thanks."

"Good arrest," Lizzie said.

John blinked as he picked her out from the crowd. "Thanks, Lizzie," he said. Then, "Will you come fishing with me at Sagamore Lake?"

After everyone was silent for a moment, Lizzie said, "Are you kidding?"

"No. Will you?"

"Get a life," Lizzie said. She turned and walked away.

But before John could quite take in what had happened, Sondra stepped forward and took his arm. She said, "I like fishing."

John looked at her. "You do?"

"Sure do, big boy," Sondra said, smiling first at John and then at his new friend, Locke.

Michael Z. Lewin, an American writer long resident in Britain, has called the city of Indianapolis his "real series character." His detectives—

police lieutenant Leroy Powder, private eye Albert Samson and now social worker Adele Buffington—all occupy portions of this territory. Books featuring them include Late Payments, Underdog, *and* Called by a Panther.

YESTERDAY'S WITCH

BY GAHAN WILSON

Agatha Christie had Miss Marple, but, except for being an elderly woman of rather deceptive mien, she bears no resemblance whatsoever to the Miss Marble of Gahan Wilson's unsettling taste of Halloween nostalgia. When you're a kid, every neighborhood has a witch in residence, and every other block can have a gauntlet to be run. And somehow, these elements always manage to come together on Halloween in ways you never quite manage to make sense of in the safe, bright daylight of the morning after. Was I awake, or was I dreaming? So you may have wondered as you lay in bed, drifting toward consciousness.

Echoes of that same half-forgotten doubt will linger when you finish this story. Enjoy them, with the wicked compliments of Gahan Wilson.

YESTERDAY'S WITCH

Her house is gone now. Someone tore it down and bulldozed away her trees and set up an ugly apartment building made of cheap bricks and cracking concrete on the flattened place they'd built. I drove by there a few nights ago; I'd come back to town for the first time in years to give a lecture at the university, and I saw blue TV flickers glowing in the building's living rooms.

Her house sat on a small rise, I remember, with a wide stretch of scraggly lawn between it and the ironwork fence which walled off her property from the sidewalk and the rest of the outside world. The windows of her house peered down at you through a thick tangle of oak tree branches, and I can remember walking by and knowing she was peering out at me and hunching up my shoulders because I couldn't help it, but never, ever, giving her the satisfaction of seeing me hurry because of fear.

To the adults she was Miss Marble, but we children knew better. We knew she had another name, though none of us knew just what it was, and we knew she was a witch. I don't know who it was told me first about Miss Marble's being a witch; it might have been Billy Drew. I think it was, but I had already guessed in spite of being less than six. I grew up, all of us grew up, sure and certain of Miss Marble's being a witch.

You never managed to get a clear view of Miss Marble, or I don't ever remember doing so, except that once. You just got peeks and hints. A quick glimpse of her wide, short body as she scuttled up the front porch steps; a brief hint of her brown-wrapped form behind a thick clump of bushes by the garage where, it was said, an electric runabout sat rusting away; a sudden flash of her fantastically wrinkled face in the narrowing slot of a closing door, and that was all.

Fred Pulley claimed he had gotten a good long look at her one afternoon. She had been weeding, or something, absorbed at digging in the ground, and off guard and careless even though she stood a mere few feet from the fence. Fred had fought down his impulse to keep on going by, and he had stood and studied her for as much as two or three minutes before she looked up and saw him and snarled and turned away.

We never tired of asking Fred about what he had seen.

"Her teeth, Fred," one of us would whisper—you almost always talked about Miss Marble in whispers—"did you see her *teeth?*"

"They're long and yellow," Fred would say. "And they come to points at the ends. And I think I saw blood on them."

None of us really believed Fred had seen Miss Marble, understand, and we certainly didn't believe that part about the blood, but we were so very curious about her, and when you're really curious about something, especially if you're a bunch of kids, you want to get all the information on the subject even if you're sure it's lies.

So we didn't believe what Fred Pulley said about Miss Marble's having blood on her teeth, nor about the bones he'd seen her pulling out of the ground, but we remembered it all the same, just in case, and it entered into any calculations we made about Miss Marble.

Halloween was the time she figured most prominently in our thoughts. First because she was a witch, of course, and second because of a time-honored ritual among the neighborhood children concerning her and ourselves and that evening of the year. It was a kind of test by fire that every male child had to go through when he reached the age of thirteen, or to be shamed forever after. I

214

have no idea when it originated; I only know that when I attained my thirteenth year and was thereby qualified and doomed for the ordeal, the rite was established beyond question.

I can remember putting on my costume for that memorable Halloween, an old Prince Albert coat and a papier-mâché mask which bore a satisfying likeness to a decayed cadaver, with the feeling I was girding myself for a great battle. I studied my reflection in a mirror affixed by swivels to my bedroom bureau and wondered gravely if I would be able to meet the challenge this night would bring. Unsure, but determined, I picked up my brown paper shopping bag, which was very large so as to accommodate as much candy as possible, said good-bye to my mother and father and dog, and went out. I had not gone a block before I met George Watson and Billy Drew.

"Have you got anything yet?" asked Billy.

"No." I indicated the emptiness of my bag. "I just started."

"The same with us," said George. And then he looked at me carefully. "Are you ready?"

"Yes," I said, realizing I had not been ready until that very moment, and feeling an encouraging glow at knowing I was. "I can do it all right."

Mary Taylor and her little sister Betty came up, and so did Eddy Baker and Phil Myers and the Arthur brothers. I couldn't see where they all had come from, but it seemed as if every kid in the neighborhood was suddenly there, crowding around under the streetlamp, costumes flapping in the wind, holding bags and boxes and staring at me with glistening, curious eyes.

"Do you want to do it now," asked George, "or do you want to wait?"

George had done it the year before and he had waited.

"I'll do it now," I said.

I began walking along the sidewalk, the others following after me. We crossed Garfield Street and Peabody Street and that brought us to Baline Avenue where we turned left. I could see Miss Marble's iron fence half a block ahead, but I was careful not to slow my pace. When we arrived at the fence I walked to the gate with as firm a tread as I could muster and put my hand upon its latch. The metal was cold and made me think of coffin handles and graveyard diggers' picks. I pushed it down and the gate swung open with a low, rusty groaning.

Now it was up to me alone. I was face to face with the ordeal. The basic terms of it were simple enough: walk down the crumbling path which led through the tall, dry grass to Miss Marble's porch, cross the porch, ring Miss Marble's bell, and escape. I had seen George Watson do it last year and I had seen other brave souls do it before him. I knew it was not an impossible task.

It was a chilly night with a strong, persistent wind and clouds scudding overhead. The moon was three-fourths full and it looked remarkably round and solid in the sky. I became suddenly aware, for the first time in my life, that it was a real *thing* up there. I wondered how many Halloweens it had looked down on and what it had seen.

I pulled the lapels of my Prince Albert coat close about me and started walking down Miss Marble's path. I walked because all the others had run or skulked, and I was resolved to bring new dignity to the test if I possibly could.

From afar the house looked bleak and abandoned, a thing of cold blues and grays and greens, but as I drew nearer, a peculiar phenomenon began to assert itself. The windows, which from the sidewalk had seemed only to reflect the moon's glisten, now began to take on a warmer glow; the walls and porch, which had seemed all shriveled, peeling paint and leprous patches of rotting wood now began to appear well-kept. I swallowed and strained my eyes. I had been prepared for a growing feeling of menace, for ever darker shadows, and this increasing evidence of warmth and tidiness absolutely baffled me.

By the time I reached the porch steps the place had taken on a positively cozy feel. I now saw that the building was in excellent repair and that it was well-painted with a smooth coat of reassuring cream. The light from the windows was now unmistakably cheerful, a ruddy, friendly pumpkin kind of orange suggesting crackling fireplaces all set and ready for toasting marshmallows. There was a very unwitchlike clump of Indian corn fixed to the front door, and I was almost certain I detected an odor of sugar and cinnamon wafting into the cold night air.

I stepped onto the porch, gaping. I had anticipated many awful possibilities during this past year. Never far from my mind had been the horrible pet Miss Marble was said to own, a something-or-other, which was all claws and scales and flew on wings with transparent webbing. Perhaps, I had thought, this thing would swoop down from the bare oak limbs and carry me off while my friends on the sidewalk screamed and screamed. Again, I had not dismissed the notion Miss Marble might turn me into a frog with a little motion of her fingers and then step on me with her foot and squish me.

But here I was feeling foolish, very young, crossing this friendly porch and smelling—I was sure of it now—sugar and cinnamon and cider and, what's more, butterscotch on top of that. I raised my hand to ring the bell and was astonished at myself for not being the least bit afraid when the door softly opened and there stood Miss Marble herself.

I looked at her and she smiled at me. She was short and plump, and she wore an apron with a thick ruffle all along its edges, and her face was smooth and red and shiny as an autumn apple. She wore bifocals on the tip of her tiny nose and she had her white hair fixed in a perfectly round bun in the exact center of the top of her head. Delicious odors wafted round her through the open door and I peered greedily past her.

"Well," she said in a mild, old voice, "I am so glad that someone has at last come to have a treat. I've waited so many years, and each year I've been ready, but nobody's come."

She stood to one side and I could see a table in the hall piled with candy and nuts and bowls of fruit and plateful of pies and muffins and cake, all of it shining and glittering in the warm, golden glow which seemed everywhere. I heard Miss Marble chuckle warmly.

"Why don't you call your friends in? I'm sure there will be plenty for all."

I turned and looked down the path and saw them, huddled in the moonlight by the gate, hunched wide-eyed over their boxes and bags. I felt a sort of generous pity for them. I walked to the steps and waved.

"Come on! It's all right!"

They would not budge.

"May I show them something?"

She nodded yes and I went into the house and got an enormous orange-frosted cake with numbers of golden sugar pumpkins on its sides.

"Look," I cried, lifting the cake into the moonlight, "look at this! And she's got lots more! She always had, but we never asked for it!"

George was the first through the gate, as I knew he would be. Billy came next, and then Eddy, then the rest. They came slowly, at first, timid as mice, but then the smells of chocolate and tangerines and brown sugar got to their noses and they came faster. By the time they had arrived at the porch they had lost their fear, the same as I, but their astonished faces showed me how I must have looked to Miss Marble when she'd opened the door.

"Come in, children. I'm so glad you've all come at last!"

None of us had ever seen such candy or dared to dream of such cookies and cakes. We circled the table in the hall, awed by its contents, clutching at our bags.

"Take all you want, children. It's all for you."

Little Betty was the first to reach out. She got a gumdrop as big as a plum and was about to pop it into her mouth when Miss Marble said:

"Oh, no, dear, don't eat it now. That's not the way you do with tricks or treats. You wait till you get out on the sidewalk and then you go ahead and gobble it up. Just put it in your bag for now, sweetie."

Betty was not all that pleased with the idea of putting off eating her gumdrop, but she did as Miss Marble asked and plopped it into her bag and quickly followed it with other items such as licorice cats and apples dipped in caramel and pecans lumped together with some lovely-looking brown stuff and soon all the other children, myself very much included, were doing the same, filling our bags and boxes industriously, giving the task of clearing the table as rapidly as possible our entire attention.

Soon, amazingly soon, we had done it. True, there was the occasional peanut, now and then a largish crumb survived, but by and large, the job was done. What was left was fit only for rats and roaches, I thought, and then was puzzled by the thought. Where had such an unpleasant idea come from?

How our bags bulged! How they strained to hold what we had stuffed into them! How wonderfully heavy they were to hold!

Miss Marble was at the door now, holding it open and smiling at us.

"You must come back next year, sweeties, and I will give you more of the same."

We trooped out, some of us giving the table one last glance just to make sure, and then we headed down the path, Miss Marble waving us good-bye. The long, dead grass at the sides of the path brushed stiffly against our bags, making strange hissing sounds. I felt as cold as if I had been standing in the chill night air all along, and not comforted by the cozy warmth inside Miss Marble's house. The moon was higher now and seemed—I didn't know how or why—to be mocking us.

I heard Mary Taylor scolding her little sister: "She said not to eat any till we got to the sidewalk!"

"I don't care. I want some!"

The wind had gotten stronger and I could hear the stiff tree branches growl high over our heads. The fence seemed far away and I wondered why it was taking us so long to get to it. I looked back at the house and my mouth went dry when I saw that it was gray and old and dark, once more, and that the only light from its windows was reflections of the pale moon.

Suddenly little Betty Taylor began to cry, first in small, choking sobs, and then in loud wails. George Watson said: "What's wrong?" and then there was a pause, and then George cursed and threw Betty's bag over the lawn toward the house and his own box after it. They landed with a queer rustling slither that made the small hairs on the back of my neck stand up. I let go of my own bag and it flopped, bulging, into the grass by my feet. It looked like a huge, pale toad with a gaping, grinning mouth.

One by one the others rid themselves of what they carried. Some of the younger ones, whimpering, would not let go, but the older children gently separated them from the things they clutched.

* * *

I opened the gate and held it while the rest filed out onto the sidewalk. I followed them and closed the gate firmly. We stood and looked into the darkness beyond the fence. Here and there one of our abandoned boxes or bags seemed to glimmer faintly, some of them moved—I'll swear it—though others claimed it was just an illusion produced by the waving grass. All of us heard the high, thin laughter of the witch.

Gahan Wilson is best known as a highly original artist specializing in the ironically weird and the comically awful. His cartoons, regularly seen in both Playboy *and* The New Yorker, *have been collected in numerous volumes. He is the author of the mystery novels* Eddy Deco's Last Caper *and* Everybody's Favorite Duck.

WALPURGIS NIGHT

BY BRAM STOKER

Actually, exactly half a year separates Walpurgis Night, or May Day Eve, from Halloween, the eve of All Hallows. But both are Christian appropriations of seasonal pagan festivals, and both are fabled as occasions when the dead walk the land and witches hold riotous revels presided over by Satan himself. Besides, when the setting is the backroads of the Harz mountains, where one will encounter the sharp-toothed, hot-breathed minion of a certain Count Dracula, it's simply too irresistible not just to split the difference.

In fact, the narrator of this consummately creepy episode is Jonathan Harker, the unfortunate young hero of *Dracula*. Known alternately by the title "Dracula's Guest," it was originally to be the opening chapter of that novel but was trimmed in the interests of keeping the book's price down. After Stoker's death, it was found preserved among his papers.

Walpurgis Night

When we started for our drive the sun was shining brightly on Munich, and the air was full of the joyousness of early summer. Just as we were about to depart, Herr Delbrück (the maître d'hôtel of the Quatre Saisons, where I was staying) came down, bare-headed, to the carriage and, after wishing me a pleasant drive, said to the coachman, still holding his hand on the handle of the carriage door:

"Remember you are back by nightfall. The sky looks bright but there is a shiver in the north wind that says there may be a sudden storm. But I am sure you will not be late." Here he smiled, and added, "for you know what night it is."

Johann answered with an emphatic, "Ja mein Herr," and, touching his hat, drove off quickly. When we had cleared the town, I said, after signalling to him to stop:

"Tell me, Johann, what is to-night?"

He crossed himself, as he answered laconically: "Walpurgis Nacht." Then he took out his watch, a great, old-fashioned German silver thing as big as a turnip, and looked at it, with his eyebrows gathered together and a little impatient shrug of his shoulders. I realised that this was his way of respectfully protesting against the unnecessary delay, and sank back in the carriage, merely motioning him to proceed. He started off rapidly, as if to make up for lost time. Every now and then the horses seemed to throw up their heads and sniffed the air suspiciously. On such occasions I often looked round in alarm. The road was pretty bleak, for we were traversing a sort of high, wind-swept plateau. As we drove, I saw a road that looked but little used, and which seemed to dip through a little, winding valley. It looked so inviting that, even at the risk of offending him, I called Johann to stop—and when he had pulled up, I told him I would like to drive down that road. He made all sorts of excuses, and frequently crossed himself as he spoke. This somewhat piqued my curiosity, so I asked him various questions. He answered fencingly, and repeatedly looked at his watch in protest. Finally I said:

"Well, Johann, I want to go down this road. I shall not ask you to come unless you like; but tell me why you do not like to go, that is all I ask."

For answer he seemed to throw himself off the box, so quickly did he reach the ground. Then he stretched out his hands appealingly to me, and implored me not to go. There was just enough of English mixed with the German for me to understand the drift of his talk. He seemed always just about to tell me something—the very idea of which evidently frightened him; but each time he pulled himself up, saying, as he crossed himself: "Walpurgis Nacht!"

I tried to argue with him, but it was difficult to argue with a man when I did not know his language. The advantage certainly rested with him, for although he began to speak in English, of a very crude and broken kind, he always got excited and broke into his native tongue—and every time he did so, he looked at his watch. Then the horses became restless and sniffed the air. At this he grew very pale, and, looking around in a frightened way, he suddenly jumped forward, took them by the bridles and led them on some twenty feet. I followed, and asked why he had done this. For answer he crossed himself, pointed to the spot we had left and drew his carriage in the direction of the other road, indicating a cross, and said, first in German, then in English: "Buried him— him what killed themselves."

I remembered the old custom of burying suicides at cross-roads:

"Ah! I see, a suicide. How interesting!" But for the life of me I could not make out why the horses were frightened.

Whilst we were talking, we heard a sort of sound between a yelp and a bark. It was far away; but the horses got very restless, and it took Johann all his time to quiet them. He was pale, and said: "It sounds like a wolf—but yet there are no wolves here now."

"No?" I said, questioning him; "Isn't it long since the wolves were so near the city?"

"Long, long," he answered, "in the spring and summer; but with the snow the wolves have been here not so long."

Whilst he was petting the horses and trying to quiet them, dark clouds drifted rapidly across the sky. The sunshine passed away, and a breath of cold wind seemed to drift past us. It was only a breath, however, and more in the nature of a warning than a fact, for the sun came out brightly again. Johann looked under his lifted hand at the horizon and said:

"The storm of snow, he comes before long time." Then he looked at his watch again, and, straightaway holding his reins firmly—for the horses were still pawing the ground restlessly and shaking their heads—he climbed to his box as though the time had come for proceeding on our journey.

I felt a little obstinate and did not at once get into the carriage.

"Tell me," I said, "about this place where the road leads," and I pointed down.

Again he crossed himself and mumbled a prayer, before he answered: "It is unholy."

"What is unholy?" I enquired.

"The village."

"Then there is a village?"

"No, no. No one lives there hundreds of years." My curiosity was piqued: "But you said there was a village."

"There was."

"Where is it now?"

Whereupon he burst out into a long story in German and English, so mixed up that I could not quite understand exactly what he said, but roughly I gathered that long ago, hundreds of years, men had died there and been buried in their graves; and sounds were heard under the clay, and when the graves were opened, men and women

225

were found rosy with life, and their mouths red with blood. And so, in haste to save their lives (aye, and their souls!—and here he crossed himself) those who were left fled away to other places, where the living lived, and the dead were dead and not—not something. He was evidently afraid to speak the last words. As he proceeded with his narration, he grew more and more excited. It seemed as if his imagination had got hold of him, and he ended in a perfect paroxysm of fear—white-faced, perspiring, trembling and looking round him, as if expecting that some dreadful presence would manifest itself there in the bright sunshine on the open plain. Finally, in an agony of desperation, he cried:

"Walpurgis Nacht!" and pointed to the carriage for me to get in. All my English blood rose at this, and, standing back, I said:

"You are afraid, Johann—you are afraid. Go home; I shall return alone; the walk will do me good." The carriage door was open. I took from the seat my oak walking-stick—which I always carry on my holiday excursions—and closed the door, pointing back to Munich, and said, "Go home, Johann—Walpurgis Nacht doesn't concern Englishmen."

The horses were now more restive than ever, and Johann was trying to hold them in, while excitedly imploring me not to do anything so foolish. I pitied the poor fellow, he was so deeply in earnest; but all the same I could not help laughing. His English was quite gone now. In his anxiety he had forgotten that his only means of making me understand was to talk my language, so he jabbered away in his native German. It began to be a little tedious. After giving the direction, "Home!" I turned to go down the cross-road into the valley.

With a despairing gesture, Johann turned his horses towards Munich. I leaned on my stick and looked after him. He went slowly along the road for a while: then there came over the crest of the hill a man tall and thin. I could see so much in the distance. When he drew near the horses, they began to jump and kick about, then to scream with terror. Johann could not hold them in; they bolted down the road, running away madly. I watched them out of sight, then looked for the stranger, but I found that he, too, was gone.

With a light heart I turned down the side road through the deepening valley to which Johann had objected. There was not the slightest reason, that I could see, for his objection; and I daresay I tramped for a couple of hours without thinking of time or distance, and certainly without seeing a person or a house. So far as the place was concerned, it was desolation itself. But I did not notice this particularly till, on turning a bend in the road, I came upon a scattered fringe of wood; then I recognised that I had been impressed unconsciously by the desolation of the region through which I had passed.

I sat down to rest myself, and began to look around. It struck me that it was considerably colder than it had been at the commencement of my walk—a sort of sighing sound seemed to be around me, with, now and then, high overhead, a sort of muffled roar. Looking upwards I noticed that great thick clouds were drifting rapidly across the sky from north to south at a great height. There were signs of coming storm in some lofty stratum of the air. I was a little chilly, and, thinking that it was the sitting still after the exercise of walking, I resumed my journey.

The ground I passed over was now much more picturesque. There were no striking objects that the eye might single out; but in all there was a charm of beauty. I took little heed of time and it was only when the deepening twilight forced itself upon me that I began to think of how I should find my way home. The brightness of the day had gone. The air was cold, and the drifting of clouds overhead was more marked. They were accompanied by a sort of far-away rushing sound, through which seemed to come at intervals that mysterious cry which the driver had said came from a wolf. For a while I hesitated. I had said I would see the deserted village, so on I went, and presently came on a wide stretch of open country, shut in by hills all around. Their sides were covered with trees which spread down to the plain, dotting, in clumps, the gentler slopes and hollows which showed here and there. I followed with my eye the winding of the road, and saw that it curved close to one of the densest of these clumps and was lost behind it.

As I looked there came a cold shiver in the air, and the snow began to fall. I thought of the miles and miles of bleak country I had passed, and then hurried on to seek the shelter of the wood in front. Darker and darker grew the sky, and faster and heavier fell the snow, till the earth before and around me was a glistening white carpet, the further edge of which was lost in misty vagueness. The road was here but crude, and when on the level its boundaries were not so marked, as when it passed through the cuttings; and in a little while I found that I must have strayed from it, for I missed underfoot the hard surface, and my feet sank deeper in the grass and moss. Then the wind grew stronger and blew with ever increasing force, till I was fain to run before it. The air became icy-cold, and in spite of my exercise I began to suffer. The snow was now falling so thickly and whirling around me in such rapid eddies that I could hardly keep my eyes open. Every now and then the heavens were torn asunder by vivid lightning, and in the flashes I could see ahead of me a great mass of trees, chiefly yew and cypress all heavily coated with snow.

I was soon amongst the shelter of the trees, and there, in comparative silence, I could hear the rush of the wind high overhead. Presently the blackness of the storm had become merged in the darkness of the night. By-and-by the storm seemed to be passing away: it now only came in fierce puffs or blasts. At such moments the weird sound of the wolf appeared to be echoed by many similar sounds around me.

Now and again, through the black mass of drifting cloud, came a straggling ray of moonlight, which lit up the expanse, and showed me that I was at the edge of a dense mass of cypress and yew trees. As the snow had ceased to fall, I walked out from the shelter and began to investigate more closely. It appeared to me that, amongst so many old foundations as I had passed, there might be still standing a house in which, though in ruins, I could find some sort of shelter for a while. As I skirted the edge of the copse, I found that a low wall encircled it, and following this I presently found an opening. Here the cypresses formed an alley leading up to a square mass of some kind of building. Just as I caught sight of this, however, the drifting clouds obscured the moon, and I passed up the path in darkness. The wind must have grown colder, for I felt myself shiver as I walked; but there was hope of shelter, and I groped my way blindly on.

I stopped, for there was a sudden stillness. The storm had passed; and, perhaps in sympathy with nature's silence, my heart seemed to cease to beat. But this was only momentarily; for suddenly the moonlight broke through the clouds, showing me that I was in a graveyard, and that the square object before me was a great massive tomb of marble, as white as the snow that lay on and all around it. With the moonlight there came a fierce sigh of the storm, which appeared to resume its course with a long, low howl, as of many dogs or wolves. I was awed and shocked, and felt the cold perceptibly grow upon me till it seemed to grip me by the heart. Then while the flood of moonlight still fell on the marble tomb, the storm gave further evidence of renewing, as though it was returning on its track. Impelled by some sort of fascination, I approached the sepulchre to see what it was, and why such a thing stood alone in such a place. I walked around it, and read, over the Doric door, in German—

COUNTESS DOLINGEN OF GRATZ

IN STYRIA

SOUGHT AND FOUND DEATH.

1801.

On the top of the tomb, seemingly driven through the solid marble—for the structure was composed of a few vast blocks of stone—was a great iron spike or stake. On going to the back I saw, graven in great Russian letters: "The dead travel fast."

There was something so weird and uncanny about the whole thing that it gave me a turn and made me feel quite faint. I began to wish, for the first time, that I had taken Johann's advice. Here a thought struck me, which came under almost mysterious circumstances and with a terrible shock. This was Walpurgis Night!

Walpurgis Night, when, according to the belief of millions of people, the devil was abroad—when the graves were opened and the dead came forth and walked. When all evil things of earth and air and water held revel. This very place the driver had specially shunned. This was the depopulated village of centuries ago. This was where the suicide lay; and this was the place where I was alone—unmanned, shivering with cold in a shroud of snow with a wild storm gathering again upon me! It took all my philosophy, all the religion I had been taught, all my courage, not to collapse in a paroxysm of fright.

And now a perfect tornado burst upon me. The ground shook as though thousands of horses thundered across it; and this time the storm bore on its icy wings, not snow, but great hailstones which drove with such violence that they might have come from the thongs of Balearic slingers—hailstones that beat down leaf and branch and made the shelter of the cypresses of no more avail than though their stems were standing-corn. At the first I had rushed to the nearest tree; but I was soon fain to leave it and seek the only spot that seemed to afford refuge, the deep Doric doorway of the marble tomb. There, crouching against the massive bronze door, I gained a certain amount of protection from the beating of the hailstones, for now they only drove against me as they ricocheted from the ground and the side of the marble.

As I leaned against the door, it moved slightly and opened inwards. The shelter of even a tomb was welcome in that pitiless tempest, and I was about to enter it when there came a flash of forked lightning that lit up the whole expanse of the heavens. In the instant, as I am a living man, I saw, as my eyes were turned into the darkness of the tomb, a beautiful woman, with rounded cheeks and red lips, seemingly sleeping on a bier. As the thunder broke overhead, I was grasped as by the hand of a giant and hurled out into the storm. The whole thing was so sudden that, before I could realise the shock, moral as well as physical, I found the hailstones beating me down. At the same time I had a strange, dominating feeling that I was not alone. I looked towards the tomb. Just then there came another blinding flash, which seemed to strike the iron stake that surmounted the tomb and to pour through to the earth, blasting and crumbling the marble, as in a burst of flame. The dead woman rose for a moment of agony, while she was lapped in the flame, and her bitter scream of pain was drowned in the thundercrash. The last thing I heard was this mingling of dreadful sound, as again I was seized in the giant-grasp and dragged away, while the hail-stones beat on me, and the air around seemed reverberant with the howling of wolves. The last sight that I remembered was a vague, white, moving mass, as if all the graves around me had sent out the phantoms of their sheeted dead, and that they were closing in on me through the white cloudiness of the driving hail.

WALPURGIS NIGHT

*　*　*

Gradually there came a sort of vague beginning of consciousness; then a sense of weariness that was dreadful. For a time I remembered nothing; but slowly my senses returned. My feet seemed positively racked with pain, yet I could not move them. They seemed to be numbed. There was an icy feeling at the back of my neck and all down my spine, and my ears, like my feet, were dead, yet in torment; but there was in my breast a sense of warmth which was, by comparison, delicious. It was as a nightmare—a physical nightmare, if one may use such an expression; for some heavy weight on my chest made it difficult for me to breathe.

This period of semi-lethargy seemed to remain a long time, and as it faded away I must have slept or swooned. Then came a sort of loathing, like the first stage of sea-sickness, and a wild desire to be free from something—I knew not what. A vast stillness enveloped me, as though all the world were asleep or dead—only broken by the low panting as of some animal close to me. I felt a warm rasping at my throat, then came a consciousness of the awful truth, which chilled me to the heart and sent the blood surging up through my brain. Some great animal was lying on me and now licking my throat. I feared to stir, for some instinct of prudence bade me lie still; but the brute seemed to realise that there was now some change in me, for it raised its head. Through my eyelashes I saw above me the two great flaming eyes of a gigantic wolf. Its sharp white teeth gleamed in the gaping red mouth, and I could feel its hot breath fierce and acrid upon me.

For another spell of time I remembered no more. Then I became conscious of a low growl, followed by a yelp, renewed again and again. Then, seemingly very far away, I heard a "Holloa! holloa!" as of many voices calling in unison. Cautiously I raised my head and looked in the direction whence the sound came; but the cemetery blocked my view. The wolf still continued to yelp in a strange way, and a red glare began to move round the grove of cypresses, as though following the sound. As the voices drew closer, the wolf yelped faster and louder. I feared to make either sound or motion. Nearer came the red glow, over the white pall which stretched into the darkness around me. Then all at once from beyond the trees there came at a trot a troop of horsemen bearing torches. The wolf rose from my breast and made for the cemetery. I saw one of the horsemen (soldiers by their caps and their long military cloaks) raise his carbine and take aim. A companion knocked up his arm, and I heard the ball whizz over my head. He had evidently taken my body for that of the wolf. Another sighted the animal as it slunk away, and a shot followed. Then, at a gallop, the troop rode forward—some towards me, others following the wolf as it disappeared amongst the snow-clad cypresses.

As they drew nearer I tried to move, but was powerless, although I could see and hear all that went on around me. Two or three of the soldiers jumped from their horses and knelt beside me. One of them raised my head, and placed his hand over my heart.

"Good news, comrades!" he cried. "His heart still beats!"

Then some brandy was poured down my throat; it put vigour into me, and I was able to open my eyes fully and look around. Light and shadows were moving among the trees, and I heard men call to one another. They drew together, uttering frightened exclamations; and the lights flashed as the others came pouring out of the cemetery pell-mell, like men possessed. When the further ones came close to us, those who were around me asked them eagerly:

"Well, have you found him?"

The reply rang out hurriedly:

"No! no! Come away quick! This is no place to stay, and on this of all nights!"

"What was it?" was the question, asked in all manner of keys. The answer came variously and all indefinitely as though the men were moved by some common impulse to speak, yet were restrained by some common fear from giving their thoughts.

"It—it—indeed!" gibbered one, whose wits had plainly given out for the moment.

"A wolf—and yet not a wolf!" another put in shudderingly.

"No use trying for him without the sacred bullet," a third remarked in a more ordinary manner.

"Serve us right for coming out on this night! Truly we have earned our thousand marks!" were the ejaculations of a fourth.

"There was blood on the broken marble," another said after a pause—"the lightning never brought that there. And for him—is he safe? Look at his throat! See, comrades, the wolf has been lying on him and keeping his blood warm."

The officer looked at my throat and replied:

"He is all right; the skin is not pierced. What does it all mean? We should never have found him but for the yelping of the wolf."

"What became of it?" asked the man who was holding up my head, and who seemed the least panic-stricken of the party, for his hands were steady and without tremor. On his sleeve was the chevron of a petty officer.

"It went to its home," answered the man, whose long face was pallid, and who actually shook with terror as he glanced around him fearfully. "There are graves enough there in which it may lie. Come, comrades—come quickly! Let us leave this cursed spot."

The officer raised me to a sitting posture, as he uttered a word of command; then several men placed me upon a horse. He sprang to the saddle behind me, took me in his arms, gave the word to advance; and, turning our faces away from the cypresses, we rode away in swift, military order.

As yet my tongue refused its office, and I was perforce silent. I must have fallen asleep; for the next thing I remembered was finding myself standing up, supported by a soldier on each side of me. It was almost broad daylight, and to the north a red streak of sunlight was reflected, like a path of blood, over the waste of snow. The officer was telling the men to say nothing of what they had seen, except that they found an English stranger, guarded by a large dog.

"Dog! that was no dog," cut in the man who had exhibited such fear. "I think I know a wolf when I see one."

The young officer answered calmly: "I said a dog."

"Dog!" reiterated the other ironically. It was evident that his courage was rising with the sun; and pointing to me, he said, "Look at his throat. Is that the work of a dog, master?"

Instinctively I raised my hand to my throat, and as I touched it I cried out in pain. The men crowded round to look, some stooping down from their saddles; and again there came the calm voice of the young officer:

"A dog, as I said. If aught else were said we should only be laughed at."

I was then mounted behind a trooper, and we rode on into the suburbs of Munich. Here we came across a stray carriage, into which I was lifted, and it was driven off to the Quatre Saisons— the young officer accompanying me, whilst a trooper followed with his horse, and the others rode off to their barracks.

When we arrived, Herr Delbrück rushed so quickly down the steps to meet me, that it was apparent he had been watching within. Taking me by both hands he solicitously led me in. The officer saluted me and was turning to withdraw, when I recognised his purpose, and insisted that he should come to my rooms. Over a glass of wine I warmly thanked him and his brave comrades for saving me. He replied simply that he was more than glad, and that Herr Delbrück had at the first taken steps to make all the searching party pleased; at which ambiguous utterance the maître d'hôtel smiled, while the officer pleaded duty and withdrew.

"But Herr Delbrück," I enquired, "how and why was it that the soldiers searched for me?"

He shrugged his shoulders, as if in depreciation of his own deed, as he replied:

"I was so fortunate as to obtain leave from the commander of the regiment in which I served, to ask for volunteers."

"But how did you know I was lost?" I asked.

"The driver came hither with the remains of his carriage, which had been upset when the horses ran away."

"But surely you would not send a search-party of soldiers merely on this account?"

"Oh, no!" he answered; "but even before the coachman arrived, I had this telegram from the Boyar whose guest you are," and he took from his pocket a telegram which he handed to me, and I read:

BISTRITZ.

Be careful of my guest—his safety is most precious to me. Should aught happen to him, or if he be missed, spare nothing to find him and ensure his safety. He is English and therefore adventurous. There are often dangers from snow and wolves and night. Lose not a moment if you suspect harm to him. I answer your zeal with my fortune.—Dracula.

As I held the telegram in my hand, the room seemed to whirl around me; and, if the attentive maître d'hôtel had not caught me, I think I should have fallen. There was something so strange in all this, something so weird and impossible to imagine, that there grew on me a sense of my being in some way the sport of opposite forces—the mere vague idea of which seemed in a way to paralyse me. I was certainly under some form of mysterious protection. From a distant country had come, in the very nick of time, a message that took me out of the danger of the snow-sleep and the jaws of the wolf.

Bram Stoker, an Irish writer long associated with famed actor Henry Irving as his stage manager, published Dracula *in 1897. The best known and most influential depiction of the vampire in all of literature, it has served as the inspiration for an as-yet unstaunched flow of fiction and film.*

TRICK OR TREAT

BY JUDITH GARNER

A Halloween tale that shapes itself to our dawning awareness as gently as this one does is better off without too much of an introduction. But, along with such writers as William Golding, Richard Hughes and Shirley Jackson, Judith Garner obviously doesn't believe for an instant in the innocence of childhood.

TRICK OR TREAT

I was sitting with my American friend Bambi in our basement kitchen when the front doorbell rang. As the caretaker, I immediately rose to answer it, not for the first time cursing the necessity of taking on this job for the rent-free quarters.

It was October 30 and Mrs. Adams, my niggardly employer, had forbidden fires so early in the season. But already the chill and damp promised a fierce winter. I opened the street door to a grotesque little figure outlined against the yellow fog.

It was a small girl, about eight or nine years old, dressed as a witch in a long black university gown and pointed Welsh hat. She was not one of the tenants of our service flats, but I vaguely thought I had seen her playing in the Gardens with her nanny and a pram. I had an idea she was an American, that her father had something to do with the embassy. Not a pretty child, she had an old-fashioned rubber doll in a very dilapidated push-chair.

"Trick or treat?" she asked.

"Treat," I said firmly, thinking I was being offered a choice.

She looked at me expectantly, but when I made no move, she inquired, "Well, where is it then?"

"What?"

"My treat," she said patiently. "If you don't give me a treat, I'll play a trick on you."

"You be off now," I said crossly. "Why, it's extortion! You Americans are all gangsters at heart!"

I closed the door in her hostile little face and went down to the basement, where Bambi was lighting yet another of her cigarettes.

"Trick or treat," I explained.

"Oh!" she exclaimed. "I didn't know you had that custom in England."

"We don't. What is it, American?"

"Yes, indeed. We always used to go out in costumes trick-or-treating in New York."

"What kind of trick can I expect?"

"Well, my mother used to let us take a sockful of flour. If you hit it against the door it leaves a lovely mark."

"I thought I heard some sort of thud as I came downstairs," I said, "but it didn't sound like a sockful of flour, more like a kick."

"Well, they say things are very unpleasant in the States at Halloween nowadays. How gangs will break your windows or slash your tires if you don't give them at least a dollar."

I thought the custom simply encouraged hooliganism and I said so. "Anyhow, Halloween isn't until tomorrow."

Bambi looked put out at my unfriendliness about her national customs. "Good lord!" she said. "I've been giving away pennies for the Guy for the last month. I do think Guy Fawkes is just as peculiar. Fancy burning a human figure!"

I couldn't see it that way, but I held my tongue. Tonight I resented Bambi; poor though she was personally, I envied her the affluence of her background. Besides, I had always wanted to travel myself.

I poured her another cup of tea and she reverted to her show-business anecdotes. Then Ron, my husband, joined us, and we played dominoes with the gas money until eleven.

I was up at six the next morning, bringing Ron his tea and stoking up the boiler for the hot water. At 7:30 I went up to the ground floor for the milk. The milkman was just leaving.

"Curious decorations you have around here," he said, gesturing at our front door. It certainly was odd. Nailed to the door was a doll's hand. It had a rubber skin filled with cotton; the stuffing was coming out. It looked ugly and perverted.

"If I'd seen that in Brixton or Camden Town," the man said, "you know what I would have thought? That someone was practicing voodoo. But you don't get that sort of thing around here. Not in Gloucester Road, you don't."

I pulled the dirty thing off the door and chucked it into an open dustbin. "It's all up and down the Gardens," he continued. "Bits of a doll, nailed to the doors."

Not being superstitious, I just shrugged and went upstairs to distribute the milk. Later, having got my son off to school, I began cleaning the flats and the halls.

I did not associate the mutilated doll with my small visitor of the previous evening until, Mrs. Adams having sent me out shopping, I saw the torso just being removed from Professor Newton's door.

"Creepy, isn't it?" I greeted him.

"It's that wretched Halloween child who did it. Trick or treat indeed! Something disturbing about that family. Too much sibling rivalry is my diagnosis. I shall make a formal protest to the parents. Better yet, I shall write a letter to the *Times*, protesting about the importing of foreign customs—noxious foreign customs!" Having with some difficulty removed the nails, the professor took the grisly souvenir into the house with him and indignantly slammed the door.

The head of the doll was impaled on the railings at the corner. There I found Lady Arthwaite studying it with interest. "I wonder what the poor thing has done to be decapitated," she murmured to me as I passed. "Positively medieval, isn't it? Or, to be precise, it's—well, I haven't seen a doll like that since before the war. The skin texture is so much more lifelike than this disgusting plastic you get nowadays. I would have liked one like it for my little granddaughter."

But as it was chilly I could not wait around. Nevertheless, her homely words took something of the horror out of the incident. I did my shopping, and made Mrs. Adams's lunch. I worked until it became dark, which was very early.

A storm was brewing. The sky was very dark and threatening. My son got home from school just in time, but I made him a nice cup of hot cocoa anyhow, in case the chill had entered his bones. He is a delicate boy.

The rain came pelting down just after five. Ron was drenched when he came in half an hour later. "Halloween," he said. "I need a drink." I mixed the whiskey and hot lemonade the way he liked it.

He sat crouching over the newly stoked boiler in his secondhand smoking jacket. I began preparing the dinner—chops, chips, and peas, with fruit salad and custard for dessert.

We began to eat. Suddenly the front doorbell sounded again. Muttering angrily, I climbed the stairs.

The little American stood there, dressed like a pirate this time. "Trick or treat?" she said.

This time she had her baby brother in the push-chair.

Judith Garner, *a native New Yorker, lived in England until her untimely death. She worked as a journalist, artist's model, census taker and assistant wardrobe mistress for a ballet company. "Trick or Treat" was chosen as one of the three best "first stories" published in* Ellery Queen's Mystery Magazine *in 1975.*

ONE NIGHT AT A TIME

BY DOROTHY CANNELL

Imagine Carol Burnett doing Anne Rice, with a soupçon of Barbara Cartland thrown in, just for class, and you'll have an idea of what Dorothy Cannell is up to in this charming romp. As an All Hallows' mystery, it's completely surprising, from start to finish; as a period piece, it's wonderfully unclear exactly what its period is—and that only adds to the fun!

One Night at a Time

It was an evening in late October of the kind of which I am particularly fond. An east wind whipped around the corners of the London street, chasing off any chance wayfarers with their coattails between their legs. The moon gloomed behind a ragged curtain of cloud, and rain spat cheekily upon the windows as if in hopes I would relax my clasp of the curtains and charge off to seize up the poker, in order to challenge the peeking shadows to a duel.

I was restless to be out and about, if to do no more than explore the dark alleys and courtyards with which that part of town abounded. My rooms were at the top of a repressively humdrum building, and it is my belief that they were as tired of me as I of them. The wall lamps did their best in lending a feverish blush to the wallpaper, but the sofa and chairs sat stolidly where they always sat, like dogs told to "stay" and subsequently forgotten by an absentminded master. The books and papers on my desk had all been squared away by my secretary, before she escaped to whatever life she knew beyond these walls. Not a pencil required sharpening, not an inkwell filling. Assuming a seat by the fire, I reminded myself that this confinement to quarters was of my own making. A scant week before, I had invited an old acquaintance to take up residence with me until he could establish himself elsewhere. This offer was not made purely out of the goodness of my heart. Ours was a relationship of doctor and patient, for although I do not hang my shingle in vulgar display upon the door, I may lay claim to certain credentials as a medical practitioner.

The clock on the mantelpiece struck nine, and I arose with more alacrity than was merited by the occasion to set out a pair of decanters and some glasses. Ah, yes! My guest had awakened. A creaking sound, coupled with a nose-nipping draft, indicated the opening of the bathroom door. Upon his arrival I had strongly urged him to a more conventional medium of repose, but he had insisted he would rest more soundly in the mahogany-enclosed bathtub.

When he now entered the sitting room I perceived the chill of porcelain still upon him, heightening the somber effect of raven locks winging back from a pallid brow. The shadows beneath the sunken eyes appeared more pronounced tonight, and I made haste to play the genial host.

"Ah, Batinsky!" I spread my hands with a flourish. "I trust you slept well?"

"Tolerably, my dear Warloch." The smile he bestowed on me was as frayed about the edges as the aged smoking jacket he wore, causing me to suspect that his rest had been assaulted by dreams in which all the old, forbidden cravings reimposed themselves.

When Batinsky had first approached me seeking "a cure" I had thought him foolish indeed. I have never experienced a burning (so charming a word) desire to join the human race. But he had brought me by degrees to the realization that he had come to find his present existence intolerable. Recalling, albeit grudgingly, a service he had once performed to me at some risk to himself, I fetched down my alchemist's vials from the cupboard and set about mixing up a potion that would provide, when taken daily, the nutrients his particular chemistry required and were no longer to be ingested through his favorite libation.

I had previously had occasion for experimentation with a case similar to his. The subject had been my secretary, the inestimable Miss Flittermouse. Finding her shorthand tiptop, but her tendency to bare her fangs at me—upon being asked to work late—disconcerting, I had been moved to try to assist her in rejoining the common herd. (The particular inducement for her was a gentleman:

a curate of all unsuitables, an attachment that happily withered on the vine once Miss Flittermouse took "the cure.") I may say, without fear of correction, that hers was a success story. True, there were days when she was a little flighty, but I put this down to the time of the month, when the moon was full, and in the main was well satisfied with her.

From the outset I had known Batinsky's would be the more challenging case. Traditionally, the male sex tends to be harder to reclaim, and, unlike Miss Flittermouse, he was no recent acolyte. His addiction had been created over centuries, and no potion, however exactly compounded, could entirely rid him of a dependence both emotional and physical. His only real hope lay in total abstinence. There must be, I told him with an attempt at lightness, no social imbibing or talk of "one last nip for the road." Having explained the situation as plainly as I might, I urged him to seek out some other form of diversion for his energies, but he made no response to the suggestion, and, to my increasing irritation, seemed bent upon boring himself into oblivion.

"A drink, Batinsky?" I said now, holding up a decanter.

"Yes, but not port, I think," he smiled wryly. "I would prefer, if I may, a glass of tomato juice. If not the flavor, at least the look and consistency, my dear Warloch."

Relieved to find him up to even this meager jest, I made haste to procure him the requested beverage. "And what is your pleasure tonight, sir?" After filling my own glass, I waved him to a chair. "After we have dined, we may, if you wish, visit some friends of mine in Kensington."

"To play parlor games with a crystal ball?" Batinsky seated himself and stared broodingly into the fire. "Your efforts to entertain me are unceasing, old friend, and do you the more credit for being an infernal nuisance." At my murmured denials he paused to sip his drink. Setting it aside he said, "You cannot deny you must have been wishing me off"—a derisive chuckle—"in some belfry all week. But let me tell you now that your advice to bestir myself did not go in one ear and out the other. I have thought long and hard, through the dark reaches of the night, as to how best to redirect my life and now am come to a decision."

"Splendid!" I sat down across from him, leaned back comfortably and rested my glass of port on my waistcoat front. "Relieve my curiosity, sir! Or must I pry the whole out of you?"

"Yesterday I placed an advertisement in *The Spectre*."

"My! We *have* been industrious!"

"In it I announced my availability in matters requiring the services of a private detective."

"Indeed?" I was somewhat at a loss.

"For people of our sort."

"Of course."

Batinsky leaned forward, his bone-white hands resting upon the knees of his old-world breeches; the shadow cast by the bureau behind him lent an eagle swoop to his shoulders. "You may recall that I have upon occasion engaged in the solving of certain riddles that perplexed and troubled members of our acquaintance."

"Certainly. I am unlikely to forget your timely assistance in recovering the journals that recorded my family's history, after they were appropriated by that impudent puritan. A woman skulking under the name of Mercy, if I remember rightly!" Rising, I trod over to the window and stared fixedly out into the night. "Doubtless I would have withstood the rigors of interrogation; but I will admit to you an unmanly fear of the ducking stool."

My sharp ears picked up the sound of Batinsky's shrug. "An abominable indignity," he said. "And I do not forget that to the hunter you and I look the same in the dark. But let us return to the present. Do you wish then me success in my labors?"

In truth I was of two minds about the matter. My friend did well to contemplate an emergence from his lethargy; however, the uneasy thought occurred that he might have fallen prey to the desire to atone for his past life by embarking upon a course of good works—a most unhealthy attitude—but before I could urge him to consider the possibility of card-sharking as an alternative diversion, my attention was caught by the movement of a figure in the street below.

"A veiled woman." I followed the words with a sour chuckle. "If ours were the world of detective fiction, Batinsky, she would undoubtedly be making for our door to consult you upon a matter of gravest urgency."

"Do not despair!" Before I could turn towards him, Batinsky was at my shoulder. "Life is no less predictable than the printed page. Smooth down your shirt front, Warloch, and prepare for a visitor."

"So you make your deduction," I responded with heavy sarcasm, "because the fish-and-chip shop next door is closed, the boxing club across the way does not cater to females, and because you know the other inhabitants of this building, all in all a sterling lot, are not given to receiving callers at unreasonable hours."

"Very true." Batinsky turned to face the door.

"And next you will be telling me you can ascertain by the weary turn of the lady's head and the languid drift of her skirts that she has traveled a vast distance by means of a milk cart with a broken axle and a horse lame in the near foreleg. . . ."

"She has certainly come from far-off places," he conceded in voice of one humoring a child, holding up a hand to solicit my silence. Before I could raise an eyebrow the door-knocker sounded with a thud, causing the mantel clock to execute a series of jumps. Batinsky and I moved as one, but we were not halfway across the room when the woman walked through the door. Please understand, she did not turn the knob and enter in the prescribed manner. Rather, she passed through that door while it stood closed and barring the way, as was its earthly function.

Her voice was soft and anxious as a child's. "Which of you gentlemen is the Baron Batinsky?"

"I have that misfortune, Madam." My friend executed a low bow, and our visitor advanced upon him, her outstretched hands as transparent as her draperies, her countenance of less substance than her veil. But what she lacked in flesh and blood she more than made up for with the force of her presence. It was not only that she brought with her the dew-washed fragrance of woodland flowers; there was an urgency to her movements that charged the room with the energy of an electrical storm.

"Sir, I am come to you for help." In the heightened glare of the wall lamps, she stood with head bent. "Do not, I beg of you, send me away."

"Allow me instead," Batinsky spoke gently, "to present my colleague, Dr. Warloch."

"I am honored." The lady turned her veils in my direction, and I made the necessary responses even as I began to feel quite grumpy.

Splendid! Here I am, cast in the role of the old duffer who feeds the great detective's intellectual vanity by asking the wrong question at the right time, while he, with all due nobility, basks in the attentions of a woman whose soul is her only attraction. Trying to restrain my irritation, I asked our visitor if she would care for something to drink.

"A glass of brandy, Madam?"

"Thank you"—her voice held a hint of innocent mirth—"but I did not partake of spirits, even before I became one. I will, however, take a seat, and you gentlemen may join me." Whereupon she glided over to the settee, and Batinsky and I availed ourselves of the fireside chairs. "And now you would like me to explain my intrusion on your evening." As she spread her shadow skirts, I became convinced that she had been hardly more than a girl when events brought her to her present pass.

"You have not told us your name." Batinsky—perhaps in contrast to her vaporous form, or possibly because his boredom was deserting him—looked more alive than I had yet seen him.

"Elspeth Sinclair."

"You are"—I could not resist a smug glance at the great detective—"Lady Sinclair?"

"The same."

"Then I remember something of your story," I proclaimed triumphantly. "A dozen serving wenches may come to grief without any fuss being made; but when a lady of your quality meets an untimely end, it is a different matter. Also, the date on which calamity struck your ladyship happens to be of cultural significance to me."

Silencing me with a slight stiffening of his shoulders, Batinsky turned squarely towards our guest. "The suspicion occurred to me when you first appeared, Madam, that death had not come to you in one of its more acceptable forms."

"It was assumed I took my own life, but the cruel truth is that I was murdered." Her voice came in a whisper, even as the rest of her seemed to gain strength, so that the contours of her face were now discernable and her eyes burned through the veil. "Last year on the night of All Hallows' Eve I was thrown from a fourth-story balcony."

"An accidental fall was not considered a possibility, by those involved in the investigation?" I asked.

"The height of the railing ruled out misadventure."

"And you come to me seeking revenge upon your murderer?" Batinsky reached out a hand towards her and as quickly withdrew it.

"No!" Her cry was one of such abject despair that even my tough old heart was touched. "I want you to discover the name of the one who hated me so much that he . . . or she would want me banished from the earth, because not knowing who or why keeps me from my rest . . . were there not an even more compelling reason for the truth to be known."

"You had no enemies?" Batinsky asked.

"None."

"And what of lovers?"

"I had a husband." The mere words breathed life into her, and I saw, or thought I saw, her eyes turn the color of bluebells on a spring morning and her hair blossom into wheaten gold. Hers was the kind of beauty to which I am not usually partial, one enhanced by sweetness of temper and winsome laughter. But I had forcibly to remind myself that I could be her great-great grandfather. And that she was dead.

"Ours was one of those great loves." She was leaning towards Batinsky, her hands fleshing out as she twisted them in bitter hopelessness. "There were many who said our marriage would not work because Justin was twenty years my senior and had not lived a monk's existence before we met. But I never doubted his devotion. He told me again and again, in the most tender and impassioned way, that I had renewed his soul and that without me he was nothing."

What *you* must tell us, Lady Sinclair, I thought, with all my accustomed cynicism, is of those events leading to your unscheduled departure for the other side.

"So you must see I cannot leave Justin in the torment of believing I took my own life," she declared, spectral tears pooling.

"I will help you if I can," promised my friend, offering her his handkerchief.

"And in order that you may do so"—a stifled sob—"you will need as much information as I can provide."

"I would like to know where you were and with whom," came Batinsky's almost dreamy reply, "on the night in question."

"At a masked ball in Chiswick, given by Mrs. Edward Browne."

"Where no doubt a great many of your friends and acquaintances were present."

"I am sure of it, but you must understand we were not only masked but in costume and thus unrecognizable one to the other. And I, for one, had upheld the stricture of the invitation that we keep our disguises secret."

Batinsky did not make the obvious point that Sir Justin must surely have been privy to his wife's costume. Instead he asked, "What did you wear, Lady Sinclair, to this All Hallows' ball?"

Her answer was a moment in coming, and I saw her mouth for the first time, sweetened by the rosiest of smiles. "My husband insisted that I go as Marie Antoinette. He had a yearning to see me in a powdered wig and silk gown of sea green trimmed with forget-me-nots and French lace. What merry times we had that last month! Every fitting was an occasion because Justin made a point of being always present with suggestions—for an alteration, perhaps, to the bodice or more ruching for the skirt. Yet you must not think him a tyrant, for he lavished praise upon the little dressmaker, who entered into the spirit of the thing with her pretty, teasing ways."

"Lady Sinclair," I said, determined not to be backward in coming forward, "did this seamstress have a name?"

"Millie Tanner."

"What Dr. Warloch would intimate"—Batinsky's expression was hidden beneath his hooded eyes—"is that this young woman may, with no malice intended, have discussed your costume with one or another of her clients."

"She was a chatterbox," Lady Sinclair affirmed, yet she sounded doubtful. "Millie had sewn for me once before, and it was as much for the liveliness of her personality as her exceptional talent with the needle that we hired her back. But even if I concede the possibility that she forgot her vow of silence and let her tongue run away with her, it makes no difference, because when I was thrown over that balcony I was not in costume as Marie Antoinette."

"The peasouper thickens," I quipped, the truth being that for once a woman had me under her spell. However, I suspect it was the brooding intensity of Batinsky's silence that encouraged Lady Sinclair to approach the climax of her story.

"It was a night of one vexation after another. While my husband and I were dressing—he was to go as a Versailles dandy—his valet brought him up a letter that had been delivered to the house. Justin would have slipped the envelope into his pocket without opening it, but I insisted it must bear tidings of some urgency to have been sent round at such an hour. And so it proved. After scanning the note, Justin began to pace the floor in great agitation before gathering me up in his arms and begging my understanding. A dear friend, a member of his club, had suffered some misfortune—I do not know of what nature, and am not sure that Justin was clear on that himself—and was summoning him. What could I do but tell him in as cheerful a voice as I could muster that he should go to this friend at once?"

"Did he suggest joining you later at the ball?" Batinsky's eyes appeared to look right through her (which was, of course, entirely possible).

"Yes, but I would not allow myself to hope, for there was no knowing how long he would be detained. And no sooner had I arrived at Mrs. Browne's house than calamity struck again. A villainous-looking pirate, who was about to take his departure, reached for my hand and was bestowing a very hairy kiss upon it when I felt the seam of my gown rip all the way from my underarm to the waist. I made my excuses to my hostess, and would have gone immediately home, but she insisted that I accompany her to the attic where she was certain we could find a costume for me among the trunks. Before her marriage Mrs. Browne was for some years an actress, in musical comedies, I believe, and would seem to have held on to every flower-seller's hat and feather boa she had worn upon the boards."

"Did the good lady remain with you while you picked out a change of costume?" I asked before Batinsky could do so.

"No. She was in haste to return to her other guests. And Mrs. Browne was not an intimate friend of mine. We had met on but two prior occasions. It was Justin who knew her from his bachelor days. Indeed I think it likely there may have been more to their relationship than mere friendship, because at first he had been hesitant to accept the invitation to the ball and then, when I persuaded him, was so lovingly determined that I look my very best.

"Always I assured Justin that what had gone before meant nothing; only the present counted with me. And had I experienced any foreboding when standing in Mrs. Browne's attic that I would within minutes be consigned to the past, I would never have donned the Nell Gwyn costume I found in the first trunk I opened. But, I tell you, my skin did not prickle nor my hair stand on end. Indeed, when lacing up the bodice and abandoning my powdered wig for a mobcap with ringlets attached, I began to see the humor in the situation and think myself peevish for being so put out by one failed evening, when my life was in the main so richly blessed."

"Did you encounter anyone upon leaving the attic?" I inquired. A sound question, but one posed, I must confess, because I was strangely unwilling to take that final walk with Lady Sinclair.

"No one was about when I went down the short flight of stairs to the fourth floor where the ballroom was located. But when I was passing down the corridor something did occur to startle me. I heard a cry—a woman's voice—emanating from one of the bedrooms."

"And you investigated?" Batinsky sat like a wax exhibit in a museum.

"Yes, to my undying . . ."—a sound between a moan and a laugh—"mortification. The room would have been in darkness but for there being a full moon that night, making it possible for me to see the shapes of a pair of lovers upon the bed. I could really tell nothing about the woman, whose hair was loosened upon the pillow, because he was on top of her, his hands upon her neck or shoulders. He did look up when I was backing out the door, and I can scarcely doubt he was as embarrassed as I."

"But he, like you, was masked?" Batinsky asked.

"Yes, along with the added camouflage of some head-covering of dark cloth and a beard to hide his blushes. Once back in the corridor I made every effort to put the incident behind me. I was, after all, a married woman, not a schoolgirl. But, after entering the overheated ballroom and wending my way through the crush of gentlemen in togas and ladies clanging Gypsy tambourines, I felt

254

flushed to the point of faintness and soon escaped through one of the many doors to an anteroom, whose French doors stood invitingly open. I . . . heard footsteps approaching as I went through to the small balcony, but before I could turn, let alone experience the least flutter of panic . . ."—her voice faltered—"I was grabbed from behind and lifted up, like an offering to the gods, and hurled over the iron railing."

The wind stilled, as if it, along with Batinsky and myself, had ceased breathing, and, when I forced myself to meet Lady Sinclair's gaze, the blue had ebbed from her eyes and the gold from her hair. She was, as she had been upon entering my sitting room, but a shadow of her former self.

Gliding up from the sofa in a cobwebby drift of veils, she whispered, "My time is up, Baron Batinsky."

"Dear lady," I intervened, "you must not rush off. Our friend here does not charge by the hour."

Her sigh came as a dying breath. "My strength is all but exhausted. And I fear that this intrusion upon your time has been in vain, for I cannot think I have told you anything to assist you in discovering the identity of my murderer."

Batinsky chose not to exert his fabled power with the fair sex to reassure her; instead, he asked, "Have you been able to make contact with your husband?"

"I see him." Lady Sinclair was fading as we watched. "I see him in all his anguish. I watch him pace the house in the dead of night and I hear him crying out my name. But he does not feel me reach out to comfort him or know that I am there. Imagine, if you can, how he must feel in believing I took my own life. He must doubt his own sanity, for I know he can never doubt my love for him. I beg you, Baron"—she was now reduced to a pair of outstretched shadow hands—"discover who did this to me, so that I and my beloved may know some peace."

"It will be done, Madam."

"I have not spoken to you of payment."

"In giving my thoughts a new direction, my lady, you place me in your debt."

"Tomorrow . . ." Her voice came, soft as a raindrop, from over by the door. "I will come again at this time tomorrow night. Pray

God you will have an answer for me; and may He bless your endeavors, dear Baron."

Before either of us could murmur our adieux, the great detective and I were alone, with only the blank-faced furniture for company. Had it not been for the lingering fragrance of wildflowers, there would have been nothing to suggest we had not conjured up the Lady Sinclair out of our imaginations.

"Tomorrow," I said, pouring myself a liberal glass of port. "You know what day that is, Batinsky!"

"All Hallows' Eve."

"My feast day," I could not forbear reminding him, "and the anniversary of our . . . your client's murder."

"Timeliness is of the essence, my dear Warloch." He roamed the room in so somber a mood that even his shadow would seem to grow nervous.

"You need a drink," I told him.

"Indeed, I do"—his eyes burned into mine—"and something stronger than tomato juice."

"Your wish is my command," I said, deliberately misconstruing. "I will mix it with a splash of vodka and we'll entitle the brew a Bloody Betty . . . or Mary, given your penchant for virgins."

Taking the glass I handed him and downing the contents in a single swallow, Batinsky said, "Her perfume was both delightful and distinctive, was it not?"

"The very essence of the woman."

"It occurs to me"—he resumed his prowling—"that a husband might fail to recognize it on grounds of familiarity, whereas some-one else might well . . . pick up the scent in tracking down his . . . or her prey."

"Irrefutably." I retrieved his glass as it went past me for the fourth time. "But I do not think you should readily dismiss Sir Justin as a suspect. Church bells, Batinsky! There is no denying that when it comes to the human tragedy, the husband is always the most likely culprit."

"I hear you, my dear Warloch." He ceased his perambulations in front of the fireplace, and the clock gave a nervous ping as if asking permission to proceed with chiming the hour.

"But do not think me blind to other possibilities," I said when silence reigned once more, "blessed as I am with an evil mind, I see all the advantages to the hostess of the ball, Mrs. Browne, in removing the wife of her lover."

"Former lover, if we are to believe the lovely Lady Sinclair," countered Batinsky. "And men of Sir Justin's walk of life are not prone to marry their mistresses, who are in the main chosen from the lower orders to dispel those very aspirations."

"You forget." I sat down and planted my hands in the manner of a righteous cleric upon my waistcoat. "You forget that Mrs. Browne had already married up in the world. Her late husband, a Yorkshire mill owner, was no blueblood, it is true, but he was rich to the point of respectability, making it not implausible that his widow might set her sights even higher the second time around."

"What an invaluable source of gossip you are." Batinsky's eyes were darker than the night, and even more adept at concealment.

"One does one's best to live in the real world," I responded mildly. "And I admit the facts speak strongly against Mrs. Browne in that the Nell Gwyn costume came from her store of theatrical finery."

"There is no discounting, for all the emphasis upon the masquerade, that she may have mentioned Lady Sinclair's change of attire to one or other of the guests."

"Most probably to Sir Justin, were he to come looking for his wife," I replied with some complacency. "But in focusing upon him as our villain, do not think I fail to note the implications of Lady Sinclair's entering that bedroom to interrupt a passionate encounter, whose revelation might prove exceedingly awkward for the parties involved. Indeed, it appears to me probable that our unknown gentleman, using the term loosely, may have had sufficient glimpse of her ladyship, alias Nell Gwyn, to track her down."

"But surely murder would seem excessive under the circumstances described."

"Sometimes, Batinsky," I said, "one gets the impression that you have no inkling of how life is lived beyond the confines of your personal twilight zone. If one or both lovebirds were married and liable to be cut off without a shilling, or the male speared in a duel upon discovery, I can perceive murder to be a viable alternative."

"Your reasoning, my dear Warloch, puts me to shame." So saying, the great man paced over to the window, where he stood pleating the curtains between his bone-white fingers.

"And, pray tell"—a smirk tugged at my lips—"what are your deductions, oh Master Mind?"

"That the Lady Sinclair was a woman born to be loved."

Such were his pearls of wisdom! The man did wonders for my fragile ego, and I began to see the advantages of having him for a guest, if not as a private detective, were I ever to find myself in dire straits. After several moments of silence, I said, in hope of encouraging him to more cerebral endeavors, "It is certainly a case one can sink one's teeth into." Upon receiving no reply, I heaved out of my chair and with a pettish clanking of glass to bottle replenished our drinks.

Batinsky bestirred himself to offer a toast. "To our first client, my friend!" Encouraging. I allowed myself to hope that we would spend the rest of the night wrapping up the affair of The Veiled Lady, but it was not to be. He immediately left the room and did not reappear, leading me to the annoying conclusion that he was hiding out in the mahogany-enclosed tub until I should be driven to my bed. Being the softhearted old codger that I am, I could readily understand his embarrassment at failing to come up a brilliant solution to the case, but I resented having to make my ablutions in the little watering hole off my dressing room. It was enough of a sacrifice to do so during the day, but if Batinsky was about to make the bathroom his night quarters, as well, I could see the need to suggest he look into taking up residence elsewhere. It was in a grim mood that I eventually retired.

Shortly before noon the next day I was met by my secretary, who was exiting the bathroom. It was irksome to be forced to speak up for my troublesome guest, but I girded my dressing-gown cords about me and did my duty.

"Miss Flittermouse, I trust you did not disturb Baron Batinsky."

" 'Course I didn't." She batted her eyes at me and raked her six-inch fingernails through her tar-black hair. "To be honest, I'd quite forgot about him when I went in to wash me hands, but it makes no matter because he weren't there."

"Weren't . . . wasn't in the bath?"

"You've got it, guv'ner." Startled by my bewilderment, she scuttled for the sitting room, all the while flapping her arms as if in some futile attempt to get airborne. To the accompaniment of a crescendo being played upon the typewriter keys, I flung open the bathroom door to see for myself . . . that Batinsky wasn't there.

Not to panic, I told myself. I should take it as a promising sign that he had overcome his aversion to daylight and ventured out, perhaps for a stroll in the park. Determined to look on the bright side—and indeed there was no escaping the sun which, in defiance of the time of year, streamed ruthlessly through the windows—I drank several cups of coffee before beginning the day's dictation of my memoirs. As the hours passed, however, and Batinsky did not return, I experienced a growing alarm.

For all I knew he could have left the flat by way of the bathroom window in the middle of the night while I was still up. No one, I think, could accuse me of being a man of conscience, but my own people have been subjected to sufficient persecution over the years that I may have become a little squeamish in my old age. The thought that Batinsky might even now be sleeping off the effects of his bloodthirsty debauchery did not sit well with my luncheon. When the afternoon was over I found myself thinking that I might have done more to aid his rehabilitation. For instance, I could have suggested he meet on a weekly basis with Miss Flittermouse and others battling their particular addiction, in an atmosphere of support and fellowship.

At six o'clock my secretary placed the cover over her typewriter and vanished from the scene, leaving me to the doubtful companionship of the decanters. The prospect of facing Lady Sinclair, alone, and without the information she sought, made me feel remarkably low. I was, however, becoming resigned to my fate, when the outer door opened and Batinsky walked into the sitting room, for all the world as if he had just been out to buy a newsppaer.

"So it's you!" I sank lower in my chair, sounding very much like a shrewish wife.

"My dear Warloch." He stood unbuttoning and rebuttoning his cape with black-gloved hands. "I trust my absence did not cause you any alarm."

"You might have left a note."

"Don't pout, Warloch." A smile touched his lips. "My kind is not easily civilized, but I promise," he avowed humbly, "another time I will be more thoughtful."

"Then we will say no more on the subject."

"You must not let me off so easily." His eyes glittered with an emotion I could not read, in a face white as the walls. "And I must relieve your mind of any fears that I have suffered a relapse. The truth is I have been out and about on legitimate business, in the course of which I was able to confirm that the woman is dead."

At once my concern for his mental health reasserted itself. But before I could remind him that Lady Sinclair's state of being had never been at issue, he produced my cloak from the armoir and informed me we were going out.

"Make haste, my friend! We are off to pay a call on Mrs. Edward Browne."

"But what of . . ."

"We will be back in time to receive Lady Sinclair." Batinsky clapped my hat upon my head, draped a silk scarf about my neck, and hurried me out the door and down several flights of stairs to the pavement where he faced me under the glare of the street lamps. "It is my understanding that Mrs. Browne tonight is hosting her annual masquerade ball, an occasion not to be missed, do you not agree, Warloch?"

"Indeed!" I spoke to his back, for he was already heading past the shuttered shops and bleary-eyed dwellings towards the cross-road, his cape billowing out behind him and his feet appearing to glide at least two inches off the ground. Before I reached the corner a cab had already drawn up alongside him, whether or not of the driver's own volition I cannot say. Batinsky issued the required address to the driver, whose eyes looked ready to bolt out of his head.

"We are on our way to a fancy dress do," I said.

"Ah, that explains it!" the man replied in vast relief. "Hop aboard! And don't neither of you get any ideas of putting a hex on me if the traffic is bad and I don't make good time!" His laughter rumbled away under the turning of the wheels.

The moon poked her pale face through the window but there was little to see and nothing to hear. Batinsky did not speak a word during the short journey to the Browne residence, and by the rigidity of his posture he prevailed upon me to maintain the silence.

Upon alighting from the cab, we found ourselves facing a broad flight of marble steps leading up to what would appear from its onion domes and curlicue spires to be a tomb all in an Arabian night's work. Batinsky had barely laid a hand upon the knocker when the red lacquered door inched open with a sound like a spent sigh.

We found ourselves looking in upon a gilded cage, where flocked all manner of birds of paradise. Indeed there must have been a hundred people in the hall, whose circular walls soared two stories high to a ceiling painted with cavorting nymphs and shepherds. Immediately before us, in the light dripping from a chandelier whose spangles might have been clipped from an exotic dancer's costume, stood a plumply pretty dairymaid with very red hair and an expectant smile on her painted lips.

"Mrs. Edward Browne?" My companion raised his voice above the crowd, and her hand to his bloodless lips. "I am the Baron Batinsky and this"—a nod in my direction—"is Dr. Warloch."

"Charmed, I'm sure!" Our hostess watched in fascinated confusion as we stepped over the threshold and the door swung silently shut behind us. "You must be nice lads," she rallied, "and not mind me not recognizing you, for when all's said and done—that's the whole point of a costume party, isn't it? And your disguises are ever so good, even though you're being naughty and not wearing your masks. I'm the only one who gets to show me face round here."

She poked a finger at Batinsky's chest. "But don't think I'll be too hard on you, 'cos if I was to meet you in some dark alley, you'd scare the living daylights out of me."

"You'd have no call to worry, Madam." I made my bow. "He is in recovery."

"Now, if that don't ease my mind!" Mrs. Browne appeared not to know if she was on her head or her heels, which was hardly surprising since around her the masked figures wove in and out, as if in step to the formation of some vast minuet.

"My dear lady," Batinsky said, "your memory does not fail you. Neither Dr. Warloch nor myself was on your guest list."

"Well, we always have some of that, don't we—people barging in uninvited?" Eyes suddenly hostile, hands on her ample hips, she looked us up and down. "I never used to bother about it; but after what happened last year there's a new set of rules. People may say the lady killed herself, but who knows? So if it's all the same with you, then, I'll be showing you a shortcut to the door."

"It is on account of Lady Sinclair's unhappy demise that my colleague and I are here tonight." Batinsky fixed her with his compelling gaze. "We are private detectives employed by a client, whose name we are not free to divulge, to ascertain what really happened upon that balcony one year ago this day."

"Well, I never!" Mrs. Browne clapped her hands to her rouged cheeks. "So that's the way the wind blows! Someone thinks the lovely Elspeth didn't take matters into her own hands. And now you want me to escort you to the scene of the crime, is that it?" Without waiting for an answer she plowed through the crowd at the foot of the stairs and beckoned for us to follow her.

Up she went, always three steps ahead of us, her skirts bunched in her hands, her words rattling down upon our heads. "I was downstairs this time last year, right where we was just standing, when I heard that scream what made my blood run cold. I tried to get up the stairs, but it was jammed with people not knowing whether they was coming or going, and when I almost saw my way clear—down came some poor pirate (we always have a lot of pirates) with a swooning female in his arms. Seems she'd been overcome by the heat of the ballroom—as if I can help it getting stuffy up there!" Mrs. Browne nipped around the bend in the staircase, her feet keeping pace with her words. "It's a tragedy whatever way you slice it. Still, I must say I'd feel better knowing Elspeth Sinclair didn't take her own life."

"I have it from an unimpeachable source that she did not," Batinsky replied.

"Well, tell that to Sir Justin! Word is that he's scarcely left the house in a year. And his butler turns everyone away from the door. I went round several times myself but it weren't no use. . . ."

"Was the suggestion ever made," I queried, panting, "that he might have been responsible for her death?"

"Not as I heard. And anyway, why would he want to do away

with her? She was young, beautiful, and didn't have any money of her own to speak of."

Spoken like a devoted mistress, former or otherwise, I thought sourly. My disposition is never improved by exercise better suited to a mountain goat, but, happily for my creaking joints, we had by now reached the fourth floor.

Proceeding down a broad corridor hung with portraits of bogus ancestors to a set of double doors, we found ourselves at the entry to the ballroom. The musicians on the dais were, at that moment, resting their instruments, but I doubt a full orchestra could have heard itself above the babble. The room was as congested with humanity as the hall had been. Curses! I unavoidably stepped on the toes of Lord Nelson and was forced to make my apologies for elbowing aside a lady from the court of Queen Elizabeth before we came to a door providing escape. It is possible that my wits had gone begging, but I gave not a passing thought to our hostess as a prime suspect in the case.

"Here we are, lads!" Mrs. Browne stepped aside to let us enter but did not follow us into the anteroom. It contained a scattering of chairs and had curtains looped aside to reveal French doors giving onto a semicircular balcony.

"What now, Batinsky?" I asked, with an attempt at nonchalance. Blame it on the stresses of the day, but my usual delight in the macabre had deserted me, and I found myself attempting to admire the paintings upon the walls. For that reason I did not see the gentleman, sans mask and unimaginatively suited in evening dress, until he materialized ten feet from the backdrop of glass panes.

"Sir Justin Sinclair, I presume?" Batinsky arched a black eyebrow and, upon receiving no reply but a blind stare, continued in his most expressionless voice: "I am come to tell you that your wife was murdered."

"Do you think that I of all people need to be told that Elspeth did not take her own life?" The words came as if wrenched from the very soul of the man, and I found myself stirred to an unlikely pity when looking into that ravaged face. Once upon a time, he must have combined remarkable good looks with a well-nigh irresistible charm, but he was now an empty shell, a creature beyond hope of heaven or hell. As to whether or not Mrs. Browne had known of his presence, who can say? Women, for me, will always retain an element of mystery.

"You think me some avenging angel." Batinsky smiled grimly at the thought. "But there is no call for alarm, sir; my client wishes only your peace of mind."

"Who sends you?" The words were a hoarse cry.

"Your wife."

"That cannot be!" Sir Justin staggered backwards.

"Cannot be—because she is dead, or because you are the one who killed her?"

Here it was, the moment when self-congratulation was in order, for most assuredly I had led Batinsky to this conclusion. So how was it, then, that I wanted only to be home in my own armchair, drinking the first of several glasses of port?

"I loved her!"

"I believe you." Batinsky walked forwards until he stood only a scant few feet from his quarry. "Lady Sinclair described the love between the two of you as one of the grand passions. But, being the man you are, that did not prevent your enjoying a frolic with Millie Tanner, the seamstress who came to sew Lady Sinclair's costume for the masquerade ball. She had worked for your wife once or twice before, and this time you contrived to be present at every sitting, turning the girl's head with your blandishments. A harmless diversion in your mind, no doubt, but on the night of the ball she sent you a letter . . ."

"She demanded that I meet her within the hour, or she would go to Elspeth and inform her of our liaison." Sir Justin covered his face with his hands.

"I first suspected Miss Tanner's involvement," Batinsky said, "when I learned that the seam of Lady Sinclair's costume ripped apart within moments of her entering this house. An inexperienced needlewoman might be given to such lapses, but surely not a sea-soned dressmaker! I recalled your pocketing the note when it was delivered and only reading it when pressed to do so by Lady Sinclair. The whole business smacked of the surreptitious. But, tell me, how did Millie conduct herself at your rendezvous? Was she amenable to being fobbed off with a few pounds a week in return for her silence?"

"She wept, and said she was sorry for causing me embarrassment. I believed her assurances that there would be no future difficulties."

"With what a light heart you must have arrived at this house, Sir Justin," Batinsky remarked, as if making polite conversation. "And what a stroke of good fortune it must have seemed when you encountered one of the guests, dressed as a pirate, heading down the house steps as you were about to mount to the front door. You had not your valet with you to assist you into your costume, but I am sure you managed the bushy beard and head scarf without undue difficulty. Your mask in place, you must have believed the evening a success and your marriage secure, until you discovered that Millie had followed you into the house. A most enterprising young lady, although, according to Mrs. Browne, others have achieved the same feat."

"I panicked," Sir Justin said drearily.

"So you took the girl up to one of the bedrooms and strangled her." Batinsky pressed on. "And when a woman dressed as Nell Gwyn pushed open the door, you had no way of knowing that she was your wife, or that she thought herself to be witnessing not a deathbed scene but a pair of lovers sharing a moment of passion. So you followed her from the room, and the very familiarity of her fragrance was against you: no warning sounded as you caught up with her upon the balcony and hurled her down four stories to the pavement. Still unknowing, you returned to the bedroom for your first victim and carried her down the stairs, informing passersby that the girl had just swooned from the heat."

Locating my voice at last, I said, "I am to understand, Batinsky, that when you spoke to me this evening of having confirmed upon investigation that the woman was dead, you were speaking of Millie Tanner."

"Who else, my dear Warloch?"

"Elspeth would have forgiven my involvement with Millie"— Sir Justin lifted his hands as if to ward off the awfulness of memory—"but I could not conceive of causing her such pain."

"I believe you," Batinsky told him, "and you may believe me that she loves you still."

"You said"—the words came in a strangled blend of bewilderment and hope—"that she sent you. Oh, if that were but true! For I would have you know that since that night a year ago I have been one of the living dead." He turned from us on the last word, and while Batinsky and I stood like two statues anchored in several feet of concrete, he walked slowly through the French doors, climbed onto the balcony railing, stood upright for a moment arms spread wide, and then leaped into night.

From the ballroom behind us came the soft strains of a Viennese waltz and from the street below the beginnings of pandemonium. "Time to go home." In a rare attempt at intimacy I reached out a hand and placed it on Batinsky's shoulder. "We must not keep Lady Sinclair waiting."

"She will not keep the appointment." He moved away from me to stand staring out at the sky, from which the moon had hidden her face, and all the stars had disappeared—as if they were hand-held candles blown out by the wind.

"You are no doubt correct," I said. "But keep in mind that there will be other cases, other clients."

"But none"—he spoke in a voice of utmost wistfulness—"quite like the late lamented Lady Sinclair; she must, I think, have had a lovely neck."

Dorothy Cannell's *comic novels of crime and mystery include* The Thin Woman, The Widows Club, *and* How to Murder Your Mother-in-Law, *all featuring the engaging amateur sleuth Ellie Haskell.*

NIGHT OF THE GOBLIN

BY TALMAGE POWELL

Here's another pointed tale in which a child,
stretched to the breaking point, feels compelled to
take adult matters into his own small hands. The
Halloween setting, naturally, is crucial to the plot's
machinery, not only because a night of masks makes
a perfect cover for any suspicious activity, but because it's also a time of relative freedom from
rules—when, for example, accepting candy from
strangers is considered entirely appropriate. And little Bobby instinctively understands that all he need
do to accomplish his goal is to tap into the fears that
are already in place around him.

Encouraging paranoia: It's child's play, really.

Night of the Goblin

Bobby palmed the packet of razor blades and dropped his hand in his pocket as he sidled on toward the candy racks. It was the first time in his eight years he'd stolen anything, and he had the sudden sickening expectancy of sirens and flashing lights.

He dawdled at the tier of small bins holding candy bars while the feverish upsurge of guilty sweat cooled on his forehead. Two other people were in the neighborhood convenience store, a woman paying for a bottle of milk and loaf of bread, and Mr. Pepper, the pleasant old man who clerked in the store.

As the woman went out, Bobby chose a Karmel King, crossed to the counter, and dropped a coin from his damp palm.

"Hi, young fella!" Mr. Pepper, as always, had a warm smile for Bobby. Sometimes, when traffic was slow, they would chat while Bobby sipped a soda pop. The old man seemed forever fascinated, delighted, bemused by Bobby's wit, intelligence, and scope of knowledge. Kids nowadays . . . smarter than scientists used to be . . . weaned on moon walks, fourth dimensions, space warps, atomic fission, computers, TV classrooms, nuclear bombs . . . Saganian witchcraft . . .

Bobby supposed that Mr. Pepper had to work because his social security wouldn't keep up with inflation. He wondered what it was like to be old.

"Guess you'll go trick-or-treat tonight, Bobby."

Bobby nodded, his throat a bit dry. With the razor blades in his pocket, he didn't want to linger in the tall gray presence.

"Halloween ain't what it used to be." Mr. Pepper held Bobby's Karmel King in one hand, Bobby's coin in the other. "When I was a boy Halloween was a kind of street carnival, folks dressing up like spooks and pirates and swarming through the streets of old downtown. You might get your face throwed full of flour, or have somebody drop a paper sack full of water on your head from an upstairs window. Merchants got their store windows all soaped over, and if you didn't take the swing off the front porch you might find it atop a lamppost next morning. It was a night for turning over outhouses and letting the air out of tin lizzie tires—but there weren't the creeps around to drug or poison the stuff dropped in a little child's trick-or-treat sack."

"Please, sir . . . You don't have to bother putting my Karmel King in a bag." Bobby took the candy bar, and fled.

Jethro "Jet" Simmons, lead guitar with the rock group Iceberg, lately employed six nights at the Asphalt Cowboy Disco, slouched in the recliner and watched the quarterback keep the ball on an option play. The TV commentator explained that it was an option play with the quarterback keeping the ball, which brought a sneer to Jet's thin lips. Bunch of dumb creeps, those sports announcers.

"Hey, Judy," he yelled, dropping the empty beer can on the chairside table, "make with a brew."

"I just brought you the last one from the fridge," Judy Clark called from a bedroom.

"Be a kitten," Jet called back, "and get us a six-pack. The goons are right in the middle of the second quarter."

Judy appeared in the inner doorway of the small living–dining room. "And I'm up to my elbows in black crepe paper, trying to fashion some sort of little-old-man suit, pants and jacket yet, to hang together for one evening."

In their deep sockets, Jet's moody eyes frosted. "Why the hell can't the kid put on a bedsheet and be a ghost, like any normal kid? All this crap about turning into a gnome, a goblin for Halloween . . ."

"His heart's set on it, Jet. You know kids at Bobby's age. Things that don't matter to grown-ups can be terribly important to them. He's a good boy, and Halloween is only one night out of the year. Is it asking so much?"

Who wants to know kids, Jet asked himself tightly, especially the brat by her ex-husband that Judy should have aborted the day after she missed her period. Little fink. No tantrums. No open challenges. Just that glint of wisdom and hatred Jet sometimes caught in the bright brown eyes.

But two can play that game, brat. Pretense and smiles.

While the quarterback threw an incomplete forward pass, Jet stretched, yawned, stood up. He was tall, lean, pantherishly muscled, with a rawboned face framed in shoulder-length waves of glossy brown. He washed his hair at least once a day and enjoyed drying and brushing it out. He was equally vain of the flatness of his belly, the leanness of hips in his brushed denims, the biceps that bulged the short sleeves of his black knitted shirt.

"Grab a six-pack at the convenience store during the halftime break," Judy suggested. Trim, attractive, the emerald softness of her eyes highlighted by the deep auburn of her hair, she worked five days a week as a respiratory therapist in the huge hospital nearby. Robert, her husband, had walked out three years ago. ("Sorry, nothing personal, Judy; just up to here with the marriage bit. You can tell Bobby I went off to the wars, or something.") Great for the ego. She hadn't heard from Robert since.

"And while you're buying the beer," Judy added, "pick up a Karmel King candy bar. It's Bobby's favorite, and it would be nice if you dropped it into his trick-or-treat bag yourself, Jet."

Her gaze lingered on the closed door after Jet went out. He had moved into the apartment across the hall two months ago. They'd met a week later, coming into the building, and a thing had quickly developed. Last week Jet had carried his personal belongings, guitar and amplifier, clothing, stereo, tennis racket, barbells across the corridor into her apartment.

Even though the arrangement was acceptable nowadays, Judy had suffered a twinge of conscience, due to a somewhat old-fashioned upbringing and her deep love for Bobby.

A block away, Ed Travis walked into his kitchen. In paint-splotched work pants and T-shirt, he had worked up a steamy sweat even though October was closing on a crisp autumn note. He yanked a paper towel from the holder beside the sink and mopped his craggy face. He was a big, powerful man, feline in his movements in the way of a leopard. A plainclothes detective, he was devoting several off-duty hours to wedge and sledge, bursting down to wood-stove size the sawn circular sections of oak tree trunk piled in his backyard. Wheelbarrow load at a time, he was stacking the firewood neatly alongside the garage. Piecemealing the job over the next few weeks he'd have plenty for the winter, and the fuel oil dealer could spit in the tank.

Blond and slender, so very perfect for his dark heft, Marian was at the kitchen table arranging the punch-bowl set as a centerpiece for the trays of Halloween cookies. She glanced over her shoulder, smiling. "I'll bet I know someone who could use something tall and cool and wet."

Marian turned toward the refrigerator, poured an iced-tea glass almost full of orange juice, leaving room for a couple of ice cubes and a half-inch of sour mash whiskey.

She handed Ed the finished drink, and he sank onto a kitchen chair with a pleasantly tired grunt. He took a long pull and exhaled gustily. "Now, that's a drink for the old woodsman!"

"How's it going?"

"Fine. About another half-cord cut and stacked today. Guess I'll knock off. Have a good, hot bathtub and get ready for dinner. Potluck?"

"You know it."

Ed looked at the homemade cookies iced in greens, oranges, blacks. He wondered if he could get away with eating a couple of the little chocolate jack-o'-lanterns? Probably. But Marian had the trays so beautifully arranged. He let his stomach rumble, unrequited.

"How many kids you taking trick-or-treat?"

Marian shrugged. "All that show up by seven-thirty. Esther and I invited the eight close by."

"Probably have a dozen," Travis said. "More the merrier. I got some extra-nice red Delicious for the apple dunking when you bring them back here for the party."

"Ed," Marian said, turning to fill the coffee maker, "why the hell don't you give in and eat some jack-o'-lanterns? Plenty more over there on the sideboard."

"You ought to be a parole officer," he said, reaching. "Head off a lot of trouble, way you read impulses in the criminal mind."

"One for me, too," Esther squealed from the doorway. She flashed across the room, climbed up on him, plopped against him. Five years old, her daddy's dark coloration was in her large, happy eyes and hair that lay in soft ringlets. The rest of her, the grace of limb and lovely piquancy of face, was sheer Marian. Ed's heart jumped pleasurably every time he looked at her. If the depth of feeling was a little unmanly, the hell with manliness.

"Cookie yourself," Ed said. "Take a bite out of you!"

He growled ferociously, and Esther wriggled, giggling in delight. They tussled and brawled, Ed tickling her ribs and nibbling the back of her tiny neck while she writhed and filled the kitchen with her laughter, and Marian tossed a fond smile their way.

Finally, Esther fell back against his massive arm, looking up at him, gasping through parted lips. "Daddy, I laughed so hard I almost went t-t in my pants!"

"Well, I'm glad you didn't. Very unladylike. You know, Mama's been so busy doing for this party, why don't we do something for her?"

Esther half raised. "What, Daddy?"

"Go to the fried chicken place and bring back a barrel for dinner. Like a party of our own."

Bobby cleared a spot on the small table in his room by setting his microscope and a box of parts for a half-finished model temporarily on the floor. He turned on a gooseneck lamp and laid the Karmel King, purchased, and the razor blades, stolen, in the glare.

He tried not to think of the way he'd gotten the blades, while he sat in a straight wooden chair and pulled himself hard against the edge of the table. He picked up the dime store magnifying glass normally used to examine used postage stamps purchased, when affordable, from a dealer's penny-nickle-dime barrel. He laid the Karmel King with the lettered topside of the wrapper against the table, and studied for a moment the way the gold and tan wrapper was folded and sealed.

One of Mommy's old tweezers, stamp tongs, lay beside a perf gauge, amid a clutter, orderly to its owner, of stamp sheets, science fiction comic books, and experiments with a little rubber-type printing machine.

Carefully he inserted a tweezer tine under the imperfectly joined folds in the candy bar wrapper. Lower lip pressed between his teeth, he applied gentle pressure. The fold popped loose. Bobby drew a long breath before attacking the wrapper further.

In a few moments, he had opened the wrapper without marring it with a single tear. The Karmel King lay exposed, dark and naked in its skin of chocolate.

He rested briefly; then he picked up the candy with one hand, a razor blade in the other. Face set in intense concentration, he started at a corner and made a thin cut around the thinner perimeter of the candy bar, along the sides and across the ends. Gently. The chocolate must not chip. The cut must be even and straight.

He repeated the cut, deepening the surgery. The Karmel King came apart in two perfect layers. He eased them onto the table, top and bottom, insides facing the ceiling.

Breathing through his mouth, he cuffed sweat from his forehead with the back of his hand. So far, perfect. Once the halves were rejoined into a whole candy bar, the perimeter cut could easily be wiped away with a careful stroking of a warm thumb along the chocolate surface. Then back into the undamaged wrapper . . . cautiously preserving the original folds . . . a touch of model airplane glue to reseal . . . And no one could tell by looking at the candy bar that it hadn't just come from the factory.

But before that, prior to the restoration, came the part that Bobby dreaded most.

He set his teeth, snapped his head in a shake, and rummaged his needle-nosed pliers from among the tools in the table drawer—

wood carving set, small ball peen hammer, screwdriver, jack-knife.

He slipped the remaining razor blades from their plastic casing one by one onto the tabletop. With the pliers he broke a blade in half, lengthwise, then into shorter pieces. He embedded a piece vertically into the bottom half of the Karmel King . . . then another . . . another . . . another . . . working tirelessly while the supply of blades dwindled.

"Bubble, bubble, toil, and trouble," Ed Travis boomed, flinging open the front door, peering through the eyeholes of a Frankenstein monster mask. "What have we here? A witch with an expired broomstick license and her scary helpers with loaded trick-or-treat sacks."

Eight assorted miniature beings from Star Wars, Brothers Grimm, and other folklore trooped into the Travis living room, where a paper donkey was hung for the tail-pinning, an armada of apples floated in an old-time washtub, a white crepe-paper ghost danced in midair, a candle inside a jack-o'-lantern cut from a real pumpkin shed unreal light and shadows.

There was Timmy Brock as R2D2, little Cara Norman beneath a skeleton costume, Bucky Steadman an obvious Rip Van Winkle, Laurie Jameson as a witch, Junior Roberts a cowboy without his hi-yo Silver. Ed's own Esther was a black kitty cat, and Bobby Clark had to be, Ed supposed, a gnome in the little-old-man black outfit, wrinkles eyebrow-penciled on his face, a knotted top from a nylon stocking tightly capped on his head to give him the bald look. Chaperoning the group on the trick-or-treat trek, Marian had ventured forth in a commonplace pants suit.

She closed the door as the final child scurried in, looked at Ed's mask, and nodded approval. "Quite an improvement."

"Thought you'd like it," Ed said. He slipped the mask off, turned toward the room. "Okay, kids . . ."

Ed looked at Marian and grinned. The witching hour creatures scattered about the Travis living room, more interested in treasure troves right now than in anything Esther's papa had to say. They peered into trick-or-treat sacks, plunged in their hands, rummaged, popped candies and gum in their mouths.

"Mr. Travis?" said the goblin.

"Yes, Bobby?"

"I've a Karmel King!"

"Great!" Ed smiled at the expression on the gnome face.

Bobby reached up, holding the candy bar. "I would like to share it with Esther."

"Bobby, I'm sure she has more than . . ."

"Please, sir. My treat. You and Mrs. Travis and Esther are so nice . . . this party and all . . ."

The small, extended hand was insistent. Ed laughed. "Sure, Mr. Goblin, I know what you mean."

Ed took the Karmel King and peeled off the wrapper.

"If you break it a little lopsided," the goblin said, "you may give Esther the big half."

Holding the Karmel King between thumbs and fingers, Ed applied mild pressure to pull the semisoft bar apart. Suddenly he yelped, jerking his finger hand free. He stared at the bright, seeping redness on his left thumb, a glowing ruby of blood. The thought seemed foolish, unreal: the candy bar had cut him.

He whirled toward an occasional table and turned on a lamp. In the spill of light, he stretched, pulled, separating the Karmel King carefully. Frowning, Marian stepped to his side. "What is it, Ed?"

He looked up, his face itself a white, vicious Halloween mask. "Razor blades . . . the damned candy . . . Marian, somewhere along the trick-or-treat route we've got an absolute sonofabitch! Bobby!"

"Yes, sir?" said the gnome, suddenly bewildered, frightened.

Ed bent his knees to put himself on eye-level. "Have you any idea where you got the Karmel King? Which house, apartment? Who?"

"Yes, sir," Bobby said. "Jet gave it to me."

"Jet?"

"Jethro Simmons, Mr. Travis. He's Mommy's boyfriend."

"I see . . . Bobby, this is very important. You mustn't make a mistake. Are you absolutely sure he gave you the Karmel King?"

"You can ask Mrs. Travis," Bobby said. "Jet said, 'Here is your favorite,' and handed me the Karmel King." It was the moment of crisis, showdown, and Bobby was sweating lightly. His mind sparked with the memory of covertly dropping Jet's Karmel King in a street gutter and slipping the candy he'd prepared into his trick-or-treat bag.

"That's right, Ed," Marian said tightly. "Bobby is telling the truth."

"Is that the only Karmel King in your bag?" Ed asked, his detective's mind covering all details.

"Yes, sir, I'm sure it is. But you can look."

Ed spilled the contents of the bag on the table; candy kisses, bubble gums, an apple, cookies, and lollipops.

Ed lifted his stony eyes. "Marian, get me a piece of aluminum foil to wrap this candy in." He glanced about the room. "Sorry . . . it was to be such a fine party. . . . Well, they can still have the games and refreshments. Gather up every bit of this trick-or-treat stuff . . . I'm going back on duty as of now. . . ."

Bobby lay in the silence of his room looking at the softness of moonlight framed in his window. He shifted on his mattress, thinking of the way Mr. Travis had looked as he'd phoned police headquarters and left the house. Wow! Bobby sure wouldn't want Mr. Travis coming after *him* with that kind of look on his face!

But it was all right. Everything had worked out okay. Aside from the little cut on Mr. Travis's thumb, nobody had got hurt, and it was okay. A goblin's goal is to protect his treasure, and the treasure was safe. Mama was upset, of course, but she would shape up. Grown-ups got over things almost as well as kids.

It was real nice to have Mama alone in the very next room once more.

A splintery, thudding sound from outside caused Bobby to rear upright. He swung his bare feet from the bed and padded to the window.

In the driveway just below lay the ruins of Jet's stereo. A dark, lumpish shadow swooped out and down, falling beside the stereo. Jet's clothing. Mama had opened the window and was throwing all of Jet's things out.

When the guitar hit the driveway cement, it emitted a skirling discord, a ghostly note exactly right for a Halloween midnight.

Talmage Powell *began his career as a writer for the pulps in the 1940s, publishing in magazines with names like* Crack Detective *and* Dime Mystery. *He has continued to be prolific ever since, concentrating for over thirty years on short mystery fiction with an output that nearly rivals that of Ed Hoch. In the early 1960s he produced a five-book series of paperback originals featuring Tampa private eye Ed Rivers; these include* The Girl's Number Doesn't Answer *and* Start Screaming Murder.

TRICK-OR-TREAT

BY ANTHONY BOUCHER

Murder comes in many shapes and sizes and it makes its most successful appearances when it catches its victims unawares. In this tale of a missing witness and a timeless motive, Anthony Boucher delights in misdirecting our attention. But one thing he forces us to look at closely is the awkward finality of sudden death. For all its studied strangeness, Halloween is also a time of well-orchestrated comings and goings and, when this familiar rhythm is interrupted by violence, it truly is obscene, much like a skeleton at a banquet. This is, in fact, quite a hard-boiled story, with a murder sequence that's as taut and tough as hangman's rope.

TRICK-OR-TREAT

The radio said, "So remember, folks: murder, though it has no tongue, will speak." A deep voice on a filter mike echoed it horribly: *"Murder—will—speak!"* Then the electric organ music came up loud.

Ben Flaxner clicked the switch. He said, "That's a cheerful thought," and the outside corner of his left eye began to twitch again.

Rose looked up from mending her pink housecoat. "I don't see why you've got to keep listening to stuff like that. As if it wasn't bad enough to be living in this dump with your nerves all shot and—"

She broke off and gasped, "Oh!" as a terribly twisted face goggled leeringly at the glass in the window. The doorbell rang and Ben jumped. Then he saw the face and grinned. "Kids," he said.

He answered the door and a high voice outside on the sidewalk said, "Trick or treat!"

Ben laughed. "You kids got you a good racket. A shakedown, we used to call it back in—" He glanced back at Rose and stopped the sentence.

"Trick or treat!" the voice repeated.

"Treat," Ben said. He went across to the kitchen, which was a

281

part of the same room as the living room, and the bedroom too, for that matter. He came back with a double handful of hard candy.

Ben grinned as he shut the door. "Sometime I'll have to hold out on 'em," he said. "I'd like to see what they do for a trick. Usually they soap the windows, and with ours all soaped up already—"

"That's it," Rose snapped. "Remind me!" In repose her features were pretty, especially if she remembered all her makeup. Now they looked sharp and tight and a lot older. "Remind me I've got to live here in one little room with you *and* your brother, and it isn't even a room. A store, facing right on the street, where you've got to soap the windows so the customers won't look in and think you're an ad for tomato juice!"

Ben spoke a little slower even than usual. "Look, baby! Where's there a safer place to hole up? Berkeley's full of transients now— defense workers, service families. Nobody keeps an eye on strangers; there's too many of 'em. With Joe already working here, it was a natural."

"For how long?" Rose flared up.

Ben said, "So long as the heat is on."

"The cops couldn't pin it on you," she said.

Ben waved a big fist vaguely. "Yeah, but—"

The doorbell rang again. Ben's body jerked and his hand moved toward his hip. Then he relaxed, seeing another masked face.

He opened the door and heard "Trick or treat!" and went through all the routine again. When it was over, he fetched out a fifth and showed it to Rose. She shook her head and sat sullen. He poured himself a slug and held it up and said, "Here's to Halloween." He downed it and gasped. "I got to make some good contacts out here. This stuff . . . Rrrrr!"

"You won't make contacts sitting in here all day scared of your shadow."

He didn't hear her. "But damned if I don't like Halloween. I remember when Joe and me was kids. We used to have us a time, all right. And sometimes I think maybe that's what got me started— trick or treat. You walk up to some dope and you tell him '. . . or else!' It's all the same . . . Come on, honey, just one snort? For Halloween?"

"You couldn't get me something hot on that radio, could you? Or does it just play murders?"

The doorbell rang again, and Ben grinned happily at the little sheeted, masked figure outside. Rose groaned, and got up and fiddled with the dial herself. She heard Ben open the door and she heard the little voice say, "Trick or treat!" Then she heard the shots. When she turned, all she could see was a wisp of white sheet whisking away in the darkness, and Ben squatting there on the floor, holding his stomach with both hands.

He started to roll over backward as she reached him. Somehow it seemed very important to hold him up. Men aren't dead till they're stretched out. His lips were making noises, but there was a choking rattle in his throat that kept the lip noises from being words. Rose knelt there beside him, propping him up, and the tear she'd just mended ripped open again with the tension on her housecoat where she was kneeling on it, but with all that blood you could never clean it, anyway.

She thought silly thoughts like that because you can't think: He's dying here in my arms and the last words I said to him were mean. Then there weren't any more lip noises and she let go. But the body didn't just keel over backward. She'd been holding it somehow off balance and it started to topple toward her. She screamed one short, sharp, high scream and pushed at it. This time it did go over backward. She screamed again, and then after a while it seemed that screaming was all she could do—ever.

A key clicked, the door opened, and Joe was standing there. He slapped her face and said, "What do you want to do? Bring the whole street in here? What's Ben been—"

Then he saw the body and stopped. His next movements were quick and efficient. He shut the door behind him, making sure the latch caught. He went to the kitchen part of the room and brought her water. Then he fetched the fifth from the table. After a minute he said, "All right?"

She nodded and gulped. "All right."

Joe said bluntly, "Did you—?"

She choked. She tried to tell him, even if it didn't make any sense. "It was one of those kids, I thought. You know: 'Trick or treat!' And then it shot—"

Joe looked her over carefully. "All right," he said at last. "I'm not asking any questions. I don't know what it was Ben got mixed up in back in Chicago, and I don't want to know. I do know he was hiding out here and scared of his skin, and now something got him. It's tough but we've got to keep our noses clean."

Rose said, "You're strong, Joe. You've got sense, not like—"

"Whose gun is that?"

Rose hadn't seen the gun before. She shook her head.

Joe said, "I'll get rid of it."

She nodded dumbly.

Joe thought aloud, sharply, decisively. "Nobody's showed up, so I guess they didn't hear you screaming. Lucky the stores on either side of us are still stores, and dark at night. You give me five minutes, then go up to the drugstore and call the police from there. Understand?"

Rose nodded again. Joe went close to her and put his hand on her soft upper arm. She pulled away. "We can't, Joe! Not with Ben—"

He shrugged his shoulders and walked out of the store.

She looked at her watch and took a drink. She tried not to look at what was on the floor. She sat there looking at the watch. Then the doorbell rang and a shrill voice said, "Trick or treat!"

When Joe came back, she was lying on the floor. She came to when he shook her, muttering, "It came back. It came back, Joe!"

"Huh? Oh, another trick or treat?"

"Joe, don't be so hard. How can you stand there—"

He gripped her by both shoulders. "Rose," he said, "I gave my brother a hideout. That's one thing. From now on I'm rid of him. I'm looking out for me—and you. Understand?" He went on rapidly. "The gun was easy. I got a San Francisco train, paid a local fare, rode to the next stop, and walked back. I left the gun there. It may turn up in San Francisco. Much more likely, some Halloween drunk'll pick it up and we'll never hear of it again. We're rid of it—too," he added. "Now, get on that phone."

This is where I came in. You always come in late when you're on Homicide, so sometimes when you tell the story it's better to start in earlier and give out with a lot of stuff we didn't learn for a long time. That way, when you're reading it, you can get a picture a lot quicker than I did when I walked into that store.

There isn't anything uncommon about people living in stores in Berkeley. You walk down Telegraph and that's what you see every place. Little one-man stores closed up because the President sends greetings, and meanwhile all the defense workers pile into town and there's no place to sleep. Sure, it was tough—a man and his wife and his brother all living in a one-room store, but at least they didn't have any kids.

I've been in some of the stores—professionally and otherwise— and they've looked real nice. Trim and neat and damned near like home. I walked into this one, and the first thing I thought was how glad I was I wasn't married to this woman. Squalor's the word, I guess. Everybody's junk everyplace.

The people's name was Flaxner and she was the corpse's wife and this was her brother-in-law. She was average height and pretty in a thin, sharp way. The brother-in-law looked like Humphrey Bogart or was going to die trying. He worked in a plant out at Richmond. The dead husband was unemployed, which was a word I haven't written down on a form in years. Well, he was unemployed now, all right.

I went over the story with each of them alone and both of them together, and it still made just as much or as little sense. They didn't either of them seem afraid of the police. They answered questions clearly and readily, but not too clearly and readily. I don't know what made me think they were covering something.

Rose Flaxner timed the shot about seven-forty because the radio chiller they'd been listening to was over at seven-thirty. I asked Joe Flaxner where he was then.

"I was at a movie—Halloween horror bill up at the Campus Theatre. Don't go."

"Thanks," I said. "Times?"

"Let's see—I get in from Richmond in the car pool about four thirty. The show probably runs about four hours, but I couldn't stick it all. I walked out around seven thirty. That's a quarter of an hour from here by foot."

The doctor said seven forty was as likely as anything. All the time I was getting the story he was busy, and so was the fingerprint man (feeling kind of annoyed because there really wasn't anything to print but the corpse), and the boys were covering the block hunting for a gun or anything else.

They didn't find the gun, but they found something else. Down at the corner, stuffed into a trash can, Rourke found a sheet and a mask. I showed them to Rose.

She shuddered. She wouldn't ever think masks were funny again. She said, "I wouldn't know. They all look alike. But it could be the same. I don't know."

I asked the usual one about has your husband got any enemies.

To hear them talk, there wasn't ever anybody alive that had so few enemies as the late Ben Flaxner. I looked at his ugly puss and I looked at Rose and I didn't believe it. But all I said was, "All right. Everybody loved him and I don't doubt they're taking up funds for a Flaxner memorial right now. But somebody killed him. All right. Who'd you know five feet or under?"

They looked at me and I got patient like George Burns trying to explain something. I said, "This is maybe the smartest killer I've ever run up against. He picks the one night in the year when he can go around completely disguised without bothering anybody. Then he ditches the sheet and the mask and there's not a thing to tie him to the crime. But to bring it off, he'd have to be little. You saw the trick-or-treater; so did your husband. Both of you would've thought there was something screwy if it hadn't looked like a kid. So who's under five feet? The killer has to be."

I was watching Rose, and something scared her and scared her bad. But I could see from the way she compressed her lips that I wasn't going to be able to find out what, just by asking. So I let it slide for the moment.

Then, suddenly, Joe exclaimed, "The hunchback!"

Rose looked suddenly relieved and she said, "The hunchback!" too.

"Of course," Joe went on. "I don't know who he is, but I've seen him around this neighborhood a lot. And one day when I came home he was having some kind of row with Ben. I don't know what. Ben wouldn't talk. But he's—oh, hell, he isn't over four eight, I'd say."

I wrote it down and waited. Finally Rose said, "Helen?"

Joe said, "Hell no. Why?"

I asked, "Who?"

"Helen Kirk," Rose said. "She's a friend of ours, works out where Joe does. She didn't hardly know Ben, but she *is* little—not over five feet. You know—the cute type."

I wrote down the name and the address she gave me and drew a cat in the margin, which was nice for Halloween.

"We're not on the same shift," Joe said. "She's on swing—she'll be getting home about twelve thirty or one. So of course she was working when—"

I said, "Of course."

There wasn't much more to say right then. I finally said to Joe, "Richmond's in the next county. That's out of my territory. If it won't hold up national armament too much, I'd just as soon you stuck around here tomorrow. I'll want to see you again."

Joe said, "Can do, I guess."

The next hour or two was a lot of routine. There were forms to fill out and then waiting while they dug out the bullets. There were three of them, all from the same .32. I put the ballistics description and the corpse's prints on the wires to Washington, where the big file is, and to Cheyenne, where Rose Flaxner said they'd come from, and to Chicago, because she'd said "Ch—Cheyenne" and that was the likeliest name for her to've almost let slip.

When I got through, it was about time for Helen Kirk to be getting off work. She was a rare lucky woman in Berkeley. She had an apartment—on Alcatraz, not too far from the Flaxners' shop. I got into the apartment house without troubling anybody and camped in front of her door.

She showed up at two thirty and there was a Marine with her. They'd been bowling. The Marine looked as if he'd like to use me to knock down a few pins, but my badge calmed him down a little. He went away and Helen let me into the apartment.

She was little—four eleven, I'd guess—and just plump enough. She wasn't too cute, either. Just sort of lively. She liked an adventure like a policeman at two in the morning, but she didn't like it when I told her about Ben Flaxner. She took it harder than the people who knew him better, and maybe that proved something about Ben.

"It was Joe you mostly knew in the Flaxner family?" I asked.

"Yes. I used to see a lot of him." She stopped and then added, "Before Rose came out here." She didn't say anything more, just let it sink in unornamented.

I said, "That's a break for the Marines."

She asked, "But why did you come to see me, Lieutenant? I told you I scarcely knew Ben. He was grumpy and nervous and afraid; you couldn't know him."

"Afraid?"

"Like a child sometimes, that thinks something's going to get him. He was—oh, I don't know—funny."

I turned that around in my mind. I asked, "You clock in on time tonight?"

She said, "I guess so. I've never been docked yet."

I thought of a lot of swell possibilities on the way home. Maybe there was some way of faking a time clock at the Richmond plant. Sure it was possible, but it took a lot of believing. Those plants aren't run for fun.

Or maybe there never was a trick or treat. Joe and Rose made up the whole story between them, and there wasn't anybody under five feet. But would they make up such a wild story and carry it out so far as to plant a mask and a sheet?

Well, there was still the hunchback. If there was a hunchback. And in the meantime I could use some sleep.

The phone woke me up. It was Rose Flaxner. I guess they gave her my number at headquarters. She sounded half-crazy. She kept saying he was gone and she was all alone and it would come back and she was scared of what sounded like an angel; I didn't know for sure. I boiled it down to where Joe hadn't been able to get off at Richmond and had gone on out there.

I said, "I'll talk to the plant manager and send a man out there to bring him back. Keep quiet about it, because it isn't strictly legal, but I think it'll work." I didn't tell her she was safe enough, anyway, because there was a man watching the storefront.

"Thank God!" she said in a kind of gasp. "Because it might come back."

"Lady, Halloween's over. This is November first."

"Yes—but you said it had to be little, and the—" She stopped short, then added, "I want to get out of this place. I'm afraid." Then suddenly she hung up.

You can't get anywhere on a phone anyway. I brushed my teeth, shaved and fixed breakfast and wondered what it was like to be a private eye like you read about, and have whiskey instead of coffee. I didn't think it'd work, but you never know till you try.

They had reading matter for me at headquarters. There wasn't anything yet from Cheyenne, not that I expected it, but there was plenty from Washington and Chicago. It started out like routine and it ended with cold fingers on my spine.

They knew Ben Flaxner's prints both places. That was his real name, and maybe it's smart to use your real name sometimes. Back before Repeal, they knew him very well in Chicago. Nothing big— just a young punk getting his start. He didn't do so good for a while after that; the depression hit all kinds of business. He got really going again with the war, and in the meantime he'd grown up.

He was 4-F and there was some suspicion of fraud, but his draft board had never been able to get hold of him for a re-physical. He got into the black market in Chicago—mostly liquor, which was a racket he knew backwards. He was doing swell until Johnny Angelino got his. The Chicago cops never pinned anything on him, but Johnny's friends had their own ideas. I began to see why he was out here and why he was jumpy and scared the way Helen Kirk said. It looked clear enough until you read the ballistics report.

It said that the type and make of the gun that had killed Flaxner was not too common and that the same sort of gun had been used on Johnny Angelino. They'd like to take a look at the slug in a comparison.

I didn't like the implications in that. But what really started the ice-fingers playing with my vertebrae was this:

Johnny Angelino—the Angel, they called him, not just from his name but from that round sweet face with the curls—was a dwarf.

Four feet one, it said. Just the right size for a trick-or-treat.

Ghosts don't come back and kill their murderers with the same gun. I know better than that. So do you. So did Ben Flaxner.

289

I didn't pay any attention to it. I didn't give it another thought. But if Berkeley had bars, which it doesn't, I might have tried the methods of a private eye before I started out hunting for the hunchback.

Joe Flaxner said he'd seen the hunchback around the neighborhood a lot, so I tried the neighborhood stores—the ones that were still really being stores. The drugstore never saw him, neither did the service station man. The barber saw him a couple of times— he remembered because he thought it brought him luck with the gee-gees—but he didn't know anything.

Then I tried the butcher. He was all alone with some brains and tripe and his memories. He said, "Hunchback? Well, he *has* been in here."

"Lately?" I asked.

"Not for a week or so."

He looked like he wanted to talk and still he didn't. I tried showing my badge and it worked. He said, "So you got him, huh?"

I deadpanned it with a grunt.

He said, "You see how it is, officer. I want to see him get it, but I don't want to start anything, see? I don't want any trouble."

"I understand."

"That foreigner up the street, now; I bet he took some of them hens. Made a nice profit on 'em, too, I'll bet you. But I don't want to go breaking ceilings. I don't want any trouble."

"Sure," I said. "There's a war on."

"That's it, officer. That's exactly it. So I told him to take his black market chickens and—well, I sure told him. But I didn't want to go to the OPA about it and report it because—"

"—you don't want any trouble."

"That's it."

"Supposing you changed your mind?"

"Huh?"

"Supposing you wanted some hens, after all. He leave any instructions?"

It took five minutes after that. I timed it by the wall clock. He kept going back and forth between "there was a war on" and he "didn't want any trouble." Finally he dug out the card from under the cash register and I thanked him and told him I'd be in as a customer next time I wanted some tripe, and I hope I live that long.

The address was over in West Berkeley, across the railroad tracks. It was in the basement of an old house made into flats. I knocked on the door the way it said on the card and he opened up, and sure enough he was a hunchback and only about four nine.

He had a long face with a Roman beak and his voice was Italian. He asked, "What you want?" and I said, "In, first of all."

He backed away and let me in. His room made the Flaxner store look elegant, but it was cleaner. He sat down by the grappa bottle, but I kept standing near the door.

He said, "What you want?" again.

I said, "Talk. We can do it here if you like. If you don't, they've got rooms as nice as this down on McKinley Avenue."

He snarled a word in Italian that maybe meant copper, only I think it went a little deeper than that. He made a move with his right hand, and I had my .45 in mine.

I said, "You're handling black-market poultry. That's none of my business. My business is corpses. And you had a row with a corpse of mine, and it just so happens he used to play black-market games, too. It takes some clearing up."

He wasn't talking. He hunched himself over a little more than nature had done and sat there. I smelled secondhand garlic and olive oil. He leaned forward a little and spat at my feet. I didn't care. It was his carpet.

I said, "All right. You won't talk to me, you'll talk to the boys."

He said, "Will I?" and just then I felt the rod in my spine.

I hadn't heard the newcomer make his entrance; he was good. I didn't argue when he said, "Drop." I let the .45 go; I slipped the safety catch back on first.

He let me turn around then. He was tall and moon-faced. He asked, "What've we got here, Gino?"

Gino grunted. Moon-face ran a hand over my clothes and felt my badge. Then he laughed. It was a full, clear laugh and the little room rang with it. He took a wallet from his pocket and handed it to me.

I read it and laughed, too. I reached down for the .45 and nobody minded.

Lafferty (that's what it said on his identification) said, "Isn't there trouble enough about local and federal government without city police and the FBI playing cops-and-robbers with each other?"

I said, "That's all right. But what's a G-man doing stooging for a black-market operator?"

He grinned. "Put it the other way round. Gino's our stooge, and a hell of a good one. I thought you were from the gang he's working with. Someday, God help him, they're going to get wise."

Gino showed three and a half teeth. "Your country free mine from Nazis. I help."

Lafferty asked, "And what did you want with him?"

I told him. When I was through I said to Gino, "And what were you doing with Flaxner?"

"One of the black-market boys see him, tell me he use to work with Johnny Angelino, maybe he work with us. I feel him out; he tell me he think about it."

I can't help it; routine's routine. I asked, "And where were you last night at seven forty?"

Lafferty said, "With me, making out a report."

"That leaves *me* with a ghost."

Lafferty shook his head. "I'm not trying to run your business, Lieutenant; but doesn't it look as if there never was a trick-or-treater? It's a put-up job."

I said, "I've heard terror in a woman's voice before. Rose Flaxner's mortally afraid of what she saw. And I'm beginning to be myself."

Back at the office I read the report from Richmond. Helen Kirk arrived at work on time last night—eight o'clock. From South Berkeley to there in twenty minutes isn't possible. And the clocks, they swore, can't be faked.

I was left with the ghost, all right.

I hunted out the mask and the sheet. They didn't tell anything. A sheet is shapeless and sizeless. So's a mask. There was no laundry mark on the sheet and no makeup inside the mask. The lab hoped it could do something with identification from sweat-groups; but the courts aren't sold on that one yet, and, anyway, first I'd have to make a pinch.

I tucked the mask under my arm.

I went to every house in a five-block radius of the Flaxners' store. I asked every mother did her kid go trick-or-treating last night. And if the answer was yes, I said what time did he get home and was he all right or did anything funny happen to him.

They mostly got home at nine if they were due at eight, and ten if they were due at nine. And nothing happened.

Until at last on Ellsworth Street a Mrs. Mary Murdock, housewife, said Terry got home before eight. It worried her; he was so early. And he had terrible nightmares last night and was so upset this morning he didn't go to school. It wasn't like Terry; he wasn't one of these sensitive children.

I said, "Lady, it wouldn't take a sensitive kid to have nightmares, if what I think happened. Could I use your phone?"

When I was through phoning I went in to see Terry. I showed him my badge and we talked shop. He was a Junior G-man and he knew some things I didn't. When everything was going smooth, I let him see the mask.

It took me ten minutes to quiet him down, and then I got the story, after I promised he could wear my badge all day, because nothing could get him then.

I had them all there when I walked into the Flaxners' store. Rose was sniffling and nervous. Joe was comforting her like a big brother, only not quite, and Helen Kirk was watching them. Gino and Lafferty sat apart, saying nothing.

I walked in and said, "Well, I've found him."

Rose sat up and asked, "Who?" as if she was afraid of the answer.

I said, "The trick-or-treat. The one that rang the doorbell last night."

Rose half-screamed. She said, "You can't. He's dead."

I walked back to the door and fetched in the kid. I said, "This is Terry. He—"

I didn't get any further, because just then Lafferty, following my suggestions on the phone, quickly and carefully shot the gun out of Joe Flaxner's hand.

"Gee, it was awful," Terry told us. This was after the squad car took Joe away. "There I was ringing the doorbell, and all of a sudden there was this Thing behind me. It was just like what I was playing at being was all of a sudden real, and it was too big. And the man opened the door and the Thing fired at him and he fell down holding his stomach, and then the Thing grabbed me in its long arms and ran away. And when we were out of sight, it told me not to say a word ever or it'd come and get me the way it got him. I ran all the way home and I felt funny all night."

I said, "Joe was smart. His scheme meant we'd be looking for a little killer, and his height alibied him. But he wasn't smart; he should've picked a better witness than Rose. Only the fact that I believed she was really scared to death kept me from throwing the whole story out. She was a natural for an accessory, and I'm still not too sure—"

"I'll show you," Rose said wildly. "I wouldn't help—a murderer. I'll even tell you where the gun went."

She did, and then I said, "Now I'll tell you. I'll give you five to one it's this rod right here that Joe pulled today. I'm pretty sure that San Francisco train story was a gag to make you think he was the big strong man to rely on in time of murder."

Lafferty said, "Okay. But what put you on the trail of Joe?"

I said, "It wasn't the ghost, I hoped, and it wasn't Helen Kirk and it wasn't Gino. Their alibis stood up. So it wasn't under five feet. So it wasn't the trick-or-treat. So it used a real trick-or-treat for its front. So find the one that got scared last night.

"It had to be Joe. He had a strong motive—it was obvious he wanted Rose—and no alibi. And it *was* Joe. You know, it's the damnedest thing: nine times out of ten, it just naturally is the guy it has to be."

The trail was easy. The gun was almost enough, but Terry's identification of the voice and even the sweat-type testimony helped. And Joe's big, silent, tough-guy act didn't help him, not even with Rose.

I was some worried about Terry. So was his mother, and for a while she didn't like me much. But once he found out it wasn't a Thing, but just a murderer, like any Junior G-man can take in his stride, it was all right. In fact, the last time I saw him he was mad at me. I wouldn't try to get him a ticket to Joe's execution.

TRICK-OR-TREAT

Anthony Boucher is a celebrated pen name for mystery fiction fans who know that behind it lurked the versatile William Anthony Parker White. A critic as well as an author, he maintained equal visibility in the field of science fiction and fantasy literature, and was also a well-respected authority on opera. Fergus O'Breen and Sister Ursula are the two detectives he gave to the genre, but his long stint as an influential, widely syndicated mystery reviewer comprised probably his most significant contribution. The now hugely popular annual gatherings of mystery enthusiasts from around the world known as Bouchercons were created to honor his legacy.

PORK PIE HAT

BY PETER STRAUB

As the narrator of this haunting novella begins
to spin his story, we are quickly lost in a shifting
landscape of the past. Evoking the atmosphere of
smoky New York jazz clubs, where a man's secrets
are there in his music if only one knows how to hear
them, Peter Straub shows how a chance encounter
might give rise to speculations lasting a lifetime. And
Halloween is both central, and incidental, to the
"great mystery" that lies at the heart—or heartbreak—of "Pork Pie Hat."

Pork Pie Hat

PART ONE

1

If you know jazz, you know about him, and the title of this memoir tells you who he is. If you don't know the music, his name doesn't matter. I'll call him Hat. What does matter is what he meant. I don't mean what he meant to people who were touched by what he said through his horn. (His horn was an old Selmer Balanced Action tenor saxophone, most of its lacquer worn off.) I'm talking about the whole long curve of his life, and the way that what appeared to be a long slide from joyous mastery to outright exhaustion can be seen in another way altogether.

Hat did slide into alcoholism and depression. The last ten years of his life amounted to suicide by malnutrition, and he was almost transparent by the time he died in the hotel room where I met him. Yet he was able to play until nearly the end. When he was working, he would wake up around seven in the evening, listen to Frank Sinatra or Billie Holiday records while he dressed, get to the club by nine, play three sets, come back to his room sometime after three, drink and listen to more records (he was on a lot of those records), and finally go back to bed around the time of day people begin thinking about lunch. When he wasn't working, he got into bed about an hour earlier, woke up about five or six, and listened to records and drank through his long upside-down day.

It sounds like a miserable life, but it was just an unhappy one. The unhappiness came from a deep, irreversible sadness. Sadness is different from misery, at least Hat's was. His sadness seemed impersonal—it did not disfigure him, as misery can do. Hat's sadness seemed to be for the universe, or to be a larger than usual personal share of a sadness already existing in the universe. Inside it, Hat was unfailingly gentle, kind, even funny. His sadness seemed merely the opposite face of the equally impersonal happiness that shone through his earlier work.

In Hat's later years, his music thickened, and sorrow spoke through the phrases. In his last years, what he played often sounded like heartbreak itself. He was like someone who had passed through a great mystery, who *was passing* through a great mystery, and had to speak of what he had seen, what he was seeing.

2

I brought two boxes of records with me when I first came to New York from Evanston, Illinois, where I'd earned a B.A. in English at Northwestern, and the first thing I set up in my shoebox at the top of John Jay Hall in Columbia University was my portable record player. I did everything to music in those days, and I supplied the rest of my unpacking with a soundtrack provided by Hat's disciples. The kind of music I most liked when I was twenty-one was called "cool" jazz, but my respect for Hat, the progenitor of this movement, was almost entirely abstract. I didn't know his earliest records, and all I'd heard of his later style was one track on a Verve sampler album. I thought he must almost certainly be dead, and I imagined that if by some miracle he was still alive, he would have been in his early seventies, like Louis Armstrong. In fact, the man who seemed a virtual ancient to me was a few months short of his fiftieth birthday.

In my first weeks at Columbia I almost never left the campus. I was taking five courses, also a seminar that was intended to lead me to a Master's thesis, and when I was not in lecture halls or my room, I was in the library. But by the end of September, feeling less overwhelmed, I began to go downtown to Greenwich Village. The IRT, the only subway line I actually understood, described a straight north-south axis that allowed you to get on at 116th Street and get off at Sheridan Square. From Sheridan Square radiated out an unimaginable wealth (unimaginable if you'd spent the previous four years in Evanston, Illinois) of cafes, bars, restaurants, record shops, bookstores, and jazz clubs. I'd come to New York to get an M.A. in English, but I'd also come for this.

I learned that Hat was still alive about seven o'clock in the evening on the first Saturday in October, when I saw a poster bearing his name on the window of a storefront jazz club near St. Mark's Place. My conviction that Hat was dead was so strong that I first saw the poster as an advertisement of past glory. I stopped to gaze longer at this relic of a historical period. Hat had been playing with a quartet including a bassist and drummer of his own era, musicians long associated with him. But the piano player had been John Hawes, one of *my* musicians—John Hawes was on half a dozen of the records back in John Jay Hall. He must have been about twenty at the time, I thought, convinced that the poster had been preserved as memorabilia. Maybe Hawes's first job had been with Hat—anyhow, Hat's quartet must have been one of Hawes's first stops on the way to fame. John Hawes was a great figure to me, and the thought of him playing with a back number like Hat was a disturbance in the texture of reality. I looked down at the date on the poster, and my snobbish and rule-bound version of reality shuddered under another assault of the unthinkable. Hat's engagement had begun on the Tuesday of this week—the first Tuesday in October; and its last night took place on the Sunday after next—the Sunday before Halloween. Hat was still alive, and John Hawes was playing with him. I couldn't have told you which half of this proposition was the more surprising.

To make sure, I went inside and asked the short, impassive man behind the bar if John Hawes was really playing there tonight. "He'd better be, if he wants to get paid," the man said.

"So Hat is still alive," I said.

"Put it this way," he said. "If it was you, you probably wouldn't be."

3

Two hours and twenty minutes later, Hat came through the front door, and I saw what he meant. Maybe a third of the tables between the door and the bandstand were filled with people listening to the piano trio. This was what I'd come for, and I thought that the evening was perfect. I hoped that Hat would stay away. All he could accomplish by showing up would be to steal soloing time from Hawes, who, apart from seeming a bit disengaged, was playing wonderfully. Maybe Hawes always seemed a bit disengaged. That was fine with me. Hawes was *supposed* to be cool. Then the bass player looked toward the door and smiled, and the drummer grinned and knocked one stick against the side of his snare drum in a rhythmic figure that managed both to suit what the trio was playing and serve as a half-comic, half-respectful greeting. I turned away from the trio and looked back toward the door. The bent figure of a light-skinned black man in a long, drooping, dark coat was carrying a tenor saxophone case into the club. Layers of airline stickers covered the case, and a black porkpie hat concealed most of the man's face. As soon as he got past the door, he fell into a chair next to an empty table—really fell, as if he would need a wheelchair to get any farther.

Most of the people who had watched him enter turned back to John Hawes and the trio, who were beginning the last few choruses of "Love Walked In." The old man laboriously unbuttoned his coat and let it fall off his shoulders onto the back of the chair. Then, with the same painful slowness, he lifted the hat off his head and lowered it to the table beside him. A brimming shot glass had appeared between himself and the hat, though I hadn't noticed any of the waiters or waitresses put it there. Hat picked up the glass and poured its entire contents into his mouth. Before he swallowed, he let himself take in the room, moving his eyes without changing the position of his head. He was wearing a dark gray suit, a blue shirt with a tight tab collar, and a black knit tie. His face looked soft and worn with drink, and his eyes were of no real color at all, as if not merely washed out but washed clean. He bent over, unlocked the case, and began assembling his horn. As soon as "Love Walked In" ended, he was on his feet, clipping the horn to his strap and walking toward the bandstand. There was some quiet applause.

Hat stepped neatly up onto the bandstand, acknowledged us with a nod, and whispered something to John Hawes, who raised his hands to the keyboard. The drummer was still grinning, and the bassist had closed his eyes. Hat tilted his horn to one side, examined the mouthpiece, and slid it a tiny distance down the cork. He licked the reed, tapped his foot twice, and put his lips around the mouthpiece.

What happened next changed my life—changed me, anyhow. It was like discovering that some vital, even necessary substance had all along been missing from my life. Anyone who hears a great musician for the first time knows the feeling that the universe has just expanded. In fact, all that happened was that Hat had started playing "Too Marvelous For Words," one of the twenty-odd songs that were his entire repertoire at the time. Actually, he was playing some oblique, one-time-only melody of his own that floated above "Too Marvelous For Words," and this spontaneous melody seemed to me to comment affectionately on the song while utterly transcending it—to turn a nice little song into something profound. I forgot to breathe for a little while, and goosebumps came up on my arms. Halfway through Hat's solo, I saw John Hawes watching him and realized that Hawes, whom I all but revered, revered *him*. But by that time, I did, too.

I stayed for all three sets, and after my seminar the next day, I went down to Sam Goody's and bought five of Hat's records, all I could afford. That night, I went back to the club and took a table right in front of the bandstand. For the next two weeks, I occupied the same table every night I could persuade myself that I did not have to study—eight or nine, out of the twelve nights Hat worked. Every night was like the first: the same things, in the same order, happened. Halfway through the first set, Hat turned up and collapsed into the nearest chair. Unobtrusively, a waiter put a drink beside him. Off went the pork pie and the long coat, and out from its case came the horn. The waiter carried the case, pork pie, and coat into a back room while Hat drifted toward the bandstand, often still fitting the pieces of his saxophone together. He stood straighter, seemed almost to grow taller, as he got on the stand. A nod to his audience, an inaudible word to John Hawes. And then that sense of passing over the border between very good, even excellent music and majestic, mysterious art. Between songs, Hat sipped from a glass placed beside his left foot. Three forty-five minute sets. Two half-hour breaks, during which Hat disappeared through a door behind the bandstand. The same twenty or so songs, recycled again and again. Ecstasy, as if I were hearing *Mozart* play Mozart.

One afternoon toward the end of the second week, I stood up from a library book I was trying to stuff whole into my brain—*Modern Approaches to Milton*—and walked out of my carrel to find whatever I could that had been written about Hat. I'd been hearing the sound of Hat's tenor in my head ever since I'd gotten out of bed. And in those days, I was a sort of apprentice scholar: I thought that real answers in the form of interpretations could be found in the pages of scholarly journals. If there were at least a thousand, maybe two thousand, articles concerning John Milton in Low Library, shouldn't there be at least a hundred about Hat? And out of the hundred shouldn't a dozen or so at least begin to explain what happened to me when I heard him play? I was looking for *close readings* of his solos, for analyses that would explain Hat's effects in terms of subdivided rhythms, alternate cords, and note choices, in the way that poetry critics parsed diction levels, inversions of meter, and permutations of imagery.

Of coruse I did not find a dozen articles that applied a musicological version of the New Criticism to Hat's recorded solos. I found six old concert write-ups in the *New York Times*, maybe as many record reviews in jazz magazines, and a couple of chapters in jazz histories. Hat had been born in Mississippi, played in his family band, left after a mysterious disagreement at the time they were becoming a successful "territory" band, then joined a famous jazz band in its infancy and quit, again mysteriously, just after its break-through into nationwide success. After that, he went out on his own. It seemed that if you wanted to know about him, you had to go straight to the music: There was virtually nowhere else to go.

I wandered back from the catalogues to my carrel, closed the door on the outer world, and went back to stuffing *Modern Approaches to Milton* into my brain. Around six o'clock, I opened the carrell door and realized that *I* could write about Hat. Given the paucity of criticism of his work—given the virtual absence of information about the man himself—I virtually had to write something. The only drawback to this inspiration was that I knew nothing about music. I could not write the sort of article I had wished to read. What I could do, however, would be to interview the man. Potentially, an interview would be more valuable than analysis. I could fill in the dark places, answer the unanswered questions—why had he left both bands just as they began to do well? I wondered if he'd had problems with his father, and then transferred these problems to his next bandleader. There had to be some kind of story. Any band within smelling distance of its first success would be more than reluctant to lose its star soloist—wouldn't they beg him, bribe him, to stay? I could think of other questions no one had ever asked: who had influenced him? What did he think of all those tenor players whom he had influenced? Was he friendly with any of his artistic children? Did they come to his house and talk about music?

Above all, I was curious about the texture of his life—I wondered what his life, the life of a genuis, tasted like. If I could have put my half-formed fantasies into words, I would have described my naive, uninformed conceptions of Leonard Bernstein's surroundings. Mentally, I equippied Hat with a big apartment, handsome furniture, advanced stereo equipment, a good but not flashy car, paintings . . . the surroundings of a famous American artist, at least by the standards of John Jay Hall and Evanston, Illinois. The difference between Bernstein and Hat was that the conductor probably lived on Fifth Avenue, and the tenor player in the Village.

I walked out of the library humming "Love Walked In."

4

The dictionary-sized Manhattan telephone directory chained to the shelf beneath the pay telephone on the ground floor of John Jay Hall failed to provide Hat's number. Moments later, I met similar failure back in the library after having consulted the equally impressive directories for Brooklyn, Queens, and the Bronx, as well as the much smaller volume for Staten Island. But of course Hat lived in New York: Where else would he live? Like other celebrities, he avoided the unwelcome intrusions of strangers by going unlisted. I could not explain his absence from the city's five telephone books in any other way. Of course Hat lived in the Village—that was what the Village was *for*.

Yet even then, remembering the unhealthy-looking man who each night entered the club to drop into the nearest chair, I experienced a wobble of doubt. Maybe the great man's life was nothing like my imaginings. Hat wore decent clothes, but did not seem rich—he seemed to exist at the same oblique angle to wordly success that his nightly variations on "Too Marvelous For Words" bore to the original melody. For a moment, I pictured my genius in a slum apartment where roaches scuttled across a bare floor and water dripped from a rip in the ceiling. I had no idea of how jazz musicians actually lived. Hollywood, unafraid of cliché, surrounded them with squalor. On the rare moments when literature stooped to consider jazz people, it, too, served up an ambiance of broken bedsprings and peeling walls. And literature's bohemians—Rimbaud, Jack London, Kerouac, Harte Crane, William Burroughs—had often inhabited mean, unhappy rooms. It was possible that the great man was not listed in the city's directories because he could not afford a telephone.

This notion was unacceptable. There was another explanation—Hat could not live in a tenement room without a telephone. The man still possessed the elegance of his generation of jazz musicians, the generation that wore good suits and highly polished shoes, played in big bands, and lived on buses and in hotel rooms.

And there, I thought, was my answer. It was a comedowm from the apartment in the Village with which I had supplied him, but a room in some "artistic" hotel like the Chelsea would suit him just as well, and probably cost a lot less in rent. Feeling inspired, I looked up the Chelsea's number on the spot, dialed, and asked for Hat's room. The clerk told me that he wasn't registered in the hotel. "But you know who he is," I said. "Sure," said the clerk.

"Guitar, right? I know he was in one of those San Francisco bands, but I can't remember which one."

I hung up without replying, realizing that the only way I was going to discover Hat's telephone number, short of calling every hotel in New York, was by asking him for it.

5

This was on a Monday, and jazz clubs were closed. On Tuesday, Professor Marcus told us to read all of *Vanity Fair* by Friday; on Wednesday, after I'd spent a nearly sleepless night with Thackeray, my seminar leader asked me to prepare a paper on James Joyce's "Two Gallants" for the Friday class. Wednesday and Thursday nights I spent in the library. On Friday I listened to Professor Marcus being brilliant about *Vanity Fair* and read my laborious and dimwitted Joyce paper, on each of the five pages of which the word "epiphany" appeared at least twice, to my fellow-scholars. The seminar leader smiled and nodded throughout my performance and when I sat down metaphorically picked up my little paper between thumb and forefinger and slit its throat. "Some of you students are so *certain* about things," he said. The rest of his remarks disappeared into a vast, horrifying sense of shame. I returned to my room, intending to lie down for an hour or two, and woke up ravenous ten hours later, when even the West End Bar, even the local Chock Full O' Nuts, were shut for the night.

On Saturday night, I took my usual table in front of the bandstand and sat expectantly through the piano trio's usual three numbers. In the middle of "Love Walked In" I looked around with an insider's foreknowledge to enjoy Hat's dramatic entrance, but he did not appear, and the number ended without him. John Hawes and the other two musicians seemed untroubled by this break in the routine, and went on to play "Too Marvelous For Words" without their leader. During the next three songs, I kept turning around to look for Hat, but the set ended without him. Hawes announced a short break, and the musicians stood up and moved toward the bar. I fidgeted at my table, nursing my second beer of the night and anxiously checking the door. The minutes trudged by. I feared he would never show up. He had passed out in his room. He'd been hit by a cab, he'd had a stroke, he was already lying dead in a hospital room—and just when I was going to write the article that would finally do him justice!

Half an hour later, still without their leader, John Hawes and other sidemen went back on the stand. No one but me seemed to have noticed that Hat was not present. The other customers talked and smoked—this was in the days when people still smoked—and gave the music the intermittent and sometimes ostentatious attention they allowed it even when Hat was on the stand. By now, Hat was an hour and a half late, and I could see the gangsterish man behind the bar, the owner of the club, scowling as he checked his wristwatch. Hawes played two originals I particularly liked, favorites of mine from his Contemporary records, but in my mingled anxiety and irritation I scarcely heard them.

Toward the end of the second of these songs, Hat entered the club and fell into his customary seat a little more heavily than usual. The owner motioned away the waiter, who had begun moving toward him with the customary shot glass. Hat dropped the pork pie on the table and struggled with his coat buttons. When he heard what Hawes was playing, he sat listening with his hands still on a coat button, and I listened, too—the music had a tighter, harder, more modern feel, like Hawes's records. Hat nodded to himself, got his coat off, and struggled with the snaps on his saxophone case. The audience gave Hawes unusually appreciative applause. It took Hat longer than usual to fit the horn together, and by the time he was up on his feet, Hawes and the other two musicians had turned around to watch his progress as if they feared he would not make it all the way to the bandstand. Hat wound through the tables with his head tilted back, smiling to himself. When he got close to the stand, I saw that he was walking on his toes like a small child. The owner crossed his arms over his chest and glared. Hat seemed almost to float onto the stand. He licked his reed. Then he lowered his horn and, with his mouth open, stared out at us for a moment. "Ladies, ladies," he said in a soft, high voice. These were the first words I had ever heard him speak. "Thank you for your appreciation of our pianist, Mr. Hawes. And now I must explain my absence during the first set. My son passed away this afternoon, and I have been . . . busy . . . with details. Thank you."

With that, he spoke a single word to Hawes, put his horn back in his mouth, and began to play a blues called "Hat Jumped Up," one of his twenty songs. The audience sat motionless with shock. Hawes, the bassist, and the drummer played on as if nothing un- usual had happened—they must have known about his son, I thought. Or maybe they knew that he had no son, and had invented a grotesque excuse for turning up ninety minutes late. The club owner bit his lower lip and looked unusually introspective. Hat played one familiar, uncomplicated figure after another, his tone rough, almost coarse. At the end of his solo, he repeated one note for an entire chorus, fingering the key while staring out toward the back of the club. Maybe he was watching the customers leave— three couples and a couple of single people walked out while he was playing. But I don't think he saw anything at all. When the song was over, Hat leaned over to whisper to Hawes, and the piano player announced a short break. The second set was over.

Hat put his tenor on top of the piano and stepped down off the bandstand, pursing his mouth with concentration. The owner had come out from behind the bar and moved up in front of him as Hat tiptoed around the stand. The owner spoke a few quiet words. Hat answered. From behind, he looked slumped and tired, and his hair curled far over the back of his collar. Whatever he had said only partially satisfied the owner, who spoke again before leaving him. Hat stood in place for a moment, perhaps not noticing that the owner had gone, and resumed his tiptoe glide toward the door. Looking at his back, I think I took in for the first time how genu- inely *strange* he was. Floating through the door in his gray flannel suit, hair dangling in ringletlike strands past his collar, leaving in the air behind him the announcement about a dead son, he seemed absolutely separate from the rest of humankind, a species of one.

I turned as if for guidance to the musicians at the bar. Talking, smiling, greeting a few fans and friends, they behaved just as they did on every other night. Could Hat really have lost a son earlier today? Maybe this was the jazz way of facing grief—to come back to work, to carry on. Still it seemed the worst of all times to approach Hat with my offer. His playing was a drunken parody of itself. He would forget anything he said to me; I was wasting my time.

On that thought, I stood up and walked past the bandstand and opened the door—if I was wasting my time, it didn't matter what I did.

He was leaning against a brick wall about ten feet up the alleyway from the club's back door. The door clicked shut behind me, but Hat did not open his eyes. His face tilted up, and a sweetness that might have been sleep lay over his features. He looked exhausted and insubstantial, too frail to move. I would have gone back inside the club if he had not produced a cigarette from a pack in his shirt pocket, lit it with a match, and then flicked the match away, all without opening his eyes. At least he was awake. I stepped toward him, and his eyes opened. He glanced at me and blew out white smoke. "Taste?" he said.

I had no idea what he meant. "Can I talk to you for a minute, sir?" I asked.

He put his hand into one of his jacket pockets and pulled out a half-pint bottle. "Have a taste." Hat broke the seal on the cap, tilted it into his mouth, and drank. Then he held the bottle out toward me.

I took it. "I've been coming here as often as I can."

"Me, too," he said. "Go on, do it."

I took a sip from the bottle—gin. "I'm sorry about your son."

"Son?" He looked upward, as if trying to work out my meaning. "I got a son—out on Long Island. With his momma." He drank again and checked the level of the bottle.

"He's not dead, then."

He spoke the next words slowly, almost wonderingly. "No-body—told—me—if—he—is." He shook his head and drank another mouthful of gin. "Damn. Wouldn't that be something, boy dies and nobody tells me? I'd have to think about that, you know, have to really *think* about that one."

"I'm just talking about what you said onstage."

He cocked his head and seemed to examine an empty place in

the dark air about three feet from his face. "Uh huh. That's right. I did say that. Son of mine passed."

It was like dealing with a sphinx. All I could do was plunge in. "Well, sir, actually there's a reason I came out here," I said. "I'd like to interview you. Do you think that might be possible? You're a great artist, and there's very little about you in print. Do you think we could set up a time when I could talk to you?"

He looked at me with his bleary, colorless eyes, and I wondered if he could see me at all. And then I felt that, despite his drunkenness, he saw everything—that he saw things about me that I couldn't see.

"You a jazz writer?" he asked.

"No, I'm a graduate student. I'd just like to do it. I think it would be important."

"Important." He took another swallow from the half pint and slid the bottle back into his pocket. "Be nice, doing an *important* interview."

He stood leaning against the wall, moving further into outer space with every word. Only because I had started, I pressed on: I was already losing faith in this project. The reason Hat had never been interviewed was that ordinary American English was a foreign language to him. "Could we do the interview after you finish up at this club? I could meet you anywhere you like." Even as I said these words, I despaired. Hat was in no shape to know what he had to do after this engagement finished. I was surprised he could make it back to Long Island every night.

Hat rubbed his face, sighed, and restored my faith in him. "It'll have to wait a little while. Night after I finish here, I go to Toronto for two nights. Then I got something in Hartford on the thirtieth. You come see me after that."

"On the thirty-first?" I asked.

"Around nine, ten, something like that. Be nice if you brought some refreshments."

"Fine, great," I said, wondering if I would be able to take a late train back from wherever he lived. "But where on Long Island should I go?"

His eyes widened in mock-horror. "Don't go nowhere on Long

Island. You come see me. In the Albert Hotel, Forty-ninth and Eighth. Room 821.''

I smiled at him—I had guessed right about one thing, anyhow. Hat did not live in the Village, but he did live in a Manhattan hotel. I asked him for his phone number, and wrote it down, along with the other information, on a napkin from the club. After I folded the napkin into my jacket pocket, I thanked him and turned toward the door.

"Important as a motherfucker," he said in his high, soft, slurry voice.

I turned around in alarm, but he had tilted his head toward the sky again, and his eyes were closed.

"Indiana," he said. His voice made the word seem sung. "Moonlight in Vermont. I Thought About You. Flamingo.''

He was deciding what to play during his next set. I went back inside, where twenty or thirty new arrivals, more people than I had ever seen in the club, waited for the music to start. Hat soon reappeared through the door, the other musicians left the bar, and the third set began. Hat played all four of the songs he had named, interspersing them through his standard repertoire during the course of an unusually long set. He was playing as well as I'd ever heard him, maybe better than I'd heard on all the other nights I had come to the club. The Saturday night crowd applauded explosively after every solo. I didn't know if what I was seeing was genius or desperation.

An obituary in the Sunday *New York Times*, which I read over breakfast the next morning in the John Jay cafeteria, explained some of what had happened. Early Saturday morning, a thirty-eight-year-old tenor saxophone player named Grant Kilbert had been killed in an automobile accident. One of the most successful jazz musicians in the world, one of the few jazz musicians known outside of the immediate circle of fans, Kilbert had probably been Hat's most prominent disciple. He had certainly been one of my favorite musicians. More importantly, from his first record, *Cool Breeze*, Kilbert had excited respect and admiration. I looked at the photograph of the handsome young man beaming out over the neck of his saxophone and realized that the first four songs on *Cool Breeze* were "Indiana," "Moonlight in Vermont," "I Thought About You," and "Flamingo." Sometime late Saturday afternoon, someone had called up Hat to tell him about Kilbert. What I had seen had not merely been alcoholic eccentricity, it had been grief for a lost son. And when I thought about it, I was sure that the lost son, not himself, had been the important motherfucker he'd apothesized. What I had taken for spaciness and disconnection had all along been irony.

PART TWO

1

On the thirty-first of October, after calling first to make sure he remembered our appointment, I did go to the Albert Hotel, room 821, and interview Hat. That is, I asked him questions and listened to the long, rambling, often obscene responses he gave them. During the long night I spent in his room, he drank the fifth of Gordon's gin, the "refreshments" I brought with me—all of it, an entire bottle of gin, without tonic, ice, or other dilutants. He just poured it into a tumbler and drank, as if it were water. (I refused his single offer of a "taste.") I made frequent checks to make sure that the tape recorder I'd borrowed from a business student down the hall from me was still working, I changed tapes until they ran out, I made detailed backup notes with a ballpoint pen in a stenographic notebook. A couple of times, he played me sections of records that he wanted me to hear, and now and then he sang a couple of bars to make sure that I understood what he was telling me. He sat me in his only chair, and during the entire night stationed himself, dressed in his pork pie hat, a dark blue chalk-stripe suit, and white button-down shirt with a black knit tie, on the edge of his bed. This was a formal occasion. When I arrived at nine o'clock, he addressed me as "Mr. Leonard Feather" (the name of a well-known jazz critic), and when he opened his door at six thirty the next morning, he called me "Miss Rosemary." By then, I knew that this was an allusion to Rosemary Clooney, whose singing I had learned that he liked, and that the nickname meant he liked me, too. It was not at all certain, however, that he remembered my actual name.

I had three sixty-minute tapes and a notebook filled with handwriting that gradually degenerated from my usual scrawl into loops and wiggles that resembled Arabic more than English. Over the next month, I spent whatever spare time I had transcribing the tapes and trying to decipher my own handwriting. I wasn't sure that what I had was an interview. My carefully prepared questions had been met either with evasions or blank, silent refusals to answer—he had simply started talking about something else. After about an hour, I realized that this was his interview, not mine, and let him roll.

After my notes had been typed up and the tapes transcribed, I put everything in a drawer and went back to work on my M.A. What I had was even more puzzling than I'd thought, and straightening it out would have taken more time than I could afford. So the rest of that academic year was a long grind of studying for the comprehensive exam and getting a thesis ready. Until I picked up an old *Time* magazine in the John Jay lounge and saw his name in the "Milestones" column, I didn't even know that Hat had died.

Two months after I'd interviewed him, he had begun to hemorrhage on a flight back from France; an ambulance had taken him directly from the airport to a hospital. Five days after his release from the hospital, he had died in his bed at the Albert.

After I earned my degree, I was determined to wrestle something usable from my long night with Hat—I owed it to him. During the first seven weeks of that summer, I wrote out a version of what Hat had said to me, and sent it to the only publication I thought would be interested in it. *Downbeat* accepted the interview, and it appeared there about six months later. Eventually, it acquired some fame as the last of his rare public statements. I still see lines from the interview quoted in the sort of pieces about Hat never printed during his life. Sometimes they are lines he really did say to me; sometimes they are stitched together from remarks he made at different times; sometimes, they are quotations I invented in order to be able to use other things he did say.

But one section of that interview has never been quoted, because it was never printed. I never figured out what to make of it. Certainly I could not believe all he had said. He had been putting me on, silently laughing at my credulity, for he could not possibly believe that what he was telling me was literal truth. I was a white boy with a tape recorder, it was Halloween, and Hat was having fun with me. He was *jiving* me.

Now I feel different about his story, and about him, too. He was a great man, and I was an unworldly kid. He was drunk, and I was priggishly sober, but in every important way, he was functioning far above my level. Hat had lived forty-nine years as a black man in America, and I'd spent all of my twenty-one years in white suburbs. He was an immensely talented musician, a man who virtually thought in music, and I can't even hum in tune. That I expected to understand anything at all about him staggers me now. Back then, I didn't know anything about grief, and Hat wore grief about him daily, like a cloak. Now that I am the age he was then, I see that most of what is called information is interpretation, and interpretation is always partial.

Probably Hat was putting me on, jiving me, though not maliciously. He certainly was not telling me the literal truth, though I haev never been able to learn what was the literal truth of this case. It's possible that even Hat never knew what was the literal truth behind the story he told me—possible, I mean, that he was still trying to work out what the truth was, forty years after the fact.

2

He started telling me the story after we heard what I thought were gunshots from the street. I jumped from the chair and rushed to the windows, which looked out onto Eighth Avenue. "Kids," Hat said. In the hard yellow light of the streetlamps, four or five teenage boys trotted up the Avenue. Three of them carried paper bags. "Kids shooting?" I asked. My amazement tells you how long ago this was.

"Fireworks," Hat said. "Every Halloween in New York, fool kids run around with bags full of fireworks, trying to blow their hands off."

Here and in what follows, I am not going to try to represent the way Hat actually spoke. I cannot represent the way his voice glided over certain words and turned others into mushy growls, though he expressed more than half of his meaning by sound; and I don't want to reproduce his constant, reflexive obscenity. Hat couldn't utter four words in a row without throwing in a "motherfucker." Mostly, I have replaced his obscenities with other words, and the reader can imagine what was really said. Also, if I tried to imitate his grammar, I'd sound racist and he would sound stupid. Hat left school in the fourth grade, and his language, though precise, was casual. To add to these difficulties, Hat employed a private language of his own, a code to ensure that he would be understood only by the people he wished to understand him. I have replaced most of his code words with their equivalents.

It must have been around one in the morning, which means that I had been in his room about four hours. Until Hat explained the "gunshots," I had forgotten that it was Halloween night, and I told him this as I turned away from the window.

"I never forget about Halloween," Hat said. "If I can, I stay home on Halloween. Don't want to be out on the street, that night."

He had already given me proof that he was superstitious, and as he spoke he glanced almost nervously around the room, as if looking for sinister presences.

"You'd feel in danger?" I asked.

He rolled gin around in his mouth and looked at me as he had in the alley behind the club, taking note of qualities I myself did not yet perceive. This did not feel at all judgmental. The nervousness I thought I had seen had disappeared, and his manner seemed marginally more concentrated than earlier in the evening. He swallowed the gin and looked at me without speaking for a couple of seconds.

"No," he finally said. "Not exactly. But I wouldn't feel safe, either."

I sat with my pen half an inch from the page of my notebook, uncertain whether or not to write this down.

"I'm from Mississippi, you know."

I nodded.

"Funny things happen down there. Whole different world. Back when I was a little kid, it was really a different world. Know what I mean?"

"I can guess," I said.

He nodded. "Sometimes people just disappeared. They'd be *gone*. All kinds of stuff used to happen, stuff you wouldn't even believe in now. I met a witch-lady once, a real one, who could put curses on you, make you go blind and crazy. I saw a dead man walk. Another time, I saw a mean, murdering son of a bitch named Eddie Grimes die and come back to life—he got shot to death at a dance we were playing, he was *dead*, and a woman went down and whispered to him, and Eddie Grimes stood right back up on his feet. The man who shot him took off double-quick and he must have kept on going, because we never saw him after that."

"Did you start playing again?" I asked, taking notes as fast as I could.

"We never stopped," Hat said. "You let the people deal with what's going on, but you gotta keep on playing."

"Did you live in the country?" I asked, thinking that all of this sounded like Dogpatch—witches and walking dead men.

He shook his head. "I was brought up in town, Woodland, Mississippi. On the river. Where we lived was called Darktown, you know, but most of Woodland was white, with nice houses and all. Lots of our people did the cooking and washing in the big houses on Miller's Hill, that kind of work. In fact, we lived in a pretty nice house, for Darktown—the band always did well, and my father had a couple of other jobs on top of that. He was a good piano player, mainly, but he could play any kind of instrument. And he was a big, strong guy, nice-looking, real light-complected, so he was called Red, which was what that meant in those days. People respected him."

Another long, rattling burst of explosions came from Eighth Avenue. I wanted to ask him again about leaving his father's band, but Hat once more gave his little room a quick inspection, swallowed another mouthful of gin, and went on talking.

"We even went out trick-or-treating on Halloween, you know, just like the white kids. I guess our people didn't do that everywhere, but we did. Naturally, we stuck to our neighborhood, and probably we got a lot less than the kids from Miller's Hill, but they

317

didn't have anything up there that tasted as good as the apples and candy we brought home in our bags. Around us, folks made instead of bought, and that's the difference." He smiled at either the memory or the unexpected sentimentality he had just revealed—for a moment, he looked both lost in time and uneasy with himself for having said too much. "Or maybe I just remember it that way, you know? Anyhow, we used to raise some hell, too. You were *supposed* to raise hell, on Halloween."

"You went out with your brothers?" I asked.

"No, no, they were—" He flipped his hand in the air, dismissing whatever it was that his brothers had been. "I was always apart, you dig? Me, I was always into my own little things. I was that way right from the beginning. I play like that—never play like anyone else, don't even play like myself. You gotta find new places for yourself, or else nothing's happening, isn't that right? Don't want to be a repeater pencil." He saluted this declaration with another swallow of gin. "Back in those days, I used to go out with a boy named Rodney Sparks—we called him Dee, short for Demon, 'cause Dee Sparks would do anything that came into his head. That boy was the bravest little bastard I ever knew. He'd wrassle a mad dog. He was just that way. And the reason was, Dee was the preacher's boy. If you happen to be the preacher's boy, seems like you gotta prove every way you can that you're no Buster Brown, you know? So I hung with Dee, because I wasn't any Buster Brown, either. This is all when we were eleven, around then—the time when you talk about girls, you know, but you still aren't too sure what that's about. You don't know what *anything*'s about, to tell the truth. You along for the ride, you trying to pack in as much fun as possible. So Dee was my right hand, and when I went out on Halloween in Woodland, I went out with *him*."

He rolled his eyes toward the window and said, "Yeah." An expression I could not read at all took over his face. By the standards of ordinary people, Hat almost always looked detached, even impassive, tuned to some private wavelength, and this sense of detachment had intensified. I thought he was changing mental gears, dismissing his childhood, and opened my mouth to ask him about Grant Kilbert. But he raised his glass to his mouth again and rolled his eyes back to me, and the quality of his gaze told me to keep quiet.

"I didn't know it," he said, "but I was getting ready to stop being a little boy. To stop believing in little boy things and start seeing like a grown-up. I guess that's part of what I liked about Dee Sparks—he seemed like he was a lot more grown-up than I was, shows you what my head was like. The age we were, this would have been the last time we actually went out on Halloween to get apples and candy. From then on, we would have gone out mainly to raise hell. Smash in a few windows. Bust up somebody's wagon. Scare the shit out of little kids. But the way it turned out, it was the last time we ever went out on Halloween."

He finished off the gin in his glass and reached down to pick the bottle off the floor and pour another few inches into the tumbler. "Here I am, sitting in this room. There's my horn over there. Here's this bottle. You know what I'm saying?"

I didn't. I had no idea what he was saying. The hint of fatality clung to his earlier statement, and for a second I thought he was going to say that he was here but Dee Sparks was nowhere because Dee Sparks had died in Woodland, Mississippi, at the age of eleven on Halloween night. Hat was looking at me with a steady curiosity which compelled a response. "What happened?" I asked.

Now I know that he was saying *It has come down to just this, my room, my horn, my bottle.* My question was as good as any other response.

"If I was to tell you everything that happened, we'd have to stay in this room for a month." He smiled and straightened up on the bed. His ankles were crossed, and for the first time I noticed that his feet, shod in dark suede shoes with crepe soles, did not quite touch the floor. "And, you know, I never tell anybody everything, I always have to keep something back for myself. Things turned out all right. Only thing I mind is, I should have earned more money. Grant Kilbert, he earned a lot of money, and some of that was mine, you know."

"Were you friends?" I asked.

"I knew the man." He tilted his head and stared at the ceiling for so long that eventually I looked up at it, too. It was not a remarkable ceiling. A circular section near the center had been replastered not long before.

"No matter where you live, there are places you're not supposed to go," he said, still gazing up. "And sooner or later, you're gonna wind up there." He smiled at me again. "Where we lived, the place you weren't supposed to go was called The Backs. Out of town, stuck in the woods on one little path. In Darktown, we had all kinds from preachers on down. We had washerwomen and blacksmiths and carpenters, and we had some no-good thieving trash, too, like Eddie Grimes, that man who came back from being dead. In The Backs, they started with trash like Eddie Grimes, and went down from there. Sometimes, some of our people went out there to buy a jug, and sometimes they went there to get a woman, but they never talked about it. The Backs was *rough*. What they had was *rough*." He rolled his eyes at me and said, "That witch-lady I told you about, she lived in The Backs." He snickered. "Man, they were a mean bunch of people. They'd cut you, you looked at 'em bad. But one thing funny about the place, white and colored lived there just the same—it was *integrated*. Backs people were so evil, color didn't make no difference to them. They hated everybody anyhow, on principle." Hat pointed his glass at me, tilted his head, and narrowed his eyes. "At least, that was what everybody *said*. So this particular Halloween, Dee Sparks says to me after we finish with Darktown, we ought to head out to The Backs and see what the place is really like. Maybe we can have some fun.

"Well, that sounded fine to me. The idea of going out to The Backs kind of scared me, but being scared was part of the fun—Halloween, right? And if anyplace in Woodland was perfect for all that Halloween shit, you know, someplace where you might really see a ghost or a goblin, The Backs was better than the graveyard." Hat shook his head, holding the glass out at a right angle to his body. A silvery amusement momentarily transformed him, and it struck me that his native elegance, the product of his character and bearing much more than of the handsome suit and the suede shoes, had in effect been paid for by the surviving of a thousand unimaginable difficulties, each painful to a varying degree. Then I realized that what I meant by elegance was really dignity, that for the first

320

time I had recognized actual dignity in another human being, and that dignity was nothing like the self-congratulatory superiority people usually mistook for it.

"We were just little babies, and we wanted some of those good old Halloween scares. Like those dumbbells out on the street, tossing firecrackers at each other." Hat wiped his free hand down over his face and made sure that I was prepared to write down everything he said. (The tapes had already been used up.) "When I'm done, tell me if we found it, okay?"

"Okay," I said.

3

"Dee showed up at my house just after dinner, dressed in an old sheet with two eyeholes cut in it and carrying a paper bag. His big old shoes stuck out underneath the sheet. I had the same costume, but it was the one my brother used the year before, and it dragged along the ground and my feet got caught in it. The eyeholes kept sliding away from my eyes. My mother gave me a bag and told me to behave myself and get home before eight. It didn't take but half an hour to cover all the likely houses in Darktown, but she knew I'd want to fool around with Dee for an hour or so afterwards.

"Then up and down the streets we go, knocking on the doors where they'd give us stuff and making a little mischief where we knew they wouldn't. Nothing real bad, just banging on the door and running like hell, throwing rocks on the roof, little stuff. A few places, we plain and simple stayed away from—the places where people like Eddie Grimes lived. I always thought that was funny. We knew enough to steer clear of those houses, but we were still crazy to get out to The Backs.

"Only way I can figure it is, The Backs was *forbidden*. Nobody had to tell us to stay away from Eddie Grimes's house that night. You wouldn't even go there in the daylight, 'cause Eddie Grimes would get you and that would be that.

"Anyhow, Dee kept us moving along real quick, and when folks asked us questions or said they wouldn't give us stuff unless we sang a song, he moaned like a ghost and shook his bag in their faces, so we could get away faster. He was so excited, I think he was almost shaking.

"Me, I was excited, too. Not like Dee—sort of sick-excited, the way people must feel the first time they use a parachute. Scared-excited.

"As soon as we got away from the last house, Dee crossed the street and started running down the side of the little general store we all used. I knew where he was going. Out behind the store was a field, and on the other side of the field was Meridian Road, which took you out into the woods and to the path up to The Backs. When he realized that I wasn't next to him, he turned around and yelled at me to hurry up. *No*, I said inside myself, *I ain't gonna jump outta of this here airplane, I'm not dumb enough to do that.* And then I pulled up my sheet and scrunched up my eye to look through the one hole close enough to see through, and I took off after him.

"It was beginning to get dark when Dee and I left my house, and now it was dark. The Backs was about a mile and a half away, or at least the path was. We didn't know how far along that path you had to go before you got there. Hell, we didn't even know what it was—I was still thinking the place was a collection of little houses, like a sort of shadow-Woodland. And then, while we were crossing the field, I stepped on my costume and fell down flat on my face. Enough of this stuff, I said, and yanked the damned thing off. Dee started cussing me out, I wasn't doing this stuff the right way, we had to keep our costumes on in case anybody saw us, did I forget that this is Halloween, on Halloween a costume *protected* you. So I told him I'd put it back on when we got there. If I kept on falling down, it'd take us twice as long. That shut him up.

"As soon as I got that blasted sheet over my head, I discovered that I could see at least a little ways ahead of me. The moon was up, and a lot of stars were out. Under his sheet, Dee Sparks looked a little bit like a real ghost. It kind of glimmered. You couldn't really make out its edges, so the darn thing like *floated.* But I could see his legs and those big old shoes sticking out.

"We got out of the field and started up Meridian Road, and pretty soon the trees came up right to the ditches alongside the road, and I couldn't see too well any more. The road looked like it went smack into the woods and disappeared. The trees looked taller and thicker than in the daytime, and now and then something right at the edge of the woods shone round and white, like an eye—reflecting the moonlight, I guess. Spooked me. I didn't think we'd ever be able to find the path up to The Backs, and that was fine with me. I thought we might go along the road another ten–fifteen minutes, and then turn around and go home. Dee was swooping around up in front of me, flapping his sheet and acting bughouse. *He* sure wasn't trying too hard to find that path.

"After we walked about a mile down Meridian Road, I saw headlights like yellow dots coming toward us fast—Dee didn't see anything at all, running around in circles the way he was. I shouted at him to get off the road, and he took off like a rabbit—disappeared into the woods before I did. I jumped the ditch and hunkered down behind a pine about ten feet off the road to see who was coming. There weren't many cars in Woodland in those days, and I knew every one of them. When the car came by, it was Dr. Garland's old red Cord—Dr. Garland was a white man, but he had two waiting rooms and took colored patients, so colored patients was mostly what he had. And the man was a heavy drinker, *heavy* drinker. He zipped by, goin' at least fifty, which was mighty fast for those days, probably as fast as that old Cord would go. For about a second, I saw Dr. Garland's face under his white hair, and his mouth was wide open, stretched like he was screaming. After he passed, I waited a long time before I came out of the woods. Turning around and going home would have been fine with me. Dr. Garland changed everything. Normally, he was kind of slow and quiet, you know, and I could still see that black screaming hole opened up in his face—he looked like he was being tortured, like he was in Hell. I sure as hell didn't want to see whatever *he* had seen.

"I could hear the Cord's engine after the tail lights disappeared. I turned around and saw that I was all alone on the road. Dee Sparks was nowhere in sight. A couple of times, real soft, I called out his name. Then I called his name a little louder. Away off in the woods, I heard Dee giggle. I said he could run around all night if he liked but I was going home, and then I saw that pale silver sheet moving through the trees, and I started back down Meridian Road. After about twenty paces, I looked back, and there he was, standing in the middle of the road in that silly sheet, watching me

go. Come on, I said, let's get back. He paid me no mind. Wasn't
that Dr. Garland? Where was he going, as fast as that? What was
happening? When I said the doctor was probably out on some
emergency, Dee said the man was going *home*—he lived in Woodland, didn't he?

"Then I thought maybe Dr. Garland had been up in The Backs.
And Dee thought the same thing, which made him want to go there
all the more. Now he was determined. Maybe we'd see some dead
guy. We stood there until I understood that he was going to go by
himself if I didn't go with him. That meant that I *had* to go. Wild
as he was, Dee'd get himself into some kind of mess for sure if I
wasn't there to hold him down. So I said okay, I was coming along,
and Dee started swooping along like before, saying crazy stuff.
There was no way we were going to be able to find some little old
path that went up into the woods. It was so dark, you couldn't see
the separate trees, only giant black walls on both sides of the road.

"We went so far along Meridian Road I was sure we must have
passed it. Dee was running around in circles about ten feet ahead
of me. I told him that we missed the path, and now it was time to
get back home. He laughed at me and ran across to the right side
of the road and disappeared into the darkness.

"I told him to get back, damn it, and he laughed some more and
said I should come to *him*. Why? I said, and he said, Because this
here is the path, dummy. I didn't believe him—came right up to
where he disappeared. All I could see was a black wall that could
have been trees or just plain night. Moron, Dee said, look down.
And I did. Sure enough, one of those white things like an eye
shone up from where the ditch should have been. I bent down and
touched cold little stones, and the shining dot of white went off
like a light—a pebble that caught the moonlight just right. Bending
down like that, I could see the hump of grass growing up between
the tire tracks that led out onto Meridian Road. He'd found the
path, all right.

"At night, Dee Sparks could see one hell of a lot better than me.
He spotted the break in the ditch from across the road. He was
already walking up the path in those big old shoes, turning around
every other step to look back at me, make sure I was coming along
behind him. When I started following him, Dee told me to get my

sheet back on, and I pulled the thing over my head even though I'd rather have sucked the water out of a hollow stump. But I knew he was right—on Halloween, especially in a place like where we were, you were safer in a costume.

"From then on in, we were in no-man's-land. Neither one of us had any idea how far we had to go to get to The Backs, or what it would look like once we got there. Once I set foot on that wagon-track I knew for sure The Backs wasn't anything like the way I thought. It was a lot more primitive than a bunch of houses in the woods. Maybe they didn't even have houses! Maybe they lived in caves!

"Naturally, after I got that blamed costume over my head, I couldn't see for a while. Dee kept hissing at me to hurry up, and I kept cussing him out. Finally I bunched up a couple handfuls of the sheet right under my chin and held it against my neck, and that way I could see pretty well and walk without tripping all over myself. All I had to do was follow Dee, and that was easy. He was only a couple of inches in front of me, and even through one eyehole, I could see that silvery sheet moving along.

"Things moved in the woods, and once in a while an owl hooted. To tell you the truth, I never did like being out in the woods at night. Even back then, give me a nice warm barroom instead, and I'd be happy. Only animal I ever liked was a cat, because a cat is soft to the touch, and it'll fall asleep on your lap. But this was even worse than usual, because of Halloween, and even before we got to The Backs, I wasn't sure if what I heard moving around in the woods was just a possum or a fox or something a lot worse, some-thing with funny eyes and long teeth that liked the taste of little boys. Maybe Eddie Grimes was out there, looking for whatever kind of treat Eddie Grimes liked on Halloween night. Once I thought of that, I got so close to Dee Sparks I could smell him right through his sheet.

"You know what Dee Sparks smelled like? Like sweat, and a little bit like the soap the preacher made him use on his hands and face before dinner, but really like a fire in a junction box—a sharp, kind of bitter smell. That's how excited he was.

"After a while we were going uphill, and then we got to the top of the rise, and a breeze pressed my sheet against my legs. We started going downhill, and over Dee's electrical fire, I could smell woodsmoke. And something else I couldn't name. Dee stopped moving so sudden, I bumped into him. I asked him what he could see. Nothing but the woods, he said, but we're getting there. People are up ahead somewhere. And they got a still. We got to be real quiet from here on out, he told me, as if he had to, and to let him know I understood I pulled him off the path into the woods.

"Well, I thought, at least I know what Dr. Garland was after.

"Dee and I went snaking through the trees—me holding that blamed sheet under my chin so I could see out of one eye, at least, and walk without falling down. I was glad for that big fat pad of pine needles on the ground. An elephant could have walked over that stuff as quiet as a beetle. We went along a little further, and it got so I could smell all kinds of stuff—burned sugar, crushed juniper berries, tobacco juice, grease. And after Dee and I moved a little bit along, I heard voices, and that was enough for me. Those voices sounded angry.

"I yanked at Dee's sheet and squatted down—I wasn't going any farther without taking a good look. He slipped down beside me. I pushed the wad of material under my chin up over my face, grabbed another handful, and yanked that up, too, to look out under the bottom of the sheet. Once I could actually *see* where we were, I almost passed out. Twenty feet away through the trees, a kerosene lantern lit up the greasepaper window cut into the back of a little wooden shack, and a big raggedy guy carrying another kerosene lantern came stepping out of a door we couldn't see and stumbled toward a shed. On the other side of the building I could see the yellow square of a window in another shack, and past that, another one, a sliver of yellow shining out through the trees. Dee was crouched next to me, and when I turned to look at him, I could see another chink of yellow light from some way off in the woods over that way. Whether he knew it or not, he'd just about walked us straight into the middle of The Backs.

"He whispered for me to cover my face. I shook my head. Both of us watched the big guy stagger toward the shed. Somewhere in front of us, a woman screeched, and I almost dumped a load in my pants. Dee stuck his hand out from under his sheet and held it out, as if I needed *him* to tell me to be quiet. The woman screeched again, and the big guy sort of swayed back and forth. The light from the lantern swung around in big circles. I saw that the woods were full of little paths that ran between the shacks. The light hit the shack, and it wasn't even wood, but tarpaper. The woman laughed or maybe sobbed. Whoever was inside the shack shouted, and the raggedy guy wobbled toward the shed again. He was so drunk he couldn't even walk straight. When he got to the shed, he set down the lantern and bent to get in.

"Dee put his mouth up to my ear and whispered, *Cover up—you don't want these people to see who you are. Rip the eyeholes, if you can't see good enough.*

"I didn't want anyone in The Backs to see my face. I let the costume drop down over me again, and stuck my fingers in the nearest eyehole and pulled. Every living thing for about a mile around must have heard that cloth ripping. The big guy came out of the shed like someone pulled him out on a string, yanked the lantern up off the ground, and held it in our direction. Then we could see his face, and it was Eddie Grimes. You wouldn't want to run into Eddie Grimes anywhere, but The Backs was the last place you'd want to come across him. I was afraid he was going to start looking for us, but that woman started making stuck pig noises, and the man in the shack yelled something, and Grimes ducked back into the shed and came out with a jug. He lumbered back toward the shack and disappeared around the front of it. Dee and I could hear him arguing with the man inside.

"I jerked my thumb toward Meridian Road, but Dee shook his head. I whispered, *Didn't you already see Eddie Grimes, and isn't that enough for you?* He shook his head again. His eyes were gleaming behind that sheet. *So what do you want,* I asked, and he said, *I want to see that girl. We don't even know where she is,* I whispered, and Dee said, *all we got to do is follow her sound.*

"Dee and I sat and listened for a while. Every now and then, she let out a sort of whoop, and then she'd sort of cry, and after that she might say a word or two that sounded almost ordinary before she got going again on crying or laughing, the two all mixed up together. Sometimes we could hear other noises coming from the shacks, and none of them sounded happy. People were grumbling and arguing or just plain talking to themselves, but at least they sounded normal. That lady, she sounded like *Halloween*—like something that came up out of a grave.

"Probably you're thinking what I was hearing was sex—that I was too young to know how much noise ladies make when they're having fun. Well, maybe I was only eleven, but I grew up in Darktown, not Miller's Hill, and our walls were none too thick. What was going on with this lady didn't have anything to do with fun. The strange thing is, Dee didn't know that—he thought just what you were thinking. He wanted to see this lady getting humped. Maybe he even thought he could sneak in and get some for himself, I don't know. The main thing is, he thought he was listening to some wild sex, and he wanted to get close enough to see it. Well, I thought, his daddy was a preacher, and maybe preachers didn't do it once they got kids. And Dee didn't have an older brother like mine, who sneaked girls into the house whenever he thought he wouldn't get caught.

"He started sliding sideways through the woods, and I had to follow him. I'd seen enough of The Backs to last me the rest of my life, but I couldn't run off and leave Dee behind. And at least he was going at it the right way, circling around the shacks sideways, instead of trying to sneak straight through them. I started off after him. At least I could see a little better ever since I ripped at my eyehole, but I still had to hold my blasted costume bunched up under my chin, and if I moved my head or my hand the wrong way, the hole moved away from my eye and I couldn't see anything at all.

"So naturally, the first thing that happened was that I lost sight of Dee Sparks. My foot came down in a hole and I stumbled ahead for a few steps, completely blind, and then I hit a tree. I just came to a halt, sure that Eddie Grimes and a few other murderers were about to jump on me. For a couple of seconds I stood as still as a wooden Indian, too scared to move. When I didn't hear anything, I hauled at my costume until I could see out of it. No murderers were coming toward me from the shack beside the still. Eddie Grimes was saying *You don't understand* over and over, like he was so drunk that one phrase got stuck in his head, and he couldn't say or hear anything else. That woman yipped, like an animal noise, not a human one—like a fox barking. I sidled up next to the tree

328

I'd run into and looked around for Dee. All I could see was dark trees and that one yellow window I'd seen before. To hell with Dee Sparks, I said to myself, and pulled the costume off over my head. I could see better, but there wasn't any glimmer of white over that way. He'd gone so far ahead of me I couldn't even see him.

"So I had to catch up with him, didn't I? I knew where he was going—the woman's noises were coming from the shack way up there in the woods—and I knew he was going to sneak around the outside of the shacks. In a couple of seconds, after he noticed I wasn't there, he was going to stop and wait for me. Makes sense, doesn't it? All I had to do was keep going toward that shack off to the side until I ran into him. I shoved my costume inside my shirt, and then I did something else—set my bag of candy down next to the tree. I'd clean forgotten about it ever since I saw Eddie Grimes's face, and if I had to run, I'd go faster without holding onto a lot of apples and chunks of taffy.

"About a minute later, I came out into the open between two big old chinaberry trees. There was a patch of grass between me and the next stand of trees. The woman made a gargling sound that ended in one of those fox-yips, and I looked up in that direction and saw that the clearing extended in a straight line up and down, like a path. Stars shone out of the patch of darkness between the two parts of the woods. And when I started to walk across it, I felt a grassy hump between two beaten tracks. The path into The Backs off Meridian Road curved around somewhere up ahead and wound back down through the shacks before it came to a dead end. It had to come to a dead end, because it sure didn't join back up with Meridian Road.

"And this was how I'd managed to lose sight of Dee Sparks. Instead of avoiding the path and working his way north through the woods, he'd just taken the easiest way toward the woman's shack. Hell, I'd had to pull him off the path in the first place! By the time I got out of my sheet, he was probably way up there, out in the open for anyone to see and too excited to notice that he was all by himself. What I had to do was what I'd been trying to do all along, save his ass from anybody who might see him.

"As soon as I started going as soft as I could up the path, I saw that saving Dee Sparks's ass might be a tougher job than I thought—maybe I couldn't even save my own. When I first took off my costume, I'd seen lights from three or four shacks. I thought that's what The Backs was—three or four shacks. But after I started up the path, I saw a low square shape standing between two trees at the edge of the woods and realized that it was another shack. Whoever was inside had extinguished his kerosene lamp, or maybe wasn't home. About twenty–thirty feet on, there was another shack, all dark, and the only reason I noticed that one was, I heard voices coming from it, a man and a woman, both of them sounding drunk and slowed-down. Deeper in the woods past that one, another greasepaper window gleamed through the woods like a firefly. There were shacks all over the woods. As soon as I realized that Dee and I might not be the only people walking through The Backs on Halloween night, I bent down low to the ground and damn near slowed to a standstill. The only thing Dee had going for him, I thought, was good night vision—at least he might spot someone before they spotted him.

"A noise came from one of those shacks, and I stopped cold, with my heart pounding away like a bass drum. Then a big voice called out, *Who's that?*, and I just lay down in the track and tried to disappear. *Who's there?* Here I was calling Dee a fool, and I was making more noise than he did. I heard that man walk outside his door, and my heart pretty near exploded. Then the woman moaned up ahead, and the man who'd heard me swore to himself and went back inside. I just lay there in the dirt for a while. The woman moaned again, and this time it sounded scarier than ever, because it had a kind of a chuckle in it. She was crazy. Or she was a witch, and if she was having sex, it was with the devil. That was enough to make me start crawling along, and I kept on crawling until I was long past the shack where the man had heard me. Finally I got up on my feet again, thinking that if I didn't see Dee Sparks real soon, I was going to sneak back to Meridian Road by myself. If Dee Sparks wanted to see a witch in bed with the devil, he could do it without me.

"And then I thought I was a fool not to ditch Dee, because hadn't he ditched me? After all this time, he must have noticed that I wasn't with him anymore. Did he come back and look for me? The hell he did.

"And right then I would have gone back home, but for two things. The first was that I heard that woman make another sound—a sound that was hardly human, but wasn't made by any animal. It wasn't even loud. And it sure as hell wasn't any witch in bed with the devil. It made me want to throw up. That woman was being *hurt*. She wasn't just getting beat up—I knew what that sounded like—she was being hurt bad enough to drive her crazy, bad enough to kill her. Because you couldn't live through being hurt bad enough to make that sound. I was in The Backs, sure enough, and the place was even worse than it was supposed to be. Someone was killing a woman, everybody could hear it, and all that happened was that Eddie Grimes fetched another jug back from the still. I froze. When I could move, I pulled my ghost costume out from inside my shirt, because Dee was right, and for certain I didn't want anybody seeing my face out there on *this* night. And then the second thing happened. While I was pulling the sheet over my head, I saw something pale lying in the grass a couple of feet back toward the woods I'd come out of, and when I looked at it, it turned into Dee Sparks's Halloween bag.

"I went up to the bag and touched it to make sure about what it was. I'd found Dee's bag, all right. And it was empty. Flat. He had stuffed the contents into his pockets and left the bag behind. What that meant was, I couldn't turn around and leave him—because he hadn't left me after all. He waited for me until he couldn't stand it anymore, and then he emptied his bag and left it behind as a sign. He was counting on me to see in the dark as well as he could. But I wouldn't have seen it at all if that woman hadn't stopped me cold.

"The top of the bag was pointing north, so Dee was still heading toward the woman's shack. I looked up that way, and all I could see was a solid wall of darkness underneath a lighter darkness filled with stars. For about a second, I realized, I had felt pure relief. Dee had ditched me, so I could ditch him and go home. Now I was stuck with Dee all over again.

"About twenty feet ahead, another surprise jumped up at me out of darkness. Something that looked like a little tiny shack began to take shape, and I got down on my hands and knees to crawl toward the path when I saw a long silver gleam along the top of the thing. That meant it had to be metal—tarpaper might have a lot of uses, but it never yet reflected starlight. Once I realized that the thing in front of me was metal, I remembered its shape and realized it was a car. You wouldn't think you'd come across a car in a down-and-out rathole like The Backs, would you? People like that, they don't even own two shirts, so how do they come by cars? Then I remembered Dr. Garland speeding driving away down Meridian Road, and I thought *You don't have to live in The Backs to drive there.* Someone could turn up onto the path, drive around the loop, pull his car off onto the grass, and no one would ever see it or know that he was there.

"And this made me feel funny. The car probably belonged to someone I knew. Our band played dances and parties all over the county and everywhere in Woodland, and I'd probably seen every single person in town, and they'd seen me, too, and knew me by name. I walked closer to the car to see if I recognized it, but it was just an old black Model T. There must have been twenty cars just like it in Woodland. Whites and coloreds, the few coloreds that owned cars, both had them. And when I got right up beside the Model T, I saw what Dee had left for me on the hood—an apple.

"About twenty feet further along, there was an apple on top of a big old stone. He was putting those apples where I couldn't help but see them. The third one was on top of a post at the edge of the woods, and it was so pale it looked almost white. Next to the post one of those paths running all through The Backs led back into the woods. If it hadn't been for that apple, I would have gone right past it.

"At least I didn't have to worry so much about being making noise once I got back into the woods. Must have been six inches of pine needles and fallen leaves underfoot, and I walked so quiet I could have been floating—tell you the truth, I've worn crepe soles ever since then, and for the same reason. You walk *soft*. But I was still plenty scared—back in the woods there was a lot less light, and I'd have to step on an apple to see it. All I wanted was to find Dee and persuade him to leave with me.

"For a while, all I did was keep moving between the trees and try to make sure I wasn't coming up on a shack. Every now and then, a faint, slurry voice came from somewhere off in the woods, but I didn't let it spook me. Then, way up ahead, I saw Dee Sparks. The path didn't go in a straight line, it kind of angled back and forth, so I didn't have a good clear look at him, but I got a flash of that silvery-looking sheet way off through the trees. If I sped up I could get to him before he did anything stupid. I pulled my costume up a little further toward my neck and started to jog.

"The path started dipping *downhill*. I couldn't figure it out. Dee was in a straight line ahead of me, and as soon as I followed the path downhill a little bit, I lost sight of him. After a couple more steps, I stopped. The path got a lot steeper. If I kept running, I'd go ass over teakettle. The woman made another terrible sound, and it seemed to come from everywhere at once. Like everything around me had been *hurt*. I damn near came unglued. Seemed like everything was *dying*. That Halloween stuff about horrible creatures wasn't any story, man, it was the way things really were—you couldn't know anything, you couldn't trust anything, and you were surrounded by *death*. I almost fell down and cried like a baby boy. I was lost. I didn't think I'd ever get back home.

"Then the worst thing of all happened.

"I heard her die. It was just a little noise, more like a sigh than anything, but that sigh came from everywhere and went straight into my ear. A soft sound can be loud, too, you know, be the loudest thing you ever heard. That sigh about lifted me up off the ground, about blew my head apart.

"I stumbled down the path, trying to wipe my eyes with my costume, and all of a sudden I heard men's voices from off to my left. Someone was saying a word I couldn't understand over and over, and someone else was telling him to shut up. Then, behind me, I heard running—heavy running, a man. I took off, and right away my feet got tangled up in the sheet and I was rolling downhill, hitting my head on rocks and bouncing off trees and smashing into stuff I didn't have any idea what it was. Biff bop bang slam smash clang crash ding dong. I hit something big and solid and wound up half-covered in water. Took me a long time to get upright, twisted up in the sheet the way I was. My ears buzzed, and I saw stars—

yellow and blue and red stars, not real ones. When I tried to sit up, the blasted sheet pulled me back down, so I got a faceful of cold water. I scrambled around like a fox in a trap, and when I finally got so I was at least sitting up, I saw a slash of real sky out the corner of one eye, and I got my hands free and ripped that hole in the sheet wide enough for my whole head to fit through it.

"I was sitting in a little stream next to a fallen tree. The tree was what had stopped me. My whole body hurt like the dickens. No idea where I was. Wasn't even sure I could stand up. Got my hands on the top of the fallen tree and pushed myself up with my legs—blasted sheet ripped in half, and my knees almost bent back the wrong way, but I got up on my feet. And there was Dee Sparks, coming toward me through the woods on the other side of the stream.

"He looked like he didn't feel any better than I did, like he couldn't move in a straight line. His silvery sheet was smearing through the trees. *Dee got hurt, too*, I thought—he looked like he was in some total panic. The next time I saw the white smear between the trees it was twisting about ten feet off the ground. *No*, I said to myself, and closed my eyes. Whatever that thing was, it wasn't Dee. An unbearable feeling, an absolute despair, flowed out from it. I fought against this wave of despair with every weapon I had. I didn't want to know that feeling. I couldn't know that feeling—I was eleven years old. If that feeling reached me when I was eleven years old, my entire life would be changed, I'd be in a different universe altogether.

"But it did reach me, didn't it? I could say *no* all I liked, but I couldn't change what had happened. I opened my eyes, and the white smear was gone.

"That was almost worse—I wanted it to be Dee after all, doing something crazy and reckless, climbing trees, running around like a wildman, trying to give me a big whopping scare. But it wasn't Dee Sparks, and it meant that the worst things I'd ever imagined were true. Everything was dying. You couldn't know anything, you couldn't trust anything, we were all lost in the midst of the death that surrounded us.

"Most people will tell you growing up means you stop believing in Halloween things—I'm telling you the reverse. You start to grow up when you understand that the stuff that scares you is part of the air you breathe.

"I stared at the spot where I'd seen that twist of whiteness, I guess trying to go back in time to before I saw Dr. Garland fleeing down Meridian Road. My face looked like his, I thought—because now I knew that you really *could* see a ghost. The heavy footsteps I'd heard before suddenly cut through the buzzing in my head, and after I turned around and saw who was coming at me down the hill, I thought it was probably my own ghost I'd seen.

"Eddie Grimes looked as big as an oak tree, and he had a long knife in one hand. His feet slipped out from under him, and he skidded the last few yards down to the creek, but I didn't even try to run away. Drunk as he was, I'd never get away from him. All I did was back up alongside the fallen tree and watch him slide downhill toward the water. I was so scared I couldn't even talk. Eddie Grimes's shirt was flapping open, and big long scars ran all across his chest and belly. He'd been raised from the dead at least a couple of times since I'd seen him get killed at the dance. He jumped back up on his feet and started coming for me. I opened my mouth, but nothing came out.

"Eddie Grimes took another step toward me, and then he stopped and looked straight at my face. He lowered the knife. A sour stink of sweat and alcohol came off him. All he could do was stare at me. Eddie Grimes knew my face all right, he knew my name, he knew my whole family—even at night, he couldn't mistake me for anyone else. I finally saw that Eddie was actually afraid, like he was the one who'd seen a ghost. The two of us just stood there in the shallow water for a couple more seconds, and then Eddie Grimes pointed his knife at the other side of the creek.

"That was all I needed, baby. My legs unfroze, and I forgot all my aches and pains. Eddie watched me roll over the fallen tree and lowered his knife. I splashed through the water and started moving up the hill, grabbing at weeds and branches to pull me along. My feet were frozen, and my clothes were soaked and muddy, and I was trembling all over. About halfway up the hill, I looked back over my shoulder, but Eddie Grimes was gone. It was like he'd never been there at all, like he was nothing but the product of a couple of good raps to the noggin.

"Finally, I pulled myself shaking up over the top of the rise, and what did I see about ten feet away through a lot of skinny birch trees but a kid in a sheet facing away from me into the woods, and hopping from foot to foot in a pair of big clumsy shoes? And what was in front of him but a path I could make out from even ten feet away? Obviously, this was where I was supposed to turn up, only in the dark and all I must have missed an apple stuck onto a branch or some blasted thing, and I took that little side trip downhill on my head and wound up throwing a spook into Eddie Grimes.

"As soon as I saw him, I realized I hated Dee Sparks. I wouldn't have tossed him a rope if he was drowning. Without even thinking about it, I bent down and picked up a stone and flung it at him. The stone bounced off a tree, so I bent down and got another one. Dee turned around to find out what made the noise, and the second stone hit him right in the chest, even though it was really his head I was aiming at.

"He pulled his sheet up over his face like an Arab and stared at me with his mouth wide open. Then he looked back over his shoulder at the path, as if the real me might come along at any second. I felt like pegging another rock at his stupid face, but instead I marched up to him. He was shaking his head from side to side. *Jim Dawg*, he whispered, *what happened to you?* By way of answer, I hit him a good hard knock on the breastbone. *What's the matter?* he wanted to know. *After you left me*, I say, *I fell down a hill and ran into Eddie Grimes.*

"That gave him something to think about, all right. Was Grimes coming after me, he wanted to know? Did he see which way I went? Did Grimes see who I was? He was pulling me into the woods while he asked me these dumb-ass questions, and I shoved him away. His sheet flopped back down over his front, and he looked like a little boy. He couldn't figure out why I was mad at him. From his point of view, he'd been pretty clever, and if I got lost, it was my fault. But I wasn't mad at him because I got lost. I wasn't even mad at him because I'd run into Eddie Grimes. It was everything else. Maybe it wasn't even him I was mad at.

"*I want to get home without getting killed*, I whispered. *Eddie ain't gonna let me go twice.* Then I pretended he wasn't there anymore and tried to figure out how to get back to Meridian Road. It seemed to me that I was still going north when I took that tumble downhill, so when I climbed up the hill on the other side of the creek I was still going north. The wagon-track that Dee and I took into The Backs had to be off to my right. I turned away from Dee and started moving through the woods. I didn't care if he followed me or not. He had nothing to do with me anymore, he was on his own. When I heard him coming along after me, I was sorry. I wanted to get away from Dee Sparks. I wanted to get away from everybody.

"I didn't want to be around anybody who was supposed to be my friend. I'd rather have had Eddie Grimes following me than Dee Sparks.

"Then I stopped moving, because through the trees I could see one of those greasepaper windows glowing up ahead of me. That yellow light looked evil as the devil's eye—everything in The Backs was evil, poisoned, even the trees, even the air. The terrible expression on Dr. Garland's face and the white smudge in the air seemed like the same thing—they were what I didn't want to know.

"Dee shoved me from behind, and if I hadn't felt so sick inside I would have turned around and punched him. Instead, I looked over my shoulder and saw him nodding toward where the side of the shack would be. He wanted to get closer! For a second, he seemed as crazy as everything else out there, and then I got it: I was all turned around, and instead of heading back to the main path, I'd been taking us toward the woman's shack. That was why Dee was following me.

"I shook my head. No, I wasn't going to sneak up to that place. Whatever was inside there was something I didn't have to know about. It had too much power—it turned Eddie Grimes around, and that was enough for me. Dee knew I wasn't fooling. He went around me and started creeping toward the shack.

"And damnedest thing, I watched him slipping through the trees for a second, and started following him. If he could go up there, so could I. If I didn't exactly look at whatever was in there myself, I could watch Dee look at it. That would tell me most of what I had to know. And anyways, probably Dee wouldn't see anything anyhow, unless the front door was hanging open, and that didn't seem too likely to me. He wouldn't see anything, and I wouldn't either, and we could both go home.

"The door of the shack opened up, and a man walked outside. Dee and I freeze, and I mean *freeze*. We're about twenty feet away, on the side of this shack, and if the man looked sideways, he'd see our sheets. There were a lot of trees between us and him, and I couldn't get a very good look at him, but one thing about him made the whole situation a lot more serious. This man was white, and he was wearing good clothes—I couldn't see his face, but I could see his rolled-up sleeves, and his suit jacket slung over one arm, and some kind of wrapped-up bundle he was holding in his hands. All this took about a second. The white man started carrying his bundle straight through the woods, and in another two seconds he was out of sight.

"Dee was a little closer than I was, and I think his sight line was a little clearer than mine. On top of that, he saw better at night than I did. Dee didn't get around like me, but he might have recognized the man we'd seen, and that would be pure trouble. Some rich white man, killing a girl out in The Backs? And us two boys close enough to see him? Do you know what would have happened to us? There wouldn't be enough left of either one of us to make a decent shadow.

"Dee turned around to face me, and I could see his eyes behind his costume, but I couldn't tell what he was thinking. He just stood there, looking at me. In a little bit, just when I was about to explode, we heard a car starting up off to our left. I whispered at Dee if he saw who that was. *Nobody*, Dee said. Now, what the hell did that mean? Nobody? You could say Santa Claus, you could say J. Edgar *Hoover*, it'd be a better answer than Nobody. The Model T's headlights shone through the trees when the car swung around the top of the path and started going toward Meridian Road. *Nobody I ever saw before*, Dee said. When the headlights cut through the trees, both of us ducked out of sight. Actually, we were so far from the path, we had nothing to worry about. I could barely see the car when it went past, and I couldn't see the driver at all.

"We stood up. Over Dee's shoulder I could see the side of the shack where the white man had been. Lamplight flickered on the ground in front of the open door. The last thing in the world I wanted to do was to go inside that place—I didn't even want to walk around to the front and look in the door. Dee stepped back from me and jerked his head toward the shack. I knew it was going to be just like before. I'd say no, he'd say yes, and then I'd follow him wherever he thought he had to go. I felt the same way I did when I saw that white smear in the woods—hopeless, lost in the midst of death. *You go, if you have to,* I whispered to him, *it's what you wanted to do all along.* He didn't move, and I saw that he wasn't too sure about what he wanted anymore.

"Everything was different now, because the white man made it different. Once a white man walked out that door, it was like raising the stakes in a poker game. But Dee had been working toward that one shack ever since we got into The Backs, and he was still curious as a cat about it. He turned away from me and started moving sideways in a straight line, so he'd be able to peek inside the door from a safe distance.

"After he got about halfway to the front, he looked back and waved me on, like this was still some great adventure he wanted me to share. He was afraid to be on his own, that was all. When he realized I was going to stay put, he bent down and moved real slow past the side. He still couldn't see more than a sliver of the inside of the shack, and he moved ahead another little ways. By then, I figured, he should have been able to see about half of the inside of the shack. He hunkered down inside his sheet, staring in the direction of the open door. And there he stayed.

"I took it for about half a minute, and then I couldn't anymore. I was sick enough to die and angry enough to explode, both at the same time. How long could Dee Sparks look at a dead whore? Wouldn't a couple of seconds be enough? Dee was acting like he was watching a goddamn Hopalong Cassidy movie. An owl screeched, and some man in another shack said *Now that's over,* and someone else shushed him. If Dee heard, he paid it no mind. I started along toward him, and I don't think he noticed me, either. He didn't look up until I was past the front of the shack, and had already seen the door hanging open, and the lamplight spilling over the plank floor and onto the grass outside.

"I took another step, and Dee's head snapped around. He tried to stop me by holding out his hand. All that did was make me mad. Who was Dee Sparks to tell me what I couldn't see? All he did was leave me alone in the woods with a trail of apples, and he didn't even do that right. When I kept on coming, Dee started waving both hands at me, looking back and forth between me and the inside of the shack. Like something was happening in there that I couldn't be allowed to see. I didn't stop, and Dee got up on his feet and skittered toward me.

"*We gotta get out of here*, he whispered. He was close enough so I could smell that electrical fire stink. I stepped to his side, and he grabbed my arm. I yanked my arm out of his grip and went forward a little ways and looked through the door of the shack.

"A bed was shoved up against the far wall, and a woman lay naked on the bed. There was blood all over her legs, and blood all over the sheets, and big puddles of blood on the floor. A woman in a raggedy robe, hair stuck out all over her head, squatted beside the bed, holding the other woman's hand. She was a colored woman—a Backs woman—but the other one, the one on the bed, was white. Probably she was pretty, when she was alive. All I could see was white skin and blood, and I near fainted.

"This wasn't some white-trash woman who lived out in The Backs, she was brought there, and the man who brought her had killed her. More trouble was coming down than I could imagine, trouble enough to kill lots of our people. And if Dee and I said a word about the white man we'd seen, the trouble would come right straight down on us.

"I must have made some kind of noise, because the woman next to the bed turned halfway around and looked at me. There wasn't any doubt about it—she saw me. All she saw of Dee was a dirty white sheet, but she saw my face, and she knew who I was. I knew her, too, and she wasn't any Backs woman. She lived down the street from us. Her name was Mary Randolph, and she was the one who came up to Eddie Grimes after he got shot to death and brought him back to life. Mary Randolph followed my dad's band, and when we played roadhouses or colored dance halls, she'd be likely to turn up. A couple of times she told me I played good drums—I was a drummer back then, you know, switched to saxophone when I turned twelve. Mary Randolph just looked at me, her hair stuck out straight all over her head like she was already inside a whirlwind of trouble. No expression on her face except that look you get when your mind is going a mile a minute and your body can't move at all. She didn't even look surprised. She almost looked like she *wasn't* surprised, like she was expecting to see me. As bad as I'd felt that night, this was the worst of all. I liked to have died. I'd have disappeared down an anthill, if I could. I didn't know what I had done—just be there, I guess—but I'd never be able to undo it.

"I pulled at Dee's sheet, and he tore off down the side of the shack like he'd been waiting for a signal. Mary Randolph stared into my eyes, and it felt like I had to pull myself away—I couldn't just turn my head, I had to *disconnect*. And when I did, I could still feel her staring at me. Somehow I made myself go down past the side of the shack, but I could still see Mary Randolph inside there, looking out at the place I'd been.

"If Dee said anything at all when I caught up with him, I'd have knocked his teeth down his throat, but he just moved fast and quiet through the trees, seeing the best way to go, and I followed after. I felt like I'd been kicked by a horse. When we got on the path, we didn't bother trying to sneak down through the woods on the other side, we lit out and ran as hard as we could—like wild dogs were after us. And after we got onto Meridian Road, we ran toward town until we couldn't run anymore.

"Dee clamped his hand over his side and staggered forward a little bit. Then he stopped and ripped off his costume and lay down by the side of the road, breathing hard. I was leaning forward with hands on my knees, as winded as he was. When I could breathe again, I started walking down the road. Dee picked himself up and got next to me and walked along, looking at my face and then looking away, and then looking back at my face again.

"*So?* I said.

"*I know that lady*, Dee said.

"Hell, that was no news. Of course he knew Mary Randolph—she was his neighbor, too. I didn't bother to answer, I just grunted at him. Then I reminded him that Mary hadn't seen his face, only mine.

"*Not Mary*, he said. *The other one.*

"He knew the dead white woman's name? That made everything worse. A lady like that shouldn't be in Dee Sparks's world, especially if she's going to wind up dead in The Backs. I wondered who was going to get lynched, and how many.

"Then Dee said that I knew her, too. I stopped walking and looked him straight in the face.

"*Miss Abbey Montgomery*, he said. *She brings clothes and food down to our church, Thanksgiving and Christmas.*

"He was right—I wasn't sure if I'd ever heard her name, but I'd seen her once or twice, bringing baskets of ham and chicken and boxes of clothes to Dee's father's church. She was about twenty years old, I guess, so pretty she made you smile just to look at. From a rich family in a big house right at the top of Miller's Hill. Some man didn't think a girl like that should have any associations with colored people, I guess, and decided to express his opinion about as strong as possible. Which meant that we were going to take the blame for what happened to her, and the next time we saw white sheets, they wouldn't be Halloween costumes.

"*He sure took a long time to kill her*, I said.

"And Dee said, *She ain't dead*.

"So I asked him, What the hell did he mean by that? I saw the girl. I saw the blood. Did he think she was going to get up and walk around? Or maybe Mary Randolph was going to tell her that magic word and bring her back to life?

"*You can think that if you want to*, Dee said. *But Abbey Montgomery ain't dead*.

"I almost told him I'd seen her ghost, but he didn't deserve to hear about it. The fool couldn't even see what was right in front of his eyes. I couldn't expect him to understand what happened to me when I saw that miserable . . . that *thing*. He was rushing on ahead of me anyhow, like I'd suddenly embarrassed him or something. That was fine with me. I felt the exact same way. I said, *I guess you know neither one of us can ever talk about this*, and he said, *I guess you know it, too*, and that was the last thing we said to each other that night. All the way down Meridian Road Dee Sparks kept his eyes straight ahead and his mouth shut. When we got to the field, he turned toward me like he had something to say, and I waited for it, but he faced forward again and ran away. Just ran.

I watched him disappear past the general store, and then I walked home by myself.

"My mom gave me hell for getting my clothes all wet and dirty, and my brothers laughed at me and wanted to know who beat me up and stole my candy. As soon as I could, I went to bed, pulled the covers up over my head, and closed my eyes. A little while later, my mom came in and asked if I was all right. Did I get into a fight with Dee Sparks? Dee Sparks was born to hang, that was what she thought, and I ought to have a better class of friends. *I'm tired of playing those drums, Momma*, I said, *I want to play the saxophone instead*. She looked at me surprised, but said she'd talk about it with Daddy, and that it might work out.

"For the next couple days, I waited for the bomb to go off. On the Friday, I went to school, but couldn't concentrate for beans. Dee Sparks and I didn't even nod at each other in the hallways— just walked by like the other guy was invisible. On the weekend I said I felt sick and stayed in bed, wondering when that whirlwind of trouble would come down. I wondered if Eddie Grimes would talk about seeing me—once they found the body, they'd get around to Eddie Grimes real quick.

"But nothing happened that weekend, and nothing happened all the next week. I thought Mary Randolph must have hid the white girl in a grave out in The Backs. But how long could a girl from one of those rich families go missing without investigations and search parties? And, on top of that, what was Mary Randolph doing there in the first place? She liked to have a good time, but she wasn't one of those wild girls with a razor under her skirt—she went to church every Sunday, was good to people, nice to kids. Maybe she went out to comfort that poor girl, but how did she know she'd be there in the first place? Misses Abbey Montgomerys from the hill didn't share their plans with Mary Randolphs from Darktown. I couldn't forget the way she looked at me, but I couldn't understand it, either. The more I thought about that look, the more it was like Mary Randolph was saying something to me, but what? *Are you ready for this? Do you understand this? Do you know how careful you must be?*

"My father said I could start learning the C-melody sax, and when I was ready to play it in public, my little brother wanted to take over the drums. Seems he always wanted to play drums, and in fact, he's been a drummer ever since, a good one. So I worked out how to play my little sax, I went to school and came straight home after, and everything went on like normal, except Dee Sparks and I weren't friends anymore. If the police were searching for a missing rich girl, I didn't hear anything about it.

"Then one Saturday I was walking down our street to go to the general store, and Mary Randolph came through her front door just as I got to her house. When she saw me, she stopped moving real sudden, with one hand still on the side of the door. I was so surprised to see her that I was in a kind of slow-motion, and I must have stared at her. She gave me a look like an X ray, a look that searched around down inside me. I don't know what she saw, but her face relaxed, and she took her hand off the door and let it close behind her, and she wasn't looking inside me anymore. *Miss Randolph*, I said, and she told me she was looking forward to hearing our band play at a Beergarden dance in a couple of weeks. I told her I was going to be playing the saxophone at that dance, and she said something about that, and all the time it was like we were having two conversations, the top one about me and the band, and the one underneath about her and the murdered white girl in The Backs. It made me so nervous, my words got all mixed up. Finally she said *You make sure you say hello to your daddy from me, now*, and I got away.

"After I passed her house, Mary Randolph started walking down the street behind me. I could feel her watching me, and I started to sweat. Mary Randolph was a total mystery to me. She was a nice lady, but probably she buried that girl's body. I didn't know but that she was going to come and kill *me*, one day. And then I remembered her kneeling down beside Eddie Grimes at the road-house. She had been *dancing* with Eddie Grimes, who was in jail more often than he was out. I wondered if you could be a respectable lady and still know Eddie Grimes well enough to dance with him. And how did she bring him back to life? Or was that what happened at all? Hearing that lady walk along behind me made me so uptight, I crossed to the other side of the street.

"A couple days after that, when I was beginning to think that the trouble was never going to happen after all, it came down. We heard police cars coming down the street right when we were finishing dinner. I thought they were coming for me, and I almost lost my chicken and rice. The sirens went right past our house, and then more sirens came toward us from other directions—the old klaxons they had in those days. It sounded like every cop in the state was rushing into Darktown. This was bad, bad news. Someone was going to wind up dead, that was certain. No way all those police were going to come into our part of town, make all that commotion, and leave without killing at least one man. That's the truth. You just had to pray that the man they killed wasn't you or anyone in your family. My daddy turned off the lamps, and we went to the window to watch the cars go by. Two of them were state police. When it was safe, Daddy went outside to see where all the trouble was headed. After he came back in, he said it looked like the police were going toward Eddie Grimes's place. We wanted to go out and look, but they wouldn't let us, so we went to the back windows that faced toward Grimes's house. Couldn't see anything but a lot of cars and police standing all over the road back there. Sounded like they were knocking down Grimes's house with sledge hammers. Then a whole bunch of cops took off running, and all I could see was the cars spread out across the road. About ten minutes later, we heard lots of gunfire coming from a couple of streets further back. It like to have lasted forever. Like hearing the Battle of the Bulge. My momma started to cry, and so did my little brother. The shooting stopped. The police shouted to each other, and then they came back and got in their cars and went away.

"On the radio the next morning, they said that a known criminal, a Negro man named Edward Grimes, had been killed while trying to escape arrest for the murder of a white woman. The body of Eleanore Monday, missing for three days, had been found in a shallow grave by Woodland police searching near an illegal distillery in the region called The Backs. Miss Monday, the daughter of grocer Albert Monday, had been in poor mental and physical health, and Grimes had apparently taken advantage of her weakness either to abduct or lure her to The Backs, where she had been savagely murdered. That's what it said on the radio—I still remember the words. *In poor mental and physical health. Savagely murdered.*

"When the paper finally came, there on the front page was a

picture of Eleanore Monday, girl with dark hair and a big nose. She didn't look anything like the dead woman in the shack. She hadn't even disappeared on the right day. Eddie Grimes was never going to be able to explain things, because the police had finally cornered him in the old jute warehouse just off Meridian Road next to the general store. I don't suppose they even bothered trying to arrest him—they weren't interested in *arresting* him. He killed a white girl. They wanted revenge, and they got it.

"After I looked at the paper, I got out of the house and ran between the houses to get a look at the jute warehouse. Turned out a lot of folks had the same idea. A big crowd strung out in a long line in front of the warehouse, and cars were parked all along Meridian Road. Right up in front of the warehouse door was a police car, and a big cop stood in the middle of the big doorway, watching people file by. They were walking past the doorway one by one, acting like they were at some kind of exhibit. Nobody was talking. It was a sight I never saw before in that town, whites and colored all lined up together. On the other side of the warehouse, two groups of men stood alongside the road, one colored and one white, talking so quietly you couldn't hear a word.

"Now I was never one who liked standing in lines, so I figured I'd just dart up there, peek in, and save myself some time. I came around the end of the line and ambled toward the two bunches of men, like I'd already had my look and was just hanging around to enjoy the scene. After I got a little past the warehouse door, I sort of drifted up alongside it. I looked down the row of people, and there was Dee Sparks, just a few yards away from being able to see in. Dee was leaning forward, and when he saw me he almost jumped out of his skin. He looked away as fast as he could. His eyes turned as dead as stones. The cop at the door yelled at me to go to the end of the line. He never would have noticed me at all if Dee hadn't jumped like someone just shot off a firecracker behind him.

"About halfway down the line, Mary Randolph was standing behind some of the ladies from the neighborhood. She looked terrible. Her hair stuck out in raggedy clumps, and her skin was all ashy, like she hadn't slept in a long time. I sped up a little, hoping she wouldn't notice me, but after I took one more step, Mary

Randolph looked down and her eyes hooked into mine. I swear, what was in her eyes almost knocked me down. I couldn't even tell what it was, unless it was just pure hate. Hate and pain. With her eyes hooked into mine like that, I couldn't look away. It was like I was seeing that miserable, terrible white smear twisting up between the trees on that night in The Backs. Mary let me go, and I almost fell down all over again.

"I got to the end of the line and started moving along regular and slow with everybody else. Mary Randolph stayed in my mind and blanked out everything else. When I got up to the door, I barely took in what was inside the warehouse—a wall full of bulletholes and bloodstains all over the place, big slick ones and little drizzly ones. All I could think of was the shack and Mary Randolph sitting next to the dead girl, and I was back there all over again.

"Mary Randolph didn't show up at the Beergarden dance, so she didn't hear me play saxophone in public for the first time. I didn't expect her, either, not after the way she looked out at the warehouse. There'd been a lot of news about Eddie Grimes, who they made out to be less civilized than a gorilla, a crazy man who'd murder anyone as long as he could kill all the white women first. The paper had a picture of what they called Grimes's 'lair,' with busted furniture all over the place and holes in the walls, but they never explained that it was the police tore it up and made it look that way.

"The other thing people got suddenly all hot about was The Backs. Seems the place was even worse than everybody thought. Seems white girls besides Eleanore Monday had been taken out there—according to some, there were even white girls living out there, along with a lot of bad coloreds. The place was a nest of vice, Sodom and Gomorrah. Two days before the town council was supposed to discuss the problem, a gang of white men went out there with guns and clubs and torches and burned every shack in The Backs clear down to the ground. While they were there, they didn't see a single soul, white, colored, male, female, damned or saved. Everybody who had lived in The Backs had skedaddled. And the funny thing was, long as The Backs had existed right outside of Woodland, no one in Woodland could recollect the name of anyone who had ever lived there. They couldn't even recall the name of anyone who had ever gone there, except for Eddie Grimes. In fact, after the place got burned down, it appeared that it must have been a sin just to say its name, because no one ever mentioned it. You'd think men so fine and moral as to burn down The Backs would be willing to take the credit, but none ever did.

"You could think they must have wanted to get rid of some things out there. Or wanted real bad to forget about things out there. One thing I thought, Doctor Garland and the man I saw leaving that shack had been out there with torches.

"But maybe I didn't know anything at all. Two weeks later, a couple things happened that shook me good.

"The first one happened three nights before Thanksgiving. I was hurrying home, a little bit late. Nobody else on the street, everybody inside either sitting down to dinner or getting ready for it. When I got to Mary Randolph's house, some kind of noise coming from inside stopped me. What I thought was, it sounded exactly like somebody trying to scream while someone else was holding a hand over their mouth. Well, that was plain foolish, wasn't it? How did I know what that would sound like? I moved along a step or two, and then I heard it again. Could be anything, I told myself. Mary Randolph didn't like me too much, anyway. She wouldn't be partial to my knocking on her door. Best thing I could do was get out. Which was what I did. Just went home to supper and forgot about it.

"Until the next day, anyhow, when a friend of Mary's walked in her front door and found her lying dead with her throat cut and a knife in her hand. A cut of fatback, we heard, had boiled away to cinders on her stove. I didn't tell anybody about what I heard the night before. Too scared. I couldn't do anything but wait to see what the police did.

"To the police, it was all real clear. Mary killed herself, plain and simple.

"When our minister went across town to ask why a lady who intended to commit suicide had bothered to start cooking her supper, the chief told him that a female bent on killing herself probably didn't care *what* happened to the food on her stove. Then I suppose Mary Randolph nearly managed to cut her own head off, said the minister. A female in despair possesses a godawful strength, said the chief. And asked, wouldn't she have screamed if she'd been attacked? And added, couldn't it be that maybe this female here had secrets in her life connected to the late savage murderer named Eddie Grimes? We might all be better off if these secrets get buried with your Mary Randolph, said the chief. I'm sure you understand me, Reverend. And yes, the Reverend did understand, he surely did. So Mary Randolph got laid away in the cemetery, and nobody ever said her name again. She was put away out of mind, like The Backs.

"The second thing that shook me up and proved to me that I didn't know anything, that I was no better than a blind dog, happened on Thanksgiving day. My daddy played piano in church, and on special days, we played our instruments along with the gospel songs. I got to church early with the rest of my family, and we practiced with the choir. Afterwards, I went to fooling around outside until the people came, and saw a big car come up into the church parking lot. Must have been the biggest, fanciest car I'd ever seen. Miller's Hill was written all over that vehicle. I couldn't have told you why, but the sight of it made my heart stop. The front door opened, and out stepped a colored man in a fancy gray uniform with a smart cap. He didn't so much as dirty his eyes by looking at me, or at the church, or at anything around him. He stepped around the front of the car and opened the rear door on my side. A young woman was in the passenger seat, and when she got out of the car, the sun fell on her blond hair and the little fur jacket she was wearing. I couldn't see more than the top of her head, her shoulders under the jacket, and her legs. Then she straightened up, and her eyes lighted right on me. She smiled, but I couldn't smile back. I couldn't even begin to move.

"It was Abbey Montgomery, delivering baskets of food to our church, the way she did every Thanksgiving and Christmas. She looked older and thinner than the last time I'd seen her alive— older and thinner, but more than that, like there was no fun at all in her life anymore. She walked to the trunk of the car, and the driver opened it up, leaned in, and brought out a great big basket of food. He took it into the church by the back way and came back for another one. Abbey Montgomery just stood still and watched him carry the baskets. She looked—she looked like she was just

349

going through the motions, like going through the motions was all she was ever going to do from now on, and she knew it. Once she smiled at the driver, but the smile was so sad that the driver didn't even try to smile back. When he was done, he closed the trunk and let her into the passenger seat, got behind the wheel, and drove away.

"I was thinking, *Dee Sparks was right, she was alive all the time.* Then I thought, *No, Mary Randolph brought her back, too, like she did Eddie Grimes. But it didn't work right, and only part of her came back.*

"And that's the whole thing, except that Abbey Montgomery didn't deliver food to our church, that Christmas—she was traveling out of the country, with her aunt. And she didn't bring food the next Thanksgiving, either, just sent her driver with the baskets. By that time, we didn't expect her, because we'd already heard that, soon as she got back to town, Abbey Montgomery stopped leaving her house. That girl shut herself up and never came out. I heard from somebody who probably didn't know any more than I did that she eventually got so she wouldn't even leave her room. Five years later, she passed away. Twenty-six years old, and they said she looked to be at least fifty."

4

Hat fell silent, and I sat with my pen ready over the notebook, waiting for more. When I realized that he had finished, I asked, "What did she die of?"

"Nobody ever told me."

"And nobody ever found who had killed Mary Randolph."

The limpid, colorless eyes momentarily rested on me. "Was she killed?"

"Did you ever become friends with Dee Sparks again? Did you at least talk about it with him?"

"Surely did not. Nothing to talk about."

This was a remarkable statement, considering that for an hour he had done nothing but talk about what had happened to the two of them, but I let it go. Hat was still looking at me with his unreadable eyes. His face had become particularly bland, almost

a tenor player and a drummer from the high school band. And the church work got more and more demanding for Hat's father."

"His father was a deacon, or something like that?"

He raised his eyebrows. "No, Red was the Baptist minister. The Reverend. He ran that church. I think he even started it."

"Hat told me his father played piano in church, but . . ."

"The Reverend would have made a hell of a blues piano player, if he'd ever left his day job."

"There must have been another Baptist church in the neighborhood," I said, thinking this the only explanation for the presence of two Baptist ministers. But why had Hat not mentioned that his own father, like Dee Sparks's, had been a clergyman?

"Are you kidding? There was barely enough money in that place to keep one of them going." He looked at his watch, nodded at me, and began to move closer to his sidemen.

"Could I ask you one more question?"

"I suppose so," he said, almost impatiently.

"Did Hat strike you as superstitious?"

Hawes grinned. "Oh, he was superstitious, all right. He told me he never worked on Halloween—he didn't even want to go out of his room, on Halloween. That's why he left the big band, you know. They were starting a tour on Halloween, and Hat refused to do it. He just quit." He leaned toward me. "I'll tell you another funny thing. I always had the feeling that Hat was terrified of his father—I thought he invited me to Hatchville with him so I could be some kind of buffer between him and his father. Never made any sense to me. Red was a big strong old guy, and I'm pretty sure a long time ago he used to mess around with the ladies, Reverend or not, but I couldn't ever figure out why Hat should be afraid of him. But whenever Red came into the room, Hat shut up. Funny, isn't it?"

I must have looked very perplexed. "Hatchville?"

"Where they lived. Hatchville, Mississippi—not too far from Biloxi."

"But he told me—"

"Hat never gave too many straight answers," Hawes said. "And he didn't let the facts get in the way of a good story. When you come to think of it, why should he? He was *Hat*."

After the next set, I walked back uphill to my hotel, wondering again about the long story Hat had told me. Had there been any truth in it at all?

2

Three weeks later I found myself released from a meeting at our Midwestern headquarters in downtown Chicago earlier than I had expected, and instead of going to a bar with the other wandering corporate ghosts like myself, made up a story about a relative I had promised to visit. I didn't want to admit to my fellow employees, committed like all male business people to aggressive endeavors such as racquetball, drinking, and the pursuit of women, that I intended to visit the library. Short of a trip to Mississippi, a good periodical room offered the most likely means of finding out once and for all how much truth had been in what Hat had told me.

I hadn't forgotten everything I had learned at Columbia—I still knew how to look things up.

In the main library, a boy set me up with a monitor and spools of microfilm representing the complete contents of the daily newspapers from Biloxi and Hatchville, Mississippi, for Hat's tenth and eleventh years. That made three papers, two for Biloxi and one for Hatchville, but all I had to examine were the issues dating from the end of October through the middle of November—I was looking for references to Eddie Grimes, Eleanore Monday, Mary Randolph, Abbey Montgomery, Hat's family, The Backs, and anyone named Sparks.

The Hatchville *Blade*, a gossipy daily printed on peach-colored paper, offered plenty of references to each of these names and places, and the papers from Biloxi contained nearly as many—Biloxi could not conceal the delight, disguised as horror, aroused in its collective soul by the unimaginable events taking place in the smaller, supposedly respectable town ten miles west. Biloxi was riveted, Biloxi was superior, Biloxi was virtually intoxicated with dread and outrage. In Hatchville, the press maintained a persistent optimistic dignity: When wickedness had appeared, justice official and unofficial had dealt with it. Hatchville was shocked but proud (or at least pretended to be proud), and Biloxi all but preened. The *Blade* printed detailed news stories, but the Biloxi papers suggested implications not allowed by Hatchville's version of events. I needed Hatchville to confirm or question Hat's story, but Biloxi gave me at least the beginning of a way to understand it.

A black ex-convict named Edward Grimes had in some fashion persuaded or coerced Eleanore Monday, a retarded young white woman, to accompany him to an area variously described as "a longstanding local disgrace" (the *Blade*) and "a haunt of deepest vice" (Biloxi) and after "the perpetration of the most offensive and brutal deeds upon her person" (the *Blade*) or "acts which the judicious commentator must decline to imagine, much less describe" (Biloxi) murdered her, presumably to ensure her silence, and then buried the body near the "squalid dwelling" where he made and sold illegal liquor. State and local police departments acting in concert had located the body, identified Grimes as the fiend, and, after a search of his house, had tracked him to a warehouse where the murderer was killed in a gun battle. The *Blade* covered half its front page with a photograph of a gaping double door and a bloodstained wall. All Mississippi, both Hatchville and Biloxi declared, now could breathe more easily.

The *Blade* gave the death of Mary Randolph a single paragraph on its back page, the Biloxi papers nothing.

In Hatchville, the raid on The Backs was described as an heroic assault on a dangerous criminal encampment that had somehow come to flourish in a little-noticed section of the countryside. At great risk to themselves, anonymous citizens of Hatchville had descended like the army of the righteous and driven forth the hidden sinners from their dens. Troublemakers, beware! The Biloxi papers, while seeming to endorse the action in Hatchville, actually took another tone altogether. Can it be, they asked, that the Hatchville police had never before noticed the existence of a Sodom and Gomorrah so close to the town line? Did it take the savage murder of a helpless woman to bring it to their attention? Of course Biloxi celebrated the destruction of The Backs, such vileness must be eradicated, but it wondered what else had been destroyed along with the stills and the mean buildings where loose women had plied their trade. Men ever are men, and those who have succumbed to temptation may wish to remove from the face of the earth any evidence of their lapses. Had not the police of Hatchville ever heard the rumor, vague and doubtless baseless, that operations of an illegal nature had been performed in the selfsame Backs? That in an atmosphere of drugs, intoxication, and gambling, the races had mingled there, and that "fast" young women had risked life and honor in search of illicit thrills? Hatchville may have rid itself of a few buildings, but Biloxi was willing to suggest that the problems of its smaller neighbor might not have disappeared with them.

As this campaign of innuendo went on in Biloxi, the *Blade* blandly reported the ongoing events of any smaller American city. Miss Abigail Montgomery sailed with her aunt, Miss Lucinda Bright, from New Orleans to France for an eight-week tour of the continent. The Reverend Jasper Sparks of the Miller's Hill Presbyterian Church delivered a sermon on the subject of "Christian Forgiveness." (Just after Thanksgiving, the Reverend Sparks's son, Rodney, was sent off with the blessings and congratulations of all Hatchville to a private academy in Charleston, South Carolina.) There were bake sales, church socials, and costume parties. A saxophone virtuoso named Albert Woodland demonstrated his astonishing wizardry at a well-attended recital presented in Temperance Hall.

Well, I knew the name of at least one person who had attended the recital. If Hat had chosen to disguise the name of his hometown, he had done so by substituting for it a name that represented another sort of home.

But, although I had more ideas about this than before, I still did not know exactly what Hat had seen or done on Halloween night in The Backs. It seemed possible that he had gone there with a white boy of his age, a preacher's son like himself, and had the wits scared out of him by whatever had happened to Abbey Montgomery—and after that night, Abbey herself had been sent out of town, as had Dee Sparks. I couldn't think that a man had murdered the young woman, leaving Mary Randolph to bring her back to life. Surely whatever had happened to Abbey Montgomery had brought Dr. Garland out to The Backs, and what he had witnessed or done there had sent him away screaming. And this event—what had befallen a rich young white woman in the shadiest, most criminal section of a Mississippi county—had led to the slaying of Eddie Grimes and the murder of Mary Randolph. Because they knew what had happened, they had to die.

I understood all this, and Hat had understood it, too. Yet he had introduced needless puzzles, as if embedded in the midst of this unresolved story were something he either wished to conceal or not to know. And concealed it would remain; if Hat did not know it, I never would. Whatever had really happened in The Backs on Halloween night was lost for good.

On the *Blade*'s entertainment page for a Saturday in the middle of November I had come across a photograph of Hat's family's band, and when I had reached this hopeless point in my thinking, I spooled back across the pages to look at it again. Hat, his two brothers, his sister, and his parents stood in a straight line, tallest to smallest, in front of what must have been the family car. Hat held a C-melody saxophone, his brothers a trumpet and drumsticks, his sister a clarinet. As the piano player, the Reverend carried nothing at all—nothing except for what came through even a grainy, sixty-year-old photograph as a powerful sense of self. Hat's father had been a tall, impressive man, and in the photograph he looked as white as I did. But what was impressive was not the lightness of his skin, or even his striking handsomeness: What impressed was the sense of authority implicit in his posture, his straightforward gaze, even the dictatorial set of his chin. In retrospect, I was not surprised by what John Hawes had told me, for this man could easily be frightening. You would not wish to oppose him; you would not elect to get in his way. Beside him, Hat's mother seemed vague and distracted, as if her husband had robbed her of all certainty. Then I noticed the car, and for the first time realized why it had been included in the photograph. It was a sign of their prosperity, the respectable status they had achieved—the car was as much an advertisement as the photograph. It was, I thought, an old Model T Ford, but I didn't waste any time speculating that it might have been the Model T Hat had seen in The Backs.

And that would be that—the hint of an absurd supposition—
except for something I read a few days ago in a book called *Cool
Breeze: The Life of Grant Kilbert.*

There are few biographies of any jazz musicians apart from Louis
Armstrong and Duke Ellington (though one does now exist of Hat,
the title of which was drawn from my interview with him), and I
was surprised to see *Cool Breeze* at the B. Dalton in our local mall.
Biographies have not yet been written of Art Blakey, Clifford
Brown, Ben Webster, Art Tatum, and many others of more musical
and historical importance than Kilbert. Yet I should not have been
surprised. Kilbert was one of those musicians who attract and maintain a large personal following, and twenty years after his death,
almost all of his records have been released on CD, many of them
in multidisc boxed sets. He had been a great, great player, the
closest to Hat of all his disciples. Because Kilbert had been one of
my early heroes, I bought the book (for $35!) and brought it home.

Like the lives of many jazz musicians, I suppose of artists in
general, Kilbert's had been an odd mixture of public fame and
private misery. He had committed burglaries, even armed robber-
ies, to feed his persistent heroin addiction; he had spent years in
jail; his two marriages had ended in outright hatred; he had managed to betray most of his friends. That this weak, narcissistic louse
had found it in himself to create music of real tenderness and beauty
was one of art's enigmas, but not actually a surprise. I'd heard and
read enough stories about Grant Kilbert to know what kind of man
he'd been.

But what I had not known was that Kilbert, to all appearances
an American of conventional northern European, perhaps Scandina-
vian or Anglo-Saxon, stock, had occasionally claimed to be black.
(This claim had always been dismissed, apparently, as another
indication of Kilbert's mental aberrancy.) At other times, being
Kilbert, he had denied ever making this claim.

Neither had I known that the received versions of his birth
and upbringing were in question. Unlike Hat, Kilbert had been
interviewed dozens of times both in *Downbeat* and in mass-market
weekly news magazines, invariably to offer the same story of having
been born in Hattiesburg, Mississippi, to an unmusical, working-
class family (a plumber's family), of knowing virtually from infancy

that he was born to make music, of begging for and finally being given a saxophone, of early mastery and the dazzled admiration of his teachers, then of dropping out of school at sixteen and joining the Woody Herman band. After that, almost immediate fame.

Most of this, the Grant Kilbert myth, was undisputed. He had been raised in Hattiesburg by a plumber named Kilbert, he had been a prodigy and high-school dropout, he'd become famous with Woody Herman before he was twenty. Yet he told a few friends, not necessarily those to whom he said he was black, that he'd been adopted by the Kilberts, and that once or twice, in great anger, either the plumber or his wife had told him that he had been born into poverty and disgrace and that he'd better by God be grateful for the opportunities he'd been given. The source of this story was John Hawes, who'd met Kilbert on another long Jazz at the Phil tour, the last he made before leaving the road for film scoring.

"Grant didn't have a lot of friends on that tour," Hawes told the biographer. "Even though he was such a great player, you never knew what he was going to say, and if he was in a bad mood, he was liable to put down some of the older players. He was always respectful around Hat, his whole style was based on Hat's, but Hat could go days without saying anything, and by those days he certainly wasn't making any new friends. Still, he'd let Grant sit next to him on the bus, and nod his head while Grant talked to him, so he must have felt some affection for him. Anyhow, eventually I was about the only guy on the tour that was willing to have a conversation with Grant, and we'd sit up in the bar late at night after the concerts. The way he played, I could forgive him a lot of failings. One of those nights, he said that he'd been adopted, and that not knowing who his real parents were was driving him crazy. He didn't even have a birth certificate. From a hint his mother once gave him, he thought one of his birth parents was black, but when he asked them directly, they always denied it. These were white Mississippians, after all, and if they had wanted a baby so bad that they had taken in a child who looked completely white but maybe had a drop or two of black blood in his veins, they weren't going to admit it, even to themselves."

In the midst of so much supposition, here is a fact. Grant Kilbert was exactly eleven years younger than Hat. The jazz encyclopedias give his birth date as November first, which instead of his actual birthday may have been the day he was delivered to the couple in Hattiesburg.

I wonder if Hat saw more than he admitted to me of the man leaving the shack where Abbey Montgomery lay on bloody sheets; I wonder if he had reason to fear his father. I don't know if what I am thinking is correct—I'll never know that—but now, finally, I think I know why Hat never wanted to go out of his room on Halloween nights. The story he told me never left him, but it must have been most fully present on those nights. I think he heard the screams, saw the bleeding girl, and saw Mary Randolph staring at him with displaced pain and rage. I think that in some small closed corner deep within himself, he knew who had been the real object of these feelings, and therefore had to lock himself inside his hotel room and gulp gin until he obliterated the horror of his own thoughts.

Peter Straub's best-selling novels of horror include Ghost Story, The Floating Dragon, *and* Shadowland. *In 1984 he coathored, with Stephen King,* The Talisman. *He has recently completed a loosely connected trilogy—*Koko, Mystery *and* The Throat, *each one less horror novel than philosophical thriller. He is himself a jazz musician.*

About the Editors

Michele Slung's books include *Crime on Her Mind: Fifteen Tales of Female Sleuths from the Victorian Era to the Forties*; *I Shudder at Your Touch: Tales of Sex and Horror*; and its sequel, *Shudder Again*. She has written about mystery and detective fiction for over twenty years.

Roland Hartman is the pseudonym of a legendary mystery bookman. In his roles as publisher, bookseller, collector and scholar, he has been one of the most influential figures in the genre.